About the Author

AJ Waines was a Psychotherapist for fifteen years, during which time she worked with ex-offenders from high-security institutions, giving her a rare insight into abnormal psychology. She is now a full-time novelist with publishing deals in France and Germany (Random House).

Her first two novels, *The Evil Beneath* and *Girl on a Train,* have been Number One in 'Murder' and 'Psychological Thrillers' in the UK Kindle Charts. *Girl on a Train* has also been a Number One Bestseller in the entire Australian Kindle Chart. In 2015, she was ranked in the Top 100 UK authors on Amazon KDP (Kindle Direct Publishing).

Alison has also written two self-help books: *The Self-Esteem Journal* and *Making Relationships Work* (Sheldon Press). She lives in Southampton, UK, with her husband.

Find out more at **www.ajwaines.co.uk** or follow her Blog at **www.awaines.blogspot.co.uk.** She's also on Twitter (@ajwaines), Facebook (AJWaines) and you can sign up for her Newsletter at: **http://eepurl.com/bamGuL.**

Also by AJ Waines

The Evil Beneath
Girl on a Train

Writing as Alison Waines

The Self-Esteem Journal
Making Relationships Work

dark place to hide

A J WAINES

Dark Place to Hide
A Novel

ISBN 13: 978-1514132371
ISBN 10: 1514132370

Find out more about the author and her other books at
www.ajwaines.co.uk

In memory of my father, Gordon Waines
(1925-2014)
You had a resolute zest for life
and were a true inspiration – always

Chapter 1
Harper

25 July

A handful of words - that's all it takes. He lays them out for me, leaning forward man to man, his palms on his knees. His tone is pacifying as if he thinks I've guessed; as if by now I must have worked it out.

'Your wife's had a miscarriage,' he says.

The doctor's words force my spine into the back of the seat, crushing me. I am being shunted further and further back, watching the floating faces of the two nurses beside him trying to reach me, their expressions creased with sympathy. Those words in themselves are ripe with disarray. A baby. It's a complete shock. I didn't know.

But there's more.

There's a moment first, when I think of what this means to you. The child you've been waiting for, hoping for, longing for - we both have. You must be torn apart.

The doctor straightens up. He's delivered the bad news and for the medical team, it is cut and dry. Shock, distress, sadness — that will be my onward journey in their eyes; hard, but inevitable. But they are wrong.

What he has told me doesn't make sense.

How can you be having a miscarriage?

You can't possibly be pregnant.

I can't remember the correct order of events after that. They said I could see you, Diane, but I must have stalled because the next minute I'm wandering off towards an open window by the stairwell with a plastic cup of water in my hand. One of the nurses must have handed it to me. She must have thought I needed time to prepare myself to face your grief, a period of quiet to find the right words of solace and comfort for you. But instead, a loud voice inside me is yelling, *How can this have happened?*

Blood is pumping hard and fast into my temples, my neck, my chest and I hate myself for letting this question fog my brain when you've been rushed here in pain, in panic. Of course, I was frantic when I got the call. I nearly sprained my ankle racing up the stairs to get to you, distraught and almost out of my mind. They said you had been found at the side of the road in a pool of blood; you were in intensive care and my mind was racing. I thought at first you'd been struck by a car or attacked in a secluded lane. I thought I'd lost you and I'd find a white sheet covering your face.

One emotional state, however, is now shaking down all the others and rising to the top. It is no longer panic or desperation, but confusion. It is starting to look like you have hidden a massive transgression from me; one that could shatter a marriage in the blink of an eye.

'This way, Dr Penn,' says the nurse. 'Diane wants you to come through, now.'

She must have mistaken my sigh for a sign that I'm impatient to see you. In fact, I need more time. I let her guide me, like a marionette, through two sets of double doors towards your bed. I find myself hiding my shaking hands from her as if I'm afraid she'll think I'm not man enough for you.

My eyes stumble on your face; worn and framed with sticky clumps of hair. You've been through a fight. My spirit dissolves at your vulnerability. I grab your hand.

'I'm okay,' you say, saving me from having to ask.

The nurse steps forward holding a clipboard. 'Your wife collapsed. She was on the verge of a haemorrhage, Dr Penn – it was touch and go there, for a while.'

You shake your head a little as if it was nothing; it's so like you to play down your own misfortunes.

'I didn't know,' you whisper. I can see no trace of remorse or guilt and I reproach myself for looking for it; I should be resoundingly and solely grateful that you are alive, able to recognise me, form sentences. Still, I probe your dewy eyes for signs, but there aren't any. You catch my frown. You think I'm perturbed because you hadn't told me.

'I'm so sorry, Harper,' you whimper.

I sit beside you. It was only a few hours since we'd laughed at breakfast; you dropping your buttered toast and catching it between your knees. You've always been quick like that – co-ordinated and sporty, like your sister. Now you look gaunt and pale – a different person.

'How are you feeling? Are you in pain?'

You rub your belly and wince. 'I had to have a D&C – it's fading now. I have to stay here for a couple of

3

days, they said.'

'What happened?' I mean the bigger question, the series of events, sweeping all my accumulated uncertainties into one giant enquiry, but you hear only one strand of it.

'We got pregnant,' you say, 'and I didn't even know.' Your face buckles at this moment of recognition. *We* got pregnant.

I thumb the tears gently away from your eyes, trying to ease away the pain. Wishing I could bear it for you.

'How many weeks?'

'Only seven…' You look down at my hand, holding on.

Seven weeks ago. My mind scatters as I try to pin the date into the calendar in my head. It would have been early June. We'd been in London the weekend of the 31st May and we'd made love – that much was true. I remember it, because I haven't been able to function in that department as often as I'd have liked. Nevertheless…

'I'm sorry,' you say, again, your eyes struggling to focus.

For what, exactly? My male pride is bursting to ask, but now isn't the time. You are my wife, hurting, suffering and in disbelief. I need to put a hold on my questions and be here for you. You need my support. There's been a baby – the one thing we've been waiting for; the dream, the rapture that would have made everything complete. And you have lost it. Your body has rejected it.

'It's not your fault,' I say, kissing your limp fingers.

All your movements are in slow motion and you can barely string two words together. I know you're playing it down; the physical pain, the distress – being brave for my benefit. I can't confront you with the rest of it – not now.

'I'm so glad you're here,' you whisper. 'Just hold me.' I scoop you into me and feel your feverish sweat roll against my cheek. We'll have to talk about it later. The answers are all there, I just have to wait. Then the truth will be laid out, not only for me, but also for you. As it happens, I have my own secret to share. I have my own concealment to lay bare.

Because there is also something I haven't told you.

Chapter 2

29 July

The day after you came home I was back at my specialist's clinic for one of the injections he prescribed. I told him what had happened and asked whether there was the slimmest sliver of a chance the baby could have been mine. He didn't falter in his response. I hoped for a tiny shard of doubt, but there was none. On the basis of my recent results, it was impossible.

It's a cliché, but I hoped you and I would tell each other everything – all the important stuff at least. This issue certainly falls into that category. Isn't it *the* most important issue: our own family, our offspring, our entire future? I should have said something to you when I made the initial appointment. I should have spoken up the moment I had doubts.

We'd never discussed infertility – well neither of us had used that word. You said something to me once – about six months ago. You were sitting on the carpet, sewing a button onto your coat, and you looked up at me. I was taking measurements of the fireplace, my hands covered in red dust from the broken bricks that keep falling down from our crumbling chimney. Your voice was matter of fact and undemonstrative as if we were continuing, out loud, the conversation you must have started in your head.

'How would we know if one of us couldn't have children?'

My reply came straight out. 'We'd need to have tests, I suppose.'

'When?' you said, squinting up at me as I stood in a spear of sunlight.

'I don't know. At a stage when we felt we'd tried long enough and nothing had happened.' You went quiet and I should have said more instead of leaving you with my clinical reply. I should have checked how concerned you were, but I moved away to fetch the dustpan for the hearth. Whilst you didn't pursue it when I returned, your words had sown their own dark seed in my consciousness. I'd started to look at dates, search on the Internet and to examine myself in the mirror. We'd got our timing right too often; the conditions had been set perfectly too many times – there had to be a problem.

The day of my first appointment came and went in May and I didn't say a word to anyone. You were at school, as usual, no doubt keeping your seven-year-olds enthralled with spelling contests or stories about the rainforest. I should have taken you with me, we should have gone together, but I was afraid. On the one hand, I hoped I'd get away with it, hoped I'd be wrong and my fears would be misplaced. I didn't want to lay doubts in your mind and worry you when the tests might show my sperm to be fit and strong, kicking hard to find their way home. But perhaps a bigger part of me already knew.

I got the results six weeks ago. Once I found out, I

was even more of a coward. I couldn't destroy your hopes, your brightest dream. How could I begin the sentence that would tell you it was never going to happen? That any child we might have could never come from me? I couldn't bring myself to do it. I kept telling myself I would when the time was right. But when was there ever going to be a *right time* to bulldoze over the rest of your life?

You spent most of yesterday asleep after I brought you home from the hospital. I made sure Alexa came to sit with you when I went to the specialist, but she said you didn't stir. This afternoon, she was here again while I went to the supermarket. I couldn't think straight, drifting blindly along the aisles and ended up with mainly dog food. Now I've returned, you're lying on the sofa, your head propped up with extra pillows, supping camomile tea.

'Has Alexa gone?' I ask, half in hope.

'Yes – literally two minutes ago.'

'She must have heard my car coming back.'

You cringe because you know I'm probably right. I can't seem to do much about the prickly relationship Alexa has with me. She's so easily offended and seems perpetually put out by the very fact of my presence.

'I wish she'd lighten up,' you say, annoyed on my behalf.

'You remember how horrified she was when you told her we were getting married?'

'I'll never forget it – she looked like someone had died.' You bite your lip like it's your fault.

'I suppose, for her, something *had* gone for good –

she'd had you all to herself for years and suddenly your priorities were elsewhere.' I don't need to remind you that she's never got over it.

You're distracted by Frank, who has brought a soggy tennis ball in from the garden and dropped it on your lap, waiting for you to throw it for him. 'Not inside,' I tell him, picking up the ball and walking with it to the open back door.

'It's okay,' you insist, 'as long as he doesn't hurt himself.' You're more worried about his welfare than any upheaval he may cause to the furnishings.

'You're too attached to him,' I say in mock rebuke as I throw the ball down the lawn. You were thrilled when Mark asked if we'd have his border collie 'on loan' while he went to Peru.

'I know.' You stare at the rug in front of the fireplace. 'I won't want to give him back. How long have we got left?'

'Three weeks.'

'Is that all?' You give a little moan; exactly the same kind of sound that Frank makes when he wants to come in from outside. It shows how natural it would be to bring a new life into our family; we both know there is space.

You're surprisingly calm after what has happened. You had to spend two more days in the ward, but you seem relaxed and unperturbed by now. I put it down to your natural resilience, but also the sedatives – they're pulling your mouth into a near smile as if you're floating in a warm, but false pool of serenity. Your expression looks odd, out of context, but if it means you feel stable, I don't care.

'How are you feeling?' I know you went through a lot of physical pain, but what you said afterwards made sense; you hadn't built up a strong emotional attachment to the baby, because you didn't know he or she was there.

'I'm shocked more than anything,' you say, as I kneel on the floor in front of you. 'They can't say if it was a boy or a girl, it was too early.' You cradle my face. 'I suppose I'm glad really. Best not to know – it would only make it more...'

'I know...' I kiss your palm.

'I think it will take me a while to process everything, because the idea is so new. I was a mum for a few weeks...' You rub your flat belly. 'I had no idea – it's so weird.'

'I always thought you'd know.'

'Me too. I'm really cross with myself. And yet, it has also saved us from building up all our hopes and excitement.' You close your eyes and have to stop every few words to swallow. 'I'll probably feel the loss a bit later, Dibs.'

You use my nickname and it knocks me off balance. You teased me with the name, after hapless Officer Dibble from 'Top Cat'. We discovered we'd both been fans of the cartoon as kids, and the name had stuck. But, I mustn't let the tenderness sway me. Now is the time.

I pause, make fists with my hands and tell you about my condition. I explain I was scared and ashamed and should have told you.

You try to sit up, but it hurts. I put my arm behind

your back. 'How long have you known?' There is no shred of animosity in your question.

'About six weeks.'

'What's the problem? Why can't you…?'

I explain the issue briefly in medical terms, but I know you're not able to take it in. The salient point is that I've been producing sperm, but the count is too low.

I shift forward to the edge of the sofa, on the edge of a cliff, waiting for your next response, waiting for it to sink in. If there is a miscarriage then what went before happened without me. Surely?

You put your finger on your lip. 'You've had tests. You did all this on your own?' Your eyes are full of sorrow for my decision to go it alone, not reproach.

'It was wrong of me. I'm sorry.'

I'd conned myself into believing I hadn't told you because I didn't want you to worry, but I know that's not true. In reality, I was terrified. Panic-stricken that my sterility would change how you felt about me. I couldn't risk seeing your eyes dip away then quickly recover – as you took the hit that your super-fit, passionate, lustful husband has been firing blanks.

'It's not your fault,' you say, pulling me back to you. It's your trademark – to so easily slip into forgiveness in your desire to protect me.

'I should have told you – we should have discussed it. My masculine ego got in the way. I thought you'd think I wasn't a proper man…'

'No – *never*…' You nuzzle into my neck. 'How could you think that?'

But, there is another issue at stake here. It's setting fire to the air around us. I want you to realise and jump to your own conclusion so I don't have to drag you towards it. *If I'm infertile – then how...?*

You laugh unexpectedly, but it's hoarse and shallow. 'Both our bodies have let us down.'

I don't want to have to spell it out. But I do need to know.

'Something had to be wrong,' I say. 'We'd had nothing at all, since you came off the pill.'

'I know. Over a year...'

You can't see what I'm getting at. You aren't hearing me. Your medication is making you detached from reality and you can't seem to grasp the enormous repercussions. Firstly, the fact that all our future plans are shattered; our road ahead has turned into rubble – it leads nowhere. Secondly, the obvious unthinkable deduction that runs alongside your miscarriage. I can't be the father. Your brain must be too foggy to take it in.

I wait. Perhaps, at any moment, you will put the two ends of the wire together and get the flash. But it doesn't come. You really are spaced out and instead you ask another question. 'There must be treatment? Something you can do?'

I can't help but smile. This is so like you: to turn towards making things better, always facing the light instead of the darkness.

'I've started having injections.'

'Do they have side-effects?'

Side-effects...we can't be having this conversation! My insides are dripping with murky, churned-up feelings and

I need to let them out. I need you to face what I'm facing. I have to turn the discussion back to where it should have been heading all along. I have to know.

'You seem to be overlooking something,' I say, trying to keep my voice even.

'What?' Your face is tilted up, the light from the window cradling it in innocence.

'Well...we've just established that I can't father a child.' I glance down at my nails. 'So how...?'

You push yourself up on the pillow, more alert. 'It must have been a freakish one-in-a-million chance, Dibs,' you conclude. 'You still produce sperm – you told me that – but a low count doesn't mean none at all. One must have slipped through. That's all it takes.' You fling down your arms in exasperation. 'Can you believe it? It was probably our one and only chance and I couldn't keep the baby.'

Your gaze drops, your face fragments into shadows.

I refuse to slip into consoling you. Not yet, not until I'm sure of what you're saying. 'So – you haven't, you know...?'

'What?' You're wide-eyed now. Incredulous. '*Slept* with someone else, you mean?'

I grit my teeth.

'God, no! Harper! How could you even think that?'

My doubt and bewilderment cluster together. 'It seems the obvious conclusion. If I'm classified as infertile and have been since the sarcoidosis diagnosis eighteen months ago, then it stands to reason...well, my assumption is...*was*...the baby couldn't have been mine.'

You grab me by both sleeves and drag me against

your chest. 'No! No way, darling. Honestly. No way! I've *never* cheated on you. It's not how we do things is it? It's not how we operate.' You shake your head, talking to the floor, rocking me, cooing; 'No…no…absolutely not…no…no way,' over and over, hammering it home to me.

I sit up and look at you, feeling my love for you rush into all the spaces in the room.

I want to believe you.

I don't tell you that I've requested a DNA test on the unformed child. Now is not the time.

'Shush,' I say, rocking you in my arms. 'I'm sorry. I needed to know…I love you. Get some rest.'

Chapter 3
Diane

Mid-June

Tara links arms with Diane as they head out of the school gates and cross the road towards the trees. She never stands on ceremony – it was one of the first things that drew Diane to her and she loves her friend's 'want-it, go-get-it' approach to life.

Tara brushes away the purple petals that have fallen from the nearby magnolia onto the bench. Diane is certain it's going to rain, but doesn't want to miss their daily walk over to the park.

She glances up at the elegant blossoms, standing proud like candlesticks, and realises she's barely noticed spring breaking through this year with its bold colours and promise of new life. In fact, spring is already on the cusp of summer.

'You wanted to borrow my phone?' Diane reiterates, remembering Tara's request as they left the staffroom. She's holding her lunchbox under one arm, her folded umbrella under the other, trying to reach into her rucksack for her mobile. She gives up and drops everything onto the bench.

'Please. Mine's on the blink. Just a quick call to tell Erica I can take the Disco-Jack class.'

'Disco-Jack? What's that?' Diane is unbuckling her rucksack.

'It's a kind of disco shuffle hip-hop thing.' Tara waves her hand dismissively and sits down, propping her handbag on her knees as if she is in a doctor's waiting room. She is dressed in an expensive canary-yellow coat, with matching high heels and a navy pencil skirt. Diane looks at the fraying strap of her own rucksack and marvels at the way Tara persistently overdresses. Tall and willowy – a former pole-dancer – Tara Nørgaard teaches older children at the same primary school.

'You can step in and take over a new dance class, just like that?' Tara loves all kinds of dancing. Her body has a natural rhythm inside it – you can see it when she walks. She has a tendency to wiggle her hips and twirl around without any intention of showing off. It's simply how her body sings.

'Yeah - well. I'll buy a DVD on the way home and find out what the steps are. How hard can it be?'

Some of the staff find Tara brash, but she seems spirited, straight talking…fearless, in Diane's eyes.

She drops the phone into Tara's hands. 'Help yourself,' she says.

Diane sits back, peels open the lid of her lunchbox and scoops a forkful of mushroom risotto into her mouth. Tara is half Danish with only the trace of an accent. Maybe it's tradition over there never to have lunch, Diane ponders, as she's rarely seen Tara eat anything other than the occasional apple during their breaks. Nevertheless, Tara generally joins her, if neither of them are stuck with playground duty. Since spring, they've been returning almost daily to Diane's favourite bench by the children's paddling pool.

While Tara makes the call, Diane is watching a small boy wave a plastic spade at a woman. His mother? His nanny? She gazes at the patches of sand that have clung to his knees and wonders how old he is.

'Tomorrow night at seven,' she tells Diane as she ends the call, 'fancy trying it?'

'Yeah, I'd love to.' Diane has an aptitude for all things sporty, but tends to play it down. Only a handful of staff at St Mary's know that, as a teenager, she was verging on Olympic standard in the pool. In 2006, she won silver in the 200-metre butterfly at the British Championships. There was a gold the following year in the GB team relay, but in 2008, a hip problem brought her competitive career to an abrupt end.

'You can show everyone how it's done.' Tara nudges her friend's elbow and laughs – a loud whoop like a teenager.

'Don't you dare!' Diane retorts.

Tara is still holding the phone. She's stopped laughing. 'What are all these?' she says quietly. Diane reaches for the phone, wet grains of rice toppling out of her mouth. 'Dee – there are loads of them…'

'It's nothing. It's okay,' she protests. 'You shouldn't…' Diane finally snatches back the mobile. She hadn't meant for anyone to see them. Probably around thirty of them by now. Photos of new-borns in carrier baskets leaving the maternity ward. Infants in buggies being wheeled into the supermarket. Toddlers in shopping centres. Heavily pregnant women waiting at a bus stop.

'That's why we always come here isn't it, during our lunch break?' says Tara, looking up. 'To watch the children in the playground?'

Diane winces.

'Does Harper know about this?'

'No.'

Tara puts an arm round her. 'I didn't know it had got so bad.'

Diane leans into her. She feels ashamed, but safe. 'It's silly, really. I'm only twenty-six. Harper's thirty. It's not like we're running out of time or anything. This maternal desire – a craving, really – has taken me over. It's filled me with a constant ache. We've been trying for over a year...and nothing's happened.'

'It *will*, though. When you least expect it. When you're relaxed and not so uptight about *trying* so hard.'

Diane rests her chin on Tara's shoulder; she can smell expensive perfume on her collar. She can never do this with Alexa. It wouldn't feel right, even though Alexa is always pushing for a closer and deeper relationship. Diane feels a flicker of confusion when she thinks of her sister – and the way much of her inner landscape feels too vulnerable and intimate to express with her own flesh and blood. 'I haven't been uptight about it...not really.'

'Taking all these photos seems pretty uptight to me.'

'Yeah – okay.' Diane pulls away. 'But otherwise, I've been doing all the right things. I've never smoked, I hardly drink. I'm fit and healthy, I've always eaten well – no caffeine, additives, no sugary rubbish.'

'From your swimming days?'

Diane murmurs in agreement.

'I know I should be patient, but I can't stop watching women with kids,' she admits, staring out at the children running for the swings. 'I've even started buying baby clothes...'

Tara squeezes her closer, rubbing her arm. 'It's going to happen one day. Of course, it is.'

'Is it normal, do you think? To wait this long? To want it so much?'

'Absolutely,' says Tara. 'You're craving a child. It's the most natural thing in the world to want to be a mother. It's turned into a bit of an obsession, that's all.'

Diane crinkles her nose. 'I'm even finding reasons to avoid Sally.'

Sally Lord is a fellow teacher at St Mary's and six months pregnant. Every day she carries around with her the treasure Diane wants more than anything. 'I'm trying to share her delight over her pregnancy. I really am...but every conversation revolves around birthing pools, baby buggies, stencils in the nursery. She's so exuberant and glowing. I can't...'

Tara nods. 'Do you want me to have a word with her?'

'Thanks. No. It's okay. I need to do it myself. I need to explain why I've been so off with her.' She shakes herself. 'I need to pull myself out of this.'

'You need to talk to Harper about it, girl. He'll understand – you know he will.'

'I don't want to put him under pressure.'

'It's not like this is just *you*. He wants kids just as much, doesn't he? You've always said it's your big shared dream.'

Diane blinks into the distance. 'It is...yes, it is.'

'Are you worried about how he'll react?'

'No, of course not.' She knows it comes out a little too quickly.

Chapter 4
Harper

30 July – 7.50pm

Alexa's face falls when I open the door.

'I thought she'd be here.'

'She is. Well, she was. She's just popped out. She'll be back shortly.' Alexa seems to have a lot of bright light behind her; I want to shield my eyes.

'You're drunk,' she says, her mouth sagging with disgust. She stomps inside, uninvited. Her white jeans are unironed and she wears a camisole top that leaves her belly button on display.

'It's been a difficult time. Diane's gone to get painkillers from the village store.'

'For you, I presume?' My self-conscious grimace gives away the answer. 'But that's miles away. She'll be ages.'

Alexa sits on the arm of the sofa, swinging a leg, and presses keys on her phone. She always has it in her hand when she's in my presence, as if speaking to me is only ever a prelude to doing something else far more important.

'It's not miles. Well – it's nearly two. She took the car, for once.'

Alexa stiffens. 'She never drives.' Her shoulders

undulate like sand dunes as she hitches up the thin straps on her top that keep slipping down.

'I know. She insisted.' I know how you feel about driving, Dee, and I would never have asked. I was quite happy to suffer with my self-induced headache. I deserve it.

'But she's taking sedatives.'

'She's stopped. She's keeping hold of them just in case.'

'When did she last take one?'

I'm used to interrogations like this. For your sake, Dee, I always try to go along with her to avoid friction. 'I don't know.' I glance at the clock on the wall, but it seems to be shifting around. 'Last night?'

'I can't believe you let her get behind the wheel – after all she's been through.'

'She seemed...'

Alexa is swimming in front of me now and I want her to go away. She's been over several times since the miscarriage. She doesn't make much effort to hide the fact she doesn't like me, but I do my utmost to make her welcome. I really do. But she's not like you. She's only ever been the palest shadow of you.

Alexa looks down at her phone, gets up and turns to the door. A muscle at the back of her arm bulges – one I never knew human beings had. She's superfit. It shouldn't surprise me now that Alexa's competing regularly in Ironman triathlons. How anyone can get excited by swimming nearly two-and-a-half miles, cycling another 112, then rounding off the day with a full marathon is beyond me. But then yours is, after all, a family of extremes.

'I've got to go,' she says.

'You're not going to wait? She'll only be a few minutes. She won't want to miss you.'

Alexa's phone has given her some urgent new mission and she's already reaching for the door handle. She doesn't say goodbye and charges down the path to her car.

I look at my watch, but there seem to be too many hands floating around the dial. Nevertheless, it feels like more time has passed than I expected. Shouldn't you be back by now? My mind tracks back to our conversation yesterday about the baby. Was your reaction genuine? I pick up the TV listings in search of a distraction. I don't want to open up the possibility that you didn't tell me the truth, that you were protecting me by being primed with a lie, although your reaction was so immediate, it's hard for me to believe you were deceiving me. I drop the magazine; I'm too unsettled to take any of it in.

Even though Dr Swann insisted my tests were conclusive, I searched the infertility forums online late last night, just in case I could prove him wrong. But there were no success stories; no miracles for men with my condition, or at least none documented. I keep hearing your words: *One must have slipped through.* I must be the exception.

If that is the case, I can't help feeling wholeheartedly cheated. Our one chance and it has slipped away. The chances of it happening again naturally...well...are virtually nil. Of course, I've started the treatment, but I haven't told you yet about the success rates. Sixty per cent at best, for activating pregnancy, but a third of these are lost through miscarriage. It's not a rosy picture. I don't want to make things any worse than they already are.

As I poured the juice for breakfast, I looked up. You were standing at the bottom of the stairs in pyjamas speckled with dancing pink fish.

'Explain it to me again,' you said. Your buckled forehead told me you'd been worrying about this instead of getting proper rest. I pressed you to sit down and laid a blanket over your knees, even though it was toasty in the sitting room with the morning sun.

'You remember when I had sarcoidosis?'

'That was ages ago.'

'Eighteen months.'

Confusion nipped the skin between your eyebrows. 'But, that was some sort of virus – wasn't it?'

'It usually affects the lungs and skin, but everyone reacts differently. What we didn't know was that it can affect testosterone production.'

'Oh…' The sound was clean and simple, like the response of a child.

'And too many of the sperm are deformed or have poor mobility.' My mouth twisted with shame at bringing these far-reaching deficiencies into your life. 'It's why my libido has been a bit iffy in the last year or so.'

You leaned back looking exhausted.

At some stage, you're going to ask me how long we have to wait before my treatment makes a difference.

The specialist says the gonadotropin injections won't have any effect for six months and possibly long after that, if I have adverse reactions. I didn't tell you that I'm already having side effects; my appetite has dropped in the past two weeks and I've had two nose bleeds at work. He told me that in rare cases the side effects – blood-clotting, fluid retention in the chest – can be fatal. He had to tell me these things. I'm hopeful, of course I am, about this coming right for us, but I'm not banking on it.

8.30pm
Another cluster of bricks tumble down the fireplace, making me jump. I've been slumped here on the sofa unaware of how much time has gone by. The bricks land in the hearth, like winning coins on a one-armed bandit. I wish I was better at DIY. You always laugh at me for my Heath Robinson-style attempts at fixing things with pieces of string and gaffer tape. At least I try. The builders are due in five weeks to rebuild the chimney. We also have subsidence in the extension at the back of the cottage with another surveyor coming next week, to see if we qualify for insurance. Our home is crumbling around us.

The light is peeling away from the sky. You left an hour ago. It takes less than ten minutes to get to the village shop in the car. You ought to be back by now.

I try your mobile, but there's no reply. Where else would you go? Surely you wouldn't stop at the pub when you know I need the painkillers? You wouldn't, anyway – not if you're driving. You wouldn't do anything to put yourself at risk. I know you are a reluctant driver at the best of times – it's down to that time you didn't swerve fast enough (your words) and hit a deer.

A surge of panic hits me. Were you still too drowsy with the medication to be driving? Is it my fault? Has something terrible happened? I should have stopped you, like Alexa said.

As soon as I set foot outside, I realise I'm too drunk to stay upright on my bicycle, so I go back for Frank, who thinks this extra romp is a special treat, and we head out on foot. Frank snuffles through clumps of dandelions at the roadside. Nettledon is split into two parts. On the south side are detached cottages, spread out, with clumps of trees, and we are the last one before the farmland stretches down towards the valley. The pub, shop and church are on the north side surrounded by terraced cottages and in-between is a stretch of road, with trees and thick scrub on both sides belonging to the council. There are tight bends on this lane and the road is narrow.

We get to the signpost for the footpath and Frank pulls on the lead, trying to drag me into the woods. I apologise and tell him we have to stick to the main road. There's no path and I need him by my side. Blades of grass gather between my toes and the heads of tufty weeds find their way inside my sandals.

What am I looking for? A black Astra at the roadside? Maybe you had a flat tyre, but wouldn't you have called if you'd broken down? I try to recall. Yes, I'm sure you took your bag; your phone would be in it.

The headache brings waves of nausea with it. Too

much vodka – idiot. It's got to stop. Everything about the baby, about my part in it, or not – and my diagnosis – has temporarily got the better of me, but it's no excuse. There are more important things at stake here. I force my eyes to search the tarmac. What else am I looking for? Skid marks? Did you have an accident?

There is a stretch of road coming up with a steep bank on the left. It drops away into woods and undergrowth. If the car left the road, the undergrowth would break the fall, wouldn't it? We reach that spot. I examine the slatted fence, the bark of the large oak tree, the turf, for signs. Nothing is damaged or disturbed. What else am I looking for? I feel like I'm in one of my own lectures; I'm used to problem solving and I've always been good at it. I invariably spot the whodunit in my detective novels way before anyone else. As a child, I was always the first to find my way out of the park maze; I always won at Cluedo. I just have that kind of mind.

Frank and I reach the crossroads. You would have gone straight on here. I check near the white give-way markings for glass, the orange plastic of a shattered light. Nothing. Frank's tongue flops to one side now. We must have speeded up. I check for fresh ruts along the verge, tyre marks in the mud outside gateposts. We reach the village green. I stride into The Eagle and ask Terry, behind the bar, if he's seen you. When I mention the shop, he points towards Marvin Baines, the owner of the one and only village shop. Marvin is sitting with three other men, all with pint glasses drained to the same point. He rolls Frank's soft ear between his finger and thumb. He hasn't seen you either. I ask around. We moved to our cottage three years ago, so all the locals know us by now. I get nothing but shakes of the head.

I come out. It's still light. I check the car park, the verges, the kerb for a black Astra. It isn't there.

Where are you?

It might be nothing, but when I get back I notice my paperback is splayed open on the coffee table. I never do that; I use a bookmark. I'm inclined to spot these things. Being a so-called expert in criminology and forensics makes you look at the world in terms of puzzles and clues. You're always telling me I'm turning into Jack Reacher, the fictional creation of Lee Child, with my ability to instantly 'read a room'.

I stand still. The laptop has moved. Have you been back? Did you wonder why I wasn't here and set out looking for me? I call your name. The place looks messy. I hate things being untidy, but we've had to clear the alcove so the surveyor can see the cracks in the wall when he comes. Piles of paperbacks crowd the fireplace and you've been very patient about 'my collection', in boxes in the porch. How do we find a new home for fifteen antique typewriters? Thank you for not suggesting the garden shed.

Frank goes looking for you, too – in the garden and upstairs – but returns alone.

I do a circuit of the garden myself, go down to the river, calling your name. The end of the day is buried in a bruised sky. I come back inside and check my phone.

There's no sign of you. I sit on the armchair nearest the front door and wait. I keep the curtains open, I don't want to shut you out.

Chapter 5

9.45pm

'Have you seen her?' I ask.

'Who?' asks Alexa.

'Diane, of course. She hasn't come back from the village. I'm worried.'

'No. I haven't seen her. Did you call her?'

'Of course – there's no reply. You didn't go after her?' I ask.

'No. I had to meet someone – in Cosham.'

'It's been over two hours.'

'Maybe she's gone to the pub.'

'I've been there – no one's seen her or the car.'

'Maybe she's broken down.'

'I walked the entire route there and back.'

'Well…then…maybe she stopped off somewhere else?'

'There *is* nowhere else. Just a shop and a pub, remember?

'Yeah, okay. But, maybe she's dropped by a neighbour's or gone to a friend's for the night.'

'She wouldn't do that without telling me.' There's a snide silence as if Alexa thinks otherwise. I wonder if she knows more than she's letting on. 'Has she rung you?'

'No.'

'Please call if she rings, won't you?'

'Sure.'

I call a couple of our friends in the village, but no one has seen you. I try the next option. It's a misconception that you have to wait twenty-four hours before contacting the police about a missing person. Maybe I've underestimated the state you are in. Perhaps you're more vulnerable than I realised. Perhaps the enormity of the situation only hit you when you were halfway down the road.

I have colleagues in the Hampshire Police; guys who consult me for forensics' analysis. I give talks for the force at training and open days and have become mates with a handful of them. They're hardworking and reliable – I'm privileged to call them friends. DI Neil Fry lets me win at squash every now and again to keep me coming back. DS Paul Whitaker, on the other hand, is a rogue and adds three kilos to my barbell at the gym when I'm tying my shoelaces. They're good blokes – they'll get on to it.

I can't reach Neil; he's on holiday, so I try Paul's mobile. His wife answers and tells me he's off work with a stomach bug and needs to sleep. I call the local police station and explain what's happened. The desk sergeant asks your age, whether you have your phone and need medication or treatment. I explain that you had a miscarriage five days ago, but that you seemed stable and had stopped taking the sedatives. I know what he is going to say before I hear the words: *Most people return within forty-eight hours. Can you do a ring-round of her friends?*

Have you rung her parents? He says an officer will be in touch to arrange a visit if you still haven't returned.

I pick up the phone again to start making more calls.

I've never been unfaithful to you, Dee, or even considered it. Even now in the mornings, I prop myself up on one elbow and quietly watch your face with the sublime satisfaction of knowing you're in my bed, inches away from me, breathing the same air. You continue to light up the room whenever you enter, even after our three years as Dr and Mrs Penn.

Nothing about your behaviour has changed in the last few months. We're so close I know I would have spotted something. A slight hesitation, perhaps, when I reached over to kiss you, excuses when I initiated sex, a dropping off in the number of times you made flirtatious remarks or sexual advances towards me, a distractedness about you, less available. None of that has happened.

It's nearly dark. I throw open the window in the kitchen and rest my elbows on the ledge taking in the grassy, dewy air, trying to slow down my breathing. I stare at the fading grey shape made by the fountain in the centre and the bird feeders idly swinging under the lilac tree. Right now, this doesn't feel like mine. Ours. It doesn't feel like home. Everything's changed.

We nearly had a baby. Just a few days ago, we were on our way to being three. And we didn't know. Neither of us. It has totally floored me.

I don't want to feel like this.

I catch my reflection in the glass, unable to recognise the person I see. In fact, everything around me seems unfamiliar as if I'm in the wrong house. I'm suddenly cold. I shut the window and scan the details of the room to make my eyes remember where I am and how I got here.

I take myself back to October 2011. It's all I can think of to ground myself. We bought this detached cottage in the small Hampshire village in Nettledon weeks after we married. We were both done with the hectic city and were already thinking ahead, wanting clean air and space for our children, instead of pollution and chaos.

'We both need to slow down,' you'd told me once, when I sank onto the bottom stair, frazzled, drained and fractious, after another arduous commute home. 'London's got too manic for us. Let's leave.' It was all the encouragement I needed.

Rosamund Cottage is certainly what you'd call a 'bijou' property – we'd both been renting in London and knew we wouldn't get a palace for our savings anywhere. But it's terribly cute and cosy with low beams, small chunky windows and sunlight that slices across the sitting room. The scattering of cottages at our end of the village are separated by trees and large magnolias and rhododendrons – so we are not overlooked and have plenty of privacy. We both fell in love with the place at first sight.

You've always wanted to live by water, Dee, and there's a river running past the end of our garden. Sometimes I find you down there sitting on the bank gazing into the ripples. You also wanted to learn to ride a horse and last summer we adopted Rupert from the local stables.

'You can come home from University to a real fire in the hearth,' you'd suggested, 'and try your hand at keeping bees. Or chickens – there's a ready-made coop at the far end of the garden.' I remember being touched that you'd listened and had held onto my dreams for me.

As it happens, my plans are as yet unrealised; other basic jobs have had to come first, like sorting out the guttering and the ongoing problems with the chimney.

It's late. The kettle boils without me realising I'd even switched it on. I must get a grip. You're going to need me to be robust and supportive when you return. You'll be home any minute with a heartfelt apology, no doubt, about meeting someone while you were out. *I'm so sorry I made you worry, Dibs. I tried to get away, but she needed to talk.*

I leave the hot water – I don't want a drink. I reach into the packet of biscuits for a digestive, then put it back. I won't go to bed; I'll lie on the sofa and wait for you.

The baby has gone. Cremated by now. The DNA results come through at the end of the week. Then I'll know for certain.

Chapter 6
Marion

13 July – 8am

'We've found her!' comes a voice from the far side of the castle grounds. 'She's in the pit.'

'Thank God,' Marion cries, squeezing the damp tissue in her hand into a pulp. She allows the police constable to guide her along the narrow path in the grass towards the woman in a high-visibility waistcoat who is waving. Rose, she thinks her name is. They stop at a low collapsed wall and Marion gets down on her knees, even though the ground is knobbly with stones. 'You okay, honey?' she shouts down into the hollow below.

Clara stares up through the railings of the pit, her fingers in her mouth, looking bemused, but unhurt.

'Mummy's here, darling. They're going to get you out.'

Marion fights back the urge to break into relief-driven tears. How did she get down there?

The official from Portchester Castle wipes a bead of sweat from his lip. He's holding the keys and has told us twice that he's made a special trip from Bournemouth on a Sunday to open up.

'It's not a pit, PC Felton,' he calls out unnecessarily. 'It's an oubliette. It means "place of forgetting"; a dungeon where prisoners were left abandoned, never to be released.'

Marion doesn't want to know that. She turns to the constable by her side. 'Thank you – thank you *so* much.' She hangs onto his sleeve. 'I was really panicking. We were here yesterday and when we got back home I felt so rough, I had to go straight to bed, but I was certain my mother had arranged to collect Clara for the night, so I knew she'd be looked after.' Her mother had started popping in with her own spare key and didn't disturb her if she was asleep. 'Staying over with people is second nature to Clara. She's so smart and independent for her age – she's only seven.'

Marion is worried about what the constable will think of her and is speaking too fast. She knows she should have called her mother that evening to check she'd collected Clara, but the pain in her back had been so bad, she'd been forced to take morphine and was out for the count. As it happened, Marion had got her days mixed up and her mother wasn't expecting Clara after all. It wasn't until her mother rang the following morning to ask if Clara might want to stay over *that* night, that Marion knew her daughter wasn't with her.

'She must have come back to the castle before it closed and sneaked back in,' Marion tells the officer. 'I called the police straight away.'

'At least the temperature didn't drop too low last night,' says the constable. He's trying to make her feel better. He's given her his name twice, but in her frenzy, she hasn't hung on to it. She's been thinking how terrifying it must have been for her daughter, no matter

36

what the temperature was, to have spent all night trapped down there in the damp with no pillow, no blanket, no food or water. She thinks of the word oubliette and shivers. She tries to imagine Clara finding her way inside then being unable to get out. She thinks of a wasp trapped in a jam jar; the frantic buzzing as it bats against the glass. She presses a palm against her chest to ward off a spasm of nausea. What a dreadful mother she is for letting this happen.

Rose appears through a gap in the rubble below and squats down in front of Clara. 'There are a lot of loose rocks down here,' she calls out. 'Part of the wall must have disintegrated after Clara got inside.' The seven-year-old looks up again to check if it's the right thing to do, to go with her.

'It's okay, sweetheart. The lady will bring you out to me. Take her hand. Be careful.'

'We'll disappear for a while,' Rose calls up from the pit. 'The only way to get out is over that way.' She points towards the other side of the site, where the remains of a tower stand at ground level.

Clara gives her mother a jolly wave as the pair scramble through a hole and vanish.

Marion had been promising Clara they'd go to Portchester's medieval castle for weeks and days when she felt well enough to go out were getting few and far between. She turns again to the constable by her side. 'She's such a daredevil. Always crawling into small spaces. She sleeps under her bed, she clambers under cars, climbs into trees. She thinks a "Keep Out" sign means "Come right in and make yourself at home." One of these days she going to do herself serious harm. I can't watch her all the time.'

Marion knows she's rattling on again. Her mouth keeps opening, her words filling in the hollow where fear and dread have been lurking.

The constable flicks away a fly that has landed on his thumb. 'It must be hard…especially with…' Marion sees the way he pretends not to notice the headscarf that covers every inch of her scalp, her missing eyebrows, her fragile white skin.

'I have good days and bad days,' she tells him, the emotional release making her reveal things she wouldn't normally tell strangers. 'I used to work part-time in the post office, but I can't even do that anymore. I often have to spend the day in bed with the pain and fatigue. Then there's the side effects from the chemo; the nausea and vomiting, the diarrhoea. The sore throat and the hair loss.' She laughs and fiddles with the knot on her headscarf. 'Sorry…'

'Don't apologise, Mrs Delderfield. You have a lot to cope with – that's for certain.' He rubs his chin and stares at the grass. 'I knew Morris. He did some training for us once. Remarkable chap. Very professional.'

Marion's husband was a skydiving instructor with over a thousand jumps under his belt when she waved him goodbye four years ago as he set out for a routine stunt display in France. He was coupled with a cameraman, Henri Clem, who claimed he was experienced, but had, in fact, only done four jumps in his life. On the way down, Henri's chute got tangled up with his camera. Morris tried to save him, but they both ran out of time.

Marion fingers her wedding band. 'The company who hired Morris that day should never have let the other guy jump,' she told the officer. 'I'm still fighting for compensation. During the periods of remission, I write letters and get on the phone – but it never seems to go anywhere.'

They watch as Clara and the female officer approach from the far end of the ruins, hand in hand.

'Do you get help with Clara?' the constable asks as they stride towards them. Marion is always on high alert about this kind of question, convinced others have got social services in mind.

'We had to move to a smaller place last year, so I had to leave a lot of good friends behind, but I have a solid network of helpers. Plenty of reliable babysitters and neighbours. My mother helps when she can.' She doesn't add that her mother hasn't been well herself and is fast becoming unreliable.

The constable is kind and doesn't look as though he's about to turn her in. There's a lame silence between them before Clara breaks away from PC Felton and comes running round the side of the moat. She buries her face in her mother's skirt and Marion wishes she had the strength to pick her up. She crouches down instead and takes a good look at her.

'Did you hurt yourself?' Marion takes in the milky smell of Clara's long mousy-brown hair and pulls her close to see if she's been crying. Clara shakes her head. She's a pretty, smiley child and looks remarkably unshaken. 'Are you hungry?'

Her daughter nods with a frown. Marion hands her a

chewy raisin bar from her handbag and she takes it politely.

Wafts of the rescuing officer's floral perfume temporarily mask the stale dank air reaching her from another dungeon below. 'There was a small gap under the stone stairwell – you can't see it from here,' Rose explains. 'A few stones have toppled down from the floor above.' She pats Clara on the head. 'Once she got inside, more of the rubble must have come down and sealed off the opening.' She brushes white dust from her sleeves. 'She looks fine, but we'll need to get Clara to the hospital for a check-up, just to be sure.'

'Of course,' Marion replies. 'I have to go home first. In the panic, I didn't bring my medication—'

'And we need to feed the fish,' chips in Clara, swinging on her mother's hand.

'No problem – we'll take you.'

PC Felton addresses the warden, who's wearing a T-shirt bearing the castle logo, that looks two sizes too small. 'You'll need to cordon the area off and make it safe,' she says. 'It's dangerous to the public as it is.' He reaches for his phone with a sullen nod.

Marion turns to thank the man with the cluster of keys and he nods, but is already speaking to someone on his mobile. The officers walk with the two of them towards the exit.

'Will the car have blue lights on and make the whoop sound?' Clara asks on the way.

Rose answers with a smile. 'I'm afraid not. We'll take it nice and slow getting you back to Nettledon.'

Clara looks disappointed and scrunches up her

mouth so her top lip brushes her nose.

Marion doesn't want a lift; she'd rather walk for a while first, she needs the air, but the police insist. They can see she isn't well and her daughter has had a nasty scare.

As they reach the main road, Clara starts to skip.

'Shall I tell you a secret, Mummy?' she whispers, pulling on her arm.

'Go on, then.'

'Being down in that mangy pit was the bestest fun *ever...*'

Chapter 7
Harper

31 July – First day missing

I'm surprised to wake, because I didn't think I'd been asleep. I've been waiting to hear your key in the front door, but it didn't come. Frank jumps on the sofa dropping the squelchy tennis ball between my knees. I toss it away half-heartedly and he flings himself after it, skidding on the polished wooden floors that are everywhere.

I'm at a loss. All my calls last night ended up getting nowhere. Tara suggested you might need space, Sally said you'd seemed distracted lately, other colleagues from school haven't heard from you since the end of term. I dreaded calling your mother, adding another thing for her to worry about when she's already preoccupied with your father, but it had to be done. She was an unlikely source of information, but I'm hanging onto the possibility of finding any clues as to your whereabouts.

The conversation with your mother took an inevitable turn after about twenty seconds. It sounds like Lucinda has gone overboard with post-it notes everywhere, leaving instructions about where Ted should hang his coat, which rooms are upstairs, where to find the toilet. She has stuck notes saying *don't drink this* on the Domestos and cleaning fluid under the sink, others saying *don't use – cracked* (on a chipped milk jug) or *cat only* (on pouches of rabbit meat). All the photographs on the fridge have stickers with names attached. His Alzheimer's has become her round-the-clock project.

Lucinda didn't know you were pregnant, of course, and before being consumed by your father's latest exploits she was only able to latch on to that part of our conversation. *What happened? Is she okay? Why didn't she call me?* She was unable to grasp the real reason I was ringing. I tried to ask if she might know where you've gone, but she kept asking if you were all right.

'I can't leave Ted,' she said, 'otherwise I'd be over there straight away. Can I speak to her? Is she well enough to talk, poor girl?'

I didn't want to worry her. 'She can't come to the phone just now…'

'I understand. Keep her nice and warm. Plenty of fluids.' There was a violent crash in the background. 'Ted…?' A scuffle followed. 'I've got to go,' she said, 'He's got into the cellar…'

Our closest neighbour is Ralph, about twenty metres away, but I've already spoken to him. He's deaf and doddery and didn't really grasp what I was asking about. Nevertheless, he invited me in for tea, but I told him I was in a rush and handed him the bottle of milk on the doorstep that looked like it'd been there for several days. After that, I tried Lorraine, your old pal from University, then I had high hopes for about twenty seconds when I suddenly remembered your new friend in the village,

43

Jackie, the osteopath. She said maybe there was a problem with your phone, but the end result was that not one person has seen or heard from you.

Are you hiding because you lied to me? Because you know the baby belongs to someone else?

No – there must be some other explanation. You have never been someone to storm off – not from me, at any rate. Always the opposite, in fact. You seek me out whenever there's something bothering you; you pester me and make me sit and listen. It's what I love about you – your openness, your willingness to lay yourself bare and be seen.

Concern and doubts roll at me like waves every few minutes; one moment, I think you've been involved in some terrible accident, the next that you've deliberately taken off. They hit me, one after the other – brimming with the unthinkable. Fear about your wellbeing seizes me and I ring the local hospital, The Queen Elizabeth in Cosham again, just in case. Maybe you crashed the car somewhere off the beaten track and have been lying unconscious at the wheel all night. Perhaps another passing motorist has finally found you. There is only one obvious way to get to the village shop from our cottage, but perhaps in your distraction, you went the wrong way – and that's why I didn't find you.

You're not at the hospital. I ask the receptionist to check twice. I ring St Luke's hospital in Portsmouth, over five miles away. Same story.

I take Frank out into the woods, but my mind isn't on it. It passes in a blur and I'm back in the kitchen. I make myself the kind of strong tea you make for me –

it's barely drinkable, but it brings me closer to you. I pour it into your mug. It's as if I'm drinking *your* tea with you.

I drag myself around from room to room. I can relate to your father now, see exactly what it must be like, losing the order of things, forgetting how to live. I keep seeing your washed-out, bewildered face when you told me you didn't know there was a baby and that you were so sorry. The potential for utter euphoria shot down before it could even register, because the baby had already left your body. You kept opening and closing your eyes as if you thought you were in a dream. I slam down the mug of tea, spilling it all over next week's *Radio Times* and realise that I'm the one to blame. I've been so caught up in my own diagnosis and doubts about being the father – I haven't reached out enough to share your pain. I'm so sorry, Dee. It's all my fault. I've driven you away.

You always tell me I'm laid-back, but it's not true – I play the part well to everyone, even you, but underneath I'm uptight, holding on. You don't know, Dee, that the day my father died, when adolescence was exploding inside my hormonally charged body, I did an abominable thing that I've never told anyone about. Blind rage can make people act in atrocious ways. In fact, I'm riddled with faults you don't appear to notice. You admire my self-discipline – my refusal to be beaten at squash, rigorously completing my fifty chin-ups at the gym, meticulously planning my lectures – but really I'm just inflexible. I'm arrogant too, believing since I became entranced by you that we were invincible as a couple.

With hindsight, my attitude seems not only pompous, but naïve – things aren't always so black and white. Is that what you've found now, Dee?

The first time I met you, five years ago now, I felt a solid certainty that we had not only met before, but that we'd existed together in some other setting and timeframe far removed from this one. I had this strong sense that we'd already been on an epic journey together, survived against the odds, so that when we met that day, in the crowd at Trafalgar Square, there was a startling familiarity and a sense of reunion. When I dared to mention it on our first proper date (bolstered by a couple of gin and tonics), you sat back with incredulity. You knew exactly what I was saying.

'We must have known each other before…' you said, breathless. 'It's so weird.'

We joked about it – played little games to see what we could guess about each other. I was right when I said I thought you were sporty and liked animals. You were spot on with my interest in Formula One and *Doctor Who*. You even guessed that I liked loud Mandela-style shirts and could do a decent Sean Connery impression. This surreal ready-made understanding was why I felt instantly sure about you, secure both about who you were and my feelings for you. Even so, the way things progressed between us has still been breathtaking.

Getting married had never been on my To Do list, but you won me over. I was convinced from the age of around seventeen that I'd always be a bachelor. I don't need a psychotherapist to tell me why. Family.

Everything comes back to family. As a young kid, I adored my dad and so did thousands of others. I had to share him. When your father is Ronnie Penn, left-back for West Ham, it's hard to have him to yourself. Everywhere, people would stop him on the pavement and ask for autographs – but we had special times just the two of us; camping trips and seaside visits. There just weren't enough of them. Mum joined us too and we had family days out at Alton Towers and London Zoo, but again, I can count them on one hand.

If I wasn't going to see much of my father, then I wanted a brother or sister. A proper family. I'm the sort of person who comes to life around other people and left to my own devices too long I'd get down in the dumps and lazy, so much so that Mum would often think I was ill. She wasn't around a lot either; she insisted on working – as an optician – even though money wasn't an issue. She was fascinated by the mechanics of the eye and didn't want to give up her career. Dad was around even less: training, matches, publicity. I don't blame anyone. They were both following their dreams. I slotted in there somewhere, but there was too much empty space around me – that books, toys, games and TV couldn't fill. I had school friends, of course, but they were more interested in my father than me.

Then dad left when I was only eight. He'd met someone else and it was all over. Mum was devastated and coiled into herself. That was when I started having problems with anger. I hid it well: never disruptive in school, never snappy with Mum. But I knew one day it was going to erupt out of control and do some damage.

In my view, my father had done a terrible thing to me and our family. I hated him for going. We met up now and again – every time away from the house, but it always felt fake. The ice cream never tasted the same, the rides on the big dipper had lost their thrill, the amusement arcades felt tacky and cheap.

Then he died of a heart attack when I was fifteen. It was a shock to everyone, but to me it was as if he had died a second time.

Amidst episodes of seething rage and grief, I made a decision. In my late teens, I vowed that I was never going to put myself at risk like that again. Marriages failed – it was inevitable – and it wasn't fair on the children who were left like pinballs, ricocheting around in the middle. I wasn't going to go anywhere near a situation like that – one which could cause so much pain.

Then you came along, Dee, and day by day, without you knowing it, you gently tugged me away from my resolution. I don't know how you did it, but before long there were new ideologies folded over my old fears and doubts. After about a year, it all became clear. The way forward was a matter of me making sure I didn't repeat the patterns in my parent's marriage, not about avoiding the situation altogether. You helped me see that I was all the things my father wasn't: reliable, consistent, hands on, keen to be involved. There was no way I was going to turn out like him and do what he did. I wanted to start a family. A 'proper' family with not just one child, but several; knitted together with support and love. I was ready, with you beside me, Dee, to be a father.

It's 5.30pm and I'm struggling. I don't know how to get through the rest of the day. I find myself in one room then the next with no recollection of getting there and no purpose behind my actions. I'm waiting for something, looking for something.

At 6pm, I can't bear the silence anymore and I try your phone again. I've lost count of the number of times I've called. I leave yet another voicemail message asking you to call. It's now almost twenty-four hours since you disappeared – this is serious. I call the police and confirm you have not returned. I speak to a female duty sergeant and give the report number I was given yesterday. I explain you've been gone too long without getting in touch.

All officers taking a report of a missing person must start with the viewpoint that it is a potentially serious crime enquiry; they'll have to do something. She tells me they will visit 'the premises' this evening.

I ring Tara and Sally again. It's useless. There is nothing new. I decide to ring your sister once more – mainly to pass the time.

'I tried to call you,' comes her steely detached voice. 'I've just heard from Diane.'

'What? You have? When?' I'm on my feet, blood charging through my body.

'About twenty minutes ago.'

'Thank God! Is she okay? Where is she?'

'She's fine. It was a text, but she didn't say where she was.'

'Did you ring her back?'

'Yes – but it just went to voicemail.'

'Why didn't you call me?'

'I did…well, I tried. You were engaged.'

'Ah – I was doing another ring-round. What did she say?' I gallop through the words greedy for answers.

'She put, "Sorry – a bit stressed. Taking time out." Then two kisses.'

My feet rapidly fill with lead. 'Is that it?'

'Yeah. I think she just needs some space to work things through.' Alexa never misses an opportunity to demonstrate that she knows you better than I do.

'Did she say when she's coming back?'

'No. No – she didn't. I think we need to respect her need to be alone for a bit. After what's happened. Don't you?'

'Did she…mention me?' I want to scream *Why didn't you contact* me, *Dee*? but I can't expect Alexa to answer that.

'No – I told you exactly what her message said.' As usual, she doesn't bother to hide her hostility. She's always been like this. I've run out of ways to try to appease her.

'You make it sound like my fault.'

'I can't believe you found out something as huge as that and didn't tell her.'

You must have told Alexa about my diagnosis sometime before you left yesterday. I don't blame you. I know you sometimes have the need to turn to others, not just me. It's often hard to say how you really feel to the person who is the source of the problem.

'I've only just found out,' I tell her, stretching the truth.

'Six weeks, she said. That's how long you've had the results and you must have had check-ups and tests long before that and never said a word.'

'I was going to.' Alexa is the last person I want to be justifying myself to.

'Of course you were.' She's short and sharp with me. 'I've got to go.'

'Ring me – please – if you hear—'

She's already gone.

I am stunned. You're not missing – you've left of your own accord. I'm struggling with the notion that you need space. I can't get my head around it. At what point did you make this decision? You left so casually – you didn't look like someone who was taking off.

I try to recall exactly what happened that night. We were hugging on the sofa discussing how we might mark the loss of our baby with some kind of ritual with candles and roses. I'd drunk too much – I apologise for that – and you offered to go to the village shop for me when I realised we were out of painkillers. It was last minute, you were just in your jogging pants. What did you say at the door? I can't remember exactly. *See you in a minute? See you soon? Back shortly?* It wasn't a grand goodbye.

You kissed me. Yes, you did. You reached up on tiptoes as I stood on the doorstep and pressed your lips against mine. Not a dismissive peck on the cheek, but a plump back-before-you-know-it kind of kiss.

You didn't take anything with you apart from your phone and your handbag. Or did you?

I hurtle up the stairs and fling open the wardrobes. Four empty hangers rattle as they swing loose. This isn't the way it normally looks; we're for ever having to double-up, because there are no hangers to spare. I check the bathroom cabinet – why didn't I do this yesterday? Your little bottle of sedatives has gone. I sit on the bed and drag at my hair. Why is there no note? At least you could have left me a few words of explanation. Were you that angry with me?

I check the top of the wardrobe – the suitcases are all still there. The holdall and overnight bags are still squashed up alongside the towels in the cupboard. I check your bedside cabinet. Your watch has gone – but you were wearing that during the day. There's a hairclip, one with a butterfly – I notice you've started wearing the one with a kingfisher instead, lately. The novel you started is still here. I pick it up, flick through the pages. That's odd. You told me you've read at bedtime ever since you were a child and can't do without it – you say it's a vital comfort that helps you get off to sleep. You always take a book when we go away. It's still here.

I call the police again and give them this new information; you've been in touch with your sister. I explain that your appointment diary isn't by the bed, but that doesn't mean a great deal. It could be downstairs. The same duty sergeant as before tells me to keep them informed, but as you've been in touch, they won't be taking any further action for the time being. 'It's not a police matter if someone chooses to leave,' she tells me. She's no doubt had specialist training in handling 'relationship breakdown' cases and is drawing her own conclusions. We must have had a terrible row, but I'm refusing to acknowledge it. You must have taken off to make some serious decisions about your future...

A new surge of energy consumes me as I start a major treasure hunt for your appointment diary, just in case it's here. It might give some indication as to your plans and whereabouts. I scour each room, not caring about the mess I make as I fling cushions aside, pull out drawers, tip piles of magazines onto the coffee table. I can't find it.

I still don't understand your message to Alexa. You haven't seemed out of sorts with me or looked like you've been putting on a brave face. I can always tell.

Have I misjudged a cause for concern between us? I trawl my memories trying to find a subject that might be more serious than I thought. If there's anything, it's the issue with my mother when I blew up at her at Christmas and fled just as she was slicing into the turkey. You assured me at first that you understood and were fine with it, but I heard the tremble of disapproval in your voice. I pressed you and it came out like poison from a wound.

'I can't believe you called Bruce a shabby loan shark.'

'Well – he is,' I said. 'He owns a payday loan company. It's called Loansafe, for goodness sake. He should rename it Loanscam.'

'And I can't believe what you did afterwards...' you said. 'Smashing her plant pots like a vandal. I was *really* shocked, Harper.' Your eyelids flickered with disbelief. 'And a bit frightened, if I'm honest. Your anger…'

'I know. It was a one-off – I don't usually get worked up like that.' I didn't look you in the eye at that point. I couldn't. It's because of what I did – once – something so shameful that I can never say it out loud. I can only ever refer to it with you, inside my head. I can't bear you to know my anger isn't as tamed as I'd like you to think. I'm still a loose cannon at times – though I've done my utmost to play it down with everyone who knows me.

'They're together now – that's how it is. Your mum waited fourteen years after your father died. She's allowed to be happy.'

'Yeah, well she won't be for long. She's made a big mistake. I don't know what she sees in him. It's only because he showed an interest in her. She's eternally grateful – that's all.'

You tugged my sleeve. 'Did she say that?'

'She's settling for him because she's in her fifties.'

'Did she tell you this?' you persisted.

'More or less. Mum said, "How many more chances am I going to get at my age?"'

You told me I had to make it up to my mother. You told me I'd regret it. You didn't hold back. You were right, of course, but I wasn't ready to give in so easily.

But even that disagreement wasn't a big deal between us. Do you remember how it ended? You punched my arm and told me I was a bully – and I hauled you into a Sumo grip and put my foot on your belly, just to prove it. You dissolved into fits of laughter and I had to kiss you. Our disagreements usually end like that – we can't stay adversaries for long and we've *never* slept with an argument between us.

That's why taking off like this is so out of character. You've never needed to be away from me before. But then, something as big as this has never happened to us before. I come back to the conclusion that I must have failed you, not paid enough attention after the miscarriage.

I take another U-turn in my thinking. This chopping and changing is making me feel unhinged.

Maybe you came back when I was out looking for you. Or perhaps you hid a few basic items in the car so you could leave empty-handed. But that implies forward planning. That in itself is out of character, but *secret* forward planning is even harder to grasp. On those rare occasions when you *do* have a plan, you've always been one to involve others; to share ideas and ask advice. Your best friend. Your sister. Your colleagues. But, none of them knew a thing.

Does this mean an underhand and conscious deception? Did you lie when you said you were only going as far as the village shop? Have you, in fact, had something bigger planned all along?

Chapter 8
Marion

13 July

'Most kids of seven straddle the world between make-believe and reality,' sighs Marion, 'but Clara has both feet firmly in make-believe.'

The nurse dabs antiseptic on Clara's left knee and presses a plaster over it. The smell catches in Marion's throat and she freezes for a moment, gripping the blanket on the bed, wondering if she's going to be sick.

'Are you okay?'

'It's the chemo,' she explains. 'I've just had another round and it's hit me hard.'

The nurse gives her a sympathetic nod and points to a grey cardboard vomit bowl, sitting on one of the chairs like a bowler hat. Marion nods; she may well need to reach for it any moment.

Dr Norman pulls aside the curtain and sits on the edge of the bed. 'Now then, Miss Delderfield – a little bird tells me you've been climbing into places where little girls shouldn't go.'

'Which little bird?' Clara asks, interested.

'A little bird who loves her little chick very much and was very upset when the chick went missing.' He glances up at Marion and winks. She likes him straight away; he's young, probably in his twenties and looks like the kind of person you might see presenting a programme on CBBC. He seems totally at ease with her daughter.

'Clara doesn't live on the same plane as other people – she always has to be higher up or lower down than everyone else.'

'Mum says she prefers it when I climb into books – she says I'm a lot safer there.'

Marion rolls her eyes. 'You bet,' she says. 'Clara's getting into reading more now, though – thank goodness. She goes to the storyteller at the library after school and on Saturdays.'

'It's really good,' says Clara. 'Helen knows all the stories in the world and doesn't even need the books.'

'That's very impressive,' says the doctor, taking Clara's pulse, then pressing the stethoscope against her back. 'What did Humpty-Dumpty have?' he says, as he holds still.

'A great fall.'

'And who put him back together again?'

Clara frowns. 'Nobody,' she says perplexed.

'Not all the king's horses and all the king's men?'

'No – silly – they *couldn't* put him back together again.'

'Don't be rude, Clara,' Marion cuts in.

Clara looks unimpressed. 'You should know that by now,' she says to the doctor.

He moves the stethoscope. 'Cough for me,' he adds. Marion is pleased to see that Clara seems barely disturbed by her ordeal. She knows they must talk about what happened; she must give her child all the time she needs to talk through her experience, but on the surface all is well. Clara is a tough little kid and seems to be finding the whole episode exciting. Nevertheless, she's still only seven and realising she was trapped like that – alone, in the cold and the dark – must have been scary for her. Just not as scary as it would be for normal kids.

Marion feels the room lurch dramatically to the right and grabs the end of the bed. 'Sorry, I need fresh air...' She turns to the nurse, 'Could you keep her here until I get back?'

'Sure,' says the nurse.

'Mummy's very sick,' says Clara in a matter-of-fact way, counting the badgers on the bed sheet.

Marion is longer than she wants to be. First throwing up in the toilet, then having to wait ages for the lift to get outside; she doesn't feel strong enough to manage the stairs. She has to get out – she needs real air, uncontaminated with disinfectant and sanitisers. She finds a bench on the grassy forecourt and sits down for a few moments. She watches two ambulances arrive delivering elderly people in wheelchairs. The second one down the ramp is a woman so shrunken and fragile she looks already dead, smothered in the blanket wrapped around her.

Marion shifts her line of sight and focuses on the car park instead. A broad man in a bib is shouting at a motorist. She's finding it hard to listen to him ranting on. These days any signs of animosity or disharmony make her want to cower and hide. It's as if the myeloma has stripped away her skin and made her too sensitive for ordinary life. She goes inside for a cup of water from the machine by the stationers. When she gets back to the room where Clara was being checked over, there's a young boy on the bed and a different nurse.

'Excuse me?' she calls out. The nurse turns and comes towards her. 'I was in here a few minutes ago with my daughter, Clara Delderfield – she's supposed to be waiting for me.'

The nurse grunts and presses her latex-bound fingers into her hairline. 'Have you tried the waiting room – down there on the right?'

Marion's heels squeal as she turns to leave. *Don't you dare do this to me again, Clara,* she mutters under her breath. She scans the faces in the waiting room, but Clara's isn't one of them. She opens the toilet door and calls out, then gets the lift down to the ground floor to the coffee shop. She isn't there either. She can't remember the name of either the doctor or the nurse they met first. She remembers looking at the nurse's name badge, but her memory is like that these days – she takes hold of information and it falls through the cracks. She heads for the main reception desk and spots a familiar pink dress, flouncing along the corridor.

'Clara! Where have you been?' She tugs at her daughter's wrist harder than she means to.

'Nowhere.'

The nurse who was asked to stay with her comes scuttling behind her. 'Ah – there she is,' she says, breathing heavily. 'I'm so sorry.' She clutches her chest as if having a mild heart attack. 'She wandered off.'

'You can't tell Clara to wait anywhere, she always disappears,' Marion scolds.

'There was an emergency,' states the nurse whose name is – of course – Natalie, she remembers now.

'Sorry. She's here – that's all that matters,' says Marion, recognising more than anyone how hard it is to keep Clara in one place.

'Dr Norman said she only has a few bruises. Nothing's broken and there's no damage done as far as he can see. Just keep an eye on her.'

Marion sighs with gratitude. 'Thank you. Easier said than done.'

Clara doesn't say anything on the way to the bus stop. Marion notices her daughter's hair needs a decent trim; she's having to use her sequined Alice band every day to keep the fringe out of her eyes. Simple tasks like this have been knocked beyond Marion's grasp since her illness.

A red bus turns the corner, halts at the kerb and they step aboard.

They settle near the back. 'What do you want to do when we get back? Watch *Paddington*? Read *Rainbow Magic*? Or play table tennis with Samuel?' Samuel is eight and lives next door. Clara is more than a match for him at football, skateboarding, climbing trees – and now table tennis. As a result, she's grown bored of him and prefers entertaining herself. While Marion is in bed, which is the only place she can be on her 'bad' days, Clara reads, watches TV or explores mysterious fantasy worlds and saves kingdoms on her Nintendo Wii. She's already tackling books and playing games designed for nine-year-olds and whilst Marion is proud of this, she also knows it's because she spends a lot of time alone –

or with her imaginary friends. More times than she'd like to admit, when Marion is supposed to be watching her, Clara slips out. Her daughter has a bunch of local friends in Nettledon, but she gets fixated on certain stories and musicals and storms off if her friends want to move on to something new. Instead, Clara wanders off exploring places, building stepping stones across the beck, collecting flowers and dead insects, performing her own plays in the deserted fields. She's an expert at losing track of time.

Clara shuffles in her seat and makes a little snuffling sound in reply. It's not like her to be this quiet and Marion puts her withdrawal down to being tired after an eventful couple of days. Marion doesn't want to make a big thing of what has happened and decides to keep everything as normal as she can. 'Scrambled egg later? What do you think?'

Clara gives a little shrug – half yes, half no.

As they get up to leave the bus, Marion sees Clara's fist is closed. 'What's that in your hand?'

After they alight, Clara tentatively opens out her palm as if she's been hiding a diamond. It's an apple core.

'Where did you get the apple from, honey?' She knows Clara had no money at the hospital.

Clara sniffs. 'The Wizard of Oz gave it to me.'

'The Wizard of Oz?'

'He said he granted wishes and when I said I wanted an apple – he gave me one.'

'When did this happen?'

'When you were sick.'

'You shouldn't talk to strangers – I've told you that

before, Clara. Remember Pinocchio? He runs into terrible trouble because he talks to strangers – even if someone seems nice, it can be *dangerous*.'

'He just gave me an apple.' Clara's bottom lip shoots out.

'Remember Snow White?'

She puts her finger against her teeth and thought about the question. 'The apple was poisoned?'

'Exactly.'

Chapter 9
Harper

1 August – Second day missing

Alexa is sitting staring out of the window when I walk into the bar. She has agreed to meet me after her day's work at the gym at Gunwharf Quays in Portsmouth. She works as a personal trainer and I imagine she relishes pushing people through the pain barrier.

'Sorry I'm a bit late,' I say. 'I came on the train – I'm having to get around everywhere without the car.'

'Poor you,' she says. I feel drained in her presence already. Talking to Alexa is like stirring thick tar with a straw. She's wearing dense black eyeliner and bright lipstick that is almost purple. Without make-up the two of you look remarkably similar, but inside you're poles apart. She's hard where you are soft; she's full of thorns and guarded, where you allow yourself to be seen.

'Can I get you another drink?' I offer, to show willing.

'No, thanks – I've just started this one.' She waves her glass of fizzy liquid at me jangling the ice, as if this fact should be obvious.

'Can I see it?' I ask. 'The text?'

She says nothing, presses a few buttons on her phone and holds up the screen about a foot away from me as though she's afraid I might run off with it. I try to set aside the fact that you decided to contact your sister instead of me. I can see in the possessive way Alexa hangs on to her phone that, to her, it is a significant factor worthy of smugness.

'When did you last see her?' I ask.

'This message was yesterday, I told you.' When she's with me, Alexa's face is never far from a scowl. It's that way now; tight and closed.

'But when did you last *see* her – in person?'

'The day of the miscarriage – Friday. In the hospital.'

'Okay – before that. The last time it was just the two of you.'

'The previous Friday. For coffee after work. You were working late.'

'What was she like? How was she?'

'Fine. A bit tired. She'd had an argument with Mum as you probably know.'

No, I didn't.

'What about? She didn't tell me.'

'Maybe she doesn't tell you everything.' Ah, the sting, that neat left hook.

She's right of course. You don't and clearly haven't told me everything. I had the phone call from the hospital to prove it – just before I left to meet your sister. It confirmed my worst fears; the miscarried foetus did not carry my DNA. I am not the father.

It was like being hit by a truck and I'm still in that surreal state where my brain knows something devastating has happened, but my body hasn't yet reacted to the impact. I need to stay that way until I can deal with the aftershock. I'm not in a position – out here

64

in a public place with someone I don't trust – to let myself take it in. Nevertheless, questions bombard me at every turn. *Was it a full-blown affair or just the once? Do I know him? When did it start? Do you love him?* I can't face them – not yet.

Alexa is checking her watch, looking like I'm wasting her time. I have to remember that her hostility comes from a desire to protect you, her younger sister. She's been like a hissing snake from the moment I came into your life. When we left London, she waited six months and, lo and behold, she found a 'nice little flat' in Portsmouth and ended up sixteen miles away.

'The argument,' I say, attempting to re-engage her. 'Do you know what it was about?'

'Dad. Mum's treating him like a helpless child.'

'Is that all?'

She shrugs. 'Yes.'

'Has Diane been in touch with you since yesterday?'

'Not personally – look here,' she taps the screen, 'she says she's *taking time out*,' she enunciates each syllable as if I'm mentally impaired. 'She wants space – from everything, by the looks of it. She'll get back to us when she's ready.'

I'm taking in what she's just said. 'You said – *not personally.*'

'She's posted a few bits on Facebook and Twitter – all very bland – she doesn't say where she is.'

'Really? Why didn't you tell me?' I pat my pockets. It hasn't occurred to me that you might get in touch in such an impersonal way. 'I didn't check. What did she put? What did she say?' I'm holding my phone, but don't know how to find what you've posted. I don't use social media.

'Like I say, just generic stuff. About the dog you're looking after. A film. Nothing important.'

Getting information from her is like trying to open a can of soup with my fingernails. 'Has she said anything else to you, recently?'

'About the pregnancy?'

'Or about – anything else?'

'I didn't know she'd conceived – for a start. *She* didn't know.'

'What about other things – has she mentioned…anything bothering her?' I really want to know if they've discussed some other man, but I daren't venture into that territory just yet. I'm still reeling after the phone call. I don't know how I'll react if Alexa admits you've been seeing someone for months. Nevertheless, my question could lead there and I can't imagine Alexa has any desire to protect me.

'No – she hasn't said anything.' I'm still hovering over her as she remains seated at the small round table, sipping her drink. I didn't get around to buying one for myself and now it feels too late. An onlooker would assume I'm hassling her and she wants me to leave.

'Tell me the instant you hear from her.'

'The same goes for you,' she says, making it sound like I've insulted her.

It seems rude to leave so soon, but it was a mistake to meet here; a place where one would normally sit back, relax and catch up with friends. I never do any of those things when Alexa is around.

On the way back to the cottage, near impossible though it is, I force myself to keep the call from the hospital at arm's length. I believed you when you said you hadn't been with anyone else. I wanted my specialist to be wrong and for my infertility not to be absolute. I thought that *must* have been what happened. If I allow the words 'negative test results' to sink in, they will blast apart my will to live. Instead, I must stay strong to work out where you've gone. I need to think about those few words you've left on Alexa's phone. They're all we have of you and the only shred of substance I can hang on to:

Sorry – a bit stressed. Taking time out XX.

Something about the wording doesn't ring true for me – I've never heard you use the phrase *take time out*, for starters. I can't hear your voice in my head saying it. I try to rationalise my doubt. We're different people depending on who we're with; perhaps you use those kinds of words with Alexa. Nevertheless, it feels all wrong, but maybe I'm simply aggrieved that you chose to let Alexa know instead of me.

Before I get home, I stop at the village shop and ask Marvin if I can look at his CCTV footage from the camera outside his shop. He lets me watch from 7pm onwards on Wednesday evening. A handful of locals I recognise and several faces I don't, cross in and out of the lens. I remember you were wearing grey jogging pants and a pink T-shirt and had your long dark hair clipped at the side like you usually do. I'd know immediately if you walked by. I watch all the footage until the digital clock at the bottom reads 20.05, when Marvin locked up and pulled down the shutters. The film is black and white and blurry, but I know that none of the individuals captured on it that evening are you.

It means you didn't arrive. Did you ever intend to go? Did you have another plan already worked out? Are you with someone else? The father of the child? Have you turned to him instead of me?

Back at the cottage, I go straight to the kitchen and pour a glass of whisky. More bricks have fallen down the chimney in my absence and there's a plateau of fresh dust on the hearth mat. There's a damp tea towel squashed beside a cushion on the comfy chair. I notice newspapers, empty mugs, unopened post and unironed clothes littering the surfaces. The coffee table, sofa, mantelpiece and book shelves are disappearing under a surge of swelling detritus. When did it get so untidy? My mess has a life of its own, self-generating, breeding around me. I can't bear it. It is going to take up all the space and squeeze me out.

I find your cardigan slung over the stool by the fireplace and press it to my face. It's only two days since you left, but it feels far longer. I breathe in the dizzy smell of you. I love that perfume that is you, Dee; a heady cocktail of vanilla, fizzy sherbet and sex.

I can't hold on any longer.

At this moment the truth hits me like a searchlight breaking open the dead of night in a prison camp. It pins me down and forces me to turn and confront it. I can't escape it – I have to face the fact that the baby, our baby, wasn't mine. I do the only thing I know how and retreat to my bolt-hole in the garden.

It's hot and smells of disinfectant in here. The

chickens left with the previous owners and only the remains of sawdust, grain caught in the cracks in the wood and the odd ginger feather indicate they were once here. My breathing sounds hollow and far away. It takes me back to that time when my father was still with us.

I was about seven and he was trying to teach me how to control a football. I was hopeless; unco-ordinated with more steps off balance than upright. Dad kept a rusty old welding mask in the shed, that used to belong to his father. He forced me into it, pulling the straps tight. He told me to keep my head up so I couldn't look at my feet. *Feel the ball,* he shouted, *don't look down.* The mask was unwieldy, making me top-heavy and I could hardly breathe. It sent me off balance even more and I tripped over the ball. I can still hear his sneering laughter as he watched me try to get up. He didn't put out his hand to help me to my feet. He was full of scorn and left me there like a beetle on its back. My father was good at walking away.

I can hear him laughing at me now as I stomp around in the chicken coop. I don't know where to put myself. I take a swipe at the wall with my fist. I punch and punch, carrying on until I make my knuckles bleed. If only I could suffocate his voice; there are barbs attached to each word, biting into my skin with pronouncements that you've slept with another man, you were carrying another man's child, you *cheated* on me. I don't know how to face this. I certainly can't accept it. It's unbelievable. But, after the miscarriage, the tests said my DNA wasn't there. It wasn't our child. End of story.

I forget my father's voice and focus on you, Dee.

More anger, more humiliation. I kick the crate I was sitting on and hurl it into a corner where I crunch it to a pulp with my feet. I feel as though I'm being thrown around on an invisible hurricane ride at the fairground, tossed first in one direction, then the other. You wouldn't have done this – *yet you did*. We were solid and complete – *yet you found love elsewhere*. Nevertheless, no matter how many times I scan my memories, I can't find a single thing that backs up what has happened. It doesn't tally with your behaviour in any way whatsoever.

I sit down on the dusty floor for ten more minutes, maybe twenty, I'm not sure, and wait as the arguments and counter arguments fight their own battle inside my head. It is only Frank barking, then howling outside the door that coaxes me out. I open the door and thumb his jowls, promising him I'll take him out later.

I head back into the house and run my knuckles under the cold tap. I feel played out and run dry. I cast aside the box from yesterday's pizza and open the laptop. I enter your name followed by 'Twitter' into the search engine and track down your recent posts. There are two tweets, the first sent yesterday at 6pm: *Anyone seen* The Grand Budapest Hotel? *Any good?* And the second from today at 10am, a quote: *'Courage is resistance to fear, mastery of fear – not absence of fear.' Mark Twain.*

They are meaningless to me – I've never heard you mention Mark Twain – are they meant to be some kind of clue to your whereabouts? On your Facebook feed, coupled with a photograph of Frank are two words *Love Life*. The photo was posted today at 2.15pm and I recognise the wooden signpost in the background. It was taken in the fields near our cottage. I remember you showing it to me last week. I'm stunned. You're still tweeting and using Facebook, but not contacting me! What's going on?

My training is never to take evidence at face value. I hammer home this message to my students – *don't assume, don't jump to conclusions, don't make new information fit what you think you know.*

I stop and think. What strikes me first is how inappropriate these posts are given your – our – circumstances. You're grieving and in shock and these posts are detached and emotionally barren. Which takes me to my next point – they're devoid of any detail that says they come from you. There is nothing of you in them whatsoever. Anyone could have written them. Except they'd need your phone and your passwords. Which would mean someone is with you.

On a roll, I check our online phone bill to see which calls you've made from home. I cross-check the numbers against our phonebook and there are two I can't find. I ring the first and get an answerphone – it is a hairdresser. I try the second. It is our local GP's surgery and I reach an out-of-hours line. I say 'Sorry wrong number' and replace the receiver. Of course, there's your mobile – but that's gone; I don't know who you've called from that and only the police can trace it.

I shut the laptop, grab Frank's lead and take him out. I'm glad he's there, he's undemanding company and never judges me. I check the landline answerphone on my return – more messages from friends and neighbours asking after you. I can't return them; I have nothing to tell them, so I take a shower. I phone two of your work colleagues, Greg and Marie and ask if they noticed anything different about you before school broke up, a week and a half ago. Greg says he thought you seemed 'a bit tired, maybe'. Marie says you seemed 'just the same'. I think back to any changes in your routine. You only had two days without school before the miscarriage. Did you do anything out of the ordinary in your time off? Did you go anywhere? Who did you see? I go to the wall calendar in the kitchen; I never did find your diary – it's probably in your handbag, which I saw you take with you. My dental appointment last Monday is marked up in pencil, there's a note in your handwriting to call your mum on Friday and a reminder to put the recycling bin out on Tuesday morning. Nothing useful.

It's late, but I'm not tired in the least. I check your social media sites again to see if anything new has been posted, leave a text for Alexa to check if she's heard from you, then go to the second bedroom, which we're using as a study. I decide to start here and treat every room in the house like a crime scene. I take the Dictaphone from my briefcase and start walking and talking, making notes about what I see and don't see.

Chapter 10
Diane

9 July

It has been raining all day, but still Tara has turned up at the cottage wearing shorts and wedge sandals with the platform made of coiled rope. They are sodden and she takes them off at the door. Frank is dozing on the hearthrug and Tara stops to stroke his tail with her bare foot before she joins Diane in the kitchen. Harper is out at a criminology department meeting and Diane has invited Tara over for homemade spaghetti bolognese.

'You always make everything so special,' Tara remarks, admiring the table in the centre of the kitchen, decorated with napkins in the shape of fleur-de-lis, a vase of sweet peas from the garden and a single pink rose tied onto each napkin ring.

'Only for special people,' Diane says with a wry smile, straightening a fork.

She brings the steaming dish to the table and serves up.

She knows as soon as she tips the first forkful onto her tongue that she's put too much chilli in it. 'Sorry…' she groans with her mouth full.

'S'okay,' Tara replies, stoically, flapping her hand in front of her mouth. 'I know you're not a natural in the kitchen. I can always get a take-away on the way home.'

Diane sniggers, slurping a long snake of spaghetti through pursed lips. She loves the way Tara says it as it is.

Tara takes a big gulp of red wine, shutting her eyes briefly as it goes down. 'Here's to the end of term,' she announces.

'I can't wait,' Diane says, tapping her glass against her friend's. She always makes one glass last while Tara has two – a habit from her swimming days. 'I still haven't got anything ready for assembly on Friday. Did you know our dear deputy head has roped me in to doing it again. Third time this term.'

'It's only because you do such a good job. *And* I think he's got the hots for you.'

Diane pulls face. 'Well – he can flipping-well pour iced water on it. He's getting on my nerves; always there when I turn around.'

Tara plucks a piece of rocket from the salad bowl. 'Morrell's a bit officious, but he's not that bad.'

'Yes, he *is*,' Diane retorts. 'He's so slimy for a start. I hate the way bits of spittle collect at the corner of his mouth when he speaks to you. Have you noticed? And he comes too close – he's far too familiar for my liking.'

'You have too much sex-appeal, Dee, that's your problem.'

'That's grand coming from you.' Most of the male members of staff and a couple of the female ones have had crushes on Tara since she arrived.

'If only.' Tara has dated regularly – a string of no-hoper boyfriends. She tends to fall for the moody silent

74

type then gets upset when they're moody and silent. She finds kind, warm men boring. Diane has never been like that. She's always wanted someone straightforward who didn't play games.

Tara makes polite in-roads into the spaghetti, then puffs out a breath and props her fork on the plate, calling it a day.

'At what point did you know Harper was the one?' she asks wistfully, sitting back twirling her wine glass.

'It's strange. I knew straight away when we met at that rally in Trafalgar Square. I never thought I'd ever find anyone like Harper. He was holding an umbrella and a bag of cherries and he offered me one casually, like we knew each other. He instantly felt like family, like someone I'd already spent time with way back in the past. It was odd and decidedly disconcerting.'

In fact she couldn't believe her luck when Harper noticed her and asked her out. He shared that same uncanny feeling that they'd met before. It was totally bizarre. Every step in their relationship seemed to her like the most incredible gift. When he asked her to marry him – she burst into tears.

'That's not the response I was hoping for,' he'd said, nervously, still on one knee in a not-very-secluded spot in St James' Park.

'It means yes,' she snivelled, half laughing, half crying.

Diane found out as soon as they started dating that Harper wasn't interested in having a family. For someone so tactile and openly generous, she couldn't understand it, but in time Harper told her everything.

Tara folds her arms. 'So he wasn't interested in

having kids until you came along?'

'It wasn't that he wasn't interested in having a family, he was terrified by the idea,' Dee tells her. 'His father had a lot to do with it. It transpired that Harper was convinced he'd repeat what he called his father's "despicable behaviour" and be incapable of sustaining a long-term relationship. Until we talked about it and I worked on him, that was. I gradually chipped away at his armour, until I broke through and steered him towards a completely new frame of mind. Soon after, he proposed.'

Tara helps herself to more wine. 'Is it that you hardly ever have arguments with Harper or that you don't tell me about them?'

Diane laughs, then becomes quiet. 'I know it sounds unlikely, but we haven't had any major rows. I expected to make tons of compromises when we got together, but I've hardly made any. He has this innate respect and decency about him I've never seen in any other man.'

Tara stares into the Rioja left in her glass. 'So you haven't had *any* bust ups?'

'No – not really – seriously. There was one tricky time over Christmas when Harper walked out of the festive meal at his mother's – you know about that – but that's the biggest one.'

'Was that when he trashed his mother's plant pots on the patio?' Tara – never one to hold back.

Diane nodded.

'Jeez – it doesn't sound like Harper,' Tara exclaims.

'It's not,' Diane protests. 'It really caught me by surprise. But it was a one-off. He's not an aggressive person in the least.'

'Has he made it up to her?'

'No, not yet. But he will, in time.' Diane turns to the fridge and slides out a chocolate tart — Tara's favourite. She sets it in the centre of the table with a jug of thick cream. 'He's not one to hold on to bad feelings and he loves his mother.'

Tara cuts herself a wedge of tart large enough for two and smothers it in double cream. She scoops a loose drip from the spout and licks her finger. 'What do you think of his new stepfather?'

'Bruce? He runs a loan company and it seems so underhand. I can see what Harper means. I'd hate to be involved in anything like that. It's so unethical, preying on people's deluded optimism that magically they're going to have the money to pay everything back as soon as they get to pay-day.'

'What's Bruce like, personally?'

'Not sure, really. He seems a bit slippery. He's got this humorous, nice-guy front all the time, but he often laughs at other people's expense and he's opinionated and sexist. Racist too, I'm afraid.'

'Oh, dear,' Tara cringes. 'What does Harper's mother see in him?'

'She seems to adore him. He appears to treat her really well; he's besotted with her too. He can't do enough around the house, fixing things up, mowing the lawn, buying her expensive jewellery, taking her on trips. They're going on a cruise in September. Lilian says it's going to be a trip of a lifetime. She's so happy.'

'I wouldn't mind a bit of that,' says Tara. 'It's your

anniversary in September, isn't it?'

'Yeah – we're not doing anything big. Just going to a new restaurant in Winchester and staying overnight. I've got a new dress.'

'You must show me!' Tara gets up; she's like a fox chasing a rabbit whenever anyone mentions fashion.

They go up to the bedroom and Tara slips her feet into a pair of stilettos Diane has left by the mirror. She flops on the bed while Diane flicks through the hangers. Tara rolls onto her stomach, her knees bent, and picks up a DVD lying on Harper's bedside cabinet.

'Not *Doctor Who*…Oh, God – the box set. My kids at school are hooked on it. What's the appeal for a grown man like Harper?'

'He likes the idea of time-travel in a police box and having a complete personality change every three or four years!' Diane laughs at the quirks of her adorable husband. She remembers she left the new dress in the wardrobe in the spare bedroom so Harper won't see it. She'll fetch it as soon as there's a lull in conversation.

'You said he works with the police sometimes,' Tara continues.

Diane is barely listening. On the dresser is the glove puppet Harper's been playing with to tease Frank and she's thinking of her husband's hands. He has beautiful long expressive fingers, like Nureyev. She loves the way he holds the phone, grips his toothbrush, stirs a sauce. Everyone notices his hands and assumes he must be artistic in some way: a dancer, a painter, a pianist. In fact, he's none of these, but she loves the way he uses his hands to sculpt her body. The way he traces his playful fingers around her lips, nipples, armpits and inner thighs. They seem to have a sensibility of their own.

She snaps herself back to Tara's comment. 'He doesn't really work with them. He has colleagues in the force – through his university work mainly, but they share research.'

'You said he goes into prisons?'

'Not for the police. That's a bit different. He goes in twice a month as a prison visitor.'

'How did he get into that?'

Diane tugs at the tassel on the curtain tie at the window. 'His best friend was sent to Wormwood Scrubs for killing his girlfriend in 2002. Harper went to visit him, then became an official visitor and he's done it ever since. What happened to his friend was a catalyst. It had the profound effect of kick-starting his career. He didn't have a clue about what he wanted to do when he left school and suddenly he was studying criminology. He wanted to understand.'

'So why didn't he become a detective? You said he loves puzzles.'

'He didn't want to be in law enforcement. He didn't want to be one of the people who could have put Victor behind bars, but he wanted to work within the system; improving it for both victims and offenders.'

'Did he understand why his friend did it?'

'It was a spur of the moment thing, apparently. Victor wasn't thinking straight – he'd had a string of bad luck. He'd recently been hit by a car and needed surgery on his knee. He'd been dropped from the college rugby team and his grades had fallen off. He was depressed and stressed; his self-esteem was suffering, then came the final straw – he caught his girlfriend with someone else. She laughed in his face and in that moment, he snapped.'

'Wow – what did he do?'

'He strangled her in a fit of jealous rage.' She was inadvertently rolling the cord from the curtain around her fingers. 'Harper told me that as soon as Victor saw her slide to the floor, he was mortified. All he wanted was for her to stop laughing at him – and that's how it ended.'

'My God – male pride. A dangerous thing, huh?'

'Yeah. He lost it. Went totally out of control. Harper says it's more common than we think. Someone rises to the bait, makes a silly mistake, takes a risk, isn't thinking – and the result is that someone else dies. For Victor, hearing Nicci laugh at him was the ultimate humiliation and it tipped him over the edge. In those few seconds, he didn't know what he was doing.'

'What do you think?'

'I've only met Victor once – earlier this year. It's hard to say. He seemed meek and unassuming – but you can never tell what people are capable of, can you?'

'Do you think Harper can spot a criminal mind?' Tara looks fascinated, leaning back on her arms, her mouth hanging open.

'He says there's no such thing as a criminal mind. No particular type as far as he's concerned. People cross the line for hundreds of different reasons; greed, a sense of entitlement, fear, revenge, passion, anger, hurt, to protect their kids. Then there are those who are mentally

80

unwell, or have a warped sense of what is right and appropriate.'

'Yes – but don't you think there are people who are pure evil and hurt because they can, without any real motive?'

Diane taps her lip with her tongue. 'I think the ones who hurt others have been hurt themselves. It's a vicious circle. It comes from their own past – they don't just make a decision to be cruel.'

Tara makes a little humming sound, as if she's not convinced. She lies back on the bed, Diane's stilettos still on her feet, as if this is her place. They both jump when a sparrow flies into the glass of the French windows that lead onto the roof terrace. The tall panes were one of the features she and Harper loved about the place. Diane rushes over, concerned the bird is seriously injured. She hovers with her hand on the handle, wondering whether to open the door to rescue it.

'You'll frighten it,' says Tara. 'See if it recovers on its own.'

Diane finds it hard to stand by when a living creature is in pain – whether it's a dog, a frog or a squirming cockroach. She watches it as it hops around, disoriented, then flies off. She holds her chest and lets out a blast of air.

'Do they ever fly in when you have the windows open?' Tara is full of questions today; Diane can barely keep up.

'Yeah – only once. A robin came in.' She stays by the window and admires the work she's done on the roof terrace – the tall grasses around the edge to create privacy, the pots of herbs, the boxes of lavender. 'Let me get that dress,' she says, suddenly remembering why they're up here.

She comes back holding it against her body. It's off the shoulder, like her wedding dress, with a ruched crossover bodice at her ample bust, in sapphire-blue silk. Tara is, however, transfixed by something else. She's knocked over Diane's bag beside the bed and a book has flopped out onto the floor.

Tara's eyes widen. '*Managing Anger with Compassion*,' she stares with curiosity. 'This can't be for you...?' she says, hooking a question mark in at the end.

Diane stalls. 'There was a programme on TV...I'm interested...'

Tara pulls her down onto the bed; Diane's still clutching the dress. 'Oh – come on – you can't brush me off like that. Not when it's right here by your bedside.'

Diane doesn't know what to say. She hadn't planned on explaining this to anyone.

Tara lets out a loud whoosh of air. 'Sheesh – Dee, it's *me* – you can tell me anything, girl.'

'I know,' says Diane, trying not to look at Tara. 'It's fine. Honestly.'

Tara looks worried all of a sudden. She jerks upright. 'God, Dee – Harper's not rough with you, is he? He's not...abusive?'

Diane laughs, flapping her hands. 'Oh no, nothing like that.' It comes out rather flat.

'What then?' Tara waits, her mouth open.

'It's, er...look, I don't want to...you know...it's between Harper and me. It's no big deal.'

Tara's voice softens. 'You don't want to talk about it?'

Diane doesn't answer straight away. She's cursing the fact that Tara has found the book – she meant to find a proper hiding place for it – with the others. 'Harper is incredibly balanced and rational, but he has a slightly...troubled edge...' she says, trailing her fingers across the bodice of the dress.

'Are you frightened of him?'

'No! It's not like that. He adores me.' Diane tries to find the right words. She knows Tara means well, but she's not ready to tell her the full story. 'I've discovered...there's a darker side to him – that's all.'

Tara doesn't seem to like the sound of it. 'Darker – how?'

Diane stands up. 'Do you like the dress or not?'

'It's gorgeous,' Tara says, dismissively, glancing again at the book.

Diane hugs the dress. 'He never hurts me.'

Tara's frown folds into mock disapproval, but she stays quiet.

'Don't say anything will you?' Diane pleads.

Tara looks coy, twisting her pout to one side. 'Your secret is safe with me.'

Chapter 11
Harper

2 August – Third day missing

In the morning, I wake and in those first fuddled moments forget you're not here. I must have been dreaming about you – a tense, erotic dream. I reach out in bed to the place your body should be. It's cold and there is no hollow. Even the bed is forgetting you.

I pick up my phone from the bedside cabinet and ring your number. I've been ringing at regular intervals every day, but no longer with any hope – it's just to hear your recorded message. Sitting on the edge of the bed, I ring your sister; I have a specific question for her.

'Have you ever heard her use those words?' I ask after my opening attempt at pleasantries.

'What are you talking about?'

'Diane's message said: *Sorry – a bit stressed. Taking time out.* Then two kisses. Have you ever heard her use those words?'

'What – *taking time out?*'

'Yeah.'

There's a gap while she thinks about it. 'I don't know. I can't remember. I don't see why not.'

Alexa doesn't see the significance like I do. I know they're not *your* words.

I end the call and stare blankly out of the bedroom window. I have to do something.

I ring Tara and we arrange to meet at St Mary's. I cycle over – it's less than five miles – and leave my bike locked to a drainpipe by the main entrance. The glass front is locked. It's the summer holidays, but I know teachers regularly pop in to clear their classrooms and prepare for the September intake. I walk round to the side of the building and look for lights. Meeting at the school is a good idea – it feels better than a bar. Even so, I feel a shiver of awkwardness when I see Tara through the window – you'd know why. We laughed about it afterwards; it's not easy to forget.

Tara waves at me from her classroom and sends me back to the main door.

'There's no one else here,' she explains, clicking the key in the lock. 'Total bliss without the kids or any teachers – although the caretaker is around.' She catches my eye as she says the last few words, as if she wants to make sure I realise we're not alone, before turning on her heel for me to follow. I consider whether I might have said something to upset her recently – or whether during one of your tête-à-têtes, Dee, you've told her something about me she doesn't like the sound of. I put it out of my mind – my focus has to be on filling in the gaps surrounding your disappearance.

When we reach her classroom, she invites me to sit on a desk at the front while she tips two curled-up spider plants into the bin. Tara is undeniably beautiful with a cute dark bob and green eyes elongated with thick black liner. She looks exotic and alluring. During our conversation she doesn't stop moving: busying herself stripping posters from the walls, clearing old books into boxes, putting out fresh exercise books for the new faces in September.

'How was Dee when you last saw her?' I ask.

'It was the last day of term, but to be honest all the staff were on auto-pilot just trying to get to the finishing post. I didn't see her to talk to. Not properly.'

'And the day before the miscarriage – your Thursday yoga class? Dee said it was cancelled.'

'Yeah – that's right.' Tara picks up the board rubber, reaches up and starts sweeping smooth arcs into the chalky remains on the old-style blackboard. 'The tutor sent round a text to say she had a stomach bug.'

Tara tells me you'd made plans to meet up for yoga, as usual, the day after you didn't come home. 'Was she vague or definite about that?' I ask.

Tara continues to caress the board with the felt rubber even though it's now clean. 'She said she'd be there, but there was something about needing a new yoga mat – I think the dog had got to hers.'

I remember now. For some reason Frank took an instant dislike to it when you rolled it out one evening. He'd started chewing it and had ripped off one of the corners.

'So, she was intending to turn up?'

'Certainly sounded like it.'

'And before the end of term, had she still been doing contact sports – hockey at lunchtime with the kids and so on?'

'Oh, yeah. No change there.' She knows why I'm

asking. 'She wasn't avoiding exercise. She didn't know she was pregnant, I'm certain. We've talked about having kids a lot – she would have told me.'

What I really want to ask is, *What about an affair – would she have told you about that? Did she tell you about that?* But I can't bring myself to ask. I don't feel ready to hear the reply.

Tara's phone rings and she looks at the screen. 'Listen, I'll be back in tick – I just need to take this.'

For a second my heart leaps and I get to my feet, but she shakes her head when she sees my expectant stare. She leaves me in silence. Not even the clock on the wall makes a sound. It feels unnerving for a schoolroom to be this quiet. I feel surrounded by the spirits of past pupils. I take my mind back to that Christmas party, purely to distract myself.

You were late and I was being chatty and friendly, largely killing time before you turned up. Tara had been working the room with a plate of vol-au-vents, but stalled when she got to me. She offered me a glass of wine.

'You're tapping your foot,' she observed. 'Do you like the track?' It was Lady Gaga, *Born this Way*.

'Too disco for me,' I said. 'Her videos are amazing, though.'

'I know – I love her,' she exclaimed. 'I *made* them put it on.' She turned to the ancient hi-fi in the corner. She'd had a bit to drink and wobbled on her high heels. 'I did a show once with one of her dancers.' She handed me her glass and instantly broke into a series of dance moves. My mouth fell open as I marvelled at the way her body melted into the rhythm.

'I'm never dancing with you,' I said.

'Aw – spoil sport.'

She reclaimed her glass and went on to tell me about her life before teaching. How her father was a theatre director in Copenhagen, but she'd been born in Epsom – how she'd been a pole dancer in Soho before finding her true vocation in the classroom.

'It's a big step from nightclubs to this,' I said.

She sighed. 'It's true. Sometimes I wonder if it's really me.'

I didn't know you'd arrived, but Tara must have spotted you and left me for a moment. You told me afterwards that Tara had pulled you to one side and whispered a few words in your ear.

'I'm going to be terribly mean and ignore you most of the night,' she'd told you. 'You don't mind do you? Only I've been chatting to this gorgeous guy in the corner and there's a real spark. He doesn't seem to be with anyone. I don't want to miss the chance – if there is one.'

You'd patted her on the arm and sent her on her way, not looking my way.

It was highly embarrassing after that.

Tara made a beeline back to me to carry on the conversation we'd started. Time went by. I checked my phone thinking you'd call about being delayed. I didn't know you were at the far side of the room, chatting to your colleagues, waiting for me. At one point, I made Tara laugh and she spun on her glossy red stilettos and dragged me across the room by the wrist. It was something she said at that point that made me realise she hadn't heard my name correctly. It was too late to put her straight; she was already tapping you on the shoulder from behind.

'Here's the charming man I was telling you about, Dee,' she said unable to disguise her eagerness. She must have decided I was a new teacher starting the following term.

'Harper, isn't it?' you said lifting an eyebrow. 'You're my husband, I believe.'

Tara barely batted an eyelid – she's resilient and quick, like that. 'Ah – the confirmed bachelor you married?'

'A few things have changed since then,' I said.

The three of us had linked arms and put the misunderstanding behind us, but you and I referred to it now and again. I thought you might be put out, but you said you liked the fact that other women found me attractive. You said it made you feel 'even luckier' that you managed to snap me up. I'll never get tired of that sense of awe in you, Dee – it's entirely misplaced, because I'm really nothing special at all, but I can't help being secretly buoyed up by it.

Tara has come back into the room. I realise she's waiting for me to ask another question.

I clear my throat. 'When did you last have a proper chat with her?'

'That would have been the Saturday before the...' she looks at me, but doesn't say the word. 'We went shopping.'

'Did she seem different at all?'

'I've been thinking about that. Actually, I'd say she

was worried about something.'

'What makes you say that?'

'You know Diane, she's never late – and she nearly stood me up that day. I had to ring her – she'd forgotten we were supposed to be meeting. She never does that.'

'You're right – it is unusual. Anything else?'

'She seemed distracted the whole time, if I'm honest. Not fully present, checking her phone a lot.'

'Did she speak to anyone? Get any calls?'

'Not when she was with me. I asked if she was okay and she shrugged me off and didn't open up. I didn't want to pry. She left about four o'clock; she said she wanted to get some ironing done.' I throw my mind back to that weekend. I don't recall any ironing.

'And she hasn't been in touch with you in the last couple of days?'

'No.'

I walk right up to her to make it hard for her to look away. 'You're not protecting her?'

'No. Honestly. I haven't heard a peep from her.' Tara steps from side to side; I can see she's worried about you. 'I've been trying her phone. It's not like Dee at all.'

'Did anything happen at school at the end of term – anything strange?'

'Not really…just…' She is holding up a dustpan looking like she is caught in a freeze-frame.

'Go on.'

'She'll kill me if I say anything…although she might have told you…' She backs away towards the cupboard behind the blackboard. I follow her.

'It's important, Tara.'

She stops. 'Well – it's the baby thing. About how fired up she's been about being a mum.'

I nod. 'Yeah – it's been a big subject for us both. I know she's keen.'

'Not just keen, Harper – I mean…the photographs…'

'What photographs?'

'Okay – this is where she'll kill me. She's been taking photos of little kids, babies, pregnant mothers – she's got about thirty of them on her phone.'

No doubt Tara can tell from my eyes that I didn't know. 'I see.'

'She's not just keen, Harper – she's *desperate*.'

I had no idea you were this obsessed, Dee. 'Okay.' I turn away from her, go back to the edge of the table. 'I haven't recognised the depth of this. It's my fault.'

She's standing in front of me, about two feet away. You've known Tara for only two years or so, but she's quickly become your best friend. You can confide in her in a way you never can with your sister. You've explained how well Tara listens, but above all you say you can both be 'real' with each other. There's a straightforward quality to Tara that makes me see how that's possible. She takes a step towards me and speaks again.

'Don't. I'm sure it's not you.' She touches my arm to make me look at her. 'She probably didn't want to keep going on about it…she said she didn't want to put you under pressure.'

'She said that?'

'Yes,' Tara assures me. I squeeze my eyes shut. Is this

the reason you've gone? You were so desperate for a child that you turned to another man? I shake my head. It still seems too far-fetched.

'Is there anything else? Anything at all? I've been backtracking over the last few weeks and, hand on heart, I can't find anything to indicate she was unhappy or different in any way. Maybe she's been trying to tell me something and I haven't been listening?'

Was it because my performance in bed has gone off the boil? You never seemed disappointed.

'No – I don't think so. What about her sister?' Tara says. 'Does she know anything?'

'Alexa is not very forthcoming.' I shake my hands in the air, trying to grasp at something. 'I keep wondering, looking back, to see if there have been a string of clues I've missed. A steady stream of hints I didn't see because I didn't...*want* to see them.'

'Don't you think her taking off like this is simply her way of dealing with the miscarriage? I mean it's a massive thing for her. Everyone knew she was looking forward to having a family. It must have been awful finding out like that – the first sign she had of her pregnancy was losing the baby...and it was already all over.'

I press my palm against my head. I don't know what to say.

Tara goes on, 'One thing is certain – she adores you. Absolutely. She's always going on about you – every day at school. I'm sure you're not the reason. Even on that Saturday, she was talking about getting you something special for your anniversary.'

I want to cry. 'That's nice.'

'What I mean to say is – she isn't...cheating on you. I just know it.'

I snap back to the phone call I received from the laboratory yesterday. Tara's words are groundless. I start to wonder what you've told her. How much does she know? I decide to tell her the truth. There's no point in keeping up the pretence.

'Did Dee tell you I'm infertile?'

'She mentioned something on the phone, just after the miscarriage.' Her voice is neutral, without Alexa's barbs. 'She said an illness had made things more difficult – not that it was impossible.'

'She was underplaying it. It's more clear-cut than that.' Tara says nothing, staying close. 'I had a DNA test done on the foetus,' I say, without looking at her. 'The baby wasn't mine.'

Tara's reaction is immediate and packs a punch. 'No! – I don't believe that. She wouldn't. She just...wouldn't.'

I shrug and draw my hands together. 'They are the facts of the matter.'

'It doesn't make sense. There must be a mistake...'

'It makes it look more and more likely that she went off with someone else...except the manner of it, the way she left...'

Tara is definitive. 'She wouldn't do that.'

'Last night, I went through every inch of the cottage with my Dictaphone.' I tell her. 'She didn't take her toothbrush.' It might sound a small thing, but it carries a lot of weight for me. 'You know Diane – she's so particular about cleanliness.'

Tara looks thoughtful. 'That's true. She's the only person I know who flosses morning and night.'

'It looks like she must have come back for a few clothes, but *not* the toothbrush – or the floss for that matter. That doesn't ring true to me.'

Tara tips her head on one side. 'She was upset…perhaps she wasn't thinking straight…'

I don't buy it.

'Can we get some air?' I say. I'm feeling uptight and restless, wanting to move my limbs. She locks up and we take off across the playing field. A workman is trundling around with a white box, re-marking the lines of the running track.

Tara is surprisingly easy to talk to and before I know it, it all comes tumbling out. 'We never discussed infertility,' I admit. 'Well, neither of us ever used that word. She asked me once, about six months ago, how we'd know if one of us couldn't have children, but that was as far as it went.'

'What did you say?'

'That we'd deal with it – if it happened.'

Your question had snagged at me at the time, but it wasn't an accusation – just a mild speculation that these things happened. 'Maybe she didn't dare bring it up again,' I say.

Tara reacted immediately with a shake of her head. 'Dee isn't like that. She comes out with what she's thinking. She doesn't hold on to things, harbour things – certainly not if they're as important as that.'

'Of course. I know. You're right.' Why do I feel like I don't know you at all, Dee? 'When she told you about the miscarriage...how did she sound? Did she seem guilty?'

It's as though everything left unsaid in your absence has been piling up in a box, like Lego, and finally I tip it onto the grass at Tara's feet. It is too late to consider whether Tara is the best person to be spilling everything to. I seem to have lost all sense of perspective regarding what is appropriate and what's not. Come what may, I'm disclosing everything to her – like I should have done to you, Dee, weeks ago.

'She certainly didn't sound guilty. Not at all. She was a bit woozy because of the medication – and she was upset about the baby, she was devastated that she didn't know. We had a long chat – she rang me when you were out with the dog.' Tara stops and turns to me to make sure I hear this part. 'She did say she thought she'd let you down.'

'Let me down?'

'Yeah.' She moves on, more purpose in her step. 'About losing the baby – she said she'd let you down, because her body couldn't keep hold of the child. She didn't sound guilty about anything else. It doesn't sound like someone about to do a runner from her husband, does it?'

'I don't know any longer. The DNA tests *prove* she was with someone else.'

We walk in silence for a while. The man with the white box has finished another circuit and starts again on the next lane, working his way inwards.

'What do you think?' I stop and look at her. I want to see her face.

She responds with another question. 'Did Diane know the DNA results before she left?'

'No. She was still talking about a medical fluke.'

'Mmm...' Tara is best friends with the truth and I can tell from her wandering gaze that she's reluctant to say what she's thinking. 'I don't know – honestly. But something isn't right.' Her voice cracks. 'We need to find her.'

When I get back I look for the one item I haven't dared think about so far. But I need to know. It isn't the kind of thing you would normally have in your handbag, Dee, so under normal circumstances there's no way you should have it with you. I try to think where we keep them. They used to be in the bureau in the alcove, then we moved them to the filing cabinet upstairs. I go into the study, pull out the top drawer and flick through the file labels; our wills, paperwork about the cottage, phone bills, gas and electricity bills, banks statements, all in separate folders. I slide out the next folder and tip the contents onto the spare bed.

That's when I know.

Chapter 12

'Thanks for seeing me,' I say. 'First day back and all.'

'No problem, mate,' says Neil Fry, my detective friend. He's just come back from ten days in Spain and agreed to drive over to The Eagle as soon as he came off duty. He's highly tanned, like polished leather, and has the appearance of someone who still thinks he's in another climate. It's 9pm and he's wearing knee-length shorts and a Hawaiian shirt in orange and lemon with sunglasses poking out of the pocket.

'Pina colada – or the usual pint of Black Sheep?' I suggest.

He groans and hangs out his tongue. 'My usual pint – if you don't mind. A man can only knock back so many glasses with pink parasols in them.'

'You and Debbie have a good time?' I say when I return.

'A bit too good.' He takes the pint and hoists himself onto a tall stool by the window. 'She wants to move there now. She thinks it would be one long stroll along the beach at sunset.' He scratches his bare knee where a red insect bite is swelling to the size of a five-pence piece. 'I'm glad to be back, to be honest.' A waft of holiday-strength aftershave hits me, as I think about how to tell him what has happened without getting emotional. I manage to start somewhere and fill him in with the details.

'And she called her sister on the day after she left?' he queries.

'It was a text.'

'And she put up posts on social media up until Friday. Nothing since?'

'No. And the posts don't feel like her – for a start it's such a flippant way to keep in touch. She's hurting too much to be that blasé.' I get out my phone and show Neil the post on Facebook with the photo of Frank. '*Love life* – I mean…she would never say anything trivial and offhand like that.' It's often the little things that don't ring true. I show him earlier posts where you've added names and places to photos of friends at festivals and sporting events. There are no throw-away comments.

He nods. 'Unless she's putting on a brave face – so you don't worry.'

I throw my hands up. 'Why not just call me?'

'Maybe she's not ready to talk to you yet. Perhaps she's got stuff to work out first. Maybe she'll get back in touch when she's ready.'

'That's what her sister says.' I start peeling the top layer off the beer mat. Alexa thinks you're communicating, Dee, but I know you better. These posts aren't from you.

'Perhaps she did it this way to let you know she was fine, but she couldn't manage anything more personal right now…because it's too upsetting.'

'Yeah – maybe…' I don't believe a word of it.

Neil gets up to get another round and in an instant, I go back to the beginning, when I first met you. We were two faces in a crowd at Trafalgar Square in 2009. I was twenty-five and just finishing my PhD in Criminology at Liverpool University. I was feeling bold and full of myself, because I was about to be called *Dr* Penn. I was in London for the Amnesty rally and to catch up with a couple of friends. Back then I was entrenched in my bachelor status, but dating a lot and I'd inadvertently broken a few hearts along the way – usually as soon as the word 'commitment' cropped up. I'd moved in with Irene during my PhD and moved out about two months later. I'd been crystal clear that I didn't want to take it further, but what I said and what she heard were in entirely different languages.

It was a grey September afternoon and I turned up to the demo on my own. It was hard not to notice you straight away – you looked strong, earnest and downright gorgeous. Your long dark hair was thick and rich with overtones of russet and chestnut. I watched the way you were standing; self-assured and defiant, with a placard that read *End all Racist Attacks*.

We were there following the stabbing of two Muslim students in central London the week before. Speakers and film footage kept everyone involved, but I found myself searching the crowd every few minutes so I could stay near enough to watch you. You seemed to be with two others – two guys, and I wondered if one of them was your boyfriend. It's silly, I know, but I was looking for signs straight away that you were already 'taken' – I couldn't believe you wouldn't be. You held yourself so well, seemed so full of conviction for the cause. I like a person with backbone. I saw the way other strangers looked at you too – their eyes lingering on you – intrigued, captivated, a little entranced by your good looks and poise. One of the guys you were with brought you a burger from the veggie van parked illegally on the kerb by the fourth plinth. I shuffled through the crowd to get closer. I wanted an excuse to speak to you, but I didn't know how to make it happen without sounding crass.

The clouds folded in and it started to rain. I had an idea. I wove further to my right and pulled out my umbrella. I held it up then pretended I'd just spotted you. The rain was gathering momentum and people were pulling on their hoods and looking for cover. You did neither, simply stood in the downpour as though you hadn't noticed. Your hair soaked up the rain and I wanted to touch it. I took a risk and held the umbrella over you and said something cheesy like; *There's room for two*. I hated myself as soon as it came out and thought I'd blown it.

'Sorry – that was dreadful. You'd probably prefer to get wet...' I was on the verge of pulling away, when you took hold of the metal spine of the umbrella to keep it where it was.

'It was a nice gesture,' you said. Your voice was soft, but firm – like the rest of you – curvy, but solid; feminine, but tough. An irresistible combination.

I had a soggy bag of cherries in my pocket and I held it open for you. You took one and I was ridiculously pleased. It was at this point that I got the feeling we'd met before, but I couldn't remember where or when or even whether to mention it.

Neil comes back from the bar bringing the present moment with him. 'She came back and took stuff from the cottage, you said?' he queries. He sounds tired, but is doing his best to be engaged.

'I think so. Some clothes are gone – just a few casual items. Her appointment diary is missing and her medication; she had her phone and purse in her handbag – and now I've discovered her passport's gone.'

'Really?' He's a bit more interested now. 'Any signs of forced entry?'

I slowly shake my head.

'Has she used a bank?'

I'd thought of this and contacted her local branch, but they wouldn't give out any information. We still have separate accounts. It was one of the things we said we'd change – to a joint one – when we had a child. 'I'm hoping she'll get her statement next week. She certainly had all her bank cards with her.'

'Let me know, eh? If she has or hasn't used her bank – either way, okay?'

'Thanks, Neil. I know this is difficult.' The strain around his eyes tells me he wants to help, but he has his job to think about. He can't afford to offer much or use police resources when there is no investigation.

'Is there a way we can trace the car?' I ask. 'It's disappeared.'

Where are you, Dee? I don't know what this silence means.

'You know I can't authorise that. There's no crime, Harper. Diane's not even regarded as missing.'

'Can we check to see whether her passport has been used?' I can't believe you've left the country – you wouldn't do that, but I have to start eliminating possibilities.

He laughs but it sounds sad. 'No way.' He's not being unhelpful, I know. 'Where would we start? Gatwick? Heathrow? Eurostar? The ferries?' I understand. Without an obvious crime our hands are tied. You're not *missing* in the eyes of the police. There's nothing to raise any suspicions. Life goes on as normal.

I spread out my fingers. 'I come back to three possibilities: she's taking *time out* and will be back when she's ready.' This is the one everyone seems to think I should believe. 'The second is that she's leaving me and this is some kind of prelude to a big announcement. The third is that something bad has happened and she's in trouble and can't reach me.'

'How was the situation between you before she drove away?'

I tell him about my infertility tests and the miscarriage. I know I have to come clean and tell people like Neil everything, if I'm going to put my all into finding you. It breaks my heart to do it. I lean forward, still looking at him. 'The baby wasn't mine. I had tests done after the miscarriage.'

Neil nods in a contemplative manner, but doesn't say anything.

My thoughts won't go in a straight line anymore. I stroke my forehead and my elbow catches my glass and knocks it over. The beer pools on the table and starts to drip onto the floor. For a moment I stay exactly where I am and follow the trail of liquid with interest, like a detached observer. It's Neil who gets to his feet and goes to the bar for a cloth. I try to take it from him, but he insists on mopping up the mess, then gets us both another half.

'Thank you,' I say, shaking my head.

'I have to say – what you've told me comes as a big shock,' Neil says. 'I've seen you two together. You know, you can tell with some couples – the way they no longer stand close together, no longer look into each other's eyes when they speak, stop touching? You two, though – you've always been like newlyweds. So devoted, inseparable.'

'I know. It's a massive shock to me, too. I had no idea. Seriously…'

He looks into his drink, shakes his head. 'I'm really sorry.'

I nip my lips together. What can I say?

'Good job it's the summer break from University, eh?' he adds, making an attempt to lighten the mood. No doubt, despite the initial astonishment, he thinks, like everyone else, that your disappearance is cut and dry.

'Too right.' I moan, shoving my empty glass away. 'There's no way I'd be able to prop myself up in front of a room full of students and deliver lectures on hate crime or advances in forensic ballistics, in this state.'

Under normal circumstances, I love my lecturing job; it was a knockout stroke of luck that there was a position going at Portsmouth University at the right time, just after we married. It's what brought us to this area. I've always felt sorry when I'm with a group of mates on a night out and they're already counting down the days to their retirement. It's tragic. Neil isn't like that. He's like me – hungry for the job that's become his lifeline. We tease each other about who is more up to date with advances in forensics.

'You involved in much cyber-crime, these days?' I ask him, changing the subject.

He folds his arms. 'We all are. Online fraud and theft is rife now, as you know – and far greater than the recorded figures suggest.' He yawns. 'I'm not the least bit intrigued by "crime by numbers", though, I prefer solving physical crime; getting out there on the street, asking questions, piecing clues together.'

'Me, too – complex crimes where the trail dries up and you have to think out of the box.' I rub my hands together and a surge of electricity inside my veins reminds me that this is where my energy lies when life isn't twisted out of shape.

'You still seeing that chap who was put away for killing his girlfriend? How many years did he get?'

'Victor? He got seven – he was out in 2010. He lives in Manchester – we've kind of lost touch now. Shame. I think he wants to be with people who don't know about his past.'

'How come you knew him?'

'He was my best friend at school, a gentle guy who played serenades on his twelve-string guitar and wrote poems.' I can see Victor's sheepish smile. 'He was broken by his crime. I went to visit him, partly because I liked the guy, but also I felt it could easily have been me banged up in there. A split second, one ill-judged reaction and it would be all over. I know he never meant to strangle Nicci; he was a victim of his own lack of self-restraint. Blind fury took hold of him. He is an unfortunate lesson to the rest of us.'

'These convicts get sent on anger-management courses,' says Neil, 'but I'm not sure what good it does. Six weeks in front of a flip chart writing down the emotions you feel…rating your anger out of ten…' He shakes his head. 'Like you say, who knows what we're all capable of if someone presses the wrong buttons at the wrong time.'

I stare at the floor and fail to admit my own anger has got the better of me more times than I'd like to remember.

He waves his empty glass at me, but I've had enough. As we reach the car park I know I can't leave things like this. 'I realise it looks like Diane has gone off with someone else, but it's four days now – something isn't right. No one has *actually* spoken to her in person. Not her sister, her best friend, her parents.'

'Maybe she's feeling guilty.'

'There's something wrong, Neil, believe me. If she was going to go, she wouldn't do it like this.'

'Okay. First thing tomorrow, if you've still not heard anything, reinstate the missing person's report at the local station. I'll have a chat with the duty sergeant. You know the score – they'll come and take a look around and ask about your relationship. They'll do a risk assessment. You must tell them everything.' His eyes linger on mine to make sure I get the message.

'Of course.' Neil pats me on the shoulder and tells me not to worry.

I pass up his offer of a lift back to the cottage, preferring instead to walk in the moonlight and think about you. I instantly switch in my mind to another walk – almost opposite in every way; in the sun, amidst crowds, together. After the rally on the day we first met, I took a chance and invited you to wander with me along the Thames. You said your farewells to the guys you'd stood with. I saw them link arms as they turned away; they were together, neither of them was with you. There was a glimmer of hope.

We strode out towards Hungerford Bridge, watching the white wheel gently roll round carrying its tiny glass capsules as we crossed the river.

'I'm ashamed to say I've never been on the London Eye,' you said.

I took a chance and said we should go one day. I don't know why. It seemed ludicrous to be making plans together.

'I'd like that,' you replied. My heart raced like a kid getting away with a risky dare.

We walked to the ferry pier and stopped to watch the boats. You asked about my upbringing and I told you how Dad was a famous footballer and that he left when I was eight, just when I was starting to get to know him. 'He taught me football, of course, but I wasn't a natural.' You turned round and leant against the railings so you were facing me, not the river. 'He set up "tests" for me –

for accuracy, judgement at distances, tackling, but I was forever falling over the ball or my own feet. It was never long before he'd get frustrated and I'd watch the disappointment on his face.'

I didn't tell you about how he humiliated me with the welder's mask; that felt too raw for this stage in our relationship.

'He wasn't very kind about it,' I said. 'For years that's why I thought he left. Because I wasn't good enough and let him down.'

I turned into the breeze and let the wind press the hair away from my face – it was longer then, almost to my shoulders. Why was I telling you all this? I tried to change the subject, but you asked for more. You managed to wheedle out all kinds of personal details about my past that I'd never dreamt I'd reveal to anyone on a first meeting. It wasn't even a date.

'How about you?' I said. 'What about your background?'

We started walking again, kept going at an easy stroll, but I don't remember much about our surroundings. I was watching you, I could barely take my eyes off you – you were so vibrant and bubbling with sexual energy.

'I was born in Leeds. I've got an older sister, two years' difference and our parents are both still together. Everyone thinks their own family is a bit mad, don't they? Well – the Toinby's are all a bit obsessive one way or another – in a good way, mostly. My mum is a florist and everything had a floral design when we were growing up – the wallpaper, the soft furnishings, even the toilet paper. Dad is an aeronautical engineer; he specialises in flight safety, but he's also a tennis fanatic.

They both live in London now – near the Wimbledon tennis courts. Alexa is incredibly fit and has just swum the Channel. She had anorexia in her teens – that's when obsession gets unhealthy.' The pavement narrowed and you leant into me to avoid colliding with a jogger. 'I'm the tame one in the family. I'm just a primary school teacher. I don't really excel at anything.'

'You look pretty sporty.'

You laughed. 'You should see my sister. Alexa is a personal trainer, whipping people into shape. I used to swim, but an injury forced me to stop.' You failed to tell me just how good you'd been in the pool. You led me to believe you splashed about a bit – didn't mention medals or international competitions. I had to find all that out later. 'I get involved with kids' assault courses and boot camps these days – I love it. I love kids of any age.'

We walked further than either of us intended, weaving through the crowds in front of Tate Britain, The Globe – cutting inland after Tower Bridge and ending up in Rotherhithe. We stopped at The Mayflower pub.

'Fancy a drink?' I ventured.

'It would be rude not to, as we're here,' you said and stepped straight inside.

My heart fluttered and hiccupped. I didn't notice the ancient latticed windows, the lanterns, pewter tankards or the barrel-edged bar. The place filled up so there was barely standing room and we talked until it got dark, wrapped inside our own private bubble where no one could touch us.

*

In real time, I've made it back from the pub to the cottage. There are no lights on inside and I can hear Frank howling from the gate. He misses you too. It's cold inside, a heavy solid chill that makes me want to go straight back out into the night, where there's a delicate breeze, sounds and signs of life. I call your name and instead Frank comes to my side, his claws clattering on the wooden floor, wheezing and slobbering with joy at seeing me. I open the freezer and take out the steak I was supposed to have for my evening meal. I wasn't hungry then and I'm not now. I defrost it in the microwave and cut it into chunks for Frank, instead. He'll appreciate it more than I will.

I climb into bed without closing the curtains and leave the bedroom door ajar, so I'll hear you if you come back. Frank is meant to sleep in the kitchen, but I let him come up onto the bed beside me. He's still licking his lips, then he settles with his chin on my arm. Is this how my life is going to be?

Chapter 13
Marion

17 July

The phone rings nearly fifteen times before Marion gets to it.

'Is that Mrs Delderfield?'

Marion has heard the voice before, but she can't place it. She's just got out of bed and is more concerned over where Clara is and what she might be up to.

'Is she all right? Where is she?' she says, still foggy from the false sleep induced by medication that leaves her feeling like she's jogged to Penzance and back rather than rested.

'Clara is at school, Mrs Delderfield. She has just left my office and returned to her classroom.'

It's the headmistress, Elizabeth Macclesfield or is it Matterson? Marion didn't have the receiver in place properly when the caller announced her name at the start.

'What's happened?' Marion hasn't warmed up enough for pleasantries yet. She's still trying to break through into the waking world.

'I'll get to the point, Mrs Delderfield. Clara has been in a world of her own at school this week, even more so than usual. She's not communicating normally at all —

not in the playground with the other children, not in class with her teachers.'

The school know about Clara's incident at the castle. Marion thought they would have cut Clara some slack as a result. 'Clara's probably a bit distracted after what happened, that's all,' Marion explains. 'Even at the best of times she tends to drift off into her own little daydreams.'

'I'm aware that Clara is a highly imaginative child, creating much of her own amusement – but I think she might need to see someone.'

'See someone?' Marion is confused. 'She's been checked over at the hospital, if that's what you mean – she's fine.'

'I mean, I think she should see someone from a...psychological point of view. Something isn't right.'

Marion reflects on how Clara has been since she was found in the oubliette. She was elated by her little escapade at first, then when they got home from the hospital, she seemed to become more withdrawn. Marion had kept her out of school for a day to check for any after-effects, but she saw nothing to alarm her. But Mrs Maddersley – is that her name? – has a point. Clara has been staying in her room lately – and it's true, she doesn't seem to want to mix with any of her friends at the moment. Come to think of it, she left most of her tea yesterday and didn't want any breakfast this morning.

The voice is in her ear again, clipped and jarring. 'She spent a night on her own, outside, scared, trapped, didn't she? Do you not think this...might have affected her?' suggests the headmistress. It feels like a telling off.

Marion senses her palms getting clammy as if she's standing in the head's office herself. She wants to tell her it isn't the first time Clara has slept alone under the stars, but she doesn't want to come across as a bad mother.

'Clara secretly enjoyed her exploit actually. She takes after her father; he was an adventure seeker.' She knows she's sounding defensive. 'She loves finding hidden places, small spaces to explore and hide away on her own.'

Mrs Mallory is talking again. 'Clara's behaviour needs looking into. She refuses to speak unless she's quoting from a fairy tale. She seems to have become fixated on *Little Red Riding Hood*. I don't know what she's like at home, but she's behaving very strangely at school.'

Marion tries to remember the last few days, but they wash into a blur. Clara stayed one night with Granny, another night she must have put herself to bed, because Marion doesn't remember anything. She can't have been well. *Little Red Riding Hood?* Now that Mrs 'M' mentions it, she does recall Clara using a silly voice when she gave her beans on toast for tea on Monday. *Come in, my dear, and look what I've got for you,* she'd said in a trembling old-age tone. Marion hadn't thought much of it; Clara was always play-acting, talking to people who weren't there and performing little homemade storylines.

The voice at the other end of the phone is starting to bang a hole inside Marion's head. 'I think she should see a child psychologist or have some kind of assessment.'

Marion gives in. 'Okay. Yes. Fine. I'll look into it. Thank you.'

She can't wait to put the phone down.

The following day, Marion takes Clara to the GP. Clara sits on a chair and swings her legs, but won't answer any of Dr Lane's questions. When she does speak, which is only three times in all, she appears to be quoting from one of her books. When Dr Lane asks if she is enjoying school at the moment, Clara appears not to hear.

'Come closer, little girl, so I can see you,' Clara says in a pantomime voice.

Marion turns to the doctor. 'I'm sorry. I don't know where this is coming from.' She touches Clara's shoulder. 'Can you answer the doctor's questions, honey?' she says calmly.

'What big eyes you have, Grandma,' Clara says in reply.

The doctor asks if Clara has been sleeping properly, eating well.

'Not in the last week.'

'Since the incident?'

'Well – she was fine immediately afterwards. Then…it must have hit her harder than I thought…'

Clara turns to Marion and points her finger sharply. 'I *told* you not to go into the woods, little girl.'

Marion bites her lip as the GP writes something down on the lined pad in front of her.

Clara is silent after that. She sits on her hands and doesn't even nod or shake her head.

'I think I'll have Dr Pike take a look at her. She's a child psychiatrist at the Queen Elizabeth Hospital. I'm sure it's just a phase, but just to be certain. Keep a close eye on Clara in the meantime, won't you.' Marion sighs at the impossibility of the task. It sounds so simple, but Marion's eyes aren't what they were. They keep closing when she least expects them to.

The next day she takes Clara to the Saturday morning kids' session at the library. Clara is developing a crush on Helen Golding, the storyteller, and usually takes her a card or handmade present, but there is no gift today. Marion usually leaves Clara sitting at the front of the group, eager and wide-eyed at the prospect of another story, but today she sits at the back, cross-legged on the floor, with her thumb in her mouth. Marion can't understand it. This isn't like Clara at all. She's tried on several occasions to drop the episode at the castle into conversations at meal times or during journeys to and from the supermarket, but Clara isn't following through. The headmistress is right – Clara keeps quoting from stories instead of engaging with her.

Marion stays in the library this time – she usually leaves Clara and does her shopping – but she wants to watch her and see how she behaves. She lurks behind the bookshelves so her daughter can't see her. At first, Clara looks tired and reluctant to be there, then after a while she starts walking her fingers across the floor in front of her. She turns to the side, facing away from the other children and appears to be talking to herself. Her hands are running through some enactment of their own, like a little puppet show, and she's clearly not paying any attention at all to Helen's story. When the children get up to go at the end of the session, Clara barely notices.

Helen can see something is wrong; apparently Clara is

known for making her presence felt in these story readings – laughing, chipping in, asking questions. Marion stays behind the palaeontology rack to see how Clara reacts as Helen, looking concerned, walks over to her. Clara gets to her feet, blinking fast and looking lost. Before Helen can open her mouth, Clara buries her face in her skirt and clutches at her legs, as if she's just been told Helen is going away for a long time. Helen strokes her head and looks up, perplexed. Marion steps out of the aisle and joins her.

'Is she okay?' Helen whispers with alarm.

'Clara's had a recent experience...' Marion explains in two sentences what has happened. 'I think it's upset her more than I thought.'

Clara is crying; a soft, keening sound. Her mother bends down beside her. 'Sweetheart – what's the matter?'

She gurgles something into the pleats of Helen's skirt that Marion can't make out. Helen bobs down alongside them.

'Don't run, because if you fall over, the cake will get dirty and the bottle will break, then Grandma will get nothing...' Clara garbles in one breath.

The adults look at each other.

'Is this a story?' asks Marion, lightly.

Clara pulls away from Helen and stands between them. 'Gretel isn't here,' she says, earnestly, her face wet. Marion hands her a tissue and Clara wipes the tears herself. She takes off her Alice band and sets it straight.

'Who's Gretel?' asks Helen.

Marion glances over at Helen and shrugs. 'She has

more imaginary friends than real ones.'

Helen faces Clara. 'You mean Hansel and Gretel?'

Clara wipes her nose on her sleeve. 'They don't belong in that story,' she says crossly. 'It's time to go, Mummy, or we'll miss the bus.' She takes Marion's hand and pulls her towards the exit. With an apologetic grimace Marion turns to thank Helen, who puts out her arms as if to say, 'Who knows?'

Dr Pike has crayons. About a hundred of them, all different thicknesses and shapes, in a shallow box on the table in the centre of the room. Clara walks in and her jaw drops, like she's been invited into heaven. The room is like a toyshop: on wall-to-wall shelving there are dolls, dressing-up clothes, books, boxes of Lego, plastic figures and teddy bears – a cornucopia of delights for a seven-year-old.

'Hello, Clara, I'm Dr Pike and we're going to have some fun.'

Dr Pike is tall, slim and far too glamorous to be a psychiatrist. Marion thinks her first name must be Selina or Marina – something silky and sensual. She has long buttery-coloured hair tied back in a ponytail and wears tight-fitting black trousers. The only concessions to her profession are the white pumps she's wearing. Presumably, so she can work with children more easily and get down to their level. Stylish court shoes would fit the look far better, but Marion assumes these are tucked under her desk somewhere.

The doctor has already explained that she'd prefer to have half an hour with Clara on her own, so Marion is waiting for a signal to indicate she should leave.

'Mummy's going to be just outside while we play, is that okay?' prompts the psychiatrist.

Clara has always been the opposite of clingy and insecure and she nods without hesitation. Marion heads for the door and finds a seat in the waiting room. She hates hospitals and finds herself having to be inside one more and more often as the months go by. Tests for this, checks on that, blood infusions, chemo, follow-up appointments – and now Clara. She wants this over with and wonders what Clara is doing, saying, behind the closed blue blinds and what Dr Pike will conclude about her behaviour. While she waits she tries to read the novel she's brought with her, but she isn't taking it in. She keeps looking at the blocked windows of Dr Pike's office and hopes there is nothing wrong with her only child.

After half an hour, Dr Pike invites her back inside again. Clara is sitting at the table with drawings in front of her. She has a fat pink wax crayon in her hand and waves as her mother comes in.

'Clara, do you want to stay here a few more minutes while I have a quick chat with your Mum?'

Clara nods gleefully at the chance to carry on and reaches for a fresh sheet of paper. Dr Pike leads Marion through an interconnecting door into a smaller office. It smells of nail polish and there is a banana on the desk. Dr Pike offers her a seat and begins speaking before Marion has settled.

'Can I ask you a few questions, Mrs Delderfield?'

Marion swallows and adjusts herself in the chair. 'Of

course.'

'Clara didn't say much in our session, but she did draw scenes from stories. When I asked her to draw her own family, she drew Goldilocks and the three bears.' She hesitates. 'Does she read a lot?'

'Yes. All the time, especially recently.' Marion smoothes her hand over the thin scarf that covers her scalp and hopes she doesn't have to spell everything out to the specialist. 'She's always liked her own company and gets swept up into story ideas…' Marion wants to sound like she's fully aware and on top of the situation. 'She…creates intricate and complex fantasy worlds.'

'Clara spends a lot of time making up stories?'

Marion clucks and rolls her eyes. 'Oh, yes. She spends most of her time in cloud-cuckoo-land.' She stops, concerned that she's making her child sound deranged. 'What I mean is, sometimes it's hard to tell fantasy from reality with Clara. She tells stories, but she's not lying, she thinks they're real in her head. She's always been like that.' Marion takes her eyes down to her tight hands. 'I envy her sometimes – most times, if I'm honest – she's able to live her life in a special, magical place and make it how she wants it to be. In her world, it's always somebody's birthday.'

Dr Pike nips her lips together in professional sympathy. 'Clara is doing fine on one level,' she says, 'but there might be some cause for concern.'

Marion has had enough of bad news delivered by doctors. In a savage flash she remembers her own specialist telling her she probably had a life-expectancy of four or five years, six at best, before the myeloma they'd discovered devoured her bones. That was eighteen months ago. Marion feels dizzy at the thought of how little time she might still have left and puts her hand out to touch the desk.

Dr Pike appears not to notice. 'At this stage, I think Clara is suffering a form of post-traumatic stress following her fall into the pit.'

'She didn't fall,' Marion corrects in a brittle voice.

Dr Pike looks down at her notes. 'No...that's right...but she was trapped all night, wasn't she?'

'Yes...'

'And this is the only incident that might have upset her, recently?'

Marion nods without needing to consider. 'Yes — there's nothing else.'

'I'd like to see Clara again, next week, but at this stage I'd say she's suffering from Dissociative Paracosm.'

Marion's brain mists over. 'What?'

Dr Pike makes a steeple with her index fingers, her elbows on the table. For a second, Marion thinks it would make a nice photograph. 'Let me explain,' she says. 'It's normal for a child Clara's age to develop a "make-believe" world.'

'That sounds like Clara.'

'This normal dissociation happens when children play, but it can also occur when they are trying to block out something unpleasant – a painful injury, for example. It would appear that Clara is using fairy tales as a form of escapism – but it's got a bit extreme.'

Marion nods – it makes sense.

'I think it's because Clara is so intelligent and

119

imaginative that the incident has affected her in this way. Some children become temporarily mute or have serious anger problems after a trauma like this – but a smart child like Clara uses resources she already has inside herself for protection.'

Marion feels the sparkle of pride prick her eyes. She doesn't want to cry.

'So this *dis...disasso...*'

'Dissociative Paracosm,' Dr Pike adds, helping out. 'This is where there's some abnormal adaptation. It's a survival technique. I think it's moderate in Clara's case. She's found a way to "escape" by blocking off – dissociating herself from the terrifying event in her memory.'

'But...she didn't seem to find it *terrifying...*'

'Sometimes responses take time to emerge and come in forms we don't expect.' Dr Pike sucks in her cheeks. 'At the moment, Clara is hiding inside the stories. She's living her life there, more than she is in the real world.'

Marion is confused. 'When Clara came out of the oubliette, she was subdued at first – the police were there and she thought she'd done something wrong, but afterwards – she said being down in the pit was great fun.'

Dr Pike hooks a loose strand of hair behind her ear. 'Like I say – it could be a delayed reaction.'

Marion finds herself shuffling forward on the seat. 'You don't think it's because she lost her father...and now with me...being ill...it's not *that*, is it?'

Dr Pike trails her finger through her notes and stops. 'Mmm...four years ago – and now your myeloma,' she taps the immaculate nail on the paper. 'It's hard to say.'

Marion nods, not wanting to look at her.

'What kinds of story does Clara enjoy most?' asks the doctor, moving on.

'Oh, anything and everything – princesses, fairies, talking creatures, Mary Poppins, The Jungle Book – Walt Disney has his perfect target audience right here with my child.'

'So, for Clara to imagine that she's living inside the story of *Little Red Riding Hood* would feel safe to her?'

'Oh, yes. Absolutely. That's one of her favourites. And she saw *The Sound of Music* on a big screen at Easter and she's been going through a Julie Andrew's phase ever since. She keeps singing the *Doh-Re-Mi* song.'

Dr Pike puts her hands flat on the desk and Marion knows she's not out of the woods yet.

'Well – this is a preliminary assessment. There are other conditions I need to consider. We'll have to see.' She gives Marion a transitory smile – one that's well-rehearsed and says *that's settled then*. 'I'll need to monitor Clara for a few weeks and see how she gets on. What usually happens is that children gradually re-acclimatise to the real world given time. Clara will shift out of this reactive behaviour once her world feels safer'.

'Does she need medication or anything?'

'Not at this stage. Let's see how she gets on. It's the end of term, so at least she won't have to cope with school.' Dr Pike leans forward and her eyes stray to the place where Marion's eyebrows should be. 'You'll be able to look after her at home over the summer vacation?'

Marion feels that familiar jolt of panic. She's terrified Dr Pike is going to tell social services she can't cope and Clara will be taken away. 'Yes. Of course. That's no problem,' she gulps. 'I have my mother and babysitters…and friends – we can all make sure she's okay.'

'You don't need to do anything differently – in fact, that's the point, really. Try to keep everything the *same* as normal. Same meal times, same bedtimes, talk to her, spend time with her. Join in with her games if she'll let you. Initiate, but don't push if she wants to be on her own. Keep doors in the house open, so she isn't isolated. Watch *The Sound of Music* together. Join in with her as best you can and bring her friends round, if she'd like that.'

'What about going out? Going to friends' houses?'

'I think at the moment it's best that Clara is always supervised by an adult, so if she visits a friend's house, make sure a responsible person is present. Don't let Clara wander off on her own. Not for a while. Keep her close.'

Marion is bursting to sigh heavily at the enormity of carrying out these instructions, but doesn't want Dr Pike to know how hard this is going to be for her. She's going to have to keep Clara under lock and key – and without her daughter being aware of it.

Dr Pike asks if she has any questions and Marion's mind goes blank in response. They get up and return to Clara who has her head down colouring in a patch of her drawing in bright green. Marion notices that there is a big tree in the centre with a palace at the top – *Jack and the Beanstalk.*

'We'll need to finish now, Clara,' says Dr Pike. 'You've made some wonderful pictures. Do you want to take them with you or leave them with me for next time?'

Clara ignores her, but puts down her crayon. She gets up and pulls on her cardigan. Marion doesn't know whether to prompt Clara into answering — her daughter is never this rude. She takes Clara's hand and falters by the door.

'Thank you, doctor. Do I make another appointment for next week?'

'Yes — that's right.' Dr Pike turns to the girl. 'See you again soon, Clara,' she says brightly, holding the door open.

Clara gives her a disdainful look, before pulling her mother out of the room. She turns back at the last moment.

'Bubble, bubble, toil and trouble,' Clara says with a frown. 'How does your garden grow?'

Chapter 14
Harper

5 August – Sixth day missing

The surface of my life is uncannily quiet and deserted. This morning I got up early and took Frank across the fields and down to the river. We saw no one the entire time. His unflagging joy and affection is the only thing keeping me going. You adore him, Dee. I've watched you rolling on the lounge floor together as you tickle his tummy and he tries to lick your face. You don't know I'm spying on you. After a while I politely cough and you look up and laugh, caught in a moment of pure bliss.

As soon as I woke, yesterday, I confirmed with the police that you were still missing. Later they sent two officers round – Sergeant Peter Howis, who I'd heard of through Neil, but never met, and PC Rose Felton, who looked fresh out of college. They asked me reams of questions: Had you mentioned suicidal thoughts? Had you gone missing before? Had you been behaving oddly? I told them what I'd told Neil: the miscarriage, the infertility, the DNA test – everything. They took a look in every room – it's called an open-door search, where every space including the loft, is checked. They inspected the shed, chicken coop, garage and examined undergrowth by the river at the end of our garden.

Sergeant Howis, the investigating officer, is a big bulky chap who doesn't convey a great deal of warmth. Neil told me he didn't often socialise with the other officers and when he did, he was never the one at the bar opening his wallet. During the visit, he confirmed that you would be registered as 'low risk' given the circumstances. He thinks, just like everyone else, that you've gone to get breathing space. The officers took your PC, however, and said they'd look for any untoward activity and would trace your phone. They'll also make house-to-house enquiries in Nettledon. At least that's something.

Before they left they asked for your hairbrush, to add your DNA and fingerprints to the database at the National Missing Persons Bureau. They asked about your bank and said they would make a request to check your accounts. As a criminology 'expert', I know these procedures inside out, but being on the receiving end of them is decidedly dreamlike.

'What about the car? Can you trace the registration?' I asked.

'We'll be making other enquiries first,' Sgt Howis explained.

'I don't care about the car itself – but it could—'

He put up his hand firmly. 'Yes, I know. Let's go one step at a time.'

Howis asked for a recent photo of you and I showed him several from frames displayed around the room and more from an album in the study. It felt uncomfortably intimate having him look at pictures of you. I glanced at a photograph of the two of us, my arm around your shoulders and almost felt jealous – I'm not that man any more.

The sergeant chose a recent one where you're wearing a checked shirt, standing in front of the shed. Your hair has blown away from your face and you're looking down to earth and relaxed. It's one of the big differences between us; you always seem so natural and genuine. I struggle to appear easy-going. I fake being in control and pretend to be better than I am – whereas you are completely open. You don't need to be guarded, to hide, to hold yourself in check. There's nothing to cover up, nothing to be ashamed of – at least that's what I've always thought.

PC Felton suggested I get some posters printed to display locally. She wrote the contact details on a card so I could liaise with their media officer, but as you're considered 'low risk' there won't be a television appeal at this stage.

That was yesterday. I've already arranged for posters to be printed; I need to collect those. Things are moving.

I go into the bathroom, roll up my sleeve and give myself the infertility injection, following the series of red 'X's' I've marked on the calendar. It seems ironic doing this, boosting my sperm count, when you're nowhere in sight. As they're three times a week, a nurse at the Queen Elizabeth taught me how to administer them myself.

I empty the waste bucket in the kitchen and put nuggets down for Frank. My body goes about these normal activities, seemingly knowing what it is doing, but my mind is somewhere else, rolling around like a lost marble inside a long hollow tube.

Quite by accident I check the clock. I have to be somewhere.

The train pulls in to Wimbledon station and I use the map in the foyer to work out where to go next. I've never been here on the train before; we always come to see your parents in the car. I know I could easily hire one, but it feels wrong. Like I'm *replacing* the one you took – filling in the gaps. It feels too much like carrying on as normal.

I head up the hill towards the Village and turn right along Lancaster Road. The houses are impressive in this area; being an aeronautical engineer must have brought with it a cushy standard of living. As I turn into their drive, I realise I've never seen them on my own before. The place itself looks foreboding without you, with its two gateways and two bay windows either side of the porch. There are miniature pine trees in terracotta urns framing the front door, but they are brown and crisp. Lucinda has obviously had her hands full with Ted; she would never normally allow her plants to get into this state. I'm glad you're not here to witness it, Dee.

I don't know which way things will go today. I've tried telling Lucinda over the phone, more than once, that you drove off and haven't been seen since, but she hasn't taken it in. I'm hoping that being here in front of her, so she can't change the subject or escape, is going to get the message across. I asked the police to hold off speaking to them until I'd been over in person. They have to be primed. They might even need a family liaison officer.

As for Ted, with his burgeoning dementia, I'm not sure how much he's going to grasp of the situation. Nor do I know how I'm going to manage things after I've dealt the blow. All the unsavoury details behind why you might have gone – do I really want them to know all that?

The doorbell chimes with a resounding *bing-bong*. I expect the trim figure of Lucinda to come scurrying to the door – she's usually super-efficient and knows I'm coming. Instead, there's silence. I ring again and peer through the coloured panes of glass. I see Ted shuffling towards me. He opens the door, but doesn't seem to recognise me.

'She's at the shops,' he says definitively, as if that's likely to cover most issues he encounters at the front door. At that moment I hear footsteps on the gravel behind me and Lucinda comes rushing to my side with a shopping bag in each hand.

'Sorry – traffic was dreadful,' she says by way of welcome. I follow her inside. I take one of the bags from her in the hall and carry it through into the kitchen. I look up and take in the scattering of Post-it notes attached to the fridge, the biscuit tin, the oven, the drawers. There was one on the back of the front door I noticed, when I came in, more on the hall table, above the coat hooks, by the phone. Your parents' house has turned into a dense forest with yellow leaves flapping in the breeze when anyone walks by.

Lucinda leads me into the lounge and leaves to put

the kettle on. Ted is already seated. I wonder what's going through his mind. I sit on the edge of the sofa, my hands on my knees, unable to keep my feet from tapping.

'Chelsea won on Saturday,' says Ted as he folds his newspaper.

'Did they?' I don't know whether he's referring to the weekend just gone or one several years ago. 'I don't really follow football,' I confess. 'It's Formula One I enjoy.'

'Father was a footballer, wasn't he?'

'Yes, that's right. Played for West Ham.' At the last minute, I avoid adding a patronising *well done* to my reply.

Lucinda returns with a tray of tea. She didn't give me any choice of hot drinks — coffee would have been better at this time in the morning. 'I've forgotten the milk,' she mutters. She looks up and instructs loudly, as if to a child, 'Can you get it, Ted? The milk — it's on the table in the kitchen?'

I remember that this was the subject of your last argument with your mother; you felt she was debasing your father by talking down to him.

There is a painful silence. I don't know how to start.

Ted brings three rattling empty cups on a tray into the lounge, replicating the ones we already have, but has forgotten the milk. I don't mention it. I make myself drink it black, but I can only manage two sips.

Ted breaks the ice. 'Diane's not with you, then?'

'No. And I'm afraid that's why I'm here. There's some difficult news...' *Difficult* comes to me as a kinder word than *bad*.

Lucinda is holding up her cup and saucer staring at me.

'She went to the village shop on July 30th and she hasn't come back,' I explain.

Ted is the first to respond. 'It doesn't sound like Diane, taking off like that.'

'No,' I said, clearing my throat. 'She hasn't been in touch – not properly.'

'What do you mean?' asks Lucinda urgently.

'Well – she left a text with Alexa and posted information on the Internet, but no one has actually spoken to her for six days.'

'I think she's married now,' says Ted, bless him. He frowns and looks bewildered. Lucinda must have seen this look more times than she can bear. I want to hug him and tell him everything is going to be all right, but I'm not sure he'll understand what's going on.

I turn to Lucinda, who still hasn't responded in a way that suggests she has grasped the enormity of the matter. 'Alexa said you and Diane had a bit of an argument about something – do you remember?' I ask.

Ted answers, although I was directing my question to Lucinda. 'Did we?' he says. 'I don't know. I don't think so. I don't always remember everything,' he admits.

'You said she had a miscarriage,' says Lucinda, ignoring my question.

'Yes – but she was coping very well.' Were you? I don't know, any more.

'And then she left.' Her words come out like hammer blows, resonant with accusation. This is all my fault.

'She didn't storm out or anything. She drove to the village shop to pick something up.' I'm reluctant to mention my alcohol-induced headache.

'But she doesn't normally drive,' Lucinda points out.

'I know.' That part was certainly out of character. 'But she seemed fine. Popped out in her running gear. No big deal.'

'And you've not heard anything since?'

'No.'

'And the police – what are they doing?'

'They're making enquiries. They'll want to come and ask you questions.'

She looks up, a childlike curiosity on her face. 'Will it be on the news?'

'No...' I've hassled Howis and Neil on this subject and got nowhere. 'Diane is considered a low risk, so the police don't think that's a good use of resources.' There's a grate of bitterness in my voice.

Lucinda looks confused more than anything. There's a long gap where we all avoid looking at each other. 'It's so unlike Diane,' Lucinda concludes. 'Where would she go?'

'I know – that's it. Where? I've contacted everyone I can think of. I've put posters up in the village.'

'I haven't seen any,' Ted says, perplexed.

'Not *our* village,' snaps his wife. 'Ted hardly goes out anyway,' she says turning to me. 'I can tell you it's a full-time job looking after him.' There seems to be a layer of resentment over everything she says.

'She didn't say anything to you at all, did she?' I ask. 'She hasn't talked about being unhappy or having problems?'

'Not really,' Lucinda says, biting her lip. 'She said the cottage was turning out to be a handful, but she was enjoying school and she mentioned...the dog...'

'Frank? Yes...he's staying with us for the time being.'

'She said she thought he was lovely and it was making her broody.'

'Right.'

'You said she lost the baby. She didn't know she was pregnant?' I'm not sure if she expects an answer – she says it mostly to herself.

'Not until she was rushed into hospital.'

Ted pipes up. 'Is she all right?'

Lucinda sighs, doesn't reply and starts returning the cups to the tray. I offer to take it out, but she shakes her head.

When she returns, I get to my feet. My job is done. Sadly, I have learnt nothing from this trip, but I've done what I came to do. I reach out to give your mother a hug, but she pulls away before we get properly into hold. She leads me to the door with Ted dragging behind like an old terrier.

I turn to him in the hall and give him a hug instead. He holds me close and I wonder how much true affection he's been getting since his illness became evident.

I call out over his shoulder as I pull away, 'You will let me know if you hear from her, won't you?'

'Yes, of course,' Lucinda replies.

Ted looks blankly at the door handle. 'Who are we talking about, again?' he queries.

Lucinda grunts through gritted teeth. 'Diane, Ted – your daughter, Diane.'

He nods looking at his slippers, but I know he's lost sight of you. But then, for once he's not alone, because we all have.

As I return briskly to the station, I have had two missed calls on my mobile. One is from Tara saying the police have spoken to her and asked lots of questions about you. The other is Sgt Howis asking me to call, but making it clear it's not urgent.

I walk along to the far end of the platform away from other passengers to make the call. As the line connects, I'm staring at a poster for the West End drama, *War Horse*. You've mentioned it several times, but we've never seen it. Under different circumstances, I would book two tickets right now.

The sergeant has no news, instead he asks about our finances. Do we have a lot of money? Do we have rich parents? Had you or I upset anyone recently? He doesn't say it, but I know where he's coming from. He's considering an abduction and a possible ransom demand. I've thought of this too, of course, but it seems so unlikely that I've more or less dismissed it. I explain that your parents are pretty well off, but there's nothing new about it. Why would someone abduct you *now*? I tell him that my mother has just got remarried to a loan shark. He sounds more interested in this.

'When was that?'

'Um…last year…August. He runs his own business – it's a payday loan company called Loansafe – based in Enfield.'

Sgt Howis informs me flatly that it will be a line of enquiry. My train rumbles in and I don't hear him end the call.

Chapter 15
Marion

6 August

The oncology department has become Marion's second home. She knows every crack in the plaster on the magnolia-coloured walls from the lift to the waiting room, knows how many footsteps it takes to get from the lift to Mr Guha's room, knows it will be the fifth strip light that flickers.

Room number three. Clara's favourite number.

Marion takes a seat outside, alongside her daughter. There was no one who could childmind this morning. Marion wonders how much Clara has taken in about her illness. She doesn't want to terrorise her daughter with talk of leaving her, but Clara needs to understand, as far as her scattered little brain will allow, that she's dying. Marion needs to tread a fine line that prepares her without panicking her and she doesn't know where to start. She can barely look to the future herself. When the cancer finally gets the better of her, Clara will become an orphan. Marion cannot bear to use the word. She knows that whilst her mother would adopt her, she's ill herself, with Parkinson's. Granny is coping now, but for how long? Other relatives are thin on the ground; she can't think of anyone she'd entrust her daughter with.

The nurse who is going to look after Clara while Marion is having her consultation, arrives. Marion prefers it this way, otherwise Clara keeps asking questions and interrupting and she can see Mr Guha getting annoyed. Clara will go to the play area in the children's department instead.

As the nurse reaches out her hand, Clara bends down to untangle her laces. 'I don't like wearing shoes, because the strings always get locked,' she explains.

'That's right – then you trip up,' replies the nurse who, according to her badge, is called Sheila.

'Mummy says my eyes are in the wrong place, because I want to see things from too high up or too low down. She says I should have been born a cat or a rat, because it's normal for them to climb trees or squeeze into small holes. She says people aren't supposed to do that so much. But it's normal for me.'

This is the first series of statements that Marion has heard in the last two days that belong in the real world. Otherwise, when she's been coaxed from her room at meal times, Clara has said nothing other than quotes from nursery rhymes or fairy tales. Marion has heard the floorboards sighing in their own regular rhythm as Clara walks backwards and forwards, immersed in solo activities in her bedroom, playing in turn the roles of Cinderella, Rapunzel and Mowgli, from the *Jungle Book*. At times she's heard Clara ranting at various invisible characters in the stories. 'My what big ears you have' and 'Don't you dare go into the woods on your own again, little girl.' In fact, Marion is recognising more and more scenes from *Little Red Riding Hood*. She has tried to join in, suggested watching musicals and animated films, but Clara has been too distracted by her own little world. She didn't want to go shopping with Granny yesterday or to feed the ducks at the park. It wasn't like her at all.

This newfound introversion worries Marion and she hopes Dr Pike is going to be able to sort it out. They've had another session, but the specialist didn't seem to have anything to add to her initial diagnosis: Clara has retreated into the world of fairy tales following her traumatic experience and only time and gentle encouragement will bring her back again.

Sheila pats Marion's shoulder. 'He's ready to see you now,' she whispers in an aside to her. 'Come and find us when you're done.'

When her mother starts to walk away, Clara's face clouds over. She nips her chin and lets out a little moan. At times like this Marion has to stand her ground and let Clara go. She has to make herself strong with the familiarity of it and teach Clara to do the same. One day, it will be forever.

'We'll have a great time,' Sheila insists. 'We can do afternoon tea or play doctors and nurses.'

Clara baulks at the idea. 'Pah...' she says.

'Okay, then, what about *The Carnation* – the story where the queen is imprisoned inside the castle by the king...'

Marion stops in her tracks and spins around. It's not Sheila's fault. She isn't to know. Marion waits to see if the mention of being trapped in the castle brings about a scream, tears or leaves Clara cowering behind the chairs.

'Oh, yes,' says Clara, giving a little skip. 'That's a *good* story. I've even been the queen in real life, haven't I, Mummy? I had all the stories to myself in the dark for hours and hours in a proper castle. I saw owls and foxes and dragons and I'd love to go and do it again.'

'You are a proper little adventurer, Miss Clara Delderfield,' Sheila says, leading her away.

Marion watches, more perplexed than ever.

Marion is walking towards the play area as Mr Guha's words pitter-patter inside her head. The period of remission is over, he tells her. The patch she's just gone through was a *good* stretch, apparently. Now things are likely to get tougher. She's anaemic for a start and her paraprotein levels are too high. Mr Guha recommends another blood infusion and more chemo.

Marion reaches the right place. Seven or eight children are making trains with rows of plastic chairs, rolling balls, tractors, trucks across the floor and pouring invisible tea into cups, but Clara doesn't appear to be one of them. Marion glances at every child. Sheila isn't there either. Maybe she's taken her to the toilet. Marion takes a seat and smiles at an Asian woman who is holding a young baby. She looks at her watch. After a second glance, she gets up and walks round to the nearest toilet, but the door is wide open. A familiar fizz kicks her in the stomach. *No, no, Clara, please – not today…*

Marion goes back to the play area and stands at the reception. A nurse comes to the desk to check something on a list and Marion speaks to her, even though she can see the woman is in a hurry. 'Sheila is with my daughter – do you know where she is?'

'Sheila – er…' the nurse backs off, opening her hands wide with a shrug. 'Sorry – I've got a haemorrhage…' She turns and paces out of sight.

Marion senses movement behind her and turns.

'Clara!' She shifts her gaze, pointedly, from her daughter to Sheila, drawing out the words. 'Where've you been?'

Sheila looks flustered and out of breath – it looks like Clara has sent her chasing all over the place. 'I found her outside,' Sheila admits. 'She must have slipped out when I took a phone call.' The nurse doesn't apologise.

Marion wants to roll her eyes and tut, but she manages to restrain herself. 'Time to go,' she says, taking Clara's hand. She says a curt *thank you* to the nurse and pulls Clara away.

It's only when they are outside that she notices Clara's cardigan is buttoned up wrongly. *Did she leave home like that?* She also sees that her knees are scraped.

'You're bleeding. You've hurt yourself.' She drops a blob of spittle on a tissue and dabs at Clara's wounds. 'What happened, honey?'

Clara sniffs, tugging at her sleeve, trying not to cry. Marion folds her into her body. 'Sweetheart, did you fall over?' She bobs down to her level.

'With silver bells and puppy dogs' tails and little maids all in a row,' Clara chants in a whisper.

'Talk properly, now. What happened? How did you hurt yourself?'

'I don't want to go back there ever again,' she says, folding her arms with a pout.

'Why, what happened?' Marion repeats.

'You're a big, bad wolf,' shouts Clara, 'and you're not going to get your supper.'

Marion straightens up. She doesn't know what's going on. It's another few days before they'll see Dr Pike again and she's tired and feeling faint and she doesn't know how to deal with this.

'Let's go home, shall we? We can tell Dr Pike all about this when we see her.'

'Here?' Clara is back in the land of the living, it appears.

'Yes. We have an appointment every week and you'll be able to do drawings and play again.'

'I don't want to go back to the lopital. I don't *want* to.' Clara twists furiously and stamps her feet.

'We have to come back, darling. Mummy's sick and she needs to get help from the doctors. And it's a good place to see Dr Pike, too.'

Clara goes quiet as they amble towards the bus stop. Marion has no idea what is going on inside her daughter's head, but whatever it is – it's not making her happy.

They get off the bus a stop early, because Marion needs to get milk. She has started to feel nauseous during the journey, but they finished the last carton at breakfast and she planned to make scrambled eggs for tea. She has to get to the village shop.

They get as far as the stone cross in the centre of the green and Marion feels her head fill with candyfloss and her knees turn to mush. One minute she's stumbling across the turf, the next her mouth is down in the grass.

She can hear the voice of a little girl, far away, crying out.

The next thing she is aware of is the face of a kind man above her. He is gently tapping her face and calling her name. She recognises him from the village; the good-looking man who teaches at the university. He has a serene wife who always has a kind word and offers to carry her shopping at the supermarket.

'Mrs Delderfield, can you hear me?'

'Where's Clara?'

'She's right here.' He brings her daughter into her line of sight. 'Are you hurt?' he asks.

Marion gives this question some thought. She feels queasy, dizzy and has a headache, but nothing seems cut or broken. If anything, she feels stupid, taking a tumble like that in the centre of Nettledon.

He helps her to sit up. 'I'm Harper Penn. I've seen you before. I live at Rosamund Cottage, at the far end of the village.' He points towards the south.

'Yes – I remember,' she says. She stands up holding onto him, because the ground is still tipping away from her. 'I'm Marion. This is my daughter, Clara.' She adjusts the scarf that has slid away from her ears. 'I've just come back from the hospital. A bit wobbly.'

Clara takes hold of her mother's hand.

'Let me get you home,' suggests Harper as he picks up her handbag.

'I need milk,' she croaks.

'No worries,' he tells her. 'I'll get you back first then bring it for you.' His voice is refined and soothing like a lullaby. Mrs Penn is a lucky lady.

The three of them make slow progress to Greenacres Cottage – it's about seven properties north of the green. The Penns live at the posh end, Marion recalls, where there's more space and lovely big oak trees. Everyone is more packed in at her end, but it does mean neighbours are close at hand if she needs help.

Harper is at Marion's elbow, barely touching her, but at the ready as if guiding a blind person. The little wooden gate is difficult to open; Harper has to push against the errant bushes and shrubs that are fighting to keep people out. On the other side is a landscape of tangled weeds; the path buried. Marion sees it through a stranger's eyes – it doesn't look like some gardens do, let loose on a happy rampage when left to their own devices. Instead it's like the plants are fighting for soil, space and water – trampling and choking each other.

'It's too much for me,' explains Marion, although Harper hasn't said a word. They step over thorny branches and broken terracotta pots to get to the front door.

Marion fumbles in her bag for her keys until Clara hands her mother a solitary one from her pocket. For six months her daughter has been able to come and go as she pleases. Marion falters as she takes it, fearful that Harper will judge her, but he doesn't appear to notice.

Harper leaves her sitting at the kitchen table and runs out to get milk from the village shop. He makes tea – Marion insists he join her – and gets a glass of orange for Clara, who hasn't yet disappeared to her bedroom. She is watching Harper, sizing him up.

'Did you save Mummy's life?' she asks him, earnestly.

'I don't think so,' he replies. 'Mummy felt faint, that's all. She's fine now.'

'What big eyes you have...' Clara says in a theatrical voice. Marion cringes. Here's when everything starts to go pear-shaped.

'All the better to see you with,' Harper replies with ease, drawing his eyes wide.

'You know it,' Clara says, impressed. She clambers onto the wooden chair, getting a little closer, her feet tucked underneath her.

There's a fly in the room; Marion can hear it. It stops somewhere, then takes off again. Blasted thing. She hasn't got the energy to chase and swipe at it with a wet cloth.

'Did you know that a bluebottle is made of two jewels joined together?' Clara points out.

'You're right,' Harper agrees. 'It looks like mother of pearl.'

'What's "mother of pearl"?'

Harper delves into his pocket and pulls out his key ring. The silver disc has a mother-of-pearl butterfly in the centre. He shows it to Clara.

'It's pretty!' she exclaims. Marion doesn't think Clara's seen this type of shell before. 'Look, Mummy – it sparkles and changes colour.'

'You've got her captivated now,' says Marion. 'She loves butterflies and anything that twinkles.'

Harper removes the keys from the metal coil, pockets them and holds the silver disc out on his palm. 'I'd really like you to have it,' he says to Clara.

'Oh, no,' Marion interjects. 'It looks like it has

sentimental value.'

'Not really,' he says. 'It came out of a cracker last Christmas – I keep meaning to get another one.' He turns back to Clara. 'If you like it. You can put your house key on it, so it doesn't get lost.'

'Can I, Mummy?' Clara queries, her mouth falling open. Her mother nods and Clara peels it carefully from his hand, as if it is a live creature she wants to protect.

She holds it up to the light, feels the weight of it, turns it over. 'Why is it called "mother" of pearl and not just pearl? Do pearls have mothers?'

'That's a good question,' he contemplates. 'Pearls are like little beads that come out of a shell, but this comes from the *lining* of the shell...'

'So, it kind of looks after the pearl, keeps it warm?'

'Like a mother – yes, I suppose you're right.'

She has another question for him. 'Why are bluebottles pretty when all they do is poo on the breadboard?'

Harper is losing his way. He glances at Marion for help. She shrugs with a half-smile as if to say you're on your own. 'I really don't know,' he concludes.

'Do you want to see my room?' Clara declares.

'Shall we ask your Mummy first?' he says. 'She might not feel like climbing the stairs just at the minute.' Marion is warming to this polite and charming man almost as much as her daughter is.

She gets to her feet to see what the world feels like from up there. The kitchen seems to stay still; she's doing a little better. 'It might not be what you expect,' she warns, as they head into the hall. 'It's not pink and cute.'

Clara's room has a carpet of thick dried leaves covering the entire floor (offerings from last autumn) with pinecones crowded on the window ledge so you can't see any paintwork at all. There are two walls painted in black matt paint and two in orange with floor-to-ceiling bookshelves, mainly full of books and stuffed animals. In the corner is a fish tank with fairy lights around the top, next to the bunk bed. Clara sleeps on the top and keeps dressing-up clothes on the bottom. There is also a large chest by the wardrobe full of costumes. Clara used to change into five or six outfits a day – a fairy, a queen, a wizard – now she seems to wear just the red cape and carries the wicker basket around with her.

'What an incredible place,' Harper exclaims. 'I've never seen anything like it.'

'As you've probably gathered, Clara loves fairy tales and make-believe. When she can, she spends the entire day in character,' explains Marion. 'She doesn't like wearing shoes and draws sandals on her feet in felt pen to make it look like she's wearing them.' Harper laughs and Marion doesn't know whether to feel full of pride or embarrassment at the creative impulses of her daughter.

He gravitates to the corner where there's an antique mannequin wearing a ballet tutu. The salmon-coloured skirt looks like it's made with overlapping chrysanthemum petals. He strokes it with care. 'Her Granny bought that for her at an auction.'

'Granny – what big teeth you have…' Clara declares.

'She's a bit…confused at the moment.'

While Clara is busy pulling hats out of the cupboard,

Marion whispers to him. 'She got trapped for the night in Portchester Castle about three weeks ago,' she says quickly. 'Long story – she's fine, but she's got a bit obsessed with certain stories. I don't really know why.'

Marion lets him examine the walls. There's a totem pole, bagpipes, an Aborigine didgeridoo and a taxidermy deer's head on one and masks of Shrek, Batman, Spiderman, Minnie Mouse and Homer Simpson on another. There is only one photograph in the room, on the bookshelf, of Clara and her father after a skydive, his arm is around her. Both of them are smiling. The purple frame is studded with little diamonds. It hurts like a flame in Marion's lungs to look at it.

'Does Clara like animals?' Harper asks.

Marion smiles. 'See adores them, especially dogs.'

'But not wolves,' Clara chips in. 'They're very bad.'

'Perhaps Clara might like to come and meet Frank one day. He's a dog who's staying with us at the moment. Very friendly. I think they'd get on well.'

'Yes, please!' shouts Clara. 'I'm going to meet Frank.'

'She'd love that,' says Marion, gratefully and senses that this is a man who keeps his promises.

Chapter 16
Harper

7 August – Eighth day missing

I'm tossing stale bread in the bin when the doorbell rings at 8am. For a moment I think it's the police. They've found you. But it's the surveyor from the insurance company. I'd forgotten he was coming early to check whether the cracks in the extension indicates subsidence. We noticed small cracks when we moved in, but the estate agent explained them away as 'rustic charm'. At that time we weren't ready to face anything detrimental – we'd fallen in love with the place and just wanted to buy it.

Mr Charles is tall and tired-looking, probably in his late thirties, wearing a long raincoat even though it's a bright morning. It's the same pale grey colour as his skin. He pulls a clipboard and camera from his briefcase. I offer him a drink, but he declines. He rattles a pen against his teeth and paces around all the downstairs rooms, sliding the curtains to one side with the biro, as if they are contaminated, and moving chairs with his foot.

He goes outside and steps into the flowerbed you filled with begonias, to get to the outside brickwork. I hear the snap as he breaks off leaves and stems with his clumsy feet. I swallow hard, fighting the irrational notion that he's hurting you in some way. I want him to leave; his presence feels gloomy, like he's about to sign a death warrant on our property.

He asks for the house deeds, which you brought down from the loft a few weeks ago. That was lucky. I wouldn't have had a clue where to look. Then he sits at the kitchen table and opens his laptop. He types in figures, flicks through the deeds and makes notes.

'The problem seems isolated to the section that was added in the 1970s to create a larger kitchen,' he says. He has a pronounced Cornish accent and curls his 'r's. 'Looks like there's too much moisture under the back end of the property. That will need to be checked out – could be a faulty drain. I'll forward my full report. You should be covered.'

That's all I need to know.

My mobile rings while Mr Charles is back tapping walls and measuring cracks again. It's Sgt Howis to say that no unidentified person meeting your description has been received by the local coroner's office – thank God.

I put down the phone and don't hear anything else; the surveyor carries on – something about woodworm in the beams and concerns about the sloping window frames. There's only so much I can cope with at any one time. He leaves and I sink onto the sofa, exhausted, as if I've just had a vicious argument with him.

I find myself by the kettle and help myself to a sachet of camomile tea, because that's what you often drink at this time in the morning. It makes me feel closer to you. It also leads me to question how well I know you. I didn't think you were the kind of person who would leave me in the lurch like this. I think of you when we first met at the demo; fresh-faced, smelling of newly washed clothes. So pure and inviting.

Our first proper date followed only two days after the rally, when we went to a restaurant in Charlotte Street for a Keralan curry. We didn't need any preliminary casual arrangements for coffee or drinks at a bar to test out whether we wanted to see each other more seriously. We knew.

During the course of the evening, I revealed to you my innermost feelings about my father.

'There was no warning about him going. There were no fights or arguments – only concrete silences in every room.'

'Tell me about it,' you said, gripping my wrist. 'If you want to…'

I took a quick swig of wine and waited for it to restore sufficient moisture to my mouth to continue. Then I told you everything in one long breath, trying not to sound sorry for myself. You had that effect on me right from the start, Dee, the ability to draw out the details without causing me to resort to my usual habit of making my life sound overly melodramatic. 'One Sunday he packed up all his stuff.' I put down my glass. 'I thought at first it was a special trip we were all going on – then he said it was only for him – a West Ham training camp in Spain. He lied. It was mid-season and they had a string of local fixtures to play. He wanted to get out of the house without fireworks, that's all. Mum sat in the kitchen the whole time. She barely moved, her chin in her hand, drinking cold tea, watching the birds on the feeder outside the window.'

You didn't say a word. I was glad about that. Instead, you squeezed my hand and stayed still with me as I let the feelings breathe.

'I hardly saw him after that. There were a handful of phone calls, the occasional present at birthdays or Christmas. Nothing consistent I could rely on. He met me a couple of times after school and took me places, but it wasn't fun anymore. It felt strained, like it was a duty, a bother for him.

'I didn't know where he lived or who he was with. Mum refused to talk about him, so I stopped asking. After a few years I didn't see him at all. He was out of our lives for good.'

Your eyes hadn't strayed an inch from my face since I'd started.

'I'd turned fifteen and I still missed him; I was confused, upset, sad. I felt like it was *my* fault; perhaps I wasn't clever enough or I'd driven him away with my ineptitude at his beloved game. I don't know what brought it on – maybe it was something my mother said, or some comment about football on the news. Anyway, suddenly one Saturday I was furious with him and hated him for what he'd done. I threw away every precious gift he'd given me – football annuals, West Ham tops, caps, scarves.'

You didn't nod with forced pity or ask questions; you were like a camera, zooming in closer and closer to get to the core. No one had ever listened to me with such sensitivity before.

'That same day, I took the train to Dover. I walked

along the chalk cliff-top with the box of news cuttings from football magazines and sports pages I'd kept since my father became famous. About two hundred carefully trimmed clippings over six years that mentioned Ronnie Penn – *my dad* – and his contribution to the West Ham team. I pulled the box out of my rucksack and turned it upside down on the grass.'

My voice stuttered to a croak. 'Then I stood on the top of the cliff and painstakingly ripped every one into tiny shreds and tossed them all over the edge into the sea.' I stopped abruptly, my jaw frozen, willing the tears to stay away. 'I had nothing left of him after that.' My voice fell to a whisper. 'I didn't know he'd be dead three months later. For years I felt like I'd brought on his death. I felt like they were his ashes I'd scattered that day. I'd done it with those scraps of paper, prematurely, and somehow brought on his heart attack.'

I bowed my head and stopped there – what I'd done next was unforgiveable – and nothing would make me tell you, or anyone else, about it. Ever. You'd run a mile.

You waited before speaking. 'You must have been *so* angry.' I could feel your fury bubbling under the surface of your voice. 'You cared for him so much and only ever wanted him to be a proper dad. Then his health failed and he died.' You sighed. 'And you were left with all that guilt.'

I trailed my fingers along your delicate cheekbone. No one had ever genuinely rooted for me like this before. It was then that I said it. It came out of the blue, unconnected to anything. 'I love you,' I whispered. It was a ridiculous thing to say, so soon after we'd met, but you smiled, a soft, slow smile that built into a dazzling sunrise. 'I know. It's good isn't it?'

The tea has gone cold by now. I tip it down the sink, but don't have the will to make a fresh one. It's only mid-morning and I have the whole day yawning ahead of me. Frank is asleep after his romp. I envy him. I wish I could lose most of the day like that. I was up just after 6am and decided fresh air was better than futile attempts to get back to sleep. I'm going to have to find constructive things to do, because sitting around waiting is driving me mad.

The post arrives and I put it on the kitchen table. The pile for you is growing, but there's nothing that looks urgent. There's a postcard from Neil – arriving after the fact. It has oily thumbprints on it and smells of coconut suntan oil. I slap my hand down on the counter. I almost forget. Our holiday. We're due to go to Rome at the end of August. You're coming back for that, aren't you?

There's a charity request from Oxfam and a reminder about the council tax. I've forgotten to pay it. See how I'm falling apart without you? I'm starting to feel like someone who doesn't have a full grip on my life. What if this is it and I never see you again?

It's thoughts like this that bulldoze me sideways – I can't let them in; they're too devastating.

There's also a letter from the bank with your name on it. I've been waiting for this. I must open it. The police are no doubt checking your details, but I need to see when you last used your debit card. I rip open the seal and flash-read the statement down to the bottom, but it only goes to the end of the month. You left on July 30th and your debit card wasn't used on 31st. This is useless – it doesn't tell me anything.

The transactions don't include your credit card – that's on a different statement, due in a couple of weeks. The details would show up on your online account, of course, but I don't have your password. Would your mother know it? Would Alexa? And would they tell me if they did?

I try your mother first as the easier option, but my call goes straight to the answerphone; I don't have a mobile number for her. I fall back on Alexa.

'Have you heard anything?' she says, warily.

'No. Have you?'

'No.'

'I wondered if you could help with something,' I venture. 'It could be useful to the police.'

'I'm at work.' I can hear a persistent boomy thud in the background; it sounds like she's in a nightclub, not a gym.

'I want to know if Diane has accessed her bank account and I don't have her online passwords.'

'Can't you wait until she gets back?'

'I'm worried about her.' I can't believe Alexa is so nonchalant. 'It's been eight days. I haven't heard a thing. It's important.'

She sounds like she's chewing gum. I can hear her tossing it around in her mouth, enjoying the power she has over me. 'You want her password?'

'I'm not going to *do* anything with her money – I just want to check it. See if she's withdrawn cash, used her cards.'

It crosses my mind that I could clear out your account, Dee, and you'd be forced to come running back, but I dismiss the thought immediately. I don't want to trick or force you like that.

'Sorry,' she says, coolly. 'I don't have it.' Chew, chew, chew. 'Why can't you leave her be? She'll come back when she's ready. I've got to go.'

The phone goes dead before I can say anything further.

I haven't told your sister that I know for certain the baby wasn't mine. She would only rub my nose in it and I refuse to give her the satisfaction, although it's silly really, she's probably worked it out given you've told her I'm infertile.

I open my laptop and stare at it, as if my resolve will be enough to open up your records. The only password I have of yours is for your email account, so I open that instead. I've never done this before and I hate myself for snooping. I may very well regret it, too – but I need to know who you've been in contact with. Have you left behind the trail of an affair; illicit messages, covert invitations, erotic exchanges? My fingers tremble and I brace myself.

I go back to the start of May and look at every sender's name. Most are people I recognise; Tara, Alexa, Jackie, Lorraine and colleagues from work. There are several receipts; you've made more donations to animal shelters than I thought and recently bought cufflinks. Are they for me? For our anniversary in September? There are a few spam emails and a message from the deputy head, Stephen Morrell, thanking you for running the assembly at the end of term. I remember you were worried about that; Dennis, the teacher who joined the school just before you did, had done a brilliant one on archaeology and you didn't know how you could compete. We'd talked it through and you'd chosen astronomy and spent hours on delivering the basics about stars and outer space in a way that would captivate six to ten-year-olds.

I hate every moment of this. Checking up on you. But investigating officers will be going through all this on your own laptop too; none of this can be kept private anymore.

There are no names cropping up I don't recognise. I scan through recent documents you've opened – most are connected to your presentation. You've also updated our Christmas address list. I check the photo file; there are several of you astride Rupert, taken at the stables, but not the one of Frank you posted on the Facebook page. That one must only be on your phone. There are several of us together in the garden, taken last summer, and they make me shiver. I feel desperately and irrationally homesick, even though I am standing right here in our own kitchen.

A brainwave slashes across my mounting resignation. I open the first page of your current back account and try the same password that you use for your emails. The police are also looking into this, but I haven't heard anything yet. I draw a sharp breath. It works. I have no option. 'I'm sorry, Dee, but I have to do this.'

The screen opens and there it is: three days after you left, a withdrawal of fifty pounds from a cash machine. I check the details:

Sat 2 August – ATM Stop'n'Shop 3918 TW6 £50

There's nothing else, but it's a start. I call Neil straight away.

'The investigating officer will look into it,' he assures me, 'but you could track down the *Stop'n'Shop* and find out exactly where it is.' There's a gap. 'TW6 is Twickenham.'

I do as he says and locate the store online.

I am no longer feeling jubilant at my discovery. The ATM is five-hundred metres from Heathrow Airport.

Chapter 17
Harper

7 August

I'm still standing in the kitchen holding the disconnected phone. Neil has gone. *Stay calm.* My head feels like a washing machine that's just jolted into fast spin mode. I mustn't run away with myself. I have to take hold of this thread carefully and follow it to see where it takes me.

You used an ATM three days after you left, within half a kilometre of Heathrow.

Using the details I found online, I ring the convenience store and ask about CCTV. The ATM is inside the store and there's no built-in camera — I know from my own criminology experience that usually only the high street banks can afford them. The shop itself has a camera, but it's currently out of order, the manager tells me. This one vital lead is a total dead end.

I'm fired up now and check through all your personal effects: pockets, bags, all the paperwork I can find. It feels like a complete violation — a savage pillaging of our relationship, but I need to find you. I'm looking for evidence of plane tickets or someone else involved. There's nothing. Not one thing to indicate an affair or imminent departure. Either you've been incredibly clever or you didn't plan on going anywhere beyond the village shop.

I return to the kitchen and fling the soggy dishcloth left on the table, into the washing-up bowl full of dirty water. It splats on the surface then disappears. I am utterly powerless. All this new information has done is clog up my mind with more questions. Why Heathrow? Did you get on a plane? Did you go of your own free will? Are you alone or is someone with you? My worries are shifting. I need to know if you've gone of your own accord or if someone has taken you.

In my frustration, I have a tremendous urge to fling my coffee mug at the wall, smash glasses and expensive dishes. I crave the sound of destruction ringing in my ears, but I mustn't give in to it, or who knows where it might lead. I shut my eyes, my fists so tight I feel like my nails are going to break through to the other side of my hand.

I unlock the back door and slam it open so hard it hits the side wall with a crash. It makes me gasp.

It reminds me of another time.

The outburst at Christmas with my mother was nothing in comparison. I try to block out the 'other' time – the shameful 'episode' when I heard Dad had died; I try to force my mind elsewhere, but images from that day flash inside my head in full colour.

Mum got the phone call as we were watching an old rerun of *Dad's Army* on television. She was laughing as she picked up the receiver then her face collapsed. The next thing I remember was the house filling with people I hadn't seen in years. Everyone was crying and upset. They talked about Dad being taken before his time, how the heart attack wasn't his choice, how he hadn't meant to go.

I was fifteen and it brought it all back. That day when I was eight, when he'd packed his bags and walked away. He must have got bored with me. In spite of Mum's reassurances, a nagging question remained and had never been answered – *If he'd really loved me, he wouldn't have left, would he?* Now he'd gone for good.

The anger I'd felt as I threw his press cuttings off the cliff, three months earlier, had nowhere to go. You don't harbour ill will towards the dead. It had to be parcelled away – it was wrong and shameful. But Dad had let us down twice and I was furious. Everyone in our sitting room was melting with grief, but I felt bolt upright; strong, my bones primed with steel. I had to *do* something.

I left the house and went to his; I'd got the address from my uncle – it was only three miles away. It was dark and no one was there, so I climbed the back fence and broke in through the kitchen window. I raided his display cabinets and took all his trophies; from the medals he'd won at school through to the end of his career. I ran off, through the side gate, carrying them in a large bin bag over to the sewage plant in Enfield. Building work was underway, but had finished for the day, so I chucked them over a temporary fence into a deep pit. That was where they belonged – buried beside all the shit. I knew it wasn't going to hurt him, but it was all I could think of.

I was lucky; no one saw me leave the gathering, everyone was too concerned for my mother, who had never stopped loving him. I got out and blended back in again without anyone noticing. Luckily for me there had been some gang-related street crimes in the area where Dad lived and the police put it down to a random hate attack.

I find myself wandering aimlessly around the garden. Ironically, reliving that episode has calmed me down in a way I can't explain. Perhaps it's because it reminds me that I can fight back when I need to. I may be infertile, but I have enough self-respect and guts to stand up for myself when the going gets really tough.

I sit on the swing and think of Marion's ravaged garden. It doesn't take long for nature to become overgrown, out of control. Ours is heading the same way, already. I haven't appreciated until now how much attention it requires. Dead flower heads need clipping off, the roses need cutting back, there are weeds in the cracks along the path and soil has tumbled on to the lawn – Frank's doing, I presume. I don't know where to start and it feels wrong to interfere. This is your domain and I'll only spoil it; get something badly wrong and when you come back you'll be furious with me.

When you come back. Those words hang around my head like an angry wasp.

My phone rings. It's Paul Whitaker.

'Hey, Harper – we had a squash match booked for twenty minutes ago…'

Shit. I'd completely forgotten. 'I'm sorry to let you down, mate,' I say. 'But as it stands, I don't think I can make any more match arrangements – until…you know…'

'Sure. No problem. I know she's not back yet. I understand.' He says what everyone else does – that you just need time on your own and you'll be back soon.

I can hear trainers squeaking on court in the background. Paul will be able to fix a game with another partner without any trouble; he's a good player and in demand at the club.

I take Frank out again; a long ramble that wipes a few more inane hours out of my day. When I get back, it's 7pm. I ought to cook the pasty I took out of the freezer this morning, but eating doesn't come naturally to me now. I'm living with a lingering nausea the whole time and have to set an alarm to remind me to eat. Yesterday, I was surprisingly resourceful and cooked oven chips from frozen. I didn't taste them. I can't taste anything. Frank had most of them. You wouldn't have been happy about that.

I pour cornflakes into a bowl and add milk. It's all I can manage. I'm here and I'm not here. I pour a whisky. I know I shouldn't, but I need something to help get me through the stark evenings. I put a notepad in front of me on the kitchen table and consider all the facts.

Everything is open to interpretation; I can find no certainties anywhere. Your bank card was used at the ATM, but was it you standing there pressing the buttons? Did you drive all the way to the airport? Did you leave the car there? Have you left the country? I think about how much you withdrew. It was only fifty pounds. It isn't much. Have you also used your credit card? I tap the page with the pen – I tried the same password I used for your current account to access your online credit statement, but it didn't work, so I won't know until the paperwork arrives – or the police come up with something in the meantime.

If you aren't taking money out, then someone is definitely with you. But who?

I'm looking at our life together and wondering where the holes are I've not seen. Did your feelings for me start mutating into tolerance and acceptance instead of love? Did you fall for someone else right under my nose? How many secret phone calls did you make? How many times did you go sneaking behind my back?

I finish the glass and pour myself another. I didn't see any of it, Dee. I've been a blind fool, living in denial, not noticing that you were drifting away from me. Thing is – it's so hard for me to believe – even now. I didn't spot *anything* to give me concern. Not. A. Thing. You have the kind of face that allows every nuance of emotion to dismantle it. I would have seen something. I notice things, I pick up details and signals. It's my job, but it's also a legacy after Dad left. If that period in my life taught me anything it was to watch, listen, to look out – and never take anything for granted.

I get nowhere. I cross through the notes I've written with big black scrawls. In the end, there is only one question I need an answer to: *Are you coming back?*

Chapter 18
Diane

The pain hits me, envelops me, consumes me; it's the first thing I'm aware of. A searing rip wrenches at my side – have I been stabbed? Has my appendix burst? Internally, I feel like parts of me are broken, twisted, buckled – I want to touch my abdomen, stroke my side, but I am unable to move. I'm feverish; a cold layer of moisture trails over my skin like a troop of wet ants – there's something badly wrong with me. There is pain in my wrist and my head. Like I've fallen from a height onto concrete.

I glance down and notice trails of liquid down my fleece. I blink. Is it orange juice? No – wrong colour – it's dried blood. I have so many tender and aching places it's hard to know where the drops have come from. Where am I? What has happened to me? It's getting dark now, but I know the light has broken through and faded several times – so days must have gone by. I don't know how many. There are great landscapes of time I know nothing about. What's been going on in all the gaps where I have no recall? What am I doing here?

I'm sitting on cold stone that eats into my bones. The light is fading, but I can make out scatterings of straw on the floor, box shapes and a tin bath. There's a leathery, oily smell. Above my head on the wall is a rack with more straw. I wriggle to try to bring feeling into my backside, but everything aches, so I stay still and lean back against the rough bricks instead. I want to cry out but my voice splits at the first attempt. I sound like a dying seagull. My mouth is dry, my lips cracked and my throat seems to have seized up. Even breathing is precarious — my airways are clogged up with mucus, blood and something acidic, like vomit. I have to coax each breath gently so I don't choke. Closing my eyes hurts, but it's all I can think of to make this go away.

This can't be real.

It must be a feverish nightmare and when I come to again, I'll be cosy in my own bed and it will all be over.

Chapter 19
Harper

8 August – Ninth day missing

My specialist is running late. I can see his office door
from the bank of seats in the waiting room and in the
last forty minutes he's been in and out twice, the second
time returning with a bulky medical monitor. A nurse
and two other doctors have also been in to see him,
carrying clipboards and charts. It makes him look
important.

Dr Swann finally calls me through, wearing an
unbuttoned white coat as if he's fresh from ground-
breaking new research in the lab. Blue biro marks, like
hairs, are growing out of his top pocket. He's hunched
over his desk, the correct shape to look straight into a
microscope, and I wonder how many hours he'll put in
this week.

'Sorry for the wait,' he says, 'We have a ridiculous
amount to do...' he tails off, looking away, as if afraid
he's being disloyal to his profession. He offers me the
seat set at right angles to his, so if I lean forward I'm
able to see the computer screen in front of him. The
room is small and sparse, with an adjoining one that
contains an examination couch draped with flimsy white
paper. On his desk is a small vase containing sprigs of

dusty lavender stems which look fake and there's a snow globe next to a selection of pens. It strikes me as odd, given it's the height of summer.

Dr Swann pulls my notes in front of him and I sense he needs a few moments to recall who on earth I am and what on earth I'm being treated for. I judge him to be in his fifties and he's just the wrong side of handsome; his nose is too big and looks like putty and his eyebrows tuft up, like the edges of a rug. His hair isn't thick, but still has all its colour – a bland tawny brown, unless it comes out of a bottle – and his skin is well worn like an overused leather sofa. I wonder if he falls into the category of 'professional counting down the days to his retirement' or whether he lives for the job. It's hard to tell. He seems efficient enough given the constraints of the NHS.

He skim reads my notes, flicks the page over and nods. 'So – how are you finding the injections?'

'Fine.' I feel his time is precious; I want to answer as concisely as I can. 'I can manage them myself.'

'You'd had a couple of nosebleeds when I saw you last – any more?'

'Yeah – I'm afraid so.' I tell him I had one in the shower yesterday and one the day before as I was taking Frank over the fields – a really bad one.

He crumples up his nose. Complications. That's not what he wants. He wants me to be a straightforward case, so he can claw back some of his time this morning and not have to miss his lunch break. At least that's what I imagine as I watch his expression rearrange itself.

'And the nausea?'

'Yeah – I've had that most days.' I hesitate about complicating matters further, but I conclude it's worth mentioning. 'But, I've also had a domestic issue that might be contributing to that, to be honest. I'm off my food.' I don't want to tell him what the reason is – I can't bring myself to have to go through it all again.

He slides a pair of weighing scales out from under the desk and invites me to step on them.

He refers to his notes and I take a peek in his open briefcase beside the desk, because I'm innately driven to snoop, it would seem. There's nothing much to pique my interest: two DVDs, a book called *The Pursuit of Conception* and a sandwich box. 'You've lost half a stone since we started the injections,' he announces. 'That's not so good.'

He types something into the computer. 'I think the nausea from the injections should wear off shortly. The nosebleeds are a common reaction, I'm afraid.' He straightens up. 'Contact me again if you're having more than around two a week, okay?'

'So, I should carry on with the injections?'

'For now. Make an appointment in a month's time and we'll review things. We'll get you in for semen tests too, to check the way things are going.'

He stands up. He looks in a hurry to get me out, but is careful not to glance at his watch.

I walk out into the maze of corridors. They seem like underground tunnels and I'm demoralised at the thought of going back to the empty crumbling cottage. It feels like it's got a mind of its own and has decided to demolish itself; it's not the solid haven I thought it would be. I get the impression that as soon as one job is fixed another will present itself. The surveyor was certainly unimpressed and one of the builders who is due to fix the chimney made a passing comment about problems with the roof. Is it a metaphor for our marriage, I wonder – showing up the cracks I haven't been able to see?

I turn the final corner towards the hospital exit and walk straight into someone. A blur of blue and lemon yellow, it's a woman with a child. I recognise them instantly: Marion and Clara.

'Hello,' I say, probably sounding too cheerful for the situation, but I'm genuinely pleased to see them. 'Back again?'

'For Clara, this time. We've just finished.'

'You're the man with Frank,' Clara says. 'Look...' She pulls the mother-of-pearl key fob I gave her out of her pocket.

'She loves it,' Marion says. 'She won't lose it...' she tips up Clara's face with a finger under her chin, 'will you?'

'Not never,' says Clara.

'You don't have time for a hot drink, do you?' I suggest on the spur of the moment. 'There's a coffee shop...but then, you probably know...'

Marion smiles. 'I'd love to. As it happens, I've never stopped here for coffee. Always in a rush to... get out.' She addresses Clara. 'Is it okay if we have a nice drink, here?'

'As long as we all go,' her daughter tells her.

She leans across and whispers, so Clara can't hear. 'Getting Clara here was a nightmare, but as soon as she saw the crayons in the doctor's office, she forgot all about kicking up a fuss.'

The coffee shop is around the next corner and Clara rushes in to find a free table by the window. 'Did you bring Frank?' she asks, looking out of the window. 'Is he tied up outside?'

'No,' I reply, 'he's at home. You can come and see him later, if Mummy says that's okay.' Anything to prevent me having to step over the threshold alone.

'Yes, oh, yes...' Clara cries.

'I think that should be okay,' Marion adds.

I queue at the counter and order two coffees and a chocolate milkshake for Clara.

'Thank you for the key ring,' Marion says, as I set down the tray. 'She's been having a bit of a rough time lately.' Clara has pink glitter on her cheeks and is playing with a stick-thin doll with hair that extends from a hole in the top of its head.

I nod, but don't know whether to enquire further. Marion looks like she's only just holding everything together. I can relate to the wild, desperate look in her eyes. She is clearly frail, suffering the effects of cancer and chemo that has taken all her hair. She's also struggling to parent her bubbly young child. I don't want to tip her over the edge by asking questions.

Marion stirs her coffee deliberately and takes a sip. 'She's been to see the child psychiatrist. Dr Pike thinks Clara is retreating into fantasy – more than usual that is – after the "incident"...you know...'

'Right, yes – the one you mentioned,' I say, making sure I avoid anything specific within Clara's earshot.

'My best friend is Rapunzel,' Clara says between sips on her stripy straw. 'She has long hair and I can climb up it to get inside the castle. We play tiddlywinks together. She tells me all about the castle and shows me all the rooms and the dungeon.'

Marion throws her eyes up. 'She has plenty of "real" friends,' she insists, stroking her daughter's soft hair. 'You haven't seen Marnie for a while, have you?' She turns back to Harper. 'Marnie likes skipping and plays the piano.'

'And tennis,' Clara adds, folding the doll's long legs so she sits on the table.

'And there's Lucy,' continues Marion, 'she likes dolls, horses and swimming. She plays the flute and has a trampoline in the garden. When did you last play with Lucy?'

'Lucy is boring and Marnie's a cry-baby,' Clara says. 'I like Helen – she reads the stories at the library. I see her on Saturdays and sometimes after school, but that's finished now.'

Marion shrugs. 'She used to be gregarious and inclusive – now she hides in her room, tells me to keep out and spends all her time locked inside her own pretend world.' Her shoulders sink. 'Anyway, enough about us,' Marion concludes. 'What about you and your wife? You're both teachers?'

Marion can't have seen the posters.

'Diane teaches children of Clara's age at St Mary's.'

'Ah. Clara goes to Trinity – it's a bit nearer.'

'I teach criminology and forensics at Portsmouth University. We've both finished for the summer.'

'Criminology? How interesting. What does that involve, exactly?'

I try to dredge up some enthusiasm. 'It's largely exploring the tools and techniques the police use to catch criminals. We examine the latest technology and how certain cases were solved and why others never will be.'

'Jack the Ripper...' she murmurs.

'Mrs Stockton says there's a skelington in her sister's wardrobe,' Clara interjects. 'I'd like to see it.'

'I don't think she means for real,' Marion says. 'It's what people say sometimes.'

'Why?'

'It means they have troubles they want to hide and they call it a skeleton in the cupboard.'

'So, how do you know if someone is telling what's real or if they only mean it as a story?'

Good question. Marion gives her an answer. 'As you grow older, you'll learn the little sayings people use when they're really meaning something else. But sometimes it's still hard to tell if someone is telling the truth or making it up.' She leans over and tugs playfully at Clara's cheeks.

'Sometimes you can't tell the truth, because it's a secret,' Clara says seriously, bending the straw at the ribbed section near the top.

'Do you have secrets?' Marion asks her.

Clara doesn't look up. 'A few.'

It goes quiet after that. I lean back ready to go; I feel like I should be doing something, making progress. I glance down at my phone, but I have no missed calls. Marion smiles. She looks at ease with me and doesn't seem to want to break away just yet.

'You have a sad face,' she says unexpectedly.

I come clean. Telling strangers my private business goes entirely against the grain for me, but the more people who know you're missing, Dee, the better. Everyone is a potential witness and Marion may have seen something.

'The truth is my wife, Diane, has gone missing. She left the cottage on July 30th, just over a week ago. I haven't heard from her since.'

'Oh my God, how awful.' Marion's pallor does the impossible task of fading even further, to a shade resembling waxy parchment. She drags her hands down her neck. 'I'm so sorry.'

'I've put posters up in the village.'

'The pretty lady?' Clara throws in. 'I saw her on the lamppost.'

Marion apologises; says she's probably walked past the notices too, but she didn't register.

'You didn't see anything did you?' I press her. 'The evening of July 30th – it was a Wednesday. She drove out of our drive around 7.30pm?'

Marion holds her head still, focusing on the pepper pot. 'No...I don't...I think I was lying down...'

'Of course. You haven't had a visit from the police yet?'

'No – but I could easily have missed them. Being here...and I spend a lot of time in bed, I don't always hear the door.'

'They're making house-to-house enquiries.'

'I'm so sorry. I can't imagine how awful that must be.'

Touched by her kindness, I end up confiding more than I mean to. I tell her that you withdrew money inside a convenience store near Heathrow airport. A thought niggles at me. 'It's odd, you know, because Dee never uses a cash machine that charges a fee,' I mutter, half to myself. I visualise the extra £1.50 that appeared on the computer screen, paid to cover the transaction. 'She has a thing about not paying when there are plenty of ATMs that don't charge.'

'Perhaps it wasn't her,' Marion suggests.

'In which case, she must have given someone her PIN number, or someone got hold of it somehow.' This is the sort of conversation I should be having with the police.

I must appear disoriented, because Marion puts her hand on my arm.

'Have you eaten a decent meal in the last few days?' she says in warm motherly tones.

'Probably not,' I admit with a smile.

'Then you're coming to us,' she says, getting up. 'My mother made a chicken and mushroom pie that's far too big for Clara and me. Would you do me the honour of sharing it with us this evening – around seven?'

'That's very kind,' I reply. 'Perhaps before that, we could see if a little girl would like to meet Frank?'

Clara skips alongside us as we turn towards the exit. 'Can Little Red Riding Hood come too?'

'Of course she can.'

It occurs to me then that Marion has been the only

person to truly question your actions.

Chapter 20
Diane

The week before the miscarriage
'I'm going to have to get a new one,' says Diane, rolling up her yoga mat. 'Frank's taken the corner off and holes are breaking out everywhere.' She walks over to the corner of the dance studio and dumps it in the bin.

The room percolates the familiar blend of sweaty feet and high-class perfume; the open windows failing to generate a through flow of air. There are little piles of socks and water bottles around the edge and one by one they are collected as everyone troops out.

'I stayed upside down for too long,' Tara complains. 'I can't see straight.' She stands barefoot in blue lycra, her weight slung to one side and waits for Diane. She'd look gorgeous in anything, Diane decides – baggy overalls, a nun's habit, fisherman's dungarees.

The changing room is humid. Someone has just sprayed deodorant and it catches in her throat.

'Fancy a drink?' Tara suggests as she runs a line of cherry-red lipstick over her lips. She ruffles up her thick dark bob and looks ready to hit the dance floor. A twenty-second transformation.

'Sure – not for long, I'm a bit tired.'

'Harper been keeping you awake?' she says coyly.

Diane gives her a stern look and doesn't answer.

The studio belongs to the gym where Alexa works at Gunwharf Quays in Portsmouth. Diane hopes they don't bump into her on the way out; she doesn't want to spend the next hour regenerating the stress she's managed to let go of in the class. Alexa is fine on her own, but as soon as other people are there, she gets prickly and possessive. She doesn't like any of Diane's friends and Harper seems to get the brunt of her animosity, purely because he had the audacity to walk into her life. She has no other reason to feel that way; Harper always tries his best to welcome her. When they get to the bottom of the stairs, Diane puts her head down and charges for the wide glass doors. Tara knows the drill – they do this every week.

'Clean and dry,' Tara confirms as they scuttle across the concourse towards *The Skipper* wine bar that overlooks the harbour. They skirt the edge of the water and cross over an inlet covered with decking. Diane loves this spot, where the refined estuary reaches out to nearby Gosport, then stretches far away into the Solent towards the Isle of Wight. On a still day like today, she feels like she could walk on the water.

They brush through people gathering at the door and manage to find an outdoor seat overlooking the water. There's a breeze and the water below curls into gentle fluffy rolls. Harper would love this, she concludes. She makes a mental note to suggest they come one weekend for lunch.

While Tara gets the drinks, Diane looks out at the picturesque view and her mind wanders off towards the idea of holidays. It's one of few areas where she and Harper are at odds. Diane likes to leave things open ended, to wait and see, whereas he likes everything to be pinned down and settled months in advance. She likes the process of mulling it over, looking at brochures and websites, exploring possibilities, trying places out in her imagination. Harper wants to book their holiday right that instant – so he knows where and when they're going. It's the same with restaurants. Diane likes to turn up to an area and see where there are free tables; Harper is not so keen to rely on fate. He likes certainty. She knows her dallying drives him mad. He's always been organised and decisive, whereas she prefers to have her head in the clouds.

Tara jogs her arm with her elbow. 'Wake up – two cool and tangy G&Ts. Dive in. Cheers.' She doesn't wait for Diane, throwing back half the glass. 'Ah – that's better.'

Tara seems to be one of those people who swings drastically between unhealthy and wholesome. She goes on carb binges then fasts, she drinks too much, then goes on a detox, slobs in front of the television for weeks, then joins a gym and resumes yoga, Pilates and kick-boxing classes in the same week. Diane feels stable in comparison. She's never had an eating disorder, like the one Alexa endured for most of her adolescence. She's only occasionally felt so stressed or overwhelmed that she's turned to alcohol as a crutch. Drugs have always been out of the question, together with any form of self-harm. She's lucky, she supposes, that circumstances in her life have never truly tested her to her limits.

Tara slaps her hand down on the table. 'So...' she says, dragging out the word. 'How about those photos on your phone – how are you coping...really?'

'I'm okay, honestly.'

Diane wonders in an oblique way, if the baby issue could ever be a situation that pushes her over the edge. If they were another twelve months down the line and there was still no pregnancy, would she be quite so calm? She tosses the idea aside. 'It's still early days,' she adds.

Tara's delving green eyes won't let her get away with a brush off. 'Have you talked to Harper yet about how much you want a baby?'

'No. Not really. I think he knows.'

'You didn't tell him about the photographs?'

'I've wiped them off, actually. It was silly...'

Tara straightens up. Diane can see that plenty of faces around the room have already fixed the two of them on their radar. 'It's not silly,' Tara insists. 'It's totally normal to want to have a child. Maybe you should have some tests or something – see if there's a problem.'

'I've been thinking that, actually – but I hadn't wanted to admit that it's got to that stage. Maybe another few months.'

'And another few months...and another few after that?'

'I know.' Diane sits back, feeling the weight of her reluctance dragging at her shoulders.

'Would you talk to Harper or just get the tests done?'

'I don't know. I haven't thought that far, yet. I'm not sure the timing is that great...with Dad being so unstable. Perhaps we should wait...'

'Don't change the subject.' Tara leans forward, her voice lowered. 'Are you concerned about how he'll react?'

'Harper? No, of course not.'

'Only – a while ago you said you were a bit frightened of him.'

Diane makes a dismissive rasping sound. 'No – *you* said that. It was your word, not mine.'

'Okay – so what exactly *did* you mean, that time?'

'It's just how he is – he has…you know – got some unresolved issues from his past.' Diane props her elbow on the table and rests her cheek. 'This is because you came across that book, isn't it?'

Tara does a see-saw movement with her head that implies Diane is right. 'There's nothing you want to tell me, is there – nothing you're worried about…?'

Diane leans forward; she can feel Tara's breath on her face. Strands of her thick hair tickle her skin. She stops to think. She doesn't want Tara to worry about her; it's something she has to sort out on her own with Harper. 'There's a side of him that's dark and enigmatic…he's got a shade of Daniel Craig in him, but there's nothing to worry about.'

She swallows loudly and hopes Tara doesn't hear. It's not the whole truth. She *is* worried, but it would feel like she was betraying him to mention it to anyone else, even her best friend.

She decides to share only part of it. 'Okay, look – sometimes Harper acts a bit oddly. It's not strange to me anymore, because I'm used to it, but it might sound weird to other people.'

'Like what?' Tara looks intrigued and horrified in equal measure.

'Now and again…he locks himself in the chicken coop in the garden. I found him by accident once when I was feeding the birds. I heard a noise in there and thought we had rats. It was…a delicate situation.'

'What was he doing?'

'Nothing much.' She doesn't want to mention that her husband was wailing like a hyena and his knuckles were torn and full of splinters from punching the walls. 'He was staring into space. I called his name, but he didn't seem to hear me. When I tapped him on the shoulder, he looked shocked as if he didn't know where he was.'

'Why does he go there of all places?'

'I don't know. It's when he's upset. He sits on a crate, he stews, rants, thinks – paces back and forth. He kind of zones out.'

'Are you worried about him?'

'Not really.' She knows she's playing it down. She doesn't want Tara to think there's a major problem and wade into their private life to try to fix it. 'We all cope in different ways. It's not harming anyone.'

Tara won't let it go. 'It sounds a bit extreme. Most people slam a door or swear, or throw something across the room when they get cross.'

'It's his way of controlling it, so he *doesn't* do something he regrets.'

'So, he's not taking it out on you?' Tara holds Diane's gaze to be sure.

'Honestly – no. He's embarrassed about it. It's an

outlet for him, like thrashing the ball at squash. It's a way for him to let off steam. Like I used to pound the water when I swam.'

'Like Neanderthal man retreating to his cave?'

'Exactly.' Diane says, crunching an ice cube. 'I think it's about his childhood. I don't think he ever got over his dad leaving when he was little. He's still knotted inside about it, more cut up than he lets on and sometimes it gets too much for him, I reckon.'

'Do you think he needs…help? Therapy or treatment or something?'

Diane sighs. 'I don't know. As I say, we both know about it and it's not harming anyone.' Diane grips Tara's long fingers. '*Please* don't say anything, will you? To him or anyone else?'

'Of course not.' She taps her nose, then her heart.

'You know when I first met Harper,' Diane goes on, 'I thought he was squeaky clean, with impeccable manners and completely without any hang-ups.'

'First impressions,' says Tara pensively, 'they can set your heart on fire, but they never warn you about the disasters ahead.'

Diane drifts away from Tara for a moment, recalling the time she met her husband. During that first encounter at Trafalgar Square, he struck her immediately as friendly and earnest. He laughed easily, but had a hint of shyness in his eyes. Diane loved that; she can't bear arrogance. Harper had a quaint public school accent, softened with northern inflections – from his time at university in Manchester, then Liverpool. He coughed and seemed embarrassed when she took up the offer of his umbrella as the rain got heavier. He was expecting her to brush him off, she was sure, and was glad she surprised him.

'There's always been a hidden restraint about him,' Diane concludes.

'It's funny, isn't it?' Tara muses aloud. 'How well do we really know anyone?'

Diane finishes her drink with a flourish. 'Okay – here's his worst habit.' She can't help smiling. 'He eats peanut butter straight from the tub with a *soup* spoon...' She bursts out laughing at the thought.

'Ah – but that's cute,' Tara admits.

'See – I told you. Nothing to worry about.'

Chapter 21
Harper

9 August – Tenth day missing
When I get back from taking Frank out the following morning, there's a parcel from the police on the doormat. It's your hairbrush, back from the lab. I sit on the back step, slip it out of the package and press it against my chest, like it's alive. I look at the strands caught up in the prongs – all long and dark – and I pull one out, then don't know what to do with it. It's part of you. It seems wrong to discard it, so I drape it over my shoulder. Who knows where it will end up?

If you've chosen to be with someone else, who is he? What has he offered you that outweighs everything we have here? You're not interested in money, so it wouldn't be that. Nor would you be enticed by a flashy lifestyle – a big car, a boat, the promise of cruises or cocktails on Malibu Beach. That's where I get stuck. I can't see anything that would tempt you away from me. We've just started. We are in the process of building our nest, making it warm and dry in readiness for the next stage – aren't we? I know we've hit a rocky patch – but it's salvageable, isn't it? I still love you – more than anything – and I thought you loved me enough to overcome something like this, devastating as it has been.

I feel a chill and come inside. The calendar in the kitchen flaps open as I close the door and I notice a scribble to indicate my next prison visit is tomorrow. I'd forgotten all about it. I call the volunteer co-ordinator at Parkhurst and tell the woman who takes my call I have to cancel my trips over to the Isle of Wight for the time being, for 'personal reasons'. She doesn't sound overly impressed, but I refuse to go into details. Every time I utter the words *My wife has gone missing*, I have to recognise yet another day without you must be added to the tally and it's a further stab in my flank.

To appease my conscience over letting them down, I look up Victor's number and give him a call. I'm hoping he has some good news about his life to inject into my flagging morning.

After the initial opening banter, he tells me he's working as a painter and decorator.

'That's great,' I say, fully aware that Victor's intellectual capabilities are being wasted, but he probably hasn't had a great deal of choice in the matter.

'Not that far from you, actually,' he adds, 'in Gosport.'

That really isn't far and I struggle with how I feel about it. Victor was manageable when he was in Manchester, at a distance – the idea of him being round the corner feels too onerous. It's not because of his past – he's paid heavily in regret, guilt and even self-harm for his crime, it's more that he can be emotionally needy and clingy. In my current situation, I don't have reserves deep enough to cope with him.

'It's just a start,' he says. 'I'm doing a few guitar gigs

at the weekends, too. You and Diane should come sometime.' He's only met you once, but I could see how bowled over he was. He let it slip, not long ago, that he thought you were one of the most 'divine creatures' he'd ever met.

'Definitely,' I say, trying to keep my voice buoyant. I don't want to tell him about you. I don't want him rushing over here intending to help, then getting in the way as he sinks into his habitual maudlin navel-gazing.

Our conversation takes a detour through sport, TV programmes, art-house films, his new interest in ancient maps, my ongoing inexplicable love of old typewriters and finally grinds to a halt. 'Listen, mate,' he says after an awkward pause. 'I'll never forget what you did for me.'

'You deserved it,' I tell him. 'You worked hard to turn your life around.'

'You never once missed a visit – did you know that? Not once did you let me down.' His voice falters. 'I don't know how I can ever repay you.'

'You don't have to, Vic. What happened to you was a terrible mistake that got out of hand. As it happened, you helped open up a whole new career for me,' I laugh, wanting to avoid any further outpouring.

'Let's meet up then, eh?' he suggests.

'Sure.'

'Give me a ring.'

'Yeah…'

I end the call before we can fix anything more definite and instantly feel soiled with shame. I should never have rung him. It was a mistake when I have so little to give.

Frank yawns and stretches in front of the fireplace, then tucks his head into his tail in a soft croissant shape. It's barely 10am and I don't know what to do with myself. All my interests – squash, cooking, rugby, Formula One, crime novels – are meaningless to me. I can't even listen to music; my old favourites – Dido, Coldplay, Moby – seem to have an instant connection that takes me straight to you.

I go out into the front garden and start cutting flowers: roses, heather, lupins, two large peonies, with sprigs of cotoneaster and fern for decoration. I know someone who will appreciate these far more than I'm able to.

Marion takes a while to come to the door. She's not wearing her headscarf today. It isn't difficult to see the hair isn't her own; there is something about its gloss that makes the texture all wrong. Besides, when I saw her yesterday, she was blonde. I hold out the flowers and a bag of provisions I've bought from the village shop. Her initial embarrassment melts into gratitude and she pats her heart.

I speak first. 'I noticed you were low on cheese and butter – I hope you don't mind.' I put them on the kitchen table. 'In exchange for the magnificent pie we had yesterday.'

'That's so kind – thank you.' She invites me to sit as she opens the fridge to put things away. 'Any news?' she says, 'I've been thinking about you.'

'No – nothing concrete. The police are hoping to trace her phone and find out if she's used her credit card.'

'Oh, Lord. I wish I could do something.' She puts the

flowers in a vase and stands them in the centre of the table.

I nod, unable to smile. 'Clara been all right?'

'I'm not sure. All Dr Pike thinks is that she's got fixated on certain fairy tales to help her retreat from the trauma of being trapped in the castle that night.'

'You don't look convinced.'

Her eyes narrow; she's leaning against the sink. 'Every time Clara mentions the night in the pit she sounds excited. I would have thought that if it had upset her that much, she would either avoid talking about it – or get upset when she did.'

'I'm afraid I don't know enough about children.' I lean forward and stroke the leaves of the peony. 'Isn't she improving?'

'No – I don't think so. Maybe the diagnosis is wrong. Maybe she's banged her head or developed some kind of mental…you know…psychosis, or something.'

'She seems too normal for that, Marion. You saw her with Frank – she adores him and was as joyful and relaxed as a kid could be.'

'I know – that's true. She said an odd thing though, on the way home.' She leans on the table as if she's just trekked a considerable distance. 'She said she could be friends with Frank, because he wasn't a wolf – and that wolves are very bad.'

'*Little Red Riding Hood?*'

'Yeah – she goes on and on re-enacting parts of the story, ignoring what I say and quoting lines from that instead. Why *Little Red Riding Hood?*'

'I wish I could help.'

She sits, letting her hands take the weight of her head. 'She's not here right now – she's got story-time with Helen at the library. It's the only activity that drags her out of her room these days, apart from appointments at the hospital – mine and hers – which have turned into regular excuses for tantrums. Once she's with Dr Pike she's fine – but she doesn't seem to like the idea of going there.' She looks at the clock. 'She should be back from the library by now. Helen said she'd bring her home.'

'And how are you?' I ask.

She scratches her scalp under the lip of the wig. She isn't hiding the fact that she wears one. I like her proud spirit. She waits. 'I'm on the decline. I'm not sure I'll see Clara reach double figures.'

'I'm so sorry. That must be awful.' I don't know what else to say.

She scratches again at her head, dislodging the wig this time. 'This bloody thing – it's giving me a rash.' She pulls it off. 'I want to spare people the embarrassment of not knowing whether to mention my health or not. I also want to spare *myself* the looks I get when people try *not* to stare at my bald head.'

'You could reinvent yourself,' I suggest. 'Blonde, red-head, brunette...' She's probably still in her thirties and has a pretty face.

She laughs. 'Cate Blanchett one week, Angelina Jolie, the next?' She tosses the wig onto the nearest chair. It lies there like a dead animal.

I look away. 'I'm beginning to think my wife might have done something similar.'

'Oh, no, surely not. She's always looked so happy when I've seen her. Radiant – you know, in a contented, peaceful way. She wouldn't want a different life.'

I want to believe Marion, but I'm not sure. Have you grown tired of me, Dee? Do you want someone more interesting, more able to discuss art, music, culture? Should I be making more of an effort to get to know modern art after Picasso? Should I be reading Will Self? Getting tickets for new music at the South Bank? Are you sick of my silly celebrity commentary when I'm cooking? Perhaps if I'd fixed that shelf in the shed, made a better Christmas pudding (you're right the one at New Year was bitter and doughy) you'd still be here. Maybe, if I'd been more outdoorsy – more interested in camping, hiring a boat. Would it have made any difference? I could go on like this for ever, examining my character and wondering which parts have fallen short.

There's a sound in the hall and Clara comes in with a young woman who introduces herself as Helen.

'My phone was out of juice or I would have rung,' she says, out of breath. 'Clara had something to show me at the church.'

Clara approaches me in a familiar manner and runs her finger along my arm. 'Hello, Frank's daddy.'

Clara met Frank yesterday and it was a match made in heaven. Marion had to drag her away. 'I found a pink, glitter heart drawn on Frank's back this morning,' I say impassively.

'Clara!' Marion exclaims.

'But I've no idea how it got there,' I add, winking at Marion.

'Only dogs who are special can have it,' chirps Clara. 'I did it near his collar so he can't lick it off.'

'Go upstairs and wash your hands, Clara.'

She obediently turns on her heels.

'I'm so very sorry,' Marion bursts out once she's gone.

'It's no problem – no harm done. I can easily brush it out, but I thought Frank could look pretty for a day or so.'

'Thank you.'

She asks Helen to sit and offers both of us a drink. We settle on lemonade, because she's already taken the bottle out of the fridge for Clara. 'What was Clara so keen to show you at the church?' Marion enquires.

'She took me to the bell tower.'

'I thought that place was boarded up,' says Marion.

'It is, but Clara has been taking planks out of the old wooden door and replacing them once she's inside. She's been going there for months, she said.'

Marion rolls her eyes. 'And you went in with her?'

'She was too quick for me – I followed her up the stone spiral staircase all the way to the top. She likes it because it's cool in summer, light enough to read and looks out over the countryside. She pretends she's a bird. She takes a kneeling cushion from the one of the pews, but says she always puts it back. She knows the schedule for the flower lady, cleaner, organist and the vicar, so she can get in and out unnoticed. Sits on the tiles at the top or in the bell room itself. I think sometimes she falls asleep.'

'Isn't it dangerous?'

'Clara kept telling me to keep away from the edge. She's very aware.'

'What an extraordinary child I have,' Marion declares with dismay.

'She's a smart little girl. No one knows she's been visiting her secret hidey-hole, until now.'

'Did she pay attention in the story, today? Is she talking normally to you?'

Helen hesitates. 'To be honest, she seems to be getting a bit worse. She sat on her own in the library and read another book altogether – *Little Red Riding Hood*, I think it was – while I was reading out *Pippi Longstocking*.'

'There's a surprise,' Marion says. 'I wish I knew what was wrong with her.' Marion wavers and I'm silently willing her to get to a chair before she falls. She grabs the back of one and slumps into it. 'In her last session at the hospital, Dr Pike asked if everything was all right at home. What does she think I'm doing to her?'

'That certainly isn't an issue,' I interject firmly. Helen shakes her head.

'I'm not terribly well; I can't be with Clara the whole time.'

Clara comes down from the bathroom and wants a toasted teacake.

'Helen says you've been spending time in the bell tower?' Marion announces.

'We went to see something – only she wasn't there.'

'Who wasn't there?' Marion enquires.

'She must be able to fly, because she was in the phone box – then she was already in the tower when I got there, but she didn't look very well.'

I watch Marion who looks mystified.

'I didn't see anyone in the tower, Clara,' Helen affirms.

'Not *this* time – when I was there before – on my own. And I saw her in the church porch – *you* saw her too, Helen, you *did*.' Helen looks uncomfortable.

'Clara, have your teacake, honey.' Marion has cut it into quarters and Carla stuffs one in her mouth.

'She was smiling in the phone box…but not later.'

'And when you got to the bell tower this…lady was already there?' Marion clarifies.

'Yes – and I ran, so she must be magical to get there first. She looked like a ghost – like sick people. She didn't say anything.'

'Well, fancy that,' says her mother, 'an imaginary friend who doesn't chat back to you? Didn't she tell you all about what it's like to be Snow White or Goldilocks?'

Clara shakes her head.

'Not a word this time?'

'She isn't a friend and she didn't talk to me. She was crying.'

'Okay, well, I don't want you to see her again, because it's dangerous to go up into the bell tower. It's sealed off for a reason – because it's unsafe and you'll get hurt. You shouldn't be up there. You've got much better friends closer to home. You can play with them instead. Now finish off your lemonade.'

Clara does as she is told.

Helen gets up to go soon after and I'm about to join her, but Marion asks me to stay a while. She leaves Clara and I in the kitchen as she takes Helen to the door.

'I want to fly – like the lady – and Daddy,' Clara tells me.

'Like Daddy? What in an aeroplane?' I ask.

'No. He's dead now. But he could just fly. In the sky on his own.' She flaps her arms and spins around the kitchen making a whooo sound.

'Right…'

Marion has been watching from the doorway.

'Too many Disney movies?' I suggest.

'Oh, no. This time she's absolutely right. Morris was a skydiver – a trainer and a stuntman.'

'I see.' Sometimes it's the way children say things that makes us think they're fibbing.

'Granny had a new knee put on, didn't she, Mummy. She was dead when they did it, wasn't she?'

'No, dear – she was asleep.'

'Didn't it hurt so much it woke her up?'

'No – in the hospital they can give you a potion to make you very, very sleepy.'

'Like Snow White?'

'Yes.'

'I know. Then the doctor has to kiss you to wake you up – right?'

'Something like that.'

The doorbell rings and Marion goes out to answer it. Clara has started sticking tiny jewelled pieces onto a butterfly mosaic. She looks up at me as I'm checking my phone.

'Can you crack walnuts with your knuckles?' she asks.

'My knuckles? How do you mean?'

'Like this – when you squeeze your hands.' She tries

to show me, folding her hands and squashing them together.

'Oh, I know,' I say. I squeeze my left hand over my tight fist, but nothing happens. 'Mine don't seem to work.'

'The wizard can do it,' she says.

'Who's the wizard?' I ask.

She ignores me and moves on to another question. 'Do you ever get so kind of upset that you get juicy behind your knees?'

'Er...yes, I suppose so.'

'And hot inside your head and your eyes steam up and your hands go like boiling flannels?' Clara has an amazing imagination. I fight to hide my smile until I realise she's trying to tell me something significant.

'And you've felt like that?' I ask, keeping my voice even.

She gives a big nod. 'Mmm.' She pulls herself away from the shape she's decorating to see what it looks like, then adds two more pieces. I marvel at her ability to be absorbed and wish some of it would rub off on me, so I could cope better with the cruel uncertainty that has become my entire life.

'When was that – when you got very...upset? Can you remember?' I can hear Marion closing the front door and I'm willing something to waylay her, so Clara can finish telling me what she wants to say.

Clara drops her voice. 'I don't like being there on my own...' She appears to lose the rest of the words in the sentence and lets out her breath loudly instead.

I open my mouth to ask a question, but Marion is

194

back in the kitchen before we can say any more. Marion claps her hands and our discussion is broken. 'That was Tessa from across the road, I'm afraid I've got to get Clara over there – she's babysitting. I'm going to the cancer support group at the community centre.'

'Right – I'll get going...'

Clara holds her mother's hand as they lead me down the hall. 'Do pop by again,' Marion says with sincerity. 'Thanks again for the lovely flowers.'

There's a moment of awkwardness at the door, when none of us is sure how to say goodbye. Clara swings against her mother's legs and I consider kissing Marion on the cheek, but the moment passes. She keeps her smile in place for longer than looks natural, holding the door. I pat Clara on the head, instead, and tell her that Frank sends his love.

Just as I turn to go, Clara pulls at my cuff and declares, 'He's not a wizard at all – he's a wolf and a very bad one.'

Chapter 22
Diane

This is the first time I've felt properly lucid in ages. I try to stay rational – it's hard, because I'm so confused and my head is woolly and full of bright lights; I can barely hold it up. I must have spent most of the time asleep or unconscious. I try again to move and I can see now, why I can't. My hands and feet are tied with orange twine; there is something sticky glued over mouth. I look down. I'm sitting on broken straw – ah, I knew this – I must have been awake before. There are bales of the stuff all around me. It smells of manure.

I try shouting for help, but it comes out as a pathetic muffled moan. It wouldn't even scare the field mice away and it certainly won't be audible beyond the heavy wooden doors at the far end.

Beside me is a dog bowl with the remains of some food – lumpy porridge oats. I must have eaten. I'm bruised and weak, but I'm not hungry. That's something. But it also means someone must be coming here and giving me food and water. Who's done this to me? Why would they keep me here like this, injured, imprisoned?

The smell of animal excreta is pungent, but there's something else that's worse. My jogging bottoms are wet. I've soiled myself. I gag at the disgusting stench of it and fight back tears of humiliation. There's a tin bucket a few feet away, but if I've been in and out of consciousness I won't have been able to use it. In fact, I need to pee now. I shuffle over on my backside. It's hard to do anything with my hands and feet tied, but I hoist myself onto a small milking stool and manage to roll down my jogging pants in tiny stages with my contorted hands. From there I tip sideways on to the bucket.

I try to think back to when this must have started. I remember an ambulance, a room full of people in gowns and masks. I'd been in hospital. Had I been in an accident? Undergone an operation? Maybe that's why I'm in so much pain. I'd come home – I remember that much and I'd been taking sedatives. I feel like I'm still on them – I've got that detached, woozy feeling of not quite being here.

The place I'm in looks like an old stable. But where? And who could have brought me here? I could be in Nettledon or miles beyond, as far away as Scotland. I try to go back but my memories are patchy, like a newspaper with huge sections ripped out. I remember leaving the house, getting in the car. I had my phone – I feel for it with my tied hands – it's not here. I was going to the village shop for painkillers. That much is clear. What happened next? Pictures start to jump around behind my eyes. A figure. There was a figure running into the bushes along the lane leading to the village green. There's nothing else. That's all. My recollections hit a brick wall.

I want to scream, but I'm afraid I'll suffocate. I fight the tears for the same reason. I'm trembling, dumped and discarded like a fish tossed onto the riverbank. What have I done wrong? What is going to happen to me?

Someone help me! Please!

Chapter 23
Harper

11 August – 12th day missing

I'm feeling proud of myself today. It's faint self-praise, I know. All I did was manage *not* to have a slug of whisky before I came out to meet your friend, Tara. It's hardly anything to write home about, is it?

I walk down the High Street in Cosham. I love the summer months, but I'm barely aware of them this year. Cricket matches, tennis tournaments, outdoor concerts are passing me by.

Once again, it's awkward at the start. Tara is exquisitely beautiful and I find myself avoiding her beguiling green eyes. She's wearing impossibly high heels, tight fifties-style capri pants in peppermint green and a stripy top. I hardly know which part of her to avoid looking at first. I don't want to be in this position when you're not with us, Dee. It feels like a betrayal.

'It was kind of you to ring,' I say weakly, to get the ball rolling. She's managed to persuade me to have morning coffee. She's on a mission to save me.

'I wanted to see whether you'd heard anything – and check you were okay,' says Tara. 'This dragging on is terrible.'

'Twelve days,' I say, leaning against the lamppost

outside the café that has a poster of your face wrapped around it with sticky tape. Many of them do around here. I trudged the streets for hours putting your picture up everywhere; billboards, shop windows, telegraph poles. I've had to cover posters advertising fetes and festivals with pictures of you.

I lean against the lamppost, my cheek against yours, Dee. I expect it to be warm, but it's in the shadows here and is cold, damp and wrinkled. I pull away.

I don't want to tell Tara I've been sleeping late and turning into a slob. I've not hoovered or laundered in the last week. The food in the fridge is off, I'm not answering the phone, not calling people back – not looking after myself. Apart from the occasional visit to Marion, I'm closing myself off from the real world. All I do is mutter to Frank and take him on long walks in such a daze that I don't recall a thing once I get back.

Most of the cafés in Cosham are of the 'greasy spoon' variety, but this one, called *Number Three*, is a cut above and doubles as a wine bar in the evenings. We sit on low leather chairs at the back with a long chunky table in dark wood at knee level. The waiter creates a fern design in the foam on my cappuccino and Tara has a hot chocolate that looks like an ice-cream sundae – I wish I'd ordered that instead. I wonder if you've been here before with Tara; I know it's the kind of place you'd like, with sparkly lights, candles and dribbling paninis.

As I sink back after sipping the coffee, I feel like I haven't let out a full breath since you disappeared. The blend is rich and has a strong aftertaste and for a second it's as though I have a faint memory that simply sitting like this can be effortless and unburdened. Then I remember that everything in my life is annihilated and I have to swallow hard to keep the coffee down.

'Growing a beard?' Tara asks. I feel my chin.

'No, not deliberately – it's just...' I realise I've done a lot of this – not finishing my sentences. I seem to run out of impetus halfway through a thought. I don't want her to know I'm regressing into monosyllabic conversations with most people. I'm not watering the plants, Dee – I've not called your parents, I've had the TV on, but I'm not watching it. I can't seem to get both eyes to stay open at the same time. I feel beaten. I'm sinking fast.

'I think I'm going to stop the fertility treatment,' I tell her.

'Why?'

'Too many nosebleeds.' The handkerchief in my pocket is already saturated with the episode I had on the way over. 'In any case, there's not much point, is there?'

'But, when she comes back – she'll be so disappointed.'

'I think we'll have other things to discuss rather than starting a family, don't you?' Tara looks like she sees my point. 'I'm going to wait until she comes back.'

'Have the police heard anything?'

'There have been no more social media messages from Dee and Alexa told me yesterday she'd not had any further texts. It wasn't a surprise when the police called to tell me they think her phone has either run out of juice by now or been destroyed.'

'Oh...'

'But they do have a last location for it – somewhere near Heathrow, like the ATM that was used, so I still don't know if she got on a plane. She might still be in this country, but it's looking more and more likely that she isn't.' I close my eyes, suddenly exhausted with the endless cycle of hoping, wondering and speculation. *One call, Dee – that's all it would take. One bloody call.* 'It makes the little posters I've dotted around look rather pathetic when she could be in Paris, New York or…Australia, for all I know.'

Tara pulls a defeated face. 'Can't the police – or passport control, or whatever – tell if a passport has been used – you know, gone through the gate?'

'They can, but whether they will or not is another matter. The police can consult the UK Border Force for details of people leaving or entering the UK by air, sea or rail. I've pressed everyone I know at the local force – even stuck my neck out and gone above them to the chief constable, but it's a no-go.'

'Why?'

'Because as far as they're concerned there is no crime. They think she's gone of her own free will – she took belongings, she had a reason to go, she's been in touch…'

Tara scrunches up her nose. She still manages to look pretty.

I make a feeble attempt to ensure we don't spend the entire time talking about my misery. 'What have you been up to?' I say in a lighter tone.

She puffs out her cheeks. 'Oh – nothing. I'm bored, to be honest. I spent all of last term willing on the school holidays and now they're here, I don't know what to do with myself.' She runs her finger inside the glass to catch the last fluff of cream. 'No boyfriend – and no best friend...' she says, casting her eyes down. 'I'm not very good on my own.'

I'm about to say something philosophical in response that I know will only sound trite, when my phone rings. I normally hate mobiles interrupting me, but I never turn it off – not now – I can't afford to miss any calls.

'Harper? She's gone.' It's a number I don't recognise, but I know the voice.

'Who's gone? What's happened?'

'Clara – she's gone missing – I can't find her,' Marion gasps.

I shuffle forward. 'When did you last see her?'

'She was at the hospital,' she blurts out, 'with my mother – she took Clara to see Dr Pike this morning, because I wasn't...feeling too well. Mum left her with the nurses there, because she had to go to see her own GP in Portsmouth. One of the nurses was supposed to see Clara into a taxi home.'

'Have you contacted the hospital? Checked she's not waiting with somewhere else?'

'I've rung everyone – the nurses, babysitters, school friends. Sheila, the nurse, was supposed to meet her, but she said she didn't see Clara come out of Dr Pike's room. When she tapped on the door, Dr Pike said they'd finished ten minutes earlier.' Marion is overwhelmed with tears. 'The taxi was...supposed to bring Clara home...but she wasn't waiting at the right place.'

Dread fills my mouth. 'Have you called the police?'

'Yes – they're on their way over.'

'I'll be there,' I tell her.

A police car is already parked outside when I arrive – the front door is wide open. In the hall, two officers are trying to persuade Marion to sit down, while an older woman – Clara's grandmother, I presume – and two younger women I recognise from the village, are holding her up. Everyone seems to be getting in each other's way and I stay on the step and consider that my presence might be one too many.

Marion spots me, breaks free and rushes at me as if I'm her missing child.

'Harper – thank goodness you've come – I'm beside myself.' The tendons in her neck flicker violently under her skin. She grabs my wrist and pulls me inside.

I recognise one of the police officers, PC Rose Felton who made a corresponding visit to our cottage. She seems to know Marion. The other one introduces himself as PC Mole.

'She'll be hiding somewhere,' Felton says, 'like last time – and she'll have lost track of time.'

Marion turns to me. 'PC Felton rescued Clara from the pit at the castle,' she explains. I'm holding her arm firmly, it's barely enough to keep her upright, so I lead her to a chair in the kitchen and lower her gently down. She looks as if she's shrunk since I saw her last.

'She gets herself into places,' Marion continues, knitting her fingers together, 'you know, she climbs in – then gets herself stuck...'

'We've got a team at the castle right now,' PC Felton

assures her, 'just in case she went back there. Where else might she have gone?'

'There's the bell tower at St Hugh's Church,' Marion croaks. 'It's cordoned off, but she's been getting in.' PC Felton presses a button on her radio and passes on the information.

'Where else?'

Marion lists various places: the allotments at Grangers' corner, the wasteland by the school, the woodlands at the beck. 'She'll go anywhere – people's garages and sheds, lofts, cellars, farm buildings…'

PC Mole has been frantically scribbling. 'Right – we're on it,' declares Felton.

I interject. 'She was last seen at the hospital?'

'Yes,' PC Mole replies. 'We're scouring the area. Stopping the cars leaving the car park, talking to hospital staff.' I know that the first forty-eight hours are crucial, especially with a young child. I hope no one says it – it would only bring a fresh cloud of doom into the room.

Marion is on her feet. 'I must go and look for her…' I grab her around the waist as she disintegrates in my arms. 'You need to be here when she comes back,' I say, firmly. She needs to be in bed, but I know that's the last place she'll go.

My phone rings. It's Tara. I move into the living room and tell her what's happened. She insists on coming over to help with the search.

'Go to the hospital,' I say. 'I'll see you there; that's where she was last seen.'

In the next few hours a major police operation is launched. Out-patients and visitors to the hospital join police in covering the area, including the car parks, the fields to the right, the supermarket, library, local shopping mall. Tara walks beside me as we help scour the playing fields and scout hut. We move on to the nearest school and carry on across the fields – all day long – until it starts getting dark. I've been in regular contact with Marion by phone; she's had a visit from her doctor following a request from worried neighbours. She is now heavily sedated, in bed.

By the following morning, everything is cranked up a level. Dogs are brought in, the house to house is extended. The main hope for information is the hospital CCTV, but management are in the process of replacing the analogue system with an Internet Protocol surveillance system. The cameras at the entrance have been faulty for days, but the powers that be have seen fit to turn a blind eye to them as the entire network is being overhauled.

Whilst there is coverage inside the corridors leading from Dr Pike's room, footage at the entrance has been reduced to wobbly black lines for the entire time Clara was at the hospital. I tell Marion a less adverse version of this when she calls me at around ten o'clock. She sounds like a different person; geriatric, slow, confused – an additional forty years seem to have passed for her, overnight.

'You don't have her?' she wails.

'I'm so sorry, no – we're checking everywhere – plenty of people have turned up this morning to help.'

'It's nearly twenty-four hours…' she whimpers.

She asks me what the police have found and I pass on what I know. 'There's CCTV footage of Clara leaving Dr Pike's room on her own. She reappears on the ground floor, but then gets lost in a crowd of people by the shops in the foyer. The fire alarm went off accidentally at the café at 10.45am and there was a big muddle about whether people were allowed into the hospital or not. There is no visual record of Clara after that and she doesn't reappear in the footage outside or in any of the car parks.'

'Where did she go?' Her voice is far away and fading.

'She was probably going to head out of the main entrance – to the taxi rank.'

'That's where she was supposed to go – with Sheila.' There's a muffled cough. 'But she's not on the film?'

'No – there's a band of about two feet outside the sliding doors that's no longer covered by the cameras. Clara could have come out of the hospital and gone left or right.'

'What did Sheila say?'

'She said she got to the psychiatrist's room at exactly 11am. There's footage of her to back that up.'

'So – Dr... you know, the psych—?'

'Dr Pike?'

'Yes – she must have let Clara go early...'

'The police have spoken to Dr Pike and she said the session had come to a natural close at about 10.50am and Clara was ready to finish.'

'What did they talk about? Did Clara get upset? Did she get any funny ideas into her head?'

'I'm sure the police will have given Dr Pike a

thorough interview.'

'Why didn't she wait for Sheila? Why did the doctor let her go so early?' I hear a heart-wrenching sob and her voice breaks. 'Please help me...'

'Of course, Marion – I'm doing what I can. I'm back in with the search this mor—'

'I mean – please *find* her – you know how everything works.'

This is hard. 'I'm not a policeman or a detective, Marion – I'm a lecturer.'

'But you know about crime and evidence – you know the system and what the police will be looking for. I'm helpless – you should see me – I can't even get out of bed. I'd be out there leaving no stone unturned if I could...'

The confusion, loss and panic of her pain – I know it only too well – tugs inside me and I know what I have to do. 'Okay – I'll do everything I can.'

I mean it. I'm going to break out of this useless self-pity I've sunk into, get a grip and start shaking some trees.

'Thank you.' The gratitude in her voice makes me want to crumple.

'There will be a television appeal later today. Are you up to it?'

'I want to be there – I might need a wheelchair – but I don't know if I can speak.'

I switch instantly into professional mode. 'Right. I'll come over now and we can work out what we need to say. When the time comes, I'll read it out in front of the cameras for you. I also want to look at Clara's room again. In the meantime, could you put together a list of *everywhere* Clara has ever been in the area – places to hide, to play, either on her own or with others?'

'Yes – of course.' There's a solemn sigh. 'Thank you.'

I feel better already. This is what I'm good at.

Chapter 24
Diane

I'm awake again and this time, I remember. The baby. I lost the baby.

Oh, God. A distraught surge of grief drags at me like too much gravity. My limbs are leaden and stiff. I'm sitting on concrete, but I feel as if I'm being sucked into it, like quicksand. I was going to be a mother and it went wrong. My body rejected the tiny jewel clinging on to me. My heart swells and burns at the memory. I don't know if I can ever forgive myself. My system failed at the time I most needed it to function properly.

I think of you. My magnificent husband. It's as though you have suddenly reappeared in all my memories. We were so happy, then two bombs fell on us one after the other. I was carrying a baby and I didn't even know. Then I lost it – washed out of me at the side of the road in a cruel swipe of fate. We couldn't even name the child to say goodbye – I didn't know if it was a girl or a boy; it was too soon to tell. But not too soon to break our hearts. I want to stroke my abdomen, to comfort and honour the place where he or she started growing, but my hands are tied, so I can only rest them there.

The other explosion was finding out about your infertility. It made no sense. I was pregnant! But there were tests and indisputable results and your specialist saying that getting pregnant was a dead-end unless 'the treatment' worked. It was so confusing.

I'm definitely being given sedatives — that's why I feel so dozy, but my side feels a little better and my head isn't throbbing as much as it was. I can move my arms up and down — they're still tied at the wrists, but they're not broken. I can straighten my legs out too, though they're still held together at the ankle. I've managed to get to the bucket and my jeans are drying out. They still stink and they're damp, but I don't think I've wet myself again in the last day or so.

How many days has it been?

Why have I been left here?

At least the sedatives have protected me — I can't remember much at all and the drifting in and out is a blessing. It's almost soothing and makes me feel lazy. Someone's left me a blanket, but right now it must be the middle of the day, because there is sunlight bleeding under the doors and it's hot. There are flies. A water bottle is on its side resting against my thigh. I must have knocked it over and it's nearly empty.

Periods of nothingness are interrupted by episodes of desperate itching. I need to scratch — under my arms, between my toes, behind my knees — but with my hands tied I can't reach the right spots. I wriggle and thrash around trying to rub against the wall or floor, but it's hopeless and it's driving me mad. I'm sure there are insects inside my clothes, crawling around. I start to imagine them nestling into warm places, eating at flakes of my skin, laying eggs so that in the end I'll be covered in a seething black mass.

I try to think of something else. Something comforting. I see us on our wedding day. I'm walking with my father at first, under an archway of white roses. It was before the dementia began eating away at his brain. I glance down at my ivory silk dress and satin shoes, then along the aisle at you as you stand tall, waiting — noble and so full of love — and I know this was the best day of my life.

210

Since then, there has only ever been one issue between us. I want to understand it, but whenever I mention it, you get defensive and prickly. What's really going on when you retreat to the chicken coop? I know it's a private way of managing your anger, but it unnerves me when I hear the sounds you make and witness the damage you do to yourself. My worry is that it seems to be getting worse, not better. You won't see anyone and you won't talk about it. I know you'd never knowingly hurt me, but what if your anger got out of control?

For months, I've pushed it into the background. It has been my one thorn in an otherwise blissful marriage. I've read book after book about displaced anger and grief. It is all there. It leads right back to your father, I'm sure – the way he abandoned you. This is all about him – if only you could see that.

I've always believed in telling all and baring the truth, but this has had me flummoxed. I haven't felt able to ask anyone else about it, not even Tara, although she spotted one of my books and I had to say something. She knows what it's about, but not the full extent. You don't seem able to open up and address it – and I don't know how I can help you.

The temperature has climbed quickly again and the place feels like a sauna. I need water, but there's only about a tablespoon left in the bottle. I can't drink it anyway, because there's tape over my mouth. How bad will it get before someone comes back so I can drink again? Already I can barely swallow and I don't know when – or even if – anyone is coming back.

Now, with nothing else to fill my mind, I recall other angry episodes – the time you kicked over the newspaper stand outside the petrol station when you saw the magazine article. It painted your father as a footballing hero and you were furious. Then there's the day I came home to find you sweeping up the pieces of the

Waterford vase your mother had given us. I didn't need to ask — your sheepish look told me you'd lashed out following some altercation with her on the phone. Maybe she'd asked if you'd visited his grave recently? Perhaps she wanted to know if you'd ever forgive him? I've no idea what caused it, because I didn't dare ask and you didn't tell me. These disturbing scenes invade my space here as I sit helpless, waiting for something to happen.

I try to remember the last few days and they all melt into one long one, punctuated with distant doors opening and closing. My memory can only hold on to the sounds of sheep and cows, farmyard smells around me, the clunk and whirr of machinery. No voices, no faces. It can't seem to fix on anything important, like where I am or who has been coming back and forth.

I track back and try to recall how I got here.

I'm driving to the village shop. I'm halfway there. Then, just after the crossroads, someone runs across the road and into the bushes down the bank into the undergrowth. A young child. Yes — that's right. A girl. Judging from the kids in my class, I'd say she was seven or eight. On her own. I remember the swerve of the car, the screech of brakes. That's it. I nearly hit her! I stop the car, swing the door open. I go to check she's all right. The undergrowth is thick and lush in the woods and I don't know where she went. I listen, but I've lost track of her. Then I see her, running, slipping. I call out and she turns. She stops, but there's someone behind her, with her now. She's safe — or is she? I'm not sure.

I need to find out.

Chapter 25
Harper

13 August – 14th day missing

It's a scorcher of a day and Marion's bedroom feels like
a tent in the desert. The windows are closed and the
curtains drawn, making the heat more enclosed and the
molecules of air glue together. I want a storm, a noisy,
tumultuous downpour, to wash away the cloying
depression. But rain might not be the best thing for
finding Clara – or for you, Dee. It might obliterate clues,
wash away vital footprints or tyre tracks.

Marion can barely hold a pen. She had to ask Tessa,
the babysitter, to write down the list I asked for. She's in
no state to get out of bed, but manages to squeeze my
hand.

'I can't believe I'm like this when my darling Clara's
missing,' she tells me. She tries to sit up, but her eyes tip
to the top of her head and she slumps back into the
pillow. 'She needs me and I'm useless,' she whispers, her
eyes slamming shut.

'You've got me instead now,' I insist. 'I'll work hard
enough for both of us.' I read out the piece I've written
for the television appeal.

She keeps her eyes closed, but tiny rivulets of tears

seep out and trickle down the side of her nose. She sniffs and tries to sound upbeat and appreciative. 'That was quick – you know all the right words.' I don't tell her it's an altered version of the one I wrote for you, Dee, when I hoped the police would set up an appeal for your disappearance.

I hold up the list Tessa has written for me. 'The police are already checking everywhere, of course,' I confirm, 'but I need to see these spots for myself.'

I check Clara's bedroom before I go, looking for anything that is different from the last time. The red cape she's been wearing is on a hanger outside the wardrobe and the wicker basket is beneath it, filled with packets of tea and biscuits she must have taken from the kitchen cupboard. Drawings on the desk predominantly depict scenes from *Little Red Riding Hood* and the book of fairy tales is held open with a stone at the opening page of that story.

What is it about this tale that has got Clara obsessed? Marion said the psychiatrist thought Clara had retreated into it to protect herself, but why *this* story? The wolf, the grandmother, the little girl. Clara is clearly identifying with the little girl by dressing up in the red cape and she quotes from the story as if through the eyes of that character, too. So is this connected to the night in the oubliette, I wonder? I visualise Marion's skin; her face is the texture of dried rose petals. I can almost smell death in the air. Has Clara been hit by the recognition that her mother is not going to be here for much longer? Or is it something else, altogether?

Helen arrives shortly afterwards to ask if there's

anything she can do. She offers to take me along the exact route she and Clara took on Saturday. Several of Clara's favourite places are on the way. I have a detailed map in my pocket so we get going.

'Tell me what you know about seven-year-olds,' I ask, as we walk towards the centre of the village. I'm wearing long shorts and a loose T-shirt in deference to the heat. Helen, however, looks like she's expecting a different climate altogether, with a long brown skirt, a high-necked blouse, cardigan and flat sandals. I can picture her as a nun. She appears to be in her twenties, but has little about her that suggests she's been living in the twenty-first century. Her hair is long and pulled back hard against her head, as if she wishes she didn't have any. I think of Marion.

'In terms of social and emotional development, seven-year-olds are confident and love showing off their talents,' she says. 'That's Clara – she's always bringing me cards she's made, showing me little dances she's learnt.'

'What about her fantasy world?'

'In my experience, it's normal for a seven-year-old to have invisible friends and to talk about stories as if they're real and they're actually in the narrative themselves. They give animals human characteristics, such as suggesting what a worm might be thinking, or that a ladybird has eyelashes.' She's looking at her feet the whole time she's talking to me, sounding like she's reading from a textbook. 'Predictable routines are important sources of stability and security for children that age. I think she might have gone somewhere she knows.'

'Have you come across this kind of behaviour before in other children?'

'A fixation with certain stories, you mean?'

I nod.

'No – I've heard about it.' She laughs self-consciously. 'I'm just a librarian, but you pick up a lot about kids' development.'

'Did she tell you about the incident at the castle?'

'Yeah. It's odd – but she seemed thrilled about it and was talking about going back.'

'That's what Marion said.'

'Can you get me a copy of *Little Red Riding Hood*? The same version that Clara has? I don't want to take hers.' Helen says it's the picture-book edition by Ron Holleson and she'll drop it through my letterbox.

We reach the first location on our route: the allotments. There are about fifteen sheds in two rows.

'Has Clara been here lately, do you think?' I ask.

'When we walked past on Saturday, she said she'd shaken hands with the scarecrow, over there, last time she came. She mentioned a couple of people she's met here – I can't remember their names, but a youngish chap with a beard waved at her that day.'

We approach a handful of gardeners and ask to look inside their sheds. Everyone is obliging, but most are locked and unattended. An elderly chap with a walking stick curtly informs us that officers and dogs have already covered this plot. This is where the police have powers I don't – they can get permission to search inside each and every one, whereas I can only peer through the murky windows.

We check the paths for anything Clara might have dropped. Marion said she was wearing a pink headband the day she went missing, with a pink cheesecloth dress, a pink cardigan, bare legs and red jelly sandals. She thought she may have had some coloured bangles around her wrist and the key-ring I gave her was definitely attached to a loop in her pocket.

We move on to the old farm buildings to the right of the crossroads. We pull abandoned breeze blocks aside, check under tarpaulin, inside an old cupboard, chest freezer, under a door laid flat on bricks – upsetting a family of feral cats in the process. Again, we are following in the footsteps of the police – there's nothing here. We go across the green where there's the phone box with your face smiling out at me. I have to look away. There's another poster on the wall at the garage on the far corner. Clara's face will be joining these soon.

'The bell tower is next,' says Helen, as we skirt the green and head towards the church.

Just as Helen described, the place is dotted with *Keep Out* signs and cordoned off with yellow tape, but that wouldn't stop an inquisitive child. We lift planks out of the heavy wooden door and squeeze through. Helen leads the way up the crumbling spiral staircase and we reach another door at the top. Inside is a wooden platform and chamber for the bell above us. The rope is tied up out of reach and there are thin windows without glass and a ladder leading to a small door that gives access to the roof. A dirty blanket is screwed up in the corner and there are crisp packets, empty drinks cartons and cigarette butts. Clara hasn't been the only one up here.

I climb the ladder and step out onto the roof. I can see why Clara was drawn to this place; there are expansive views of the entire village from up here and the ledge is warm in the sun. A tatty sofa cushion has been left out here. The slate tiles slide under my feet and I have to grab on to the crenelated wall that runs around the edge to break my fall. It's a long way down the other side.

'You okay?' Helen calls from below. She must have heard the scuffle.

'It's really unsafe up here. A lot of the tiles are broken and falling away.'

Just as I'm about to retreat inside, my sandal catches on a lose piece of guttering and I end up on my backside. Several tiles have parted and I can see something glittering underneath. I reach into the gap and hold it up. All my thoughts swerve in a new direction. This isn't what I was expecting. I feel an oppressive need for air, even though I am already outside. I sit clutching my knees and take deep breaths, my heart battering my ribcage.

'Have you found something?' Helen calls up, presumably confused by the sudden silence.

I crawl back to the hatch on my hands and knees and climb down the ladder. Vertigo is trying to spin me sideways. I hold out my palm and she picks it up.

Helen's shoulders drop. 'Ah – of course, it doesn't mean much – we know Clara has been here – many times – she could have dropped it any time.'

'It's not hers,' I whisper, my throat closing up. I re-examine the hair clip, stroking the familiar multi-coloured kingfisher design on one side. I've seen it so many times in your hair. 'It belongs to my wife,' I tell her.

Helen is silent. We make our way down the stone steps and my mind is running rings around itself.

'She was here!' I declare as we break out into the air at ground level. 'That's who Clara was talking about – the *lady* she saw in the bell tower.' Helen stands, her hand over her mouth, staring at her sandals again, mystified.

'She said she saw someone in the phone box – smiling...' she says tentatively.

'Yes – it must have been the poster of my missing wife.'

'Oh – of course, I'm so sorry...Diane Penn – I didn't make the connection with your surname.' She bangs her palm into her forehead looking distraught. 'Oh, God, I'm so sorry...I should have...'

I pull her hand away. 'Please – it's okay.' Her body is rigid and I can see she doesn't know where to put herself.

'Can you remember what Clara said, exactly?' I say, wishing I'd paid more attention when Clara told us about the bell tower.

'She said the last time she was here – she didn't say when – there was a woman, looking sad, crying – like a ghost. She didn't speak, she said.'

'Diane must have been ill – or injured...' I'm thinking aloud; we're on the move back to the green.

'Oh, and Clara said she saw the woman at the

219

church…' Helen continues. 'Of course – there's another poster of your wife in the foyer – she and I both walked past it. That's why she insisted I'd seen her too.'

'Clara was telling the truth in her own way,' I say absently. 'Kids do that don't they? They mix up what's concrete and what's reproduced.'

The enormity of this revelation hits me head on as the hairclip cuts into the skin of my palm. Until now, it's as if I've been wandering along the hard shoulder. Now the time has come to step into the path of the truth.

You're in trouble. I know now. You've been hurt and you need me.

I ring the police straight away and they send a team up to the bell tower to lift material for forensics, looking for evidence not only of Clara now, but also of you, Dee.

The television appeal for Clara on the evening news cranks the search operation up several more notches and at least a hundred members of the public are gathering to help with searches and putting up posters. All main routes from the hospital to Nettledon have been combed on foot with dogs or by car. I try not to feel bitter that none of this was activated for you; only now that I've found evidence that you were at the church are the police paying attention. It feels far too late. We can't even ask Clara. We don't know which day you were up in the tower, how you got there or where you went afterwards. What were you doing there? How does it link to Heathrow?

Sgt Howis tells me that they've looked into all your bank records now and you've not accessed your account, apart from the fifty pounds you withdrew more than ten days ago. Howis claims, however, that you could have been hoarding cash beforehand to avoid suspicion and to avoid a trail of bank transactions.

'That would imply a huge amount of forward planning, sergeant,' I suggest testily.

'Maybe she knew about the pregnancy a lot earlier than she admitted, Dr Penn.'

I grit my teeth and shake my fist at the mouthpiece, but my mouth can't form any words in response. He doesn't know you. He doesn't understand. You are still registered as a 'missing person', but he admits that you remain in the 'low risk' category, which I know translates into 'low priority' in terms of police action.

Howis is not the least bit convinced about my discovery in the bell tower, claiming that a seven-year-old child is not a reliable witness and that you could have lost the hairclip or given it to Clara weeks ago. Howis also tells me they have looked into Bruce's loan company and have found no irregularities. I feel like I'm back to square one.

Marion is being looked after by her mother and friends, so I go back to our cottage. Frank is cross and barks at me; he's been left too long. I don't blame him. I take him out for a short, but energetic duty romp to pacify him. I want to get back and get things moving.

This new discovery has fired up my fears for you and I embark on another search, more detailed, more finely tuned, to find out *anything* about what could have happened. I drag everything out of wardrobes and drawers this time. I tip out all your bags and pockets, pull out sofa cushions, check behind bookshelves.

At the bottom of the pile of mounting laundry, next to a screwed-up handkerchief in the pocket of your dressing gown, I find something. It's a folded scrap of paper with a few words scribbled on it: *Surgery, June 6th, 1.15pm.*

Chapter 26

I call Tara straight away and ask her to check her diary.

'Yeah...work as usual that day,' she tells me. 'It was the first week after the half-term break.'

'I know it's a while ago, but can you remember Diane going to her GP in the lunch break?'

She lets out an uncertain hum. 'Hold on – I keep a school record of key events and stuff...' There's a gap filled by the rumble of traffic. 'No – there's nothing about Diane. I assume she was at school as usual. We often go for lunch together, but sometimes one of us has a meeting or is on playground duty, so...'

'Can you remember that day at all – what she was like? Her mood?'

'Sorry, Harper...I can't.'

'Yeah. Okay. Thanks.' I tell her about finding the hairclip.

'Oh, God – so what does that mean?'

'It's difficult to know. It means she was up there – and Clara saw her, recently.'

'When, do you think?'

'It's hard to say – and Clara isn't here to ask, but I'm certain it was sometime *after* she left the house that evening in the car. I remember she started wearing that clip again after the miscarriage. What worries me is that

Clara said she wasn't well. She said she wasn't smiling like she was on the posters – that she was crying.'

'Oh, Harper – it sounds awful – what are the police doing?'

'Not a great deal, by the look of it. They're checking out the bell tower to see if there's any definitive evidence. I think they're putting all their resources into finding Clara and hoping they might come across Dee on the way. The more I think about it, the more I can't believe the police don't see a link between the two disappearances.'

'Maybe they do.'

I'm not convinced and let out a corresponding grunt. 'Where are you now?'

'With one of the search groups near the hospital, but the police are sending us away. There are too many volunteers and we're messing things up, apparently.'

'Speak soon, okay?' I end the call and pace up and down, tearing skin off the side of my thumbnail. I ring Neil. I don't care if I'm pestering him. He's been co-ordinating the house to house in the village and is trying not to sound annoyed at my interruption.

I come straight out with it. 'What's happening with the search for my wife?'

'It's ongoing, mate.'

'Howis still seems to think she's taken off of her own accord. She hasn't contacted any of us properly, she hasn't accessed any bank accounts since that first Saturday, she was seen recently in a bad way at the top of a fucking bell tower – what are you guys doing about it?'

'Harper – there's not a lot I can do,' he stresses.

'Howis is the SIO on this one and he's got forensics over at the tower now, checking it out. He'll keep you posted.' I know Neil is bursting to remind me that there's a seven-year-old child who's been missing for thirty hours, but he's too much of a mate to do that to me. We leave it there.

I ring the surgery, but the receptionist is adamant she won't let me have confidential information, so I hop on my bike and cycle over there.

I ask to see the surgery manager when I arrive and I'm told to take a seat. People are coughing and wheezing all around me and I wonder what nasty bugs I'm going to take home with me. Twenty minutes later the receptionist informs the remaining patients that the surgery is closing in ten minutes. I ask again about speaking to the manager and refuse to sit down this time, trying to fill up as much space at the desk as possible. A woman finally comes bustling round the corner and folds her arms at me.

'Can I speak to you privately?' I enquire.

She gives me a look that suggests I've asked her to remove her clothing. The words *inconvenient* and *nuisance* are etching their way into the skin around her eyes. She turns her back on me, which I take to be a sign to follow her. We go into an empty consulting room and she indicates the seat by the desk, while she continues to stand.

'I need some information about an appointment my wife made in June,' I state. I hold out the torn scrap, but she fails to register it.

'I'm afraid that information is protected by patient

confidentiality, Mr…'

'Dr Penn. Harper Penn.'

'I suggest you ask your wife directly about it.'

I get to my feet without meaning to. Blood is hurtling too fast past my ears and I feel like I'm inside a long tunnel. An image of Victor putting his hands around his girlfriend's neck bursts into my mind. I shake my head in a bid to wipe it away and force my voice to be as neutral as I can manage. I spread the words out with exaggerated enunciation and end up sounding like I'm speaking to someone who is not only deaf, but also has learning difficulties. 'My wife has been registered as missing with the police for two weeks and I don't know if she's alive or dead.' I take another breath, feeling it judder in my chest. 'Any lead…' I read her name pointedly from her name badge, '…Penelope Hodder, is extremely important. Do you understand?'

'Of course, I do. But then the police should be making this request through the proper channels.'

I pull out what I hope will be my trump card and although it carries no real weight, I show her my university ID. 'I am a specialist in criminology and forensics with connections to the police force in Hampshire and I could make life very difficult for you, Ms Hodder, if you don't assist me with this matter.'

I sound more officious than I intended, but it seems to do the trick. She takes her eyes away from mine for the briefest moment, but long enough for me to know she is faltering.

'What is it you need to know?' Her arms are still folded, her chin jutting out.

'I want to know who my wife saw that day and I want to speak to that person.'

She sniffs and moves over to the computer. 'If you would sit down, Dr Penn,' she instructs, clawing back a vestige of power. 'Your wife saw the nurse. Lesley. I'll see if she's here. Please wait.' She turns away sharply and leaves the room.

Lesley is wide-eyed and nervous at being brought before me and I feel sheepish interrogating her. Ms Hodder stands her ground, staying with us to make sure I don't intimidate her.

'My wife came to see you on the sixth of June,' I say. 'Can you tell me what it was about?'

Lesley looks terrified at the prospect of being expected to remember the encounter. Ms Hodder steps in.

'You can refer to your records, Lesley – it's not a test.'

Lesley logs herself on to the computer and scrolls down. 'Okay. Yes, I remember.' She turns to us, her hand still on the mouse. 'Am I allowed to say?'

'Yes – go ahead,' says Ms Hodder, who now appears to have changed sides and is doing half my job for me.

'Diane was worried when she woke up feeling terrible after a work do,' Lesley informs me. I remember now, you rolled in very late one night, Dee, after a retirement party at work and you were sick before you got into bed. It wasn't like you. You never overdo it with alcohol. 'She passed out at a party and she didn't know why.'

'*Passed out?*' I exclaim. I thought it was a rogue hangover. 'Had she mixed her drinks or something…?' I ask.

227

'Diane said she hadn't drunk anything alcoholic at all. I asked if she was particularly stressed, had had any headaches lately, any other symptoms, like a temperature or flu. She said no to all those. I said it might be food poisoning.' She lowers her eyes. 'We tested for the only other thing I thought it could be.'

'Which was?' I ask.

'We did a pregnancy test. But it was negative.'

What Lesley has said makes my mind flip an internal calendar and I consider the dates. The miscarriage was on July 25th – and seven weeks before then would have been around the time of this appointment.

Of course, there was always going to be another possibility – that you were forced into something without your consent. This idea has been fluttering round my head like a lethal mosquito right from the beginning, but I'd refused to allow it to settle and brushed it away. I couldn't let it in. I couldn't allow my thoughts to go down that route – it's been too upsetting to contemplate.

Lesley carries on, 'I suggested she see her GP if she wanted to run any further tests, but from her records it looks like she didn't.'

I'm not hearing anything coherently now; my mind has leapt elsewhere. I thank them both, even squeeze Ms Hodder's arm and hurry out. By the time I'm on the pavement, Tara is answering my call.

'Yeah – there was a school retirement party in early June, for Doreen Passmore, but I was taking my Salsa class that night and I didn't go.'

'Did Diane mention it at all? Talk about it?'

'Not really.' She hesitates. 'She mentioned it in passing, but it didn't sound like she'd had a particularly good time. Sometimes, these after-work dos are a pain. All paper plates and stale sandwiches. You feel you have to go, but it's all a bit of fake camaraderie. I don't think many people liked Doreen that much, to be honest.'

'Well - apparently, Dee passed out at some point. She didn't mention that?'

'No...'

'Who went to it – do you know?'

'Not off hand – but I'll try to find out for you.'

I cycle back home and before I know it, I pour myself a whisky. I don't mean to, but my nerves are crying out for it. It's standing on the draining board; golden and full of promise. I knock it back in one and wait for the dynamic rush – soothing and electrifying all in one.

I've barely eaten all day. This can't be good for me. I check the freezer – there are ice-cubes – trays and trays of them for some party or barbeque that is never going to happen. There are frozen peas and a packet of apple sauce. That's all. I pour out a bowl of Shredded Wheat instead; my mainstay for the last two weeks. I open a can of dog food and fill Frank's bowl. His head nuzzles my hand as it's holding the fork, so that half of it ends up on the floor. I pat him, then throw both arms around him, overwhelmed suddenly with the need for warmth and comfort. He half ignores, half tolerates me, his body jerking with every gulp of food.

'Oh, mate – I don't know how much more of this I can take,' I tell him. He turns and licks my face with meaty breath and I leave him to it.

The doorbell rings and a round of shots blast around my ribcage. I'm always expecting news, yet the sound still makes me jump.

For a split second I think it's you. The same height, the long dark hair tied back at the side with a clip, the broad sculpted shoulders. It's Alexa.

'Peace offering...' she says, holding out a bottle of red wine, not looking at me. She nudges the door open with her foot and steps inside without my invitation. She's wearing denim shorts like the pair you have and a black lacy top I'm sure I've seen upstairs.

'That bloody dog still here?' she chides. Frank charges towards her, his tail wagging and she draws her arms into her body to avoid him. 'Please – can you?' She huddles against the sofa hoping I'll take him away. I enjoy a rare, but brief, moment when Alexa looks vulnerable.

'Frank – here boy...' I entice him with chews and he curls into his basket. I return from the kitchen with two glasses and a corkscrew, although I'm not convinced that Alexa turning up like this, is a good idea.

'Have you heard anything?' she says helping herself to the centre of the sofa. 'I feel like I'm out of the loop.' She kicks off her sandals and slides her feet beneath her, like she lives here. It irritates me more than it should.

I put the glasses down beside the unopened bottle and sit on the arm of a comfy chair a foot or so away from her. 'I don't know what the police have told you, but it looks like Diane was in the bell tower at the church recently.'

'What? The church here?'

'Yes. A little girl saw her – in fact the same little girl who has just gone missing from the village – it's extraordinary…' I fold my arms.

Alexa shuffles forward, bringing her legs out from under her. 'What was she doing there?'

'No one seems to know.' I tell her Clara's story – that she said you weren't well and were upset – and explain about the hairclip. 'I had a call about half an hour ago – the forensics team found one of her hairs on the rooftop, too.'

'So what does that mean?'

I think back to the call I took from Howis as I was putting my bike away. 'The senior investigating officer thinks it could have been attached to the hairclip I found. There was no blood or anything. It doesn't give us any time frame.'

'And this kid who says she saw her – have you spoken to her?'

'Yeah – she's very bright and sparky – Clara, she's seven.'

Alexa turns her nose up. 'Oh, God – that's no use. She's probably making it all up.'

'I don't think so.'

'Can't you pull any strings? Diane said you knew guys in the local force.'

'For God's sake, Alexa – I'm doing everything I can…' Sweat prickles like a tribe of ants under my armpits.

Alexa leans forward and opens the bottle of wine. She fills both glasses almost to the brim and passes one to me.

'Here's to finding her safe and well,' she says, clinking it against mine. Several drips fall to the carpet and she rubs them in with her toes. Alexa normally leaves the instant she gets what she wants, so I'm perplexed by the fact that she looks set in for the rest of the evening. Is this some kind of reconciliation? I take a long slug of the wine – it tastes expensive – and sink back. I don't have much scope for conversation and I'm happy to sit in silence until she decides it's time to leave.

Alexa's voice breaks into my consciousness. '...or Chinese?'

'Sorry?' I'm feeling slightly woozy and don't want to be in this state with Alexa here.

'Do you fancy Indian or Chinese? A take-away – I assume you haven't eaten.'

'No – I'm fine thanks.' I don't want to sit eating out of cartons, like we're mates. What's she doing here? We never spend social time together – ever – she hates me.

Alexa's glass is empty and she is helping herself to more. When she leans forward I catch sight of the dip in her milky cleavage. It looks just like yours, Dee – so do the nipples poking out of the silk camisole. I blink to make sure it's not you. I take a small sip then put the glass down on the table. Following the whisky on a near-empty stomach, this is not a good idea.

'Did Diane ever talk about a retirement party at the beginning of June?' I ask, determined to make better use of this uncomfortable situation.

'June?' She scratches her head. 'Don't think so. Why, what happened?'

'I'm not sure – but she went to see a nurse the next

day. She passed out, apparently.'

Alexa laughs. It has an unkind ring to it. 'Doesn't sound like my virtuous sister,' she says. She's starting to slur her words and it occurs to me that she might have had a drink before she arrived. She straightens up, 'Now you mention it, she was a bit down for a day or so. I thought she had flu, or something. Did she get herself pissed?'

'You know Diane – she's not one for overindulging.'

'Maybe she was letting her hair down for once,' she gives me a knowing look and reaches for the bottle again, her glass empty once more.

'What do you mean by that?' I lean forward, glaring at her. 'What do you know, Alexa?'

'Oh – this and that...'

A wave of rage rolls over me. 'Come on! Tell me what you know. This is important.'

'Diane has said a few things...' I stab my fingers into my hair unable to believe what I'm hearing. 'She hasn't mentioned anyone else exactly – but she did say something about having doubts.'

'What doubts?' I protest.

'About her marriage.'

It's like she's dealt a blow to my gut. I can't possibly take this in – where were the signs? The little excuses, the absences, the avoidances? There were none.

'I think you might have had a bit too much to drink, Alexa.'

'You've known all along, haven't you?'

'What?' I snap, taking a step back.

'That you couldn't father a child – that you and my

233

sister could *never* have kids.'

'That's rubbish, I told you – I only found out a few weeks ago.'

'That's why, at the start, you weren't keen on having children, isn't it? Because, back then, you knew you *couldn't* have them!' She flings her arm up in a wild gesture. 'You know that more than anything she wanted children and you *cheated* her – you knew before you met her.'

I don't bother to grace her outrageous accusation with a response. I shift my weight to one leg, sticking my hip out. 'Why can't you accept I'm here to stay? Eh?' I snap my arms down defiantly and lean towards her. 'Why am I such a big problem for you?'

Alexa throws back the last of the wine and does the one thing I least expect. She launches herself at me, wrapping her arms around my neck, pressing her breasts into me.

'Why do you think having you around has been so bloody hard for me?' she hisses into my face.

'What are you doing?' I try to shake myself free without hurting her.

'You can't have *her* – she's gone,' she says, 'but you can have me...' With that she plants her lips firmly against mine.

I am so taken aback I don't react immediately. She pulls away for air. 'I hate the fact that you fell for her and didn't see me. Why couldn't it have been me?'

I step away from her, put my arm out to keep her at bay. 'Alexa, this is not helping – this is not what I want.'

In an instant, her eyes harden.

'You could have hurt her,' she accuses, waving her finger at me. 'After she had the miscarriage.' I shake my head, jutting my jaw out in desperation at these ridiculous conclusions. 'I can see the anger in you, Harper,' she persists, coiling her hair around her finger, seductively. 'Even if no one else can. I know that what you did at your mother's house is only the tip of the iceberg. Smashing up her plant pots – Diane told me everything.' She moves behind the sofa, stroking the top of it, keeping it as a barrier between us. 'Is that why you visit those guys in prison – because you think "there, but for the grace of God go I?"' She's slinking, like a cat, making her way behind another chair towards the front door. 'Did you kill her?' she finally snarls at me. 'Was it during one of your violent outbursts?'

I try to hold my voice steady. 'This is preposterous, Alexa – it's the drink talking.'

'You couldn't face the truth, could you? Your wife turning to another man to get pregnant, because you couldn't get it up?'

Something snaps – I'm sure I hear it inside my head. The next moment my wine glass explodes in a frenzy of crystals and Alexa is flat against the wall right beside where it landed, a stream of red cascading towards the carpet.

'See?' she says, running her finger through the trickling wine and licking it. She doesn't move another inch. Alexa is strong and fit – her muscles are twice the size of mine. She doesn't fear me. Her eyelashes flutter and a smile creeps across her lips. She's enjoying this. 'You killed her, didn't you? You got angry *like this*, because you couldn't cope knowing she was going to have another man's child.'

For a split second, everything in the room goes underwater – thick and blurring.

'That's NOT true!' I bellow, my hands clutching at my scalp.

I take a step towards Alexa and her eyes widen, the whites expanding like fried eggs in a pan. Then she breaks into peals of laughter and sits down on the edge of the sofa. She tosses her hair back, as if we've been playing a game.

'Why are you doing this, Alexa?'

Her eyes close in a prolonged drunken blink and I realise there's no point in trying to reason with her.

She lurches towards the front door.

'I'm not sure you should be driving,' I say.

She stares at me. '*Don't* tell me what to do.' She takes a step back into the room and pulls a mouldy nectarine from the fruit bowl on the window ledge. She tosses it up like a tennis ball. 'I don't know where she is – but I know one thing.' She drops the nectarine back in the dish and steps onto the mat. 'If she's got any sense – she won't be coming back.' With that she swings her hair in a fan-shaped blur and slams the door.

I find myself here again. It's cold and damp – there's no light inside, no creature comforts. I don't know what got into me. I can't believe I lost it like that, with your sister. Sometimes I don't know what I'm capable of. I have to sit here – in solitude, in punishment, for what I have done.

Alexa's words were outrageous, of course they were; she was angry at my rejection of her and she wanted to hurt me – but I shouldn't have overreacted like that. I'm ashamed – thoroughly mortified – about what just happened. She *knows* about my anger. She can read me in a way that others don't seem to. Even more than you perhaps, Dee. That's because you're so forgiving and see the best in people. Alexa sees the truth. It's unnerving. She sees me for what I am.

I'm shivering, even though it's a barmy night. The old chicken coop is the best place for me. It's been my point of refuge since we moved here; my primeval cave. Alexa knows my anger is deep-rooted and dangerous. I think back to the blind rage I felt when my mother got the call to say my father had died. I allow myself to relive the trembling fury that claimed me as I ransacked his house. It feels now like a black and white dream; I watch it from a distance and can't believe it was me. No – that's not true. The worst thing is – I *can* believe it was me.

I admit it. There is a side to me that is out of control. I don't seem to have the middle ground others have, where they feel their anger brewing and let it out. I hate seeing people shout, slam doors, swear; I can't seem to give my anger expression in those ways. Instead, I squash it down, hold it in – then I explode like a cannonball with contemptible behaviour. It's a side I do my utmost to hide, but Alexa has seen it and revels in her discovery. Mr Nice Guy isn't so nice after all. She's right.

There are no excuses.

Chapter 27
Harper

14 August – 15th day missing

Clara went missing on Monday; it's now Thursday and the police have no leads whatsoever. An adult going missing is bad enough, but a child…I feel the weight of Marion's desperation settle in a layer over mine as I enter her cottage.

Her bedroom is almost dark when I walk in. So still and gloomy that for a moment I wonder if Marion's passed away and no one has told me. I stop in the doorway and hear the catch of her breath; it snags in her throat in a regular rhythm.

Marion has given me a key so I can let myself into the house and speak to her whenever I need to. It's nice to feel so trusted. I clutch on to small gifts such as this – there are not many joys in my life at the moment.

As I grow accustomed to the darkness I see she's sitting up in bed. It's an improvement, but she doesn't look like she's going anywhere. Her body is so thin, I can barely see how it can contain all her organs.

'I've covered all the places on the list you gave me,' I tell her. I set out early that morning with Frank and we checked everywhere I hadn't already been. 'The police have, too. We haven't found anything…yet.' I want to keep any shreds of optimism alive, but it's a losing battle.

She nods, gripping the blanket, her knuckles blueish-white, pure bone.

'Have the police asked you about all the people Clara knows?' I ask.

'Yes,' she says, sounding bleak.

'Can I do the same? Sometimes things can come to you differently on a new day.'

I'm trying to inject hope where I feel none. I feel numb after my encounter with Alexa last night – I must have spent over an hour in the chicken coop stewing it over – and, right now, I'm going through the motions. Marion hands me a photocopied list of the names she gave to Sergeant Howis; all the people in Clara's life – school friends, parents of friends, teachers, tutors from Sunday school and after-school clubs, the library, nurses and babysitters. There are twenty-seven names in all. 'Oh – and Dr Pike,' she adds, holding out a pen. 'At the hospital.'

'And your own doctor, there?'

'Ah, he's Dr Nivan Guha. There's the local GP, too. Dr Geraldine Lane.'

'Clara seems to know people at the allotment,' I inform her.

'Does she? I'm not surprised. She's friendly with everyone.' She draws in a sob. 'That's the problem.'

'Can you think of anything – anything at all in the last few weeks that's been odd or unusual, in connection with any of these people?'

'You're just like the police,' she says almost smiling.

I'm tempted to point out that the police will cover all

bases far more efficiently than I ever could. They have sniffer dogs, fingerprinting equipment and all the right gear. They have the right to walk into people's lives and fire questions at them about where they were and what they were doing. I have no right to do that. I'm doing this because she's asked me to – and to give myself something useful to do. Without this, I will only be staring at blank walls in a house I used to call home.

'You might see something they don't,' she says, as if reading my mind. 'You notice things. And you've met Clara. Something might strike you that slips past the police.'

'I know. I'll try.' I pull up a chair to show I mean business. 'So – what can you tell me?'

'Well – two nurses at the hospital were supposed to be looking after Clara during the last few visits – Natalie and Sheila – they both lost track of Clara.' I take down the details: times, dates, a brief summary. 'Tessa is a new babysitter from across the road. I used to have Lorna, but I had to stop using her. She let it slip her boyfriend was round while she was supposed to be focusing on my daughter. Clara came back upset one time recently.'

'When was that?'

'It was before we went to the castle. She said something about the boy 'helping' when Lorna gave Clara a bath once. I didn't like the sound of that at all, so I knocked it on the head.' I took the boyfriend's name – Wayne Right – he's seventeen.

'Do the police know this?'

'Oh, yes.'

'They'll run a thorough check on Wayne, for certain.'

'There is something else, now I'm thinking. I didn't mention this to the police. It may be nothing.'

'Every little thing is worth investigating,' I remind her.

'At the hospital, when Clara had to get a check-up after she was stuck in the castle, we saw someone called Dr Norman. He was sweet with Clara, joked with her – you know. But she said something that I took to mean something else at the time.'

'Carry on.'

'Dr Norman was joking about the nursery rhyme Humpy Dumpty – he pretended to get the story wrong and Clara said "You should know that by now". I thought she meant that *at his age* he should have understood the story, but what if it meant something else? What if it meant Clara and Dr Norman had already met and he'd recited it before?'

I stand up. 'I'm going to pass this on straight away. In the meantime, keep thinking, keep writing things down.' I nod to the notebook beside her bed.

'I will – don't worry.' She wafts a paper-thin hand at me as I make a move to leave. 'Before you go, I want you to have this.' She leans down beside the bed and pulls something out of a paper bag – it's a big effort for her. 'Clara wanted you to have it.' She hands me the butterfly mosaic Clara had been making in the kitchen when I last saw her.

The butterfly is mostly purple with pink and silver pieces, catching the light. 'She made it into a mobile for you to hang in your kitchen...'

'It's gorgeous,' I whisper, my fingers trembling as I take it.

I can't look at her face. I'm completely overcome and I don't want to upset her by dissolving into an emotional heap at her bedside. 'I'll go and pin it up right now.'

On the way back to the cottage, I call Neil and pass on the details about Dr Norman. He sounds neutral in his response so I can't work out whether he's grateful for my input or finds it interfering. I don't care. I'll carry on until we get somewhere.

Tara rings soon after, just as I'm fending off Frank at the front door.

'I managed to find someone who went to the retirement party in June,' she says. 'Her name is Elaine Passmore and she was happy to give me her number to pass on to you.'

I thank her and before I do anything else, I find a drawing pin and take Clara's gift into the kitchen. I stand on a chair and fix the loop of cotton thread onto the beam that runs inside the window. The mobile sparkles as it turns. Apart from Frank, it feels like the only thing that isn't dead in the place.

I make the next call. Elaine is driving, but pulls in at the roadside to speak to me.

'Yes, I remember seeing your wife at the party. Tedious affair, to be honest. We were only there to put in a polite appearance.'

'Was she okay? Did anything unusual happen?'

'I don't think so.'

'Did she drink much, do you know?'

'Oh, I don't know.' Her voice catches and I realise she's nervous. 'I remember she had a glass in her hand at the start. We all did to try to get into the party mood. She didn't usually drink much, did she?'

'No – not usually.' She seems to be stalling. I want her to get on with it.

'What else happened? Did she look unwell, upset?'

'I'm not sure…'

'Please, Elaine. She's missing. Anything could have happened to her.'

She takes a staggered breath. 'I saw her talking for ages to Stephen Morrell, the deputy head. She was drinking a blue lagoon cocktail. Yes – that's right – I remember, because it spilt on her dress.'

A blue lagoon cocktail? That doesn't sound right at all. You don't normally like cocktails, Dee.

There's a break in the connection. 'I'm not sure Diane was looking a hundred per cent, now I think about it,' she goes on, assuring me there's nothing further she can tell me. The phone cuts off – through loss of signal or by design, I'm not sure – but I've heard enough.

There is somewhere I need to be.

'I shouldn't be doing this,' Tara points out, a half-smile on her face.

'I know, but…' She opens the first door and finds the key for the second. I flip the light switch; it's one of those gloomy buildings that needs constant strip lighting.

'No – turn them off,' she says, flapping her arms. 'I know my way around without them.'

She turns left along the corridor and I follow her. I

marvel at the way the smell of sprouts is still in the air weeks after the end of term. It's as though the place has a life of its own – a kind of ghost town – after all the children have gone.

'Has Diane ever mentioned Stephen Morrell to you?' I ask.

'Not with any affection. He's the deputy head. She thinks he's creepy.'

'Married, Elaine told me.'

'Yeah – with two kids, I think.'

'Elaine said Diane was talking to him at the party...'

We push through a pair of swing doors. 'Diane never said anything.' The thud of the closing door echoes along the corridor, like a train coming. 'I know for a fact that Elaine has a bit of a thing for Stephen, so I wouldn't read too much into what she says. She's probably jealous.'

'Have you ever known Diane to drink cocktails?'

She laughs. 'Only rarely. She likes the idea of them, more than the taste, I think – you know – the colours and the bits and pieces that go in them.'

That makes sense. You love bright greens and turquoise – and pretty little trinkets.

'She thinks they're overrated,' she adds.

Tara has a key to the staffroom; it's the only place teachers can get hot drinks so everyone is allowed one, but the secretary's office is another matter. I, however, have come prepared.

'You must leave it exactly as you found it,' Tara insists. 'I could get sacked for this.'

'I know. I'm sorry.'

I take the set of skeleton keys from my rucksack and choose the one suitable for Yale locks. I only ever use them to show my students – I give a demonstration in their first term, then they are forgotten.

Once inside the office, I check the blinds are drawn and wave Tara in. She hangs in the doorway reluctantly, but her eyes give her away. They're sizzling with daring now, not fear.

'I've never committed a crime before,' she whispers.

The place is compact and has a shiny new desk as the centrepiece. On the corner is a dead fern. I check the Rolodex beside it, but it contains details of electricians, heating engineers, glaziers and other maintenance services; it's not a directory of staff addresses.

'Can you shine the torch on the filing cabinet?' I ask.

She points the beam over my shoulder and I try one of the other keys. I get into the cabinet without a hitch and carefully flick through the files.

'You're good at this,' she affirms.

I try the next drawer down and find what I need. I scribble down the address and our job is done.

Tara wants to come with me, but I need to do this next part on my own.

'Phone me, okay?' she insists.

I leave her at the school gates; she heads towards Portsmouth and I hop on my bike and start cycling to the other side of Cosham. I decide it would be better not to warn him with a phone call.

*

A child of around ten answers the door and I ask if it is the right address for Mr Morrell.

'Sure,' she says, chomping roughly on a banana. 'Dad...it's for you,' she calls out. She leans against the wall, the front door half-open, chewing. Wearing a short skirt with rolled-down socks, she rests the sole of one foot against the wall. There's meanness etched around her eyes and she has an air of invincibility about her. She's at that stage between girl and bolshie teenager; the kind I'd want a sweet child like Clara to avoid.

The door widens. 'Yeah – what is it?'

I put on my good-to-meet-you face. 'Stephen Morrell?' He ignores my extended hand.

I explain who I am. Of course, he knows you're missing, Dee. All the staff at St Mary's have had visits from the police by now. He drops his head and invites me inside. I can hear a boy making plane-crash noises from a nearby room. Morrell leads me into the sitting room where everything looks expensive rather than comfortable; a curved sofa without end pieces, three top-heavy flower displays, low lamps hanging from the ceiling. I have to navigate around an asymmetrical glass coffee table that looks like it could slice a leg off. Domesticity to impress, without comfort or practicality. I'm put off already – it feels incredibly uninviting.

Morrell is tall and lean with thick black hair and black-rimmed spectacles to match. In beige trousers my father used to call 'slacks', he looks straight out of a fifties magazine advert, selling knitting patterns for men's cardigans. He's wearing one now; tightfitting in pale green, over an open-necked shirt. Not only does he appear old-fashioned, but he's awkward and unfriendly. At the door, he didn't smile or take my hand, hasn't made eye contact once and keeps looking at the floor. If he taught at secondary school, the teenagers would eat him for breakfast. Words like dork and nerd come to mind – which is unfair, because I've barely met the man.

He stands in the middle of the room without offering a seat. There is an oily smell from the new ivory-coloured carpets and a trace of cinnamon. I glance around, trying to find the source of it without success.

'What did you want, exactly?' he says.

'I understand you attended a retirement party for Doreen Passmore at the school in June?'

'That was ages ago.'

'Do you recall my wife being there?'

'Diane? Yes. Why?'

'Someone who was there remarked on the fact that you two spent a lot of time in conversation – can you tell me what you were talking about?'

He looks startled. 'Did we? I can't remember.'

How convenient.

'Diane wasn't well that evening – do you know anything about that?' I know as soon as I ask him that I'm only going to get a string of useless replies. There is a new alertness about him, however, that makes me continue.

He shakes his head. 'No – I didn't know about that. She seemed fine to me.'

'Someone said she was drinking alcoholic blue cocktails...'

He laughs in a forced way. 'Someone's got a good

247

memory.' He composes himself. 'Everyone had a glass of something or other in their hands – it's what happens at parties.' He sniffs. 'I'm sorry, I really can't remember a great deal. It was a dreary party for a member of staff. We weren't dancing on the tables – it was all very sedate.'

There is a crash of crockery somewhere in the house and Morrell sidesteps me and follows the sound. I follow him, not wishing to lose the thread of our conversation.

A casserole dish lies in pieces on the kitchen floor. 'He pushed me,' accuses the girl, putting her tongue out at a boy of around half her height.

'I didn't – it fell,' he whines in retaliation.

'Well – things happen for a reason,' Morrell says philosophically, as he crouches down and reaches for the larger pieces of the broken dish. I spot a brush standing behind the door and, in two minds about doing it myself, hand it to the girl instead. She gives me a look that suggests I've offered her an impaled cat and leaves the room.

'Sorry, Dad,' says the boy, who squats down; he watches his father handle the shards instead of helping. I hand him the brush, but he merely holds on to it.

I step back and take in the room. Just like the sitting room, it's all for show, with shiny superfluous appliances, like a waffle-maker and rotisserie, both of which look barely used, and a silver dish with four identical red apples standing on the table. The only personal touch is a corkboard next to the fridge with postcards and photos pinned to it. I look closer and see your face in one picture. Then another. There are a cluster of photos from school and you're in all but one of them.

Morrell stands up and catches me scrutinising the board.

'A lot of pictures of my wife,' I suggest, without smiling.

He puts the cut pieces into newspaper and rolls them up without answering, then sweeps the floor.

'I said—'

'I heard you,' he says, straightening up. It's the first time he's looked me fully in the face. His eyes are grey and hard like rivets. I feel compelled to look away. He puts the brush behind the door and pats the boy on the head. 'Off you go, Ben.'

He folds his arms. 'It's a coincidence,' he says lightly. 'She happens to be in the best pictures, that's all.' I stoop and look again. Your hair is shorter in two shots, you're tanned in another; they cover a wide time period.

I turn to him. 'Do you know where my wife is, Mr Morrell?' I give him my full attention, waiting to see what he does with his eyes. They go down to the floor.

'No. We're just colleagues.'

Interesting. I haven't asked him a question that would prompt that reply.

'What happened at the party?'

He shakes his head. 'I'm afraid I have to ask you to go, Dr Penn.' He makes a pretence of checking his watch. 'I have an appointment.'

I don't have much option, but once I get to the door, I ask another question. 'Where's *your* wife, Mr Morrell?'

'She's upstairs,' he says with satisfaction. He tips his head and I hear the toilet flush. 'Although I don't see why that's any of your business.'

I leave without a further word and retrieve the bike that I've locked up on the path at the side. I take everything in; the well-tended garden, the heavy side gate, the car in the garage.

He's smug and insensitive and I can see exactly why you don't like him, Dee.

I have also taught enough seminars on body language to know he's hiding something.

Chapter 28
Diane

I open my eyes, but nothing changes – everything stays pitch black. It's night-time. Either that or I'm dead now – and this is what it's like. Silent, heavy, dank and lonely. Desperately lonely. I ache for human contact; for a kind word, the gentle touch on my shoulder, a hug. What I'd give for an embrace right now from you, Harper! I miss your voice, your touch, your kisses, your breath. I ache for you deep inside my belly. I feel a tickle on my cheek and know I'm crying. This isn't good. This isn't going to help. Feeling sorry for myself isn't going to fix anything.

With nothing else to do here, other than pine and fret and wait, I force myself to try to piece the bits together. The night I went to the village, a little girl ran across the road and I almost hit her. What happened then? Did I drive off?

No.

I snatch a breath and the tape over my mouth sucks in sharply.

Of course, the little girl. I've seen her before; I remember now. Clara Delderfield – she lives in the village, over the far side near the pub. Her mother is ill with cancer.

What was she doing? God – I nearly hit her when she bolted across the road. I jammed on the brakes. I can see my foot as I stepped out of the car. The tarmac. The broken white lines in the middle of the road caught by the headlights. I got out – I remember the car door slamming. It was quiet – there was nothing else on the

251

road. That's right – I followed her into the bushes and saw her disappear down the bank. I thought she might be hurt – or lost – she was certainly too young to be out on her own.

She stopped and I thought I saw someone behind her, but I can't be sure. Was I spotted? I carried on down the bank. I wanted to be sure Clara was okay. I was going to find her and take her home.

But by then I'd lost her. There were too many bushes, a thick blanket of trees, foliage everywhere. I stopped to listen. That's right. I heard the crackle of wood underfoot and moved towards it. Tucked away in the undergrowth was an old Anderson shelter – painted a dark matt green and covered in ivy. I nearly missed it. It was the door closing that made me notice it; that single slight movement out of the corner of my eye.

I crept closer and that's when I heard him. Talking to her in a teasing, coercive voice. His tone was soft and kind, soothing and gentle at first and I was ready to be relieved. Until I got a little closer and could make out the words. He can't have seen me, after all. He wouldn't be saying those things, those words like that, if he had. I knew Clara wasn't safe at all.

I burst in on the two of them. I should have thought it through first, but my knee-jerk response was to intervene. I had to stop him. I asked what he was doing. He told Clara to stay where she was. There were blankets, toys and books inside the shelter; as if they'd used the place before. He came outside to speak to me. He sounded so convincing. They were playing a game, he said. I must have misheard him earlier. It was all completely innocent, but he understood my concerns. Her mother knew all about it, he insisted, but I was right, it was late and he admitted he ought to be getting her home.

I was almost ready to believe him, when I saw his flies were *undone. He knew that I'd noticed; he could tell by the look on my face. And I could tell by the look on his. He came towards me. I was backing off, uncertain about running, because Clara was still inside the hut. She was in danger. I didn't know what was behind me; I didn't know there was a sheer drop that should have been fenced off.*

In a split second he had a hefty branch in his hand. He was swinging it, getting a feel of the weight and working out how high he'd have to lift it in order to knock me to the ground. I got ready to run. I'd call the police as soon as I got back to the road. I'd flag down the first car that came my way and get people to Clara within minutes.

I didn't know about the ridge with sharp crags and rocks at the bottom or the fence that had been vandalised. Right behind me. He lifted the branch and as soon as I turned, I fell. I blacked out. I must have done. I can remember nothing after that.

Clara. I take in a juddering breath. I was supposed to get help.

Judging from the pain in my chest and a deep throbbing in my kidneys, I must have dropped a long way, hitting an outcrop no doubt, as I fell. I must have internal injuries. He must have brought me to this farm – wherever it is – and decided to keep me here, because of what I'd seen.

It seems like many days have passed since then, yet I have patchy details of only a couple. He must have drugged me and little by little it's wearing off. That's it - my system must be getting used to the medication. Now things are a bit clearer, I've finally worked out who is keeping me here and what this is about. I don't know what plans he has for me, but they can't be good. He can't afford for me to get back into the outside world.

I can't break the ties around my ankles and wrists, but I can shuffle. Have I tried this before?

I scrabble on my backside towards the stable door and listen. I can hear the world carrying on without me — a distant train, the hum of an occasional vehicle far away, whoops of an owl. I'm in the middle of nowhere. I turn to feel the surface of the door with my fingers. There is a slim crack; it probably wouldn't be enough to see out of, but it indicates a weakness. I'm a strong swimmer — I have good legs. I start to batter the door with both feet together. Punching hard and fast. The door is strong too, but I hear an encouraging splinter.

Then there are footsteps — he's coming back.

Chapter 29
Harper

'Morrell's a slimy bastard,' I tell Tara.

We're wandering around cobbled streets in Portsmouth, the old part of the city, where in the eighteenth century sailors on leave used to frequent the pubs and brothels. Nowadays, there are views of the new quayside bars and restaurants, the Spinnaker Tower and ferries cutting through the water. Two picturesque pubs built in the seventeen hundreds are set on the harbour front. It feels busy with modern tourism and quaint throwbacks to the past, all in one.

We walk along the walls towards the square tower built in 1494. The water is wide enough to feel like the sea at this point and it splashes into crumbling rocks beneath us.

'And he's got photos of Diane plastered all over the walls?' she says in dismay.

'Not exactly. He's got one of those noticeboards in the kitchen and there are about six photos from school – and she's in five of them.'

Tara makes an 'O' shape with her mouth. 'Shit – that doesn't sound good.'

The splash of waves accompanies our footsteps;

children ahead of us are skipping and laughing. We've walked this trail several times this year, you and I, Dee. For a brief moment, as I gaze out at the broad planes of blue in the distance, I'm fooled into thinking I'm with you and I almost reach out to take Tara's hand.

I correct myself in time and put my hands in my pockets out of harm's way. Tara hasn't spoken for a while. She seems pensive this morning.

'You seem quiet…are you okay?'

'I've been thinking, that's all. I was dying for the school holidays and now I just feel exhausted all the time.'

'You need to recharge your batteries. Teaching is a hard slog.'

'It's more than that. I'm considering whether being a teacher is the right fit for me. I used to love it, at the start – now it feels like I'm reinventing the wheel every time a new school term comes around. Don't you feel that at the university?'

'No. I know what you mean – but I think I'm so fascinated by crime and criminology that there's always something new. It's always alive and fresh. It's an exploration for me as much as it is for the students.'

'That's a great way to be.' She sounds envious. 'I'm not sure I get that feeling in my situation. Dee's different, she adores the children. She loves watching them grow and develop and learn. She relishes the part she plays in that.'

'And you don't?'

'This is going to sound selfish, but I want to grow and learn *myself*. I feel like I'm dishing out rote facts and figures for the kids to take away, but I'm not getting anything back.'

'Maybe you need to go back to college? Focus on being a student yourself?'

'Yeah, maybe.'

We walk towards the funfair where Portsmouth becomes Southsea. Jangling tunes from two, then three rides, chime together in a crazy fairground frenzy. Children emerge with candyfloss and fluffy dolphins they don't really want.

'Dee says you're a brilliant lecturer – that you've given talks up and down the country. She says you're incredibly organised and never get nervous.'

'That's not true. I fake it and try to look like I know what I'm doing. It's an act. I've learnt to hide what's really going on.' Tara gazes at me curiously. 'I am organised, though,' I add. 'Well, controlling really.'

'Dee didn't think so. She thought you were fun, candid, sincere, easy to be with.'

I feel my cheeks turn pink. 'She always saw the good in everyone.'

I feel a glow of gratification until I realise we're talking about you as if you're dead. I bow my head and try to shake off the idea.

'A friend rang this morning to invite me to Malta for a week,' Tara says suddenly. We separate to avoid a boy on a skateboard. 'But I can't go…not with…not until…'

I reach for her hand and take it, fully aware of what I'm doing. 'Thank you. It means a lot. I'm really struggling – and with you around, I feel like I'm not going through this on my own.'

She leans into my shoulder and I sense how easy it would be to put my arm around her and take in the smell of her hair. But, it wouldn't be right.

'You seem stronger, though,' she assures me. 'I got the feeling you were starting to slip away from us for a while, there.' She laughs and I smell her sugary breath. 'You've shaved!' She turns my chin towards her and gives me a look of approval.

I laugh and use the shift in mood to pull away from her. 'I'd started to wallow in self-pity and it was no good to anybody.' I admit. 'The girl going missing shook me out of it. Clara's mother, Marion, needs support. Her cancer is untreatable and it's only a matter of time. I'm trying to do all the things she isn't able to do.'

We wander over to a wall overlooking the thin band of beach and lean on it. 'What do you think's happened to Clara?' she asks.

'God knows. It's awful. The hospital seems to be at the core of it, though. Everything seems to lead back there; it's where she was last seen.' I watch a seagull dive towards a crisp packet left on an abandoned deckchair. 'It's hard for me to do much when I don't have the powers of the police, but I'm going to see Marion later. See if I can shake things up a bit.'

'Let's go back,' she says, sounding weary.

Nothing passes between us for a while, then Tara says, 'I think I'm going to leave the school. I don't think it's me. Not now.'

'Dee would be gutted if you left St Mary's. You've been such a support to her.'

There is a silence the thickness of a steel vault between us.

My words come out like a plaintive cry. 'You don't think she's coming back, do you?'

'No…I mean…' she quickens her pace. 'No…I don't think that, at all,' she stammers.

Back at the cottage, I'm on the phone. Pressing my mates in the force for another favour. I bypass Neil, this time, and see if I can get a better response from DS Paul Whitaker instead. Despite my failing to show up for our squash match, Paul owes me. I stepped in to give a talk to his team recently, with only a day's notice. *Eternally grateful*, were his exact words at the time. I remember we laughed at how formal he sounded.

I ask him to run Stephen Morrell's name through the system. He comes back to me saying there are a series of speeding offences, but nothing more. He knows I'm involved in looking for Clara and brings me up to date.

'We're still looking into Dr Norman, a child specialist at the Queen Elizabeth – there seems to be a gap in his employment history. Also, he has no alibi for the time of Clara's disappearance. Although it's been hard to pinpoint exactly who was where at the hospital, because of the mayhem following the fire alarm.'

'Anyone else?'

'Wayne Right, the boyfriend of Marion's sacked babysitter has a history of petty theft,' he informs me.

'Is that it?' I moan, discouraged.

'We're still checking the police records of all the staff at the hospital. There are hundreds of locums and agency staff to wade through.' He sounds tired. 'Of course, it could be a patient or visitor we're looking for –

someone who came and went. Or not connected to the hospital at all.'

I thank him and ring off, my tone subdued as I recognise the pool of suspects is getting wider, not smaller.

I'm in the kitchen and as I replace the phone, the pretty mobile Clara made for me swings slowly to the left and the butterfly sparkles with twinkling silver light. It feels particularly poignant, because I know you love butterflies, Dee. It's as if it belongs to both of you; joined together in your absence.

What really happened that evening you left me, Dee? Where are you?

I ring Tara. I don't have much to say – it's purely for solace; to hear a friendly voice. She's about to go to a yoga class and says she'll call me back.

In the meantime, I clear away a fresh pile of brick dust that has fallen into the hearth. Whilst I'm tipping the orange remains into the bin, I bring to mind the photographs on Morrell's family noticeboard. Something else strikes me. When Tara calls me back, I have something to tell her.

'Those photographs at Morrell's place,' I say, 'you were in most of them, too.'

'Really!' she sounds disgusted. 'Well – then maybe it doesn't mean anything.'

I'm angry with myself. I thought I'd got a lead, but it could be nothing. 'Maybe he just takes photos of pretty women,' I say.

Tara grunts. 'What does his wife think about that?'

'I don't know. He said she was upstairs – I heard

someone – but he could have been lying.'

'Maybe they're separated or getting a divorce?'

We can speculate all we like; it isn't getting us anywhere. An idea comes to me. 'Would Elaine know?'

Tara's voice brightens up. 'It's worth a try. I'll call you back.'

Tara rings me two hours later while I'm making my way over to Marion's cottage.

'Elaine is coming over to your place later – she's got a handful of photos from the retirement party – she says Dee is in a few.'

'She's coming to the cottage?'

'Yeah – I thought I'd cook something – just an easy dish. Traditional Danish, if you like the idea – tasty, not too spicy?'

I haven't had proper hunger pangs in days and my stomach rumbles in response to her suggestion. 'Sounds great. Thank you.'

'You know the best restaurant in the world is in Copenhagen? At least it got the most votes in 2012.'

'I don't need any persuading, honestly.'

Marion is sitting in the living room, making almost no shape at all under a blanket, when I arrive. Helen is there with her. Marion's eyes stop blinking and her face opens out in anticipation as I stride in. I shake my head as I pocket the key she's given me.

Helen gets up to make us all a cup of tea. Marion turns and stares out of the window as if something has caught her eye.

'Today would have been perfect for one of Morris's

skydives,' she says. 'He loved the summer. He was in love with the sky; completely at home there. I was terrified the first time I saw him tumble out of a plane. He seemed to travel such a long way – time was passing so fast – and still he didn't activate his chute. Then whoosh and it hoisted him up and transformed him into a feather so he'd float down and roll into the grass.' She picks at fluff on the blanket. 'He could never speak to me straight after a jump; he was too emotional. Being up in the sky was a powerful experience for him. He used to say it was a privilege that he had been able to do something so exclusive for a living.'

I know she's still waiting for compensation for her husband's untimely death. Her entire life has dissolved into a tragedy. Her husband, her illness and now her missing daughter. I can't imagine anyone who deserves it less. She is such a warm-hearted and sincere person. Just like you, Dee. I wish you'd known her better.

Helen hands round a plate of digestives, but none of us take any. She looks deep in thought.

'What about you, Helen? Ever tried any extreme sports?' I say. Her hair is loose today and unexpected soft curls trail inside her collar, softening her face completely.

'I've tried ice skating a few times. Does that count?' She half smiles and lets her tongue linger against her teeth. It makes me think that perhaps she isn't as prim as she seems.

'It might,' I reply with a smile. 'Depends what you do. Any spins or triple salchows?'

Her lips break into a full sunny smile. 'No way – both

skates are glued to the ice at the same time,' she says, 'I usually manage to grab the arm of an accommodating bloke to get me round the rink. It's the only way to stay upright.' She holds my gaze for a moment, as if considering whether I'd be one of those accommodating types or not.

Marion looks like she's dropping off; I imagine the doctor has given her something to keep her calm. It's time to cut the small talk and get down to business.

'I think we need to think back very carefully over the last few weeks and try to get together some kind of timeline of Clara's movements and behaviour.' I put the teacup back on the tray. 'Maybe, by tracking her, we'll discover something.'

Marion nods.

I take out my notebook. 'We need a starting point,' I say. 'When, exactly, did Clara first seem to start acting out of character?'

Marion doesn't speak, so Helen puts forward a suggestion. 'When she was trapped in the oubliette?'

'No – it was when we came out of the hospital,' Marion says with assurance. 'After she'd been checked over by Dr Norman. She got lost for a while and I found her near the main reception desk on the ground floor. One of the nurses, Natalie, caught up with us and apologised.'

'How long was Clara missing for?'

She touches her cheek, trying to think back. 'About twenty minutes. Half an hour maximum.'

'Did Natalie say where she'd been?'

'No. She had no idea.'

Marion is still hooked into the memory, so I continue. 'Anything else?'

'Yes. On the bus, on the way home – Clara was very quiet. When we were ready to get off I found out she had an apple core in her hand.' I'm writing everything down and don't look up.

'Do you know where she got it from?'

'She didn't have any money on her, so someone must have given it to her.' Marion sits forward, the most animated I've seen her in days. 'That's right. She said the Wizard of Oz had given it to her.'

'The Wizard of Oz?' exclaims Helen.

'Yes,' Marion's fingering her top lip. 'I gave her a telling off about it. You know – about accepting sweets and stuff from strangers.'

'What did she say?'

She draws back. 'I can't remember.'

'She didn't mention anyone – a nurse, doctor, cleaner?'

'No – I'm not sure she said anything else.'

I underline Wizard of Oz, because Clara had mentioned his name to me too, but I can't remember when and in what context, so I don't make a point of drawing attention to it.

'It's a start,' I say, trying to sound upbeat.

'She seemed less keen to go to the hospital after that,' Marion continues. 'Before, she was reticent about it, in a bored kind of way – you know, having to hang around and wait for me during my appointments. But then she started getting tetchy – even upset – about going.'

'There's Dr Pike, too,' Helen chips in. 'Does Clara

like her?'

'I've no idea – I've barely had any straight answers from Clara to my questions in the past few weeks.' Marion lets out a sigh. 'Dr Pike said she thought Clara's condition was getting worse. If her "trauma" – or whatever it was – had resulted from the incident at the castle, you'd have thought that, with time, she'd have been getting better, not worse.'

The mention of Dr Pike reminds me that I saw her with Dr Norman when I was last at the hospital. I didn't know at the time they had any connection with Clara; it was before she went missing and I was heading for Dr Swann's room. I heard someone shout 'Dr Pike' and it made me smile, as I recalled seeing a Dr Trout when I was a child. Dr Trout didn't look anywhere near as elegant as Dr Pike, however, who drifted out of a consulting room with a young boy as I walked by. She was an extremely attractive woman – blonde and poised; wearing a regrettably unattractive smile – all plastic.

She passed the child on to an adult with a few words and turned to a figure standing at the entrance to an adjacent office. She elbowed him inside and started arguing with him about something, without closing the door. I bent down to tie my shoelace nearby; I was early for my appointment and intrigued by the situation.

The doctor she was railing at – I discovered afterwards when I saw his name badge – was Dr Norman. I put him at around twenty-eight; he had thick floppy hair and round specs like an overgrown Harry Potter.

'Why did you leave her there on her own?' Dr Pike hissed.

'I thought you had a patient – I didn't want to disturb

you.' Dr Norman looked visibly shaken at being caught out.

'You should have buzzed me.'

'Anyway, she wasn't on her own – *I* was looking after her.'

'Well – I don't want you *looking after* my patients,' she said. She gave him a disdainful look, which suggested she knew more about him than she wanted to.

Dr Norman shook his head and stormed out into the corridor, so I backed away into the first door I could find – the gents' loo – and waited for his footsteps to pass by.

Was that conversation significant? They certainly knew each other.

Marion yawns and I realise she's waiting for me. I tap the pen on my book. 'I can't help thinking that in her own way Clara was trying to tell us something.'

'You think she *knows* the person who took her?' Marion asks.

'She's a very sharp child. We didn't get her drift at first, when she said she'd seen a woman in the bell tower, but then we found the hairclip – and, more than likely, it was my missing wife she'd seen.'

I turn to a fresh page. 'I think something strange has been going on for a while – and it may be connected to the hospital.' I've asked Paul if there's any chance I can see the CCTV footage from the Queen Elizabeth; the police might have missed something. In the meantime we only have clues from Clara herself. 'I think we need to try to remember everything Clara said.'

I ask about the last book she'd been reading, the last

DVD she'd watched. Anything that could be out of the ordinary or triggered a conversation. Helen lists various stories Clara's been hooked on lately. 'Before *Little Red Riding Hood*, there was the *Princess and the Frog, Heidi, Matilda*,' she counts them off on her fingers.

Marion adds, '*The Princess Bride, Ella Enchanted, The Dark Crystal.*'

'What's that last one?' I interject.

She smiles. 'It's a Muppet adventure. On DVD. Another one she likes is *How to Train your Dragon*.'

I point upstairs. 'Can I take another look around?'

I scour Clara's bedroom and look beside her television, then check near the one downstairs. I've seen one of the DVD's Marion's mentioned somewhere recently – *not* here in the cottage – but I'm not sure where. I check all the downstairs rooms and come across a plastic supermarket bag by the shoe-rack in the hall. The DVD I'm looking for is inside – it's the only item, but it hasn't been opened; it's still in the plastic wrapping. I get a sandwich bag from the kitchen and lift it out without touching it.

Helen pops her head out of the living room. 'Have you found anything?'

'I'm not sure.' I join them, holding up what I've discovered. '*The Dark Crystal*. When did Clara get it, do you know?'

'She saw it at a friend's house – Samuel – then she wanted her own copy,' Marion tells me. 'I meant to get it out of the library for her. I didn't realise it was already here. I don't know where it came from.'

'Did you see Clara with this bag?' I hold up the plain

white carrier bag.

She shrugs. 'She often has something with her – for bits and bobs; pens, paper, a book to read – to pass the time at the bus stop or in waiting rooms.'

'And Samuel?'

'He's the little boy in the next cottage along.' She points to the left.

Helen comes with me. I'm holding the DVD inside the transparent bag. Samuel is at the swimming pool, but his mother asks us to wait at the door.

She comes back with his copy of *The Dark Crystal* to show us.

'Clara must have got her own copy from somewhere else,' I surmise. I curse my brain for not tracing my memory back to the source. I've seen it – I know I have.

It may be nothing, but it might also be the one key that unlocks everything.

Chapter 30

On the way back to the cottage I think about the conversations I've had with Clara, to see if anything rings a bell. I notice things. I should be able to do this. Even though I don't know her well, I am in a good position, because I have only a few exchanges to recall. Marion may find it harder to remember exactly what Clara has said, and when – and furthermore, her knowledge of her daughter will contaminate the words, too. They will tend to blend into the overall persona she knows as Clara. But I should be able to recall her words objectively.

On my last visit, Clara was certainly upset about something. What did she say exactly? Something about getting 'juicy behind the knees' and 'hot in the head'. She asked me if I ever felt like that. With hindsight, it sounded like she was describing being angry more than upset. Then she said something about not wanting to 'be there on my own' – but she didn't say where. I should have asked more, but I didn't know at the time that it could be so significant.

I hear Frank barking as I press the key into the lock and fight through the mental fog to try to grasp Clara's final words to me that day. Were they about Frank? About a dog? I get inside and close the door. No – her parting words have gone.

I give Frank a bracing walk through the woods and back along the river before supper. I'm feeling uplifted by about one degree above my recurring black mood. Partly because I'm making a small contribution towards helping Marion, and partly because I've got company for supper. Tara is arriving at six to prepare everything in my kitchen. I admonish myself. Our kitchen. There are other times recently, I notice, when I've referred to joint belongings as *mine* instead of *ours*. It's like using the past tense after someone has died – the way reality gradually sinks in, reminding you that a loved one is not coming back. I push the thought away. It's not going to happen. You're not dead. You're coming back – I know you are.

Tara troops in right on time, carrying a stack of plastic boxes and bags of vegetables. She's refreshingly business-like and gets straight on with it – her only requests are a glass of red wine and music.

'What music would you like?' I call out from the sitting room.

'Latin American…salsa or bossa nova…yummy music…'

I select my playlist of Romeo Santos. 'Okay,' I tell her. 'I hope this is yummy enough.'

'That's perfect,' she laughs and swings her hips. I have to look away.

'What's with all the typewriters?' she calls out. 'What are they doing in the porch?'

'Good question,' I say, joining her at the chopping board. 'Dee thinks I'm mad. I have a weird fascination with them; I think it's mostly the sound. Do you remember those old movies set in newspaper offices, where everyone's rattling away? I used to watch them with my dad when I was little. It's so energetic, but contained somehow – the way they punch out each letter, one by one. I like the look of the machines, too – like little mechanical ribcages...'

I don't expect her to understand. 'Dee's right – you are mad,' she replies, 'pass me the garlic press.'

Elaine arrives shortly before dishing-up time and joins us in a glass of wine. From your description of her, she isn't the person I was expecting. You said she was frumpy and a little plump, Dee – but you were being generous as usual. In fact, Elaine is seriously overweight and her lemon-yellow dungarees do nothing for her. They seem to encourage rolls of fat to gather in regular intervals from her knees upwards; the colour even clashes with her ginger hair. Every area of skin that's exposed is overrun with freckles, making her look like she should be in quarantine. But, she's earnest and wants to help. That's all I can ask for.

She and I sit at the dining table talking about dogs, while Tara adds the finishing touches. She comes through with the starter – a beetroot dish with chicken livers and apples.

'The whole meal is traditional in Denmark,' she explains, telling us exactly what's in it.

The main course is lamb fricassee with turnips and goutweed (a herb in the carrot family, apparently) followed by a more recognisable rhubarb and macaroon trifle. The meal is unusual and tasty, but the best thing is that you and I have never had anything like it. It doesn't belong to *us*, it has no memories attached to it. As such, it is a relief after so many instances in my life – nearly everything I touch and see; every thought I have – where you are immutably branded in my recollections.

I'm restless as we finish the dessert and Elaine and Tara continue to chat about school. I want to turn to the real reason Elaine is here. Finally, she reaches into her bag and brings out an envelope.

'I've brought the photos from Doreen's party, like you said.' She fans them out on the table. 'I don't know if they'll be any help.'

'Are these in the order they were taken?' I ask.

She checks and then nods.

'Can you talk us through them?' I suggest.

We pull up our chairs either side of her and she holds up each snap in turn. 'This is soon after I got to the party. It was just in the staffroom at school. Diane is talking to Stephen in the first one,' she points to you and I snatch an involuntary breath – you look so ravishing in that strappy dress.

In the next shot someone has joined you. I can see the stem, but the rest of your glass is hidden behind Morrell's elbow. 'Who's the woman?' I ask.

'That's Stephen's wife, Gillian.'

In the next picture, the three of them are still standing together in a little circle and Gillian appears to have her arm around Diane's shoulder. 'Does Gillian know Diane?' I enquire.

'I don't think so. Gill's like that with everyone. She's very welcoming.'

'How are things between Gillian and Stephen, do you think?'

272

'Oh, they come across as a very strong couple...which...' She appears to debate for a second whether to tell us more. The wine appears to make the decision for her. She's had more than Tara and me. '...I'm happy for Stephen, of course – just wish things were different, that's all.'

I find it hard, after my first meeting with Morrell to recall a single attribute that could be considered appealing to any woman, but perhaps he was on the defensive with me and in other circumstances his charms are more evident.

'What happened after these photos?' I ask. 'When did you leave? Before Diane?'

'Hold on...' She looks at the row of pictures to get the order of subsequent events straight in her mind. 'Diane didn't look too well after this one was taken and Stephen's wife took her to the bathroom. They both disappeared for a bit. I was talking to Stephen at the time.'

'Diane wasn't well?'

'Yeah – she looked a bit queasy – Gillian led her out.'

'How long did they take?'

'Not long. About five or ten minutes, maybe...'

'Then what?'

'Stephen left first. The party was still going. There were a handful of people still hanging around.'

'Where was Diane?'

Elaine stops to think. 'Stephen went on his own...Gillian left a bit later with Diane – maybe she was waiting until she felt well enough.'

'Did you actually see Stephen get into his car on his

own?' adds Tara.

'It was a taxi. About five minutes later, I saw Gillian with her arm round your wife at the door as another taxi drew up.' She smiles despondently. 'That's all.'

Elaine continues to add more unnecessary details about Stephen and how he comes across as shy and withdrawn, whereas in fact he has an 'incredible' sense of humour, is kind and gentle. 'He's helped me a lot at school,' she stresses, 'with assemblies, school plays and displays...'

'She's in love...' declares Tara and Elaine laughs and knocks back more wine.

I don't hear much more. I'm trying to figure out what exactly happened at the party. I scrutinise the pictures again as Tara and Elaine clear the dishes. It's the glass in your hand I'm focussing on. It's full, then empty, then full, then empty. How many did you have? And blue lagoons – when you've never been a fan of cocktails at all?

I change the playlist several more times and we sit in comfy chairs to drink coffee. Elaine takes up Tara's offer of cheese and biscuits – fortunately she brought supplies with her – and, long overdue, Elaine calls a taxi.

As she's slipping on her denim jacket, I have one more question for her.

'The cocktails – did Diane order them herself?'

'There wasn't a proper bar, as such, we had to bring our own drinks. One of the teachers fancied himself as a barman and he was mixing drinks in a shaker by the sink.' She stops and seems to acknowledge that she hasn't answered my question. 'I think Gillian got the first one for her. Yeah...she did. Now I think of it, she didn't call it a blue lagoon — so perhaps it was something different...'

'Can you remember what Gillian said?'

The taxi Elaine's ordered draws up outside the gate. 'Not exactly,' she says, 'but — actually, I don't think it was even alcoholic — that's right...Gill said something about it tasting like vodka, but that it wasn't...'

Tara stays to help me clear up, but like me, I'm certain she is putting off the moment when she has to return to the solitude of her empty flat.

'What do you make of that?' she asks.

I don't know whether Tara has put two and two together, but I decide it's time to fill her in, if she hasn't. 'The date of the party was around the time Diane got pregnant,' I say, absently drying a glass beside her at the sink.

I should have given her more credit. 'I know.' She turns slowly, frothy suds dripping from the rubber gloves. 'Do you think it was Stephen?'

I drop my head, unable to respond.

Tara hesitates. 'Except, Elaine said he didn't leave the room at the party — she'd know, she was watching him like a hawk the whole time.'

The golden rule in my job is never to jump to conclusions. 'Whatever happened at the party certainly made Diane very ill and resulted in her passing out.'

Tara takes a deep, shaky breath. 'I hate to say this, but aren't those the perfect conditions to...rape someone?' I wince at her words. Of course, I've known all along that you could have been put through a savage attack like this. Before now, I haven't dared to breathe life into that possibility, but now Tara has uttered the word, it suddenly feels like a concrete conclusion. Furthermore, it fits the circumstances more than anything else.

'Diane swore she hadn't been with anyone,' I whisper, a sob swelling in my throat. 'I should never have doubted her.'

I can't let myself sink into this while Tara is here; I must wait until she's gone. She puts her hand on my arm. 'Don't. You weren't to know. According to Elaine, Diane thought she was drinking mocktails.'

'Question is – whatever went on between them, did it happen at the party itself, or afterwards?'

Tara narrows her eyes. 'And did Gillian get Dee straight home – or did they stop off at the Morrell's place first?'

'Dee took a pregnancy test the day after the party,' I tell her, 'but it was negative…'

'Of course it was,' Tara replies, without a breath. 'Most people think it shows up on a test straight away, but it takes about two weeks.'

'Oh…' My head is pulsating with questions and misunderstandings. I scrunch up the tea towel and drop it on the draining board. 'Let's go through this again.'

She pulls off the rubber gloves and leans back against the sink.

'Diane got pregnant at around this time. It wasn't with me, so was it consensual, or wasn't it?'

'It can't have been consensual,' Tara jumps in.

'Let's not forget she's also disappeared. If we follow the line the police are taking, she left of her own accord and hasn't been spending much of her own money. It's the perfect set-up for a woman running off with another man – a woman who doesn't want to be found.'

Tara turns up her nose. 'Was it Stephen?' she says after a long pause. 'If it was – she's certainly not gone off with him.'

'That doesn't mean he isn't keeping her somewhere.'

'But why? And if Stephen took advantage of Diane, why would Gillian be the one plying her with alcohol and pretending it's a soft drink?'

'I know – that's what confuses me.'

Tara pauses, her eyebrows raised. 'Wouldn't Dee have known if she'd been raped? You know...even if she'd passed out, wouldn't she be able to...tell?'

'Not necessarily,' I say, slowly. I clear my throat. 'She and I had...sex regularly...if he was careful, she might not have had any pain or bruising – and no memory of any of it.'

Tara trails her finger through suds on the draining board. 'Did the police find anything on Diane's computer? Have they told you?'

'They brought it back yesterday.' I point to it on the sideboard. 'There's nothing that raised any suspicion. Not a thing.'

'Well – that's good isn't it?'

We stand staring at each other, our arms folded, getting nowhere.

'I'll need to pass the information about the drinks on to the police.' I scoop up the tea towel. 'And I need to talk to Morrell's wife.'

Tara stays late, long after the dishes are cleared away.

I find her presence comforting – mostly because, as your best friend, she keeps you alive. We talk about you and I hear your voice in her words; things I didn't know. Like how much you were looking forward to the 'yellow sunlight' during our holiday in Rome and how you were secretly plotting ways to hold on to Frank. This evening, I don't want her to leave. I don't want to drop back into that lonely place I face every night without you. There are still so many unanswered questions. I still don't even know if you're alive.

I can see what you admire in Tara; she's straight talking and clean in her interactions, if that makes sense. I feel I know where I am with her. She's trustworthy; she will say if I'm crossing any lines or talking rubbish.

Tara eventually collects her plastic boxes and steps outside to meet the taxi. She reaches out to me for an embrace and I pull her close and bury my face in her hair. We hold on to one another, each soothing our own fears, until the taxi driver beeps his horn. We must look like secret lovers, forced to tear ourselves apart. I know you'll forgive me this moment of consolation, Dee. I know you'll understand.

Everything is still once the taxi pulls away. Any day now, Mark will call and arrange to collect Frank, then I really will be on my own. There is not a wisp of breeze to disturb the air. A distant owl calls out and I stare at the velvet sky, the stars like pinpricks leading through to another universe. It feels like a temple out here, but I cannot clear from my mind the image of another man's hands on you, forcing you, invading you in such a private and intimate way. I knew it was one explanation for the enigmatic pregnancy, but it had seemed so unlikely that I hadn't let it take root. Now, everything fits. It brings up a surge of vomit and I throw up outside the front door in a clump of hydrangeas. You were violated that evening and I wasn't there to protect you.

I make a decision. I don't want to be in our estranged bed without you. Using a torch, I drag out a plastic sheet from the shed and lay it on the lawn. I get into the loft to track down a sleeping bag and choose yours, hoping that it may still smell of you. My wish is in vain; it's musty and gives off wafts of paraffin, but I want it next to my skin regardless. Frank is bemused; he follows me around, wagging his tail and wondering what game we are playing. I leave the door to the kitchen open, light a candle inside a lantern and lie down for the night on the soft grass. Frank joins me, finding a warm nook between my legs.

I send a prayer up to the brightest star I can see that you are still with us, somewhere on this planet, and that we'll be reunited before I know it.

Chapter 31
Diane

The day after the party

Diane leaves the doctor's surgery and hurries back to St Mary's before afternoon classes are due to begin. She wants to find Tara before she sets up her drawing session, to tell her she won't be joining her at the new Pilates class after school – not when she feels like this.

Her stomach growls and as soon as she reaches the main gate, she has to break into a sprint and scuttle inside to the nearest toilet. She is just in time. She sits on the seat, her upper body thrust forward as hidden blades hack at her insides.

Last night, she vomited several times as soon as she got home, trying to be quiet so as not to disturb Harper. Now her intestines are letting everything go. Finally, she flushes, peels back the lock and staggers out to wash her hands, propping herself up on the sink. She stares at her sticky, grey face in the mirror. Where have the green patches under her eyes come from? She looks terrible and she is trembling all over, like someone coming out of a bad dose of flu. Except she hasn't had flu.

She was absolutely fine yesterday when she'd arrived at Doreen's party. She hadn't been particularly looking forward to it – Tara couldn't make it and she'd had the feeling that support for the brusque and prim Doreen Passmore would be thin on the ground. Diane had felt obliged to put in an appearance, but she'd planned to do a polite tour of the room, spend some jovial send-off time with the host, then slip away before it got late.

But those plans collapsed as soon as she arrived. Stephen Morrell spotted her and made a big show of bringing her into the conversation with his wife, Gillian. Then Gillian insisted on getting her a drink and it would have been rude to walk away. By the time she returned, Elaine had joined them, giggling and fawning over Stephen, insisting the Morrells pose for a couple of photographs, although she noticed Elaine took several more of Stephen when he wasn't looking.

'Oh, I'm sorry…' said Diane as soon as Gillian presented her with the blue cocktail. 'I thought you heard me say I'm on soft drinks…'

'Yah, but it's non-alcoholic, darling.' Her high-class drawl made her sound pure Kensington born and bred.

'Oh…in that case…' Diane's eyes stretched wide at the first sip. 'Whoa – it seems quite strong.'

'It's just laraha,' Gillian assured her. 'It's a bitter Caribbean orange – with tinted lemonade, ginger and mint.'

Diane stretched out her tongue. It seemed to be icy cold at the edges and on fire in the middle.

'I *adore* them,' Gillian said, taking a sip of an identical blue cocktail in a slightly larger glass. 'You know why? Because you think it's vodka or something, but there isn't a drop!' She winked.

Diane was about to slink over to the drinks' table and

swap hers for a tonic water, when Stephen embarked on a long and convoluted story about how his mother had been involved in a terrible road accident. Once again, it seemed rude to break away and soon she had another blue cocktail in her hand, thoughtfully provided by Gillian.

'It'll keep you going,' she whispered, clinking her glass against Diane's.

The tale Stephen had recounted in considerable detail eventually wound towards a tedious conclusion, but now Elaine was rattling a bowl of peanuts at her. Diane smiled, shaking her head, and bent down for her bag, ready to move on. At this point Stephen took a step towards her and clapped his hands together as if he was about to make an announcement.

'So, tell us exactly what you've got lined up for us at the sports day fayre at the end of term, Diane.'

'Oh, yes,' chorused Gillian, crowding in. 'It sounds great fun.'

'A-am I doing the fayre itself?' Diane stammered. She knew she was organising the assault course, the hockey match and the volleyball – but surely the stalls and refreshments were someone else's department.

'Yes – that's what we agreed. Don't you remember? At the meeting last Friday. The one when Tony brought up the issue of toilet duty, and his lordship over there,' he nodded towards the headmaster. 'Said he was allergic to Domestos.' He leant in too close and his nose brushed her ear.

As Diane pulled away she noticed that his words were fading in and out. He said something she didn't catch, but it was clearly meant to be funny, because he nudged her elbow and the drink she'd nearly finished splattered down her dress.

Stephen started fussing immediately, trying to dab at her chest with a napkin.

'It's fine...honestly...' Diane was blinking fast, trying to shift what felt like layers of wax from her eyes. Her head was feeling too heavy for her neck; it seemed to want to roll to one side and stay there. She needed to sit down. She turned to try to locate a seat, but before she could make a move, Gillian was back at her arm with another full glass of blue liquid.

'Here, have a sip of this – it will make you feel better.' The glass looked to Diane like an infinity pool. 'It's been a long day. You look like you need perking up a bit.'

'It's okay...thanks...I'm...' She drew to a halt unable to find the next word – it had entirely slipped away from her. Gillian held the glass to Diane's lips and tipped it towards her. She wanted to fight it, but her arms had turned to lumps of solid lead. She felt her eyes roll shut, but the liquid went down. She didn't seem to be able to stop it. She swallowed and nearly gagged. It didn't taste right at all.

'I'm...not feeling...' She was forced to reach out for Gillian's arm. The room was pulling away from her, the floor sinking, and she was suddenly so sleepy. She heard a buzz of concern hover around her, then the scene changed; it was darker and colder, there were posters on the walls. She must be in the corridor. The images disappeared and all she was aware of now were footsteps on lino. Everything was cloudy inside her head and

Gillian was twittering on like a bird at her shoulder.

'Fresh air…taxi soon…home before you know it…nice party,' came the chirping.

Diane didn't remember any fresh air. She had a vague recollection of being bundled into the dark, leathery recesses of a taxi, but after that the curtains inside her mind closed altogether and it was night for a long time.

When she woke the next morning, her head was like a spinning top, but she was determined to get to school. She hated being off sick – it threw the school into turmoil and messed so many people around. If she was under par, she could set the class work to do and sit quietly at the front. She was hardly at death's door.

She left Harper asleep and stepped into the shower. She didn't want to worry him. She was probably overreacting, but as soon as she'd dried herself down, she rang the local surgery. She'd never felt like this before and a tiny glimmer at the back of her mind was telling her she might be pregnant. She felt a tingle all over. Could that be it? How amazing! The beginning of something new and incredible for both of them. All the more reason not to mention it to Harper – she didn't want to raise his hopes if it came to nothing.

Thankfully, the surgery could fit her in that day over lunch, but only with a nurse. Diane decided that if it was anything serious, she could book an appointment with a doctor straight away. One step at a time. She wrote the time down on a scrap of paper, even though she knew she would remember it, then she put it in the pocket of her dressing gown while she cleaned her teeth.

By lunchtime her dreams are over. There is no baby.

The nurse says it was probably something she ate. Even so, the symptoms she'd had the night before were exceedingly odd and came on so suddenly. It was like a combination of nausea, intense disorientation and complete exhaustion. She knows that for a period last night she'd blacked out altogether. Perhaps she'd caught one of those short-lived bugs that the kids were always going down with. Or maybe she'd had an allergic reaction to whatever Gillian said was in the drink she'd had – something beginning with 'I'...? – she can't remember. At least the Morrells were kind enough to get her home. Gillian had been particularly attentive, she recalls – and Diane makes a mental note to thank her with a little card.

Chapter 32
Harper

16 August – 17th day missing

I'm woken early the following morning by soft kisses, then I realise it's Frank licking my face. Somehow he's managed to squeeze himself inside the sleeping bag with me. I have one arm around him and he's wriggling, trying to get out.

My phone rings as I'm still on the lawn, stretching. Paul has gone the extra mile for me and arranged for me to view the CCTV footage in the hospital. 'Obviously, we've already examined it,' he tells me, 'as you know, it was the last place Clara was seen before she went missing.'

'Thanks, Paul – it means a lot.'

'If we don't offer you a few hidden extras, you'll only pester us and make our lives hell,' he says.

'That's true,' I say, unzipping the sleeping bag and getting to my feet.

Tara is on her way. She's called to say she'd left her measuring spoons behind, but when I told her where I was heading, she insisted on coming.

'Four eyes are better than two,' she insisted.

We arrange to meet by the hospital café, but I'm early and wander around looking at the position of the CCTV cameras. As I return, I see Dr Swann, his open white coat flapping as he strides along the corridor towards me. He's carrying a bundle of files and looks harassed and out of breath.

'Ah, er...am I seeing you today?' he says as his shoes squeak to a halt. I can see he doesn't really want to stop.

'No...' I drop my gaze. 'I'm not continuing with the injections, I'm afraid.'

'Oh,' he looks personally slighted. 'You're not? That's such a shame – we haven't discussed it, have we?' He stares at my face, trying to place me, trying to fix me amongst a myriad of other patients. 'Too many nosebleeds is that it?' he adds, suddenly. I'm impressed he's remembered.

'It's not just that. It's...a personal matter.'

He steps out of the line of pedestrian traffic and beckons me to follow him. I don't want to keep him – I know he's busy.

He lowers his voice. 'Is everything all right?' I'm touched he's taking the trouble.

'Not exactly.' I let out a noisy breath. 'My wife has gone missing and – er, well, until she comes back there doesn't seem much point in...you know.'

His mouth drops open. *'Missing.* No. I'm so sorry,' he says. 'How did...how long...is she...?' He doesn't seem to know where to start.

'It's a police matter now. It's all very distressing.'

'I can imagine.' He shakes his head and fiddles with the edge of the folders. 'I'm so sorry,' he says again. He looks at me imploringly. 'If there's anything I can do...' There's an awkward silence. 'And do consider continuing the treatment. If you don't it will mean starting over again – and that would cause a further delay in…'

'I know. Thank you. I'll let you know.'

Tara joins me seconds after he's gone.

'Who was that?'

'Dr Swann – my specialist.'

We watch as he's almost mown down by a trolley piled high with towels. 'Looks frazzled – you've definitely decided about the treatment?'

'Yeah.'

She rubs my arm. 'Do you think he's any good? In case you change your mind, I mean.'

'Seems to have a good track record – a lot of research behind him. I found an article he wrote in *The Lancet* before I had my original tests.'

'Checking up on him?'

'Sort of…just wanted to make sure I was in good hands.' Swann scuttles into the distance. 'I think he's rushed off his feet, poor guy.'

'Who isn't, in a place like this?'

I reach into my bag. 'Thanks again for dinner last night,' I say, handing over the spoons. 'It was my best meal in weeks.'

'*Det var intet – en fornøjelse*,' she replies in a mock snobbish tone. 'A pleasure,' she translates.

The security office, Paul has told me, is on the second floor. Tara pulls me in the direction of the stairs. 'Got to make up for all the gym sessions you're missing,' she says.

We pass the lifts; one is out of order. It is stuck above

us out of sight and there are bollards and tape across the gaping hole where the doors should be closed. I step over the criss-crossed tape and bypass the *keep out* sign, to take a closer look down.

'You're not very good at doing as you're told, are you?' says Tara.

'Lifts intrigue me,' I confess, 'as do disused railway lines and abandoned sections of the London Underground.'

'And you sit on train platforms in your anorak and copy down the numbers on the locomotives, I suppose?' she says, pulling at my sleeve.

'No – of course not.' She tosses me a glance which implies she has given up attempting to understand men.

Clive, the guy on duty in the security office, is an inch or two shorter than me, but tough looking. He wears a white, short-sleeved shirt over his bulging biceps. The room is dark, hot and stuffy and I'm not surprised to see grey half-moons under his armpits. He doesn't wear a wedding ring – not that this, in itself, indicates he's not married, nevertheless there's something about him that makes me think he's a bachelor. There's a can of deodorant and a tube of toothpaste on a shelf behind his desk and a shirt and tie on a coat hanger on the back of the door. Maybe he sleeps here sometimes.

He fixes up the footage for the day in question from 10.45am.

'The little girl appears in the foyer just before eleven,' he explains. He runs the film forward to that spot, but I ask him to take it back a few minutes. I want to see what was going on before Clara reached this point. 'There's congestion,' he says, 'because of the fire alarm. False alarm, thankfully – just an electrical fault, but no one was allowed in for a while.'

A group of around thirty people have congregated outside the main doors with about the same number inside, between the main doors and the reception desk. We watch as the film jolts forward in slow motion. 'The bell has stopped, but no one is quite sure whether the public are allowed in,' he tells me.

For a split second I see Clara. I recognise her dress and the thin Alice band holding back her hair. The crowd closes around her and she is lost again. I remember the local officers telling me that there's no visual record of Clara after that and she doesn't reappear in the footage in any of the car parks. I look at the people milling around in the foyer. There's a man on crutches, two women in wheelchairs, an ambulance trolley being pushed by a paramedic, patients sitting, standing or leaning against the walls, hanging around until they're told they can go through to their appointments.

Because of the poor quality of the black and white camera it's hard to distinguish faces; it's largely what people are wearing that makes them stand out. There's the white coat of a doctor and I recognise several nurses' tunics. A man in a security uniform opens the main doors just after 11am and the crowd outside surges into the building. I try to watch the path of people leaving as everyone weaves through. There's a point at which the footage is truncated. Everyone disappears off the edge of the screen.

'That's where the next camera should take over,' Clive says when I ask. 'Two cameras are down at this point, the last one on the inside and the first one outside, covering the main entrance.'

The two cameras that would hold vital shots of Clara leaving the building.

Tara lifts her hand like a schoolgirl. 'How come those particular cameras stopped working?'

'The police asked me about that. I said the managers told us not to worry about them too much, because the system is being upgraded. It should have been finished by now. The technical guys have taken a look, though, and it seems like there was dodgy wiring on both of them.'

I go back to the mass of people in the foyer.

'Have you spotted anything?' I ask Tara.

'There's that one glimpse of Clara,' she says, 'but then she disappears. I can't tell whether she doubles back or carries straight on to the main exit.'

'Me neither...'

I follow the trail of several male figures near the spot where Clara stood to see what happens. One joins a woman and baby, another heads towards the café, another has his hands in his pockets. When he takes his hands out of his pockets, I ask Clive to stop the footage.

'Can we go back – see that bit again?' I point on the screen to alert Tara. 'Keep your eye on him, okay?'

The man repeats his steps, first with his hands in his pockets; we watch closely as he takes them out. His face is turned away – his hair looks...normal, unremarkable – he could be any one of thousands of men who visit the hospital, especially as the quality of the film is poor and makes almost everything look like a fuzzy grey blob.

'Look...there – what's that?' I can only see one side of his jacket – the left side.

'It could be a tennis ball...' says Tara, squinting at the screen, 'an orange, or an apple...'

'The Wizard of Oz...' I say to myself. 'Do we know who this guy is?' I ask Clive.

'Him?' He taps his knuckle on the screen. 'No – the officers asked me that. We haven't been able to identify him. Looks like a patient rather than a member of staff.'

'Because he's not in uniform?'

'I guess so.'

The size of the man is hard to judge too, his jacket is open, so it's difficult to see whether he's thin or well built. Unhelpfully, he also appears to be of average height, perhaps a bit on the short side. His shoes look commonplace, but they don't look like trainers, he has nothing in his hands.

'Didn't you say Clara took an apple from someone in the hospital?' Tara wants to know.

'Yeah, but that was the day she was rescued from the castle pit – over a month before this.'

'Maybe the guy makes a habit of offering fruit to kids,' Clive suggests.

'You think this guy could have taken her?' Tara reasons.

I crouch closer to the screen. 'After the doors open, those who have been waiting around suddenly become more purposeful.' I ask Clive to rewind again. 'See – this is 11.01am – people are being allowed in and out. Now watch the paths of the men on their own.'

The three of us are glued to the footage. 'See, *this* guy still looks like he's waiting.'

'He could be waiting for anyone,' says Tara.

'He's scanning faces, he's not just waiting for someone.' I straighten up.

'You don't think Clara has gone off on her own somewhere and got locked in – like she did at the castle?' Tara asks, hopefully.

'For five days?' Clive adds with a sigh.

None of us say anything. We can all imagine a worst-case scenario. We watch the rest of the footage until the man disappears and the crowd thins out. Clara is nowhere to be seen and the timer on the edge of the screen reads 11.10am. I sit back, my arms folded.

'We watched every screen in the hospital,' Clive says wearily. 'Right through until the end of the day.' He shrugs. 'Nothing.'

It's time to go. As I take my jacket from the chair I notice a photograph of a group of school kids on a filing cabinet.

'You have kids?' I ask.

'No.' Clive turns the word down at the end with finality, sending a clear message that my question is off limits.

'Thanks,' I say dismally, as Tara and I leave.

'So what do we do now?' asks Tara as we retrace our steps to the stairs.

'I don't know. But I've just remembered the last words Clara said to me, a couple of days before she went missing.'

She stops and grabs my wrist. 'What?'

'She said "He's not a wizard at all – he's a wolf and a very bad one."'

Tara looks disappointed. 'And that means…?'

I huff. 'Who knows?

Tara pulls a face. 'I see…'

'I'm going to take another look around,' I tell her.

She has to go to teach a dance class at the community centre and leaves me on my own.

I don't know what I'm looking for. I'm staying here largely because I don't know what else to do and I can convince myself I'm being useful. I find Dr Pike's office and consider knocking, but I hear a child's voice inside and retreat. She wouldn't tell a complete stranger anything anyway.

I change my mind and decide to go; I could wander around here aimlessly for hours. One thing is certain, however: it's too much of a coincidence that Clara went missing when there happened to be a fire alarm causing havoc and crucial cameras were down. Someone *knew* about those cameras – maybe even engineered the alarm.

But there's one thing I'm *not* certain of.

Am I closing in on the truth about Clara – or you, Dee?

Chapter 33
Diane

I'm back where I was. So much for the breakout. He flung the door open, slapped me hard and threw me back against the wall like I was a sack of flour. He must have given me something to knock me out and while I was comatose, he screwed thick planks of wood across the bottom of the double doors. It's as strong as Fort Knox now.

I snap fully awake as another memory clicks into place. It's like a dream, but I'm way up high on a roof somewhere. I'm in dreadful pain, coming in and out of consciousness. Where was I? I close my eyes and try to picture what I can see. It's bright, I'm outdoors, my feet are in a gutter. But there's no chimney – in fact I'm looking down on chimneys, cottage roofs – familiar roofs. Yes – Nettledon, I'm sure of it! The village green, the pub. I'm looking down from the church tower, the old bell tower that's been sealed up, because it's collapsing.

How did I get up there? When was it? It was after I fell in the woods – I'm sure – I remember seeing the cuts and bruises on my arms. I can feel my legs being dragged across the floor, then I'm lifted over a shoulder, fireman's style and carried up stone steps. I must have been sedated or I'd have fought back. There's a huge bell inside the roof; it catches the light and I ache to find a stone to throw at it, so it will ring out and people will come running to find me. The next moment I'm outside, on the ledge. Oh my God – it's him — and he's trying to push me off. I hold on, clutching at the iron grips, digging my heels against the exposed battens with all the strength I have left.

Then Clara is right there in front of me. Did I dream that? She is on the ledge and there is no one else around. I am lying on the tiles. She crouches beside me and strokes my hair as she tells me she comes there often: to play, to read, to look at the sky, to see the whole village in one. 'It's the only place where you can look down on birds,' she says. 'You can be higher than them, for a change.'

She tells me her father used to fly out of aeroplanes — I remember her mother telling me her husband had died during a skydiving stunt. I want to speak to her, but I'm too weak and drowsy. I can't even be sure she is really there. She appeared out of nowhere like a guardian angel.

After that — there is white space in my recollections. I am no longer in the bell tower. Clara has gone and I am in a stable lying amongst the bales of straw.

Chapter 34
Harper

17 August – 18th day missing

Saturday breaks with splinters of white light across my pillow. It wakes me, like someone is shining a torch into my eyes, and I take Frank on his best romp yet, across the far side of the village, through dense undergrowth, over stiles, along the edges of swollen wheat fields ready for harvest. I throw sticks for him, we wrestle with long branches, race over the beck. I don't want it to end. It is our final time together. I am going to have to say goodbye.

Mark arrives, tanned and rugged from his escapades in the jungle. His hair is long and matted; he has a beard and coffee-coloured skin that's been creased by the elements. Frank is beside himself with joy. I am glad. Two souls are reunited. Mark tells me snippets from his tales in Peru, but I find it hard to take in. He sees my eyes drifting away and asks where you are. When I tell him, he jumps to his feet and paces around shaking his head, his breathing heavy, unable to say a word at first. Then he does the same as everyone else – what more can people offer? – and says 'get in touch anytime, if you need anything'. I assure him I will. Then, they are both gone.

I am bereaved all over again. There is no other living thing in the house. From now on I'm going to find more and more excuses not to be here; already I eat most of my meals on the hoof – sandwiches from corner shops, snacks from chip shops and vending machines. Apart from the supper at Marion's and the one Tara made, I can't remember when I had a proper meal. I've spent a few evenings in The Eagle, but I won't be going again. Whenever anyone mentions family or home life, the conversation inevitably disintegrates into awkward silences that slice into the atmosphere like a guillotine.

For something to do, I vacuum the entire house and do a circuit of the back garden, pulling off the dead heads on the dahlias and lupins. Some of these flowers you've never seen, Dee; you'll miss them altogether.

The ringing of the phone brings me back inside. To my surprise it's Dr Swann. I'm touched that he's calling when I am no longer his patient.

'I'm sorry if I'm disturbing you,' he says. There's a lot of machine noise in the background: bleeping and sporadic tapping. 'I was filing away your notes and remembered…how is…has your wife returned?'

I clear my throat. 'I'm afraid not.'

'I'm sorry to hear that. I can't imagine how dreadful that must be. You hear this kind of thing on the news and never think it could…well…'

'I know.' I appreciate the way he's struggling to find the right thing to say.

'I rang to say that if you wanted to consider resuming the treatment, it's not too late.'

For a moment I wonder if Dr Swann is banking on

me as some kind of guinea pig in his research and by dropping out I've messed up his results.

'I'm sorry if it's letting you down. I can't face it at the moment.'

'I do understand. That's fine. Insensitive of me to ask. Sorry. I wish you both well.'

He rings off and part of me is disappointed – he sounds like the kind of man I could have more of a conversation with – like he'd listen and understand, without asking too many questions. Anyway – it's too late; he's gone.

To take my mind off my solitude, I note down the times I've met Clara and try to recall what she'd been doing and what she said. It's the words children use sometimes and the way they say things that can make adults think they're making things up when they're not. Like when Clara said her father flew without wings. As I jot down places and dates, I write down her last statements to me word for word.

Your mother rings before lunch wanting to know if there is any news. She talks about your disappearance as though it's my fault. It's not long before your father becomes the centre of the conversation.

'He went missing on Wednesday,' she says. 'I couldn't find him anywhere.'

I find it hard to respond when 'missing' means 'temporary absence' in your father's case.

'Turns out he'd found his way to the chess club. Caught two buses – the first one going in the wrong direction. He doesn't have a membership card anymore and they rang me as soon as they recognised him.'

'Must be a worry for you,' I say dryly. I must curb my annoyance; one of these days he may get himself lost for good.

'Absolutely.' Her breath catches in her throat.

She seems to have done a magnificent job of relegating your disappearance to a separate part of her brain, so she doesn't have to acknowledge it. She doesn't ask how I am or what I'm doing. She has to go – Ted has switched on the lawnmower and it's out of bounds.

I call Alexa – for no other reason than to check she's not hiding anything from me. She's inevitably frosty, but claims she's not heard from you. I can't bring myself to ring back all the people who have left messages on the answerphone – it's too painful to go into your disappearance over and over again. I call my mother instead. Life is too short to stay angry with her. I find myself inviting her and Bruce over for supper at some vague point in the future when this is all over. She's delighted to hear from me. It makes me think she's been waiting for this call for some time. It's heart-warming to make someone happy.

I'm washing up the bowls I used for Frank, when Tara rings to see how I'm coping without him. She's remembered and I tell her how grateful I am.

'At least I know he's safe,' I say.

'No news about Dee or Clara, I suppose?'

'No. I've just been going over everything.' As I'm talking to her, I watch Clara's butterfly come to life in the breeze from the back door. 'You remember what Clara said to me...?'

She waits.

'"He's not a wizard, he's a wolf – and a very bad one."'

'Oh, yeah – I still don't get it.'

'Marion said that when Clara came away from the hospital with an apple, she told her the Wizard of Oz gave it to her.'

'Okay – I'm still none the wiser.'

'Clara was talking about him again, but saying he *isn't* actually a wizard...'

'Right – he's a *wolf* – whatever that means...so this ties up with *Little Red Riding Hood* somehow?'

'I think it does, but—'

Tara breaks in: '"He's not a wizard, he's a wolf – and a very bad one" – it's like she's saying he tricked her or did something to shock or harm her? Which is exactly what the wolf does in the story – all the kids in my class know it. He disguises himself as a lovely old grandmother, then pounces on the little girl.'

'That's it. Maybe Clara was identifying with the story,' I say. 'That's why she was stuck on that particular fairy tale.'

'You think it's someone pretending to be nice who is actually very nasty?'

'Maybe. And by reliving the story, she can keep going back to the beginning where everything is innocent and she's walking through the woods to go and see her grandmother.'

There's a short silence. 'It's a bit tenuous, isn't it?' she says.

'I know,' I sigh, realising it sounds ridiculous. 'It's just a theory.'

'It's possible, though.' She sounds like she's humouring me. 'You should run it past Marion – see if it triggers any connection.'

'And I need to see Gillian Morrell,' I add. 'See what she has to say about the retirement party.'

'Let me ring Stephen Morrell,' she jumps in, 'I'll find some pretext about school and call you back.'

Within minutes, Tara is on the line again. 'Stephen's playing golf today, somewhere near Chichester and Gillian is at home packing. They're off on holiday tomorrow.' Her tone is urgent. 'She's on her own. We've got to go today.'

'We?' I laugh.

'Of course. I'm coming with you.'

As soon as Gillian Morrell opens her front door, she strikes me as belonging to a superior league when compared to her husband, in several ways: looks, social class and people skills, for a start. She exudes elegance, wearing a silk kimono-style dress that shows off lean long legs and her hair is coiffured into a blonde chignon. She looks at least five years younger than the grumpy Morrell. Her accent is upper crust and polished. She swings the door wide and welcomes us in as if we're lifelong friends. I hastily wipe away the frown that is querying what she sees in him.

We're offered the choice of tea, coffee, homemade biscuits or toasted teacake before we even get over the threshold. 'I'm sorry the choice is limited,' she explains. 'We're going away tomorrow.' Her accent wouldn't be out of place in the royal family. 'I'm packing. The children, of course, have disappeared off somewhere, leaving it all to me,' she chuckles.

'A glass of water is fine,' I say. Tara nods. We don't want to be wasting time while Gillian faffs about in the kitchen putting together a full-blown Michelin-star platter.

'You work with Steve, I understand,' she says to Tara, as she sweeps us into the lounge and indicates the not-so-comfy low chairs without armrests, by the highly decorated fireplace. I see now that the white surround has been added; it looks far older than the house. I also understand how the décor would work around Gillian; designed solely for sophistication with a total lack of crumpled cosiness. I assume the children aren't allowed in here. You'd hate it, Dee. I think back to the first day Frank arrived with us, soggy from a rainy-day romp and paws sticky with mud. He bounded in through the front door and leapt up onto the sofa to lick your face. You laughed and embraced him, giggling at the messy crumbs of mud he was leaving on the fabric. I dread to think what kind of reception Frank's antics would get in this sitting room.

'And Harper is Diane Penn's husband,' Tara says.

Gillian covers her mouth in polite horror. 'Such a terrible situation. I can't imagine...' Her words go with her as she drifts off into the kitchen. She returns with a tray holding two tall glasses, a jug containing water with ice and slices of lemon, beside a plate of chocolate-chip cookies.

'Where are you going on holiday?' I ask for openers.

'Oh, Monaco,' she says dismissively. 'It's a favourite

haunt of mine. We're all going – Ben and Cherie, too.'

I let out an involuntary moan as the chocolate-chip cookie crumbles and melts in my mouth.

'They're my favourite,' she acknowledges, gratified, perched on the edge of the sofa, her knees together and slanted to one side, as though she's ready for a fashion shoot. She discretely glances at the clock over the fireplace. 'Steve said you wanted to borrow his book on marine archaeology for the start of term,' she says. She reaches into the bookshelf behind her and hands the heavy volume to Tara. 'And you wanted to ask about Doreen Passmore's retirement party?'

'Diane was there and you were too, I believe,' I say, watching her intently.

'Yes. I spoke to your wife – really lovely woman – about swimming. Ben is doing well in the pool and so I asked about private tuition and training for a boy his age.'

'Do you remember what she was drinking?'

'Drinking?' She tucks a loose strand into the back of the otherwise perfect twist of hair. 'I've no idea.'

'How did Diane seem?' I ask. 'Was she getting a bit tipsy or was she completely sober in your view?'

'Gosh… I don't really know your wife. That was only the second or third time we've met – always at that kind of school do. She seems so chatty and friendly. Laughing a lot, you know.'

I'm too agitated to be pussy-footing around like this. I get to the point. 'Did you give her a cocktail?'

She tosses the thick gold bracelet around on her wrist and speaks without looking up. 'It was…many weeks ago, now.'

Tara chips in. 'Elaine took several photos at the party. She said you handed a fresh drink to Diane.' I know for certain there was no photo showing Gillian handing over a drink to you, but Tara is clever, implying there is.

Gillian appears to be caught off balance and rests her finger across pursed lips.

'Oh, wait - I know what you mean. Yes – there were some non-alcoholic cocktails being passed around at the beginning – blue mocktail things. I do remember passing one over to Diane, now you mention it. I had the same, before I moved on to the Chardonnay.'

I ask about the rest of the party and Gillian's version tallies with what Elaine said. Her husband left first in a taxi – then you and she took a taxi together. 'It was nearer for me to be dropped off first, so I gave her some cash for her part of the fare and waved her goodbye. She hadn't looked too well. I assumed the taxi driver took her straight home.'

I ask for the name of the taxi firm she used and she hands me a business card without prevarication.

'Can you remember what time the taxi came to collect you?' I ask. I've already checked this with Elaine, so I'm waiting to see if the times tally.

'It was ten past eleven – or thereabouts.' That's what Elaine had said. It shouldn't be too hard to track down the driver.

I ask as tactfully as I can about the photos on the kitchen noticeboard. I point out that you and Tara are in nearly all of them.

'Stephen likes keeping a record of work events,' she tells me, assuredly. 'He always has.'

305

'They seem to be only of female members of staff,' I point out.

She smiles. 'Stephen is a discerning man. He likes attractive women,' she says, without any apparent irritation. 'I have no problem with that!'

Before we arrived, Tara suggested that we should settle on a signal I could give her to indicate she should distract Gillian, so I could have a subtle poke around the place. I put my empty glass on the coffee table and pull my phone out of my pocket as if it has buzzed against my leg.

'Sorry, I need to make a quick call.'

Tara responds to the signal and stands up. 'I'd love to see your conservatory,' she says, turning on the enthusiasm. 'I caught a glimpse of it when we came through the gate.'

'Of course, but I can't be too long. I've got so much to do.' They head out into the hall. 'We've just had new French windows put in.'

I go through the motions, pacing by the fireplace, pretending to make a call. As soon as I hear the back door click shut, I creep upstairs. I'm calculating that anything incriminating is unlikely to be left downstairs, although I have no idea what I'm looking for.

I find the study and step inside. I pull open drawers in the filing cabinet – everything is neat and labelled – and look for the most benign-sounding files: family, household, drains. I check inside these folders, but everything is what it claims to be. I can see nothing in the room that is locked or inaccessible.

I slip into the master bedroom and press myself

against the curtains by the window. Tara is doing a great job of admiring the flowerbeds. There's a half-filled suitcase open on the king-sized bed and another on the floor. I check Stephen's bedside cabinet – there's an appointment diary, so I turn back the pages to the day you went missing. The words *Speech for PET Awards* are written in for 8pm that day, but I make a note to check to be sure. I look inside his briefcase behind the door, check the top of the wardrobes, the shelves, slide my hand under the mattress. Everything looks inordinately above board, but I have a feeling about Stephen that irks me. The guys in the Hampshire Constabulary call it 'the itch'; that sixth sense that someone is hiding a dark transgression.

At the bottom of his sock drawer, squashed at the back are a stack of dirty magazines. No big deal – it's what I would expect. I give them a cursory flick through until a voice below alerts me.

'...must have gone to the loo,' Tara declares loudly, for my benefit.

I shove them back inside and make for the bathroom. Straight on cue, I flush the toilet and apologise for taking the liberty, as I descend the stairs. Gillian is looking perturbed, holding on to the newel post at the bottom.

'We've taken up enough of your time,' I confess. 'You must have lots of packing to do.'

We share gracious farewells and Tara and I walk back in silence to her red mini, parked with the back wheel on the kerb.

'Come on then – what did you find?' she probes, rattling her keys.

I climb into the passenger seat and I'm about to tell her my search was fruitless, when I bang my hand on the dashboard. 'Stupid...damn...'

'What...what's happened?'

'You'd better drive off – I'll tell you as we go.' Tara puts the car into gear and releases the handbrake. As we pass the house, Gillian gives us a polite wave from the bay window. I wave back.

'I've been looking in the wrong place.'

'What do you mean?'

'I've broken the golden rule of good detective work: *don't* jump to conclusions and always keep an open mind.'

Tara pulls away from a T-junction with a squeal. 'Will you please tell me what's going on?'

'I found porn magazines in his drawer. Nothing odd about that, of course. But I've been stupid. I should have been looking through *her* things, as well as his.' I glance at the wing mirror – it's angled incorrectly and gives a great view of the passenger door. 'Gillian was the one plying Diane with alcohol that night without her knowledge or consent. They could have been in it together.'

'Don't we need to check out the taxi driver first?'

'Yes – I'm onto that.' I'm already pressing the digits.

I reach Cosham Cars and give the details.

'That's going back a bit, mate...' comes the reply.

'I know, but it's very important – don't you keep a record of all your drivers and the fares they pick up?'

'Yeah – of course we do.' He spins me a line about not giving out 'that sort of information', so I tell him I work with the local police. At the mere mention of the word, he seems able to locate what I need straight away.

'That would have been Dobson...Micky Dobson. Only, she's in hospital right now.'

'She?'

'Yeah – Michaela. She's having a hip replacement – won't be back with us for a while, I don't suppose.'

I thank him and turn to Tara. 'I'll get someone at the station to look into it, but it looks like a dead end.' I look up 'PET Awards' on my phone and sure enough there's a press release stating that Stephen and his wife were present, sitting beside the mayor, and that Morrell's opening speech was 'witty and inspiring'. I find that hard to believe.

'The Morrells have both got an alibi for the evening Dee went missing,' I tell her. 'I'm missing something. I'm going back.'

Tara brakes in the middle of the road. 'What – now?'

'No. Tomorrow night. They're all going on holiday. The house will be empty. I'll get in with my skeleton keys – I had a look at the lock on the back door. I always check out people's security – just a strange habit of mine.'

'I'm coming too.' She moves off again without checking her mirrors and at the end of the road, she nearly fails to pull up at a red light. We come to an abrupt halt.

'No. It's too dangerous.'

'I'll be your lookout person. Don't argue. It's settled.' She puts her foot down and we peel away from the car beside us with ease.

Chapter 35
Diane

All I want to do is curl up and sob my heart out, but I'd suffocate if I let myself go. Every moment is a fight not to break down. I can't go on like this. I'm beaten. Beaten and crushed, thinking only the worst. I'm just waiting here to die, aren't I? He's going to return and finish what he's started. Surely, there's no other way for him. I was a witness and I would bring him down.

Part of me wants it all to be over. An overdose of sedatives? A point-blank bullet to my head? Please let it be quick. I hate to admit it, but it's true. I'm sorry, Harper, I know I'm letting you down. I'm usually the optimistic one — full of determination, but I'm losing the will to keep going. I want the hoping and daydreaming to stop, because all they do is remind me of what I've lost.

I've made so many plans to get out of here. I run through them in my head, but they're all futile. I'm strong by nature — my legs and arms are thick with muscle, but with my injuries and the medication I'm way under par. I've been too weak so far to fight back.

There's a dull ache in my belly and think again of the baby we lost. I could never know, but I'm convinced it was a girl. I spend time in this endless cavity of darkness, thinking of what we would have called her. I've always loved the name Marianka or Florence — and I run little fantasies about what she would have been like.

She would have been pretty, I'm certain, with your dreamy eyes, the colour of roast chestnuts, and your sharp mind. She would have been fearless and intrepid. Like Clara.

My thoughts tug me back to her. She was so innocent, standing there holding a toy rabbit, when I caught him with you at the Anderson shelter. She looked pretty; her hair tied back under an Alice band, little butterflies on her dress. I shouldn't have retreated when he came at me. I should have got past him somehow and rushed inside to grab her. But then what? He might have beaten both of us to a pulp with the huge branch he swung in his hands.

Is she with her mother? Is she well away from him? If I am ever to get out of here that's the first thing I'll do – find her and check she's safe. She's the one everyone needs to be concerned about. Then I'll report him and make sure he pays for his despicable acts.

The first time I met Clara was in the village. I was surprised to see her on her own and asked where her mother was.

'Mummy is lying flat, like an ironing board,' she said.

'Is she okay?'

'Oh, yes. Well – sort of. She's like that nearly every day. She's got cancer and it's pulled out her hair. She lies down because the cancer gets inside her body and steals the food, so she has no energy.'

'Right.' I walked with her towards the green. She had a wicker basket and told me she was going to the village shop to buy eggs.

'Is there anyone else to look after you?' As soon as I said it, I remembered about her father.

'Oh – lots of people. Helen at the library. Lorna and Tessa who usually sit with babies, but also sit with me at bedtime. Then there's Gaggy – my gran – she comes over a lot.'

'No brothers or sisters?'

'I don't want any,' she said disparagingly.

We came to a wooden telegraph pole and Clara looked up. 'Down by the river, the grass is as high as the lines across the sky.'

I didn't follow her. 'What lines across the sky?'

'Where the birds sit.'

'Oh – the telegraph wires.' I looked up too, but I wasn't sure what she was getting at. 'But the grass is short – it's down here.' I pointed to the blades, three or four inches high beside our feet. 'It isn't that tall,' I said.

'It is – when you lie on the floor and look up at the sky – the grass is the same size as the telly-path wires.'

'Ah – I see what you mean – that's called perspective. It's because you're looking up from right down close to the earth.'

'I was being a mouse.'

'Right.'

'Mummy says I can be a mouse sometimes, as long as I'm a quiet one.'

I laughed and she skipped and took my hand.

For a few moments, it's as though I feel those golden rays on my face as I blink into the sun. Our daughter would have been just like her: bold, funny, precocious. Then I'm back here and she's out there somewhere, being preyed on by that bastard.

My mind wanders off like this all the time now. Down little alleyways into weird thoughts, slivers of memory, fantasies and half dreams. I might be going mad, but I have no way of knowing. Is today the day he doesn't come back? Have I eaten my last pile of porridge? Had my last drop of water? Is this it? Has he left me to die?

In spite of the sweaty heat, I shiver. I want to go home. I've had enough.

Chapter 36
Harper

19 August – 20th day missing

It's two o'clock in the morning and we pull out into the deserted lane away from the cottage. I open the car window and will the balmy night breeze to take the edge off my jitters. I meant to stay awake, but I fell asleep on the sofa a few hours ago. I woke with a jolt, thirsty and sweating, breaking a fretful dream.

'You look like shit,' Tara kindly points out as we turn left towards Cosham.

I pull my fingers through my hair. 'Thanks. Shall we change the subject?'

She asks if I've spoken to Marion about Clara's final words to me.

'She agreed with us,' I tell her, 'she thinks the "Wizard of Oz" must be someone Clara's met at the hospital, who knew she made regular visits and wasn't always at her mother's side...' I stare at the pools of light on the road made by our headlamps. 'Marion feels terrible about it – blaming herself.'

'Poor woman – it's not her fault, she's been too ill.' She glances over at me and I know what she's going to ask. 'In your experience with the police, how likely is it that Clara...?'

'It's a week since she was last seen. The odds are not good for a seven-year-old child, but we can't give up.'

'Of course not.' She takes her eyes off the road again to pat my knee. 'For a fully grown woman, things are different,' she insists, squeezing my hand before putting hers back on the wheel.

Tara parks in the church car park and we walk the five hundred metres from there to Morrell's house. We keep our heads down, but she slips her arm through mine, so we'll look like a couple coming home from a party. There's no one about; it's the secluded and up-market part of town.

We don't hesitate at the gate, going straight in as if we have every right to be here. People tend to notice unusual behaviour – and if you belong somewhere, it's not normal to start looking behind you, loitering, looking up at windows or appearing indecisive. Everything seems still at the front of the house and there are no signs of a burglar alarm – I don't remember a control box in the hall. I check the garage as we pass – the car has gone and there are no lights on in the properties across the road.

I slip on my thin gloves as we reach the side gate. It is bolted as well as locked, but there's room to slide my hand underneath to slip the bolt across. I'd logged these details with my 'criminology consciousness' when we were here before, but I still can't believe I'm doing this – actually breaking in to someone's house.

We're in the shadows now and I stand on an upturned plant pot to undo the top one, then use my 'open-sesame' keys to get into the patio area. Tara stays the other side of the gate. She's hidden from the road, eagerly watching for any sign we've been spotted. I freeze as I hear a car approaching, but the sound fades into the distance.

The conservatory is equally simple to open up with my special keys and within seconds I'm inside the kitchen. I climb the stairs and, one by one, open the closed doors and search inside using my pencil torch. This time I root around carefully through Gillian's belongings: her drawers, bedside cabinet, packages and shoeboxes. I'm also drawn back to Stephen's appointment diary on his bedside cabinet. During my snoop last time, I noticed an entry marked 'QE' for 11am on August 8th. It occurred to me afterwards that 'QE' could mean the Queen Elizabeth Hospital. I take out my phone and take photos of the earlier pages for August and all those in June and July.

I move on and find what I'm really looking for in a make-up bag on the dressing table. It's hidden inside packaging for stomach antacids. I'd spot them anywhere – the manufacturers revised their formula so they are easier to detect, following cases of drink spiking. The capsules have a green coating with a strong blue dye – but in a blue cocktail, of course, it's flavourless and invisible. I bet those mocktails not only had vodka in them, but a dose of Rohypnol, a classic date-rape drug, too. No wonder you were ill, Dee.

My vision blurs as rage escalates to a silent roar inside my head. *What did they do to you?*

Everything in the room starts to look muddy; the bed, the carpet, the dressing table are blending into each other. *No – stay calm.* I have to keep a grip. I tell myself to be professional and finish the job. I splash water on my face in the bathroom and start again. I need evidence that they've used the drug recreationally, so I make another search, checking the study, the filing cabinet, a briefcase. All I find is a photo album, stuffed with shot after shot of what look like beautiful barely clad models – on beaches, by swimming pools, at parties. In half of them, Gillian has her arm around the women – in the other half, Stephen Morrell is getting up close and personal.

Gillian wasn't just Stephen's alibi, I conclude, she was involved in the actual crime. She lied. She said the taxi dropped her off first and then you went on home. But both of you must have got out at the Morrell's. You were probably too drugged to know where you were, Dee. She might even have tipped the driver a bit extra to back up her lie – but I wouldn't be able to prove it.

My hands shake violently as I go back and snatch the make-up bag, then put it back where it was. What I've done is futile and against the law. The Morrell's are smart; Rohypnol is a class C drug and while unauthorised possession is breaking the law, it's also available legally on private prescription. There is a sticker on the back of the packet showing they were issued by a local pharmacy. It means Gillian has a legitimate private prescription, most likely for insomnia. I'm an expert in evidence and I know this won't hold up in court. The only person likely to get arrested here is me.

I leave everything exactly as it was and close the doors. Tara is waiting by the side gate and knows not to say anything until we're in the clear. I put the plant pot back, upright, on the soil and check again that nothing is out of place. We shut the front gate carefully as we leave and walk at an unhurried pace back towards the car, arm in arm again.

'You found something?' she whispers as we cross the road by the post box.

'I know what they did to Diane that night.' I explain about finding the capsules. 'Within about ten minutes the amnesia would have set in and after about half an hour, Diane would have been heavily sedated.'

'The bastards!' We round the corner of the church car park.

I'm choked with grief and vehemence; my words tumble out like a growl. 'If I discover that scum of the earth isn't in Monaco, I'm going to rip his slimy body to pieces to find out what actually happened.'

'But you found the evidence – we've got them!'

'It's not enough. Gillian has a legitimate prescription and there's no other reason for either of them to be investigated. Elaine didn't witness anything untoward at the party. It was all executed very carefully. Anyone seeing them would think Gillian was taking her home. Dee isn't even here to go to the police.'

My body is heavy as I sink into the passenger seat. Tara pulls out onto the main road.

'Right now, what I know is worse than useless, because I can't prove a thing.'

The grumbling sound of the engine hangs between us for a while.

'The party happened weeks before she went missing,'

Tara says eventually. 'Is it related?'

'That's the bit I can't work out.' I slump down, feeling numb.

'Do you think Morrell was concerned about a paternity test? Could he have known you had one?'

'If he had, he would have stepped in sooner, surely.'

'What about the results you got?'

'They can't help us. The lab team at the hospital were clear that the foetus would be cremated and they wouldn't be able to make any other DNA comparisons after mine.' My voice is strung tight with exasperation. 'And the Morrell's have an alibi for the night Dee disappeared, remember?'

'That blows that, then.' She taps her nails on the steering wheel. 'It's the last thing you'd think of, seeing Gillian – she seems so classy and proper.'

'The perfect cover.'

Tara sighs. 'She might be going along with it to please her husband – some women do, don't they? Put up with things to keep the marriage going.'

'Or maybe her sexual tastes lean that way too. You never know what couples get up to behind closed doors.' A police car passes us and I'm relieved Tara is driving within the speed limit for once. 'What it does mean is that Dee is innocent. She didn't knowingly sleep with anyone.' My voice breaks. 'She was telling the truth. She was raped and she didn't even know it.'

There is little comfort – right now – in this knowledge. I know I will be forever haunted by my guilt for doubting you.

*

There is a sharp bang at the door at first light. I feel like I've only just got into bed. I race downstairs wearing only my boxer shorts with one thought on my mind. *They've found you!*

It's the sergeant who came before to record your disappearance; Sgt Howis and another officer I remember, PC Mole.

'Dr Penn...' Howis growls.

'Yes.' This doesn't sound good.

'We'd like you to come down to the station with us, sir.'

'Why? Is it Diane? What have you found?'

'We need to ask you some questions, sir. If you could come with us.' I hadn't noticed before how intimidating Howis is. He has a pudgy face with overhanging jowls beneath tight lips that don't know how to smile.

All I could think of was my unauthorised visit to the Morrell's house. We must have been seen. Has Tara been identified and hauled into the police station, too?

'Let me put some clothes on,' I protest. The younger officer follows me upstairs and waits by the door as I slip on a pair of chinos and a polo shirt. I squint at the clock; it's not even 7am.

I pick up my phone and remember the shots I took of Morrell's appointment diary. I've been preoccupied with finding the Rohypnol and haven't looked at them yet. The officer is talking on his radio, so I slip behind the door, briefly out of sight. I haven't got long. I swiftly flick through them looking for more 'QE' entries. There are five of them altogether, and I know for certain that the final entry, August 11th, was the same date Clara was last seen at the hospital. Morrell was there too. Fancy that – he's been making regular visits. I conjure up the CCTV footage in my mind and try to imagine whether the figure of the man with the apple in his pocket could have been Morrell. It's certainly possible.

There's a tap on the door and the officer is keen to get moving.

Not now. I need to follow this up. Another officer joins us and takes my arm. I have no choice.

Once I get to the station I'm taken through to an interview room, passing faces I know in my usual role as criminologist. They look up, smile gingerly and look away as I walk past: Krishnan, one of the lads I see at the gym, Roland and Johnny Mack. I've asked for my old friend, Martin Hackett, to attend as my solicitor, knowing this is going to be rather embarrassing. Neil and Paul are probably here, too, but I won't be allowed to speak to them, it's a conflict of interest.

Martin arrives, out of breath and oily from a fresh shave. In his rush to leave the house, he's splashed on too much aftershave. We are allowed a few minutes on our own and he explains it's about my car. They've found it. He doesn't mention the Morrell's place – this isn't about that.

Two detectives join us – Neil's colleague, DS Mick Tolland and DC Susie Reichs, who is going to take notes. Martin clears his throat and straightens his jacket. DS Tolland switches on the tape and recites the usual caution. He looks mild mannered and clean cut and I could imagine being friends with him in another situation. DC Reichs looks new and eager to get scalps under her belt. She has cropped dark hair and small eyes that dart from my feet to the top of my head, taking everything in. Her voice is brittle with the effrontery of youth; she's decided I'm guilty of whatever it is, already. They start by asking for basic details like the date you went missing and when I last saw you.

'What's the registration number of your car, Dr Penn?'

I reel it off for them.

'And when did you last drive it?'

I have to think. 'Several hours before my wife went missing. I went out around lunchtime to get some vegetables from the market – the one in Horden.'

'Can you remember what belongings you had in the car?'

'Where did you find it?'

'If you could just answer the question, Dr Penn.'

'Er – there's not much. I rarely leave anything in there apart from perhaps a spare umbrella, a blanket and plastic bags for the supermarket.' I correct myself. 'But Diane was driving it – she was in it last, so she might have left something I don't know about.'

'Did you leave a pair of shoes in the car?'

'*My* shoes?'

'Yes.' DS Tolland is sitting back in the chair his arms folded. DC Reichs is poised with her pen, crouched low over the page.

'I don't...think so.'

DS Tolland produces a see-through evidence bag with a pair of brown brogues in it and places it between us on the table. 'Are these your shoes, Dr Penn?'

I know the answer, but to be doubly sure, I peer inside at the label and the size, recognising the way my heel has rubbed a V-shape at the back. 'Yes – these are mine.'

Chapter 37
Diane

I've been moved. I'm no longer in the stable. I don't know why, but I've been brought somewhere dark and stiflingly hot. There are no windows, only a hatch in the floor. It must be an attic, but where? Who knows I'm here?

It's worse than before. The air is thick with dust and I can't hear a single sound that belongs to the outside world. I have no way of differentiating night from day – it is one eternal black tunnel. I can't bear being without light – it's too much like being dead. I'm so disorientated, my mind has started to create shapes, colours and pictures to compensate – I can see how people go mad in situations like this. When will this incarceration end? What happens now? Is he waiting for something? Is he going to kill me or not?

The floor is hard and spiders make webs across my face. There are one or two bluebottles, buzzing incessantly – I can't be sure if they're real or inside my head. I'm only aware of disjointed chunks of time. I close my eyes and several hours seem to slip by. I blink and it feels like a new day, although I can't be certain, because the darkness continues. Every waking moment, I'm tormented by questions, so it's better to be asleep.

I've barely been aware of his visits. He's definitely putting something in the food, but I have to eat. He peels away my gag and pushes the dish of food under my mouth. Baked beans, soup, porridge. If I don't eat he takes it away and I've missed my chance.

I do as I'm told. It is the only way I can stay alive. I tried screaming one time, but he dropped the tray, slapped the gag back on and I was left without food for hours.

When I feel stronger, I'm going to try something different. I imagine the moment when he slides open the hatch and that's when I'll give his hands a hard kick with my feet. The problem is he's usually so quiet and I'm so drugged up that he steals up on me too quickly – every single time. I'm never ready. I can't keep my eyes open for more than a few minutes at a time.

It doesn't sound much of a plan – now I think of it – but it's the only one I've got. Even if I was primed, I might startle and bruise him, but it won't disable him. He'll probably withdraw food for a day to punish me, but at least I'll have tried. Unless I've tried it already. My mind is mush. I've been thinking about my plan so hard and so often that I wonder if I've already attempted it – and failed once again.

I have no other plan. Without any light, I can only feel my way around in a limited fashion, but it's hardly surprising that there's nothing here to attack him with. There's a water tank because I can hear it gurgling, and near-black shadows suggest a few crates. I've shuffled around on my backside, but haven't found anything but torn blankets and empty boxes. Nothing sharp.

With my hands tied together I can't use my fingers properly. I could tip the toilet bucket over him, but that would only make him furious. I've thought about the cutlery when the food arrives, but there is only ever a spoon and it's plastic. My limbs are all I've got. I've been spending most of my waking time trying to work them free, but the twine is tight. I only end up exhausted and frustrated – and make no headway at all.

Loneliness eats away at me from the inside. It takes all my strength with it and thinking of you, Harper, is a mixed blessing.

I desperately want you with me in my thoughts. I can hear your voice comforting me, telling me everything will be all right. I can feel your long fingers smoothing the hair away from my face, trailing down my neck. But a sound or smell around me breaks the spell and you're gone. A dark period of misery follows, every time. It feels like you've died — and inevitably I move on to mourning the loss of our unborn child. Those times send me into a savage despair it's getting harder to come back from.

There's a gangrenous green hole where my spirit used to be.

I think he might have broken me.

Chapter 38
Harper

19 August

The interview room is starting to feel smaller and hotter. DS Tolland leans back, his hands either side of the shoes. DC Reichs does the opposite; she leans forward ready to sweep in for the kill.

'Where are these shoes normally kept and when did you last see them?' Tolland asks.

'They would be kept in the cottage – either in the shoe rack at the front door or in the wardrobe.' I fight to stop my voice from quivering. I don't remember when I last saw them; I haven't needed them for work and I've been living in sandals or trainers since the end of term.

Tolland clears his throat and DC Reich sits up straight. Bad news is brewing.

'We found your car, Dr Penn – on a caravan site near Chichester. Do you have anything to say about that?'

'No – I mean, I had no idea...' Nowhere near Heathrow, then?

'Can you tell us why your shoes were on the floor behind the driver's seat?'

I don't know what to say. 'I don't understand it.'

DS Tolland draws a breath. 'What's more interesting is that they have your wife's blood on them.'

'Blood?' I stand up, but there's nowhere to go. I need somewhere with some air. Martin puts out his hand in a gentle but firm gesture. 'How much blood?' I ask, on the verge of panting, my hands flat on the table. Martin beckons me to sit down.

'We're not at liberty to say,' says Tolland, 'but you can see why it would raise a number of questions for us, Dr Penn.'

'I really don't know anything about this.' How did my shoes get in the car? What does this mean? The idea of your blood being found anywhere makes me want to rush out and start looking for you all over again. I throw a troubled frown at Martin. *What's going on?*

Martin isn't looking so self-assured any more. He straightens his tie as if that's going to help.

DS Tolland deals the blow. 'Given the circumstances of your wife's disappearance we're concerned that you may have harmed her, Dr Penn.'

My head is in my hands. 'No, no – absolutely not.'

'You had, after all, just found your wife was pregnant with another man's child – and she was leaving you.'

'No – that's not what happened. Diane was raped. I haven't got proof yet – but I will have.' I know I'm sounding earnest in a crazy way, rather than someone in possession of all the facts.

'You said your wife left in the car, but what if you were in the car with her and at some stage during the journey, where the roads are quiet, you got your wife to stop the car and you attacked her.'

'No – that's not what happened. I was at the cottage. I'd had too much to drink to get behind the wheel.' It was a feeble defence – it only made me sound irresponsible.

'Then you took your wife's body somewhere and left the car in a busy tourist spot where it wouldn't be noticed for several weeks.'

Everything in the room freezes. 'Oh my God – you've found her?' I launch to my feet again, cracking my knee against the table in the process.

'No…no, we haven't found her, Dr Penn.' DS Tolland assures me, allowing a touch of sympathy into his voice.

He gives me a few moments grace to settle down before resuming his persistent tone.

'You sent false texts and messages from her social media sites using her phone, then destroyed it. Then three days after she was last seen, you caught a train to Heathrow and used your wife's pin number at an ATM, making sure there was no CCTV to catch you.'

Martin finally steps in. 'This is pure supposition. Where's your evidence for this?'

'We have a warrant to search your property again, Dr Penn. This is being carried out as we speak.'

I hold out my hands. 'That's fine. I've nothing to hide.' I stab my fingers against my temples. 'I never leave shoes in the car. Ask anyone – I never do that.'

It's a stupid thing to say. Who would know that apart from you, Dee?

Tolland shrugs. 'Double bluff, perhaps. You're an expert at this game, Dr Penn.'

'But why would I be searching for Diane so frantically – calling on my mates in the force to help, if this is what I'd done?'

'Because that's what a caring husband would do. In any case – you seem to be spending most of your time looking for a young child.'

'She's missing too, from the *same* village – I think they're connected. They have to be.'

I'm taken to a cell after that. Martin sits with me for a while as we go over what I'm being accused of.

'What the hell is going on, Martin? How did my shoes get in the car?'

'It's all circumstantial,' he says, leaning forward, his elbows on his knees. I know enough about his body language to know he's perturbed.

'I've been set up,' I snap. 'Someone planted those shoes. The same person who sent the messages from my wife's phone and shifted the car.' I think about Morrell; what part does he play in all this?

'You're going to have to sit tight and wait until they've swept your house. Hold your nerve.'

'They won't find anything. There's nothing there!' I get up and sit down again.

'Good. Then you've just got to wait it out. They can only hold you for twenty-four hours without making an arrest.'

I stomp around in my cell, panic and fury bubbling up until I'm convinced it's going to overwhelm me. The car, parked on a caravan site. And the blood...your blood, Dee – what does it mean? Was it a simple scratch...as someone forced you into the car? Or is it far worse than that?

My head is burning, there's what feels like a flashing

light in my eyes; I'm certain I'm going to pass out at any moment. They think you're dead...of course, they do. Breathe...breathe... All I want to do is run, but I must stay in control, keep still...wait until this dreadful panic lifts.

It's 10am, but time no longer seems to be moving forward and I check my watch too often, thinking it must have stopped. I'm relieved when I see an hour has passed...then another. Gradually, my body is getting heavier, the air is thicker, everything is slowing down. I try my utmost to space out, imagining I'm in the chicken coop in the garden having one of my episodes where I gradually let everything go.

To my astonishment, it actually helps. Another hour goes by, then an officer comes in with a plastic tray. There's an egg sandwich and beside it, a cup of weak tea. I choke them down without tasting a thing. Mid-afternoon I'm granted a toilet break and afterwards I sit on the bench and think; about you, about Clara, the Morrells. That only starts to wind me up again, so I let my mind drift, start to wander inside my memories, catch moments from our history together, then go further back to my childhood. It is then, when a powerful new idea comes to me, out of the blue, about my father. I'm not sure where it comes from – maybe it's because I have only blank walls and a long stretch of time with no distractions, but I feel a major breakthrough taking place in my thinking.

Dee, you've always tried to convince me that I wasn't the reason my father left when I was a kid. I could never see it – never truly grasp that you were right and perhaps there was another reason he went. I'd always felt so pathetic around him, so second rate – it had to be my fault.

Suddenly, being here – all these hours to think – I can see everything differently. I know it wasn't because I was useless at football or inadequate as a son, was it? He'd stopped loving my mum and had found someone else. He made a choice to leave us as a family – I haven't been able to understand that – not until now. I didn't let him down; I was just a kid, growing up, trying my best. I'm not responsible. I can be angry with him for what he did, but I don't need to turn the anger in on myself any more. I don't need to get the anger tangled up with fear and shame and punishment.

I'm on my feet as these revelations hit me, but my brief elation gives way to despondency. I miss you more than ever. You should be here, hearing this.

Eventually, I sit down. All this can wait. I should be out there, now I know about the Morrells, the car, the blood… I need to focus on dealing with this mess I'm in. I need the police to stop wasting their time on me and find out what actually happened. I could be stuck in here until tomorrow morning, so the best thing I can do is to run through all the facts regarding the two disappearances – dispassionately. I flick through all my internal film footage and snapshots; I travel along the timelines for both incidents. I think about Dr Pike and Dr Norman; is he taking advantage of the fact that she treats a steady stream of children? And how many people had access to hospital records to find out the dates of Marion and Clara's appointments?

And you? The car was found locally, Chichester is only a few miles away – so maybe the passport and the visit to the cash machine at Heathrow were meant to throw us off the scent. You could be right here under our noses. I think again about Morrell, but he has an alibi for the time you went missing, and he's definitely gone abroad – I checked with the neighbours and rang the hotel in Monaco. I even consider Victor – he's living in the area unexpectedly and blabbed, not long ago, that he has the hots for you, Dee – has he overstepped the mark again?

As it happens, I'm held for twenty-three hours and forty-seven minutes, but I have used my time wisely. I'm released on the basis of good character and no previous offences. Tolland tells me to stay in the area and keep my nose out of the case.

'Don't worry – I'm not going anywhere,' I say, reassuring him about his first point, at least.

I'm re-energised, but it's not simply about getting my freedom back. Nor is it following my mind-blowing epiphany. During my long wait, I've remembered a vital piece of the jigsaw and it changes everything.

As soon as I'm outside, I call Tara.

'Where've you been? I've been trying to call you.'

'I'll tell you when I see you. Listen – I've got something. I think I know what was in the pocket of the guy in the foyer around the time Clara was last seen. I'm pretty sure it wasn't an apple, but I think I know what it could be. It's all in the detail.'

'What? Tell me.'

'I can't. Not yet. Not until I'm sure. Anyway, as it stands, it's purely circumstantial. We need more.'

'What do you want me to do?'

'Meet me at the hospital as soon as you can.'

Twenty minutes later, I watch Tara's red mini swoop into the car park and she leaves it, in her customary fashion, at an angle crossing the bay markings. Either she doesn't notice or doesn't care. I join her as she's aiming the key fob at it, waiting for the locks to clunk into place. Together, we begin scouring the hospital car park, outhouses and peripheral buildings. Tara scuttles after me as we go from place to place.

'Haven't the police gone over this whole area with a fine toothcomb – as the last place Clara was seen?'

'Yes, but I think our abductor may have moved her. It's one way of keeping a step ahead of the police. I think this guy is clever.'

'You know who it is?'

'I can't be sure yet, but I've got a pretty good idea.'

We cover all the external buildings, annoying several porters in the process.

'What about inside?' Tara suggests.

'There's too much risk involved in hiding a child within the main building. The chance of accidental discovery, by cleaning staff or maintenance workers, is too high. Stock rooms and broom cupboards – you never know when someone may need access.'

'So, now what?'

We're outside near the barrier by the parking booth. 'I'm not sure.'

I look up at the front façade; the relentless pattern of rectangular windows, anonymous and uniform. The sky is thick with charcoal clouds and thin shards of sunlight squeeze between them, bouncing against the glass. I slide my eyes from window to window, not really looking, instead thinking, remembering, letting my mind wander in order to crack open the answers. A movement catches my eye; a nurse is pulling the blinds down and my gaze freezes. I stray to the adjacent frame and notice a static shape in the stairwell; a figure. Only half of his body is visible, but I know he has spotted me. I step closer so I can see him better and his face melts into a half smile; smug and self-satisfied. He's been watching me and he knows I'm looking in the wrong place.

I stare at the window speculating on who will move first. I watch as he cracks his knuckles on each hand in turn, then turns to the stairs. I remember Clara asking me if I could do it – just before she went missing. She must have seen him do it, too. *In that simple act, he has given himself away.* I run through the relevant dates in my mind – everything is set into my brain by now. It adds up. I wasn't absolutely certain before, but now I am. Although once again, all the evidence I have is circumstantial and by the look on his face, he knows it.

I turn to Tara, who has been watching new casualties arrive at the ambulance bay. 'We need to go somewhere,' I tell her.

'You're really not going to tell me a thing, are you?' She stomps under the canopy as it starts spitting with rain.

'Can you drive – slowly – the back route to South

Wickham? Take the B2177 from Cosham High Street.'

'Why there?' We hurry back to the car as the rain develops into a battering deluge. 'We're looking for hiding places on the way,' I say as I snatch at the seatbelt. 'Old farm buildings, derelict properties, building sites – that sort of thing.'

'I hate to repeat myself, but haven't the police covered the whole area?' Tara points out.

'Like I said, Clara could have been moved.'

'Fine. If you give me the directions,' she says, dropping the map on my lap. 'I haven't got around to getting a Sat Nav for this old girl, yet.'

The rain is set in for good and I realise it's the first downpour since the day we lost the baby. It feels like it's been gathering in the sky for weeks, like tears, and has finally broken through. Tara's windscreen wipers are whizzing back and forth in a frantic race to catch up with each other. Water hurtles towards the gutters and within minutes puddles form in dips in the pavement, pot holes and at the roadside. Everything is on the move.

'You remember the DVD of *The Dark Crystal* I found at Clara's house?'

'Okay?'

'I knew I'd seen it before somewhere. And I've remembered. If I'm right, it will have the culprit's fingerprints all over it.' I punch the dashboard in triumph. 'That will finally be some real evidence.'

'I've no idea what or who you're talking about.'

'It doesn't matter. Let's find Clara.'

Chapter 39
Clara

Clara wakes up and finds herself in a new place. She's never been anywhere like it before – instead of a normal square, this room is round without any corners. It doesn't seem to belong inside a house either – there's no big marble 'n' around the fireplace; there are no comfy chairs. No sofas or lampstands. No wallpaper or paintings. There are blue tits and blackbirds outside; she knows what they sound like and can hear them chattering to each other. The branch of a tree scrapes the window, high up, when the wind blows. It's more like a tall, thin shed – but that makes it all the more interesting.

There is a plate on an upturned crate with tuna sandwiches and scones and a small carton of orange juice. On a rug on the floor is a dolls' house nearly as tall as she is – complete with two floors, an attic, tons of furniture and people inside having tea. Next to it is a set of farm animals, plastic trees, fences and tractors. Everything looks brand new, like a toy shop. Clara squeals – she can't believe her luck. Toys she's asked Santa for at Christmas and never got! For a second she thinks she might be in heaven. Her mother talks about it a lot. She says she might be going there herself soon and she's very pleased about it, because she says it's the best place you could ever imagine.

Beneath her is a patchwork of square padded seats taken from chairs, blankets and soft cushions. Behind her, stacks of round wooden shapes are leaning against the wall; they look to Clara like the workings of a clock. The shapes have nicks in the edges like teeth. 'I'm Alice in Wonderland,' she says out loud. 'Look at the big wheels. I'm inside Granddad's watch!'

She helps herself to an apricot, a bag of crisps and five chewy snakes left on a floppy beanbag, before losing herself in the dolls' house. The tiny sign on the door of the first room says 'drawing room', but she can't see anyone with crayons. She puts two small people and a dog into that room, with a baby's cradle and a tray of cupcakes. She designs a little story around them and another and another. When all the rooms have been visited, she turns to the farm. She builds a wall in the shape of a circle with plastic pieces that join together and puts a gate in the front. Inside the circle she puts horses and a boy with a saddle. In the space of half an hour, he learns to ride, jump over hedges and groom the pony's tail.

Eventually, the birdsong stops altogether and the world outside settles into silence. Clara runs out of steam under a gluey fog of tiredness.

It is then she realises that she doesn't know what time it is or how long she's been there. Her mother will be wondering where she is. She can't even remember how she got into the place to start with. It's like she was magicked there. She looks up at the tiny window. It's too high and small to see out of, but the colour outside has changed from blue to grey to black. Clara knows that means it's late. There is a single light bulb swinging from a beam in the ceiling keeping everything inside from being night. 'Mummy will be cross if I'm out too late,' she mutters.

It is time to go. But she'd love to come back later.

Clara goes over to the door and turns the handle. It's stuck. She rattles it and pulls and pushes, but it's jammed.

All of a sudden she wants to be at home. She's enjoyed playing farms and making up stories about the people in the dolls' house moving into their new house. She's liked the food and hiding away in this secret place – wherever it is – but it's time to go. She wants to feel the softness of her mother's apron, breathe in the café smell of baked beans on toast, let the taste of hot butter melt on her tongue. It seems a while since she's seen her mother and Clara knows she'll be worried. 'But it's not my fault,' she says, pulling at the doorknob again. The brass fastening judders and moves a tiny bit, but the door itself stays solid and firmly in place. This isn't right. How did she get in here? The moment is misty. It's like she woke up here a long time ago.

She looks around the walls for another way in or out; a broken panel, a tumble of bricks – some entrance that no one knows about, but that she'd manage to squeeze through – like she always did. She can't find any such gaps; the walls are all flat and smooth.

Then she remembers something. It makes her feel cold and sick. It makes the back of her knees go juicy and her palms damp like boiling flannels. She thought he was a wizard – he said he was. The Wizard of Oz – the kind magician who grants wishes – but he turned out to be nothing but the big bad wolf.

'My,' Clara says, picking up a pretend basket and pointing her toes. 'What big ears you have, Grandma…'

'All the better to hear you with, my child,' she continues in a snarly voice, playing both parts.

'Grandma, what big eyes you have!'

'All the better to see you with, my dearest.'

Clara makes her voice rise up high. 'Goodness me – just look at those large hands!'

'All the better to hug you with, my little one.'

'Oh, that mouth, Grandma. What big, spikey, ENORMOUS teeth you have!'

'All the better to EAT you with!'

Clara stops there. She doesn't want to think about what happened next. The wolf said it was a secret. He said if she told anyone, if she dared to breathe a word of what he did, he'd make sure her mother didn't get well. He said he would put poison in the medicine she took. All Clara had to do was keep the secret and not tell anyone about him.

The wolf tricked her and Clara hates him. More than once he has taken her to hidden places or told her to wait for him in the woods. She doesn't want her mother to get worse and die, so she has to do what he says. But she hopes he gets chopped into little pieces by the man who cuts down trees in the forest – just like in the story.

She thinks about the toys and the food instead. Everything has been left here. By the wolf? She'll have to wait for him to come back. She likes adventures in new hiding places and she's brave, but when she thinks about the wolf, her knees turn into jelly trifle.

She pulls a cushion against the wall and sits with her knees up. She can't get comfy, so, pretending she's a bird, she makes a little nest using blankets and old sofa cushions. Clara wonders if she can get a message through to her mother by saying the words out loud while holding a picture of her mother in her mind. Will she hear it? She's never heard of such a thing, except there are things like telephones and radios and people talking inside the television, so it might work. She tries it anyway: 'Mummy, don't worry. I'm visiting Grandma in the forest with my basket of bread and wine and we're having a nice chat. I'll be home soon.'

Night-time pulls her eyelids shut like blinds, and shortly afterwards, she falls asleep.

Chapter 40
Harper

20 August – 21st day missing

The rain batters the roof of the car as we stop at traffic lights. Tara is losing patience. She wants to know who we're looking for, who the culprit is.

'If you know who it is, why don't we go to his house?'

'Not yet. Our abductor has thought this through. Clara won't be locked in a cellar or a shed; wherever she's hidden, it will be set up to look like an accident. He will have manufactured the scene – somewhere dangerous or unstable – so it looks like she crawled inside of her own accord.' I recall the smile twisting his face when I saw him at the window – he wasn't scared. 'Whatever he's done, it's going to look like the sad outcome of a curious little girl exploring a hidden, forbidden place.' I flick the next page of the map over so fiercely, I almost tear it out. I rile at myself. *Come on. Where would he hide her?*

I instruct Tara to pull off the B-roads onto back-roads and narrow tracks. We've already been out of the car to explore a tumbled-down church, an old ice-cream van, a lean-to and an abandoned tractor. Neither of us has an umbrella. Tara, at least, has a hood on the nylon cagoule she's pulled on that she happened to have in the car. Nevertheless, her hair hangs like short daggers, dripping down her cheeks. The rain is warm and would be refreshing if only we could stay out in it then get dry later. As it is, my feet are squelchy in my sandals, the car seats are soaked, the map is crinkling. Thunder rolls over from the east and I stop to wonder if Clara, wherever she may be, will find the rumbling scary or exhilarating.

We drive for miles, up and down small lanes, before taking off on foot across fields towards more abandoned buildings – barns, an old milking parlour, a petrol station, a hut.

On the way back to the car, Tara breaks the regular splosh of our footsteps with an unexpected statement. 'Diane told me you go and hide in the chicken hut in your garden sometimes.' She turns back to the last place we've been to indicate where the comment comes from.

'Did she?' I laugh, knowing that not long ago I would have done no such thing. Before my breakthrough in the prison cell the issue of retreating to the chicken coop had been a serious cause for concern – now it feels like something way back in my past. 'Did she tell you why?'

'Yeah. Sort of. She said it's because you've got anger issues. It's like a man-cave.' Unlike Alexa, Tara has a way of digging into my private life that makes me feel I'm in safe hands.

'Yes, it's true. But I had a bit of a revelation when I was arrested.'

She looks intrigued. 'What happened?'

'Dee has always tried to convince me that it wasn't my fault my father left when I was a kid.' She slips into step beside me and links her arm through mine. 'I knew what she meant, but I never really felt it *here*.' I tap my chest with my fist. 'The penny dropped while I was stewing for hours at the police station. Solitude makes you think! Somehow, I don't feel responsible for my dad leaving any more. It was *his* choice. I don't need to turn the anger in on myself now.'

'Wow – that's brilliant!' She claps her hands together. 'So – the visits to the chicken hut are numbered?'

'It's called a chicken *coop*.' I grin and she nudges me affectionately. 'We'll see,' I say. 'Probably not.'

'Dee will be pleased,' she says and with the mention of her name again, we fall quiet.

We take the road down to the south coast and pull up as close as we can get to a lighthouse I've spotted on the map. It looks like the Leaning Tower of Pisa, sitting on rocks, toppling towards the water. We clamber over chunks of turf that indicate there's been a recent landslide and hold up the barbed wire for each other to climb through. We ignore the notice which says that trespassers will be prosecuted and the council won't accept any responsibility for our injuries.

The front door is boarded up and broken scaffolding that once held up part of the side now hangs loose.

'Be careful,' I warn Tara. 'This looks like it could collapse any minute.'

We pull away the planks criss-crossed over the entrance and clamber inside. The walls are scaly and green with algae as if the seawater has climbed in and swirled all the way up to the top. An iron spiral staircase curls around a central hub, which forms the base for the huge lamps at the top. We go up the stairs, but are blocked by chunks of concrete and broken glass. It's narrow at that point and velvet lichen lapping across the slabs indicates that nothing has been moved for months. We return to the ground floor; there's nowhere to hide, the place is empty.

Replacing the planks as best we can, we take off along the shale and check under several upturned boats. Tara suggests the caves and we wander inside one small inlet in the rock, before I change my mind.

'Hang on – this is too accessible – it's out in the open. She'll be somewhere enclosed, where she can't be discovered. Let's get back in the car again.'

Chapter 41
Diane

I daren't close my eyes any more. When I shut them the noise fills my ears. It takes me a while to realise it's my own breathing filling my head. It doesn't feel right. It sounds like a ruptured engine – laboured and rasping; the sound of a creature that doesn't have long to live. That scares me more than anything. Life is oozing out of me and I feel like I'm crossing over – like the grim reaper is making his way towards me and I have nowhere to hide.

I can no longer tell if I'm asleep or awake – dead or alive. Every moment feels the same: empty, desolate, flooded in darkness. Where are you, Harper? Why don't you come for me? You're an expert at solving crimes – why haven't you worked out this one? Has everyone forgotten me? When death finally claims me, I will let him take me – he's already been inside my head for a while now, making himself at home.

There is silence – no breathing at all – then I catch up with snatches of air through my nostrils. I don't feel good. I'm shivering again – on the outside my skin is cold and wet, but on the inside I'm a furnace. I need a doctor. The back of my head is peeled raw where I've tossed it back and forth on the rough wood during my sleep. Is he poisoning me, now? Is that what this is? I've lost all the strength I had left for that one tiny moment when he might have been off-guard. It's too late now. I waited and waited, but time has run out.

Behind my eyes it is thick and black — a barren night sky without any stars. My feet are numb, as though they are already lost to me. I am slowly sinking — gradually slipping inside a grave. Slumping, sliding, going under... You're not coming are you, Harper? I'm not going to get the chance to say goodbye.

Chapter 42
Clara

Clara wakes up. She can tell she's been in the same place a long time. All the food is gone. She tips up the carton of juice – two drops fall on her tongue. She's thoroughly miserable now and her cheeks are raw with crying. She shouts out. Calls for her mother. Silence creeps around her like a deadly gas. More than anything she wants to go home. This isn't fun anymore. She shakes the door handle again. She wants the game to stop.

She has no energy, is parched and listless. Her mouth feels like the floor of a rabbit hutch. It's like her throat is a fist, gradually closing up altogether and giving her a little whistling sound as she breathes. She's had a headache for as long as she can remember, and she's dizzy and disoriented when she moves. Having to pee in the corner makes her feel dirty.

Clara sleeps, wakes a while, then drifts away again. Her limbs feel like they have weights on them. It's been dark, then light, then dark again, but she has no real sense of the passing of time. She's lost a part of herself; the part that puts ideas in her mind one after the other. Her head doesn't feel like it belongs to her any more.

She's too tired to reach out for the carton of juice to check if there's anything left. She knows there won't be a drop, but sometimes magic happens.

There's a click at the door. She's lying on the cushions in the centre of the room. Even if she wanted to, she couldn't move. She can barely open one eye.

She sees him filling the hole at the doorway. The wolf.

He stares at her, doesn't say a word. There's no tray with cakes and lemonade. He doesn't do that anymore. He just watches her for a few moments. There are a bundle of black bin bags under his arm and he starts tipping the toys and games inside. It's as though it's all over. Then she hears the door close and the bolt clicks back into place.

Chapter 43
Harper

20 August

'How far are we going?' says Tara, handing me the dregs of a bag of salt and vinegar crisps. We've covered another ten miles, stopping every time we spot anywhere that looks unoccupied. 'Shouldn't we just go to this bloke's house and see what we can find. You could use your dodgy keys.'

I consider it. 'Let's give it another half an hour, then we'll get some lunch and regroup.'

Tara gives me a tight smile and we carry on across the next T-junction.

'It says on the map, there's a windmill on the right, but I can't see it.' I look at the page, then into the distance again. 'Take a right here.' I'm late giving the instructions and Tara tuts as she grazes the muddy verge.

'Sorry,' I mutter.

I follow the map, taking us down a steep, overgrown track that looks like it's a dead end. We brought several bottles of water with us in the hope of finding Clara, and I tuck one into my pocket before we pull up outside a farm gate and carry on, on foot. It's stopped raining, but that's no comfort, because it looks like it will start again any moment.

Behind thick trees, there's a clearing with piles of bricks to one side and a dilapidated windmill in the centre. There are no sails left, just a stone cone with small square windows, like buttons, up the front. On the door is a red sign: *Dangerous Building – Do Not Enter.* It's locked. I fish around in my pockets for my set of skeleton keys; they haven't let me down yet.

The ground floor is a mess, with a grindstone lying abandoned to one side of the central spindle shaft and another in pieces on top of it. There are torn sacks, ladders with rungs missing, smashed barrels and planks of wood that are black with fire. It looks as if the place has been ransacked. I take the lead, up the narrow flight of wooden steps to the first floor. Wooden cogwheels are strewn about the place and the rickety floor creaks under our weight. There's nowhere to hide here and no sign of recent habitation. There's one more floor to go; the steps are steep and I tell Tara to stay where she is. When I get to the next landing, there's a narrow platform and a door. It's locked. Outside are three wheelbarrows stacked with blocks of rubble. I try a couple of keys until I find the best fit and push the door open.

I take a moment to adjust to the difference in décor. It's as if I've stepped into a completely different building – apart from old cogwheels leaning against the wall, the place is like an abandoned playroom. It's been dusted and painted and there are a handful of toy cars and dolls lying on a rug on the floor, a rocking horse and piles of cushions. I take a step inside and see her curled into a foetal position, her socks rolled down, her hair covering her face.

'Clara, Clara! Sweetheart – are you okay?'

Tara hears me call out and rushes up the steps to join me, her hand over her mouth. The place reeks of urine. I crouch on the floor next to the inert figure.

'Oh, God...' Tara is pressing her hand against her chest. 'Are we too late?' she whispers. She kneels down and strokes Clara's hair tenderly.

'She's got a faint pulse,' I say. 'She's been left here for days.'

Clara opens her eyes. She bursts into tears and holds on to me with trembling fingers. Her dress is torn and grubby and she's no longer wearing her Alice band to hold back her hair.

I pull out the water bottle. 'Here, sweetheart – have something to drink.' I hold it for her as she takes small sips and I glance over her body to check whether she's obviously injured. A few scratches and bruises – nothing more serious than a little girl her age would have – but I know other examinations will have to follow at the hospital. Clara blinks and comes round, staring at her surroundings as if she hasn't seen them before. 'If she hasn't had fluids for a while she might have low blood pressure,' I whisper to Tara.

'Are you hurt, Clara?' I turn her face so she's looking at me. 'Clara?'

She shakes her head. 'Hungry,' she croaks, rubbing her belly.

I know that in cases of dehydration and starvation, small sips of water mixed with glucose are all that should be given, at regular intervals. I give her more water, holding her heavy head. 'When the ambulance gets here

– they'll have something nice for you,' I assure her. 'It won't be long.'

Tara calls emergency services while I phone Marion.

It rings and rings until finally she answers. My words are bursting to come out – how much I've longed to utter them: 'I've got her! We've found Clara!'

There's nothing comprehensible in response, simply a whimpering at the other end. I pass the phone to Clara. She's brightening up remarkably since seeing a friendly face and drinking a few sips of water. I marvel at her resilience.

'It would have been better if Frank found me,' Clara tells Marion, 'but Harper will do.'

I turn to Tara. 'I wanted to find her so much. It's like I've found my own flesh and blood.'

Tara informs me that the ambulance will pick up Marion on the way, so when Clara hands back the phone, I tell her we'll see her in a few minutes. I lift Clara's slight and defenceless little body, carrying her as though she might break into pieces in my arms. Nothing appears to be broken on the outside, but inside? I dread to think what he might have done to her. I manage to get her as far as the car before I break down. I set her down on the back seat and weep silently in great body-surges, as she reaches out and holds onto my legs. I try not to let her see me – but she does, of course.

'It's okay, Harper,' she remarks. 'I didn't mean it about Frank. I'm glad it was *you* – really – who came to get me.' She climbs back out of the car and is unsteady on her feet, holding on to the passenger door. I pick her up and she puts her arms around me. I'm deeply touched by her faith in me given what another man has done to her. She pulls something out of her pocket.

'Look – I didn't lose it.' It's the butterfly key-ring I gave her. It makes me weep even more. 'You mustn't cry,' she says, 'or you'll run out of tears and there won't be any left for next time.'

Her words make me laugh and I put her down. She sits on the edge of the back seat, her thumb in her mouth. I'm still in the throes of my meltdown, leaning against the car, my arms outstretched as if I'm being sick. 'You okay?' Tara asks, softly.

'I'm sorry…it's just…' She puts her arms around me. 'I know. You've got an amazing result. But there's still someone missing.'

'I don't care if Dee is with someone else. I just want her to be alive.'

As I coax Clara under the blanket while we wait for the ambulance, I catch sight of a sparkling object sliding down her arm. My heart is in my mouth. 'Where did you get this, Clara? Who gave you this?'

She twirls the bracelet around distastefully. 'The wolf gave me it. I don't want it, but I can't get it off.'

I kneel down to her level on the wet grass. 'Do you remember the lady you saw in the bell tower – the one smiling in all the posters around the village?'

She nods warily.

'Do you know where she is? Have you seen her?'

'No.' She scratches her leg. 'She was crying. She looked sad. But that was a long time ago.'

'Have you seen her since then?'

'No.'

353

'Can you remember where you've been – in the last few days, before the wolf brought you to play here, in the windmill?'

'I was in a shed for the horses on a farm – then the wolf put me into a dark place with no windows and lots of wooden triangles.'

'Triangles?'

'Over my head,' she adds.

'With wooden floors?'

'Yes – and a tin box in the corner that sounded like a toilet.'

'A water tank.' I turn to Tara. 'She was in an attic.'

Chapter 44

'I don't agree with your tactics mate – you should have kept me informed – but, bloody good result.' DI Neil Fry pats me on the shoulder as soon as he steps out of the unmarked police car into the mud. PC Rose Felton, who was involved in Clara's rescue from the oubliette, is with him. An ambulance pulls up behind. I'm poised to give Neil a man-hug, but given the circumstances, stop and shake his hand instead.

'Has Clara told you anything?' he asks.

'No.'

'I think he left her there to die,' I say out of earshot of Tara's car.

Marion is being trundled over the thick grass in a wheelchair and Clara gets up to greet her. She's weak and wobbly and flops against her mother's legs. I pick her up so she can sit on her lap. 'I'm all right, Mummy. Some of it was fun.'

Marion clutches her daughter and looks up at me. 'Harper – I don't know what to say.' She squeezes her eyes shut. 'I can't thank you enough.' She kisses her daughter's matted hair with a loud moan of relief and reaches her bony hand out towards me. I grasp it.

'The police will want to get her checked over.' I squeeze her hand hard and she knows what I mean.

Bruises and scratches are most likely not the whole picture.

'Sorry to interrupt,' PC Felton says, holding a notebook and pen, but we will need to ask you and Ms Nørgaard some questions.' I see the bracelet on Clara's wrist again. I'm eager to get going. My job isn't finished yet – not by a long way.

Tara and I give a brief statement to police – I know there's no choice – and Neil radios in for a CSI team to go over the place. He'll speak to Clara, too, once she's feeling stronger and they've given her a full examination at the hospital.

I take Neil to one side and tell him where I think we need to go next.

'Fair enough,' he says. 'But, we're going to have to take the reins from now on, mate. No more maverick efforts.'

Neil and PC Felton pull up in their unmarked car and Tara and I park about ten metres behind. There's a car in the drive. Someone is at home. A 'For Sale' sign is strapped to the gate.

Neil instructs me to stay in the car, but as soon as they're out of sight, I get out and follow them. I hover behind a cherry tree, halfway along the drive, while they wait for response at the front door. They go round the back and when they don't return, I take it they've made a forced entry. I take the same path around the side and creep in through the open back door. There's glass on the back mat. Felton is checking downstairs while Neil takes the stairs.

I overhear Felton whispering into her radio, 'Five suitcases in the hall, sir, someone is taking a lot of stuff with them.'

The radio crackles and Neil is requesting another ambulance.

On hearing his request, I can't stand back any longer and I take the stairs two at a time. Neil is angry. 'I told you to wait in the car. You shouldn't be in here.'

'Arrest me,' I say defiantly, pushing past him on the landing. The ladders to the attic are pulled down and the hatch is half open; a leg is splayed across the gap, inert. Neil puts his hand out firmly to tell me to wait and goes up himself. I wait a couple of seconds and climb up, right behind him. Neil pulls himself inside and finds a light switch. The leg is covered in light grey wool – it belongs to a man.

'She's here,' Neil announces sounding grave.

Nothing can stop me now and he knows it.

I burst up through the hatch and see you, Dee, pale, still, lying next to Dr Swann, blood coming from your nose. Neither of you are moving.

I cradle your head, remembering Tara's earlier words when we found Clara: *Are we too late?*

Please, God, no.

I carefully cut your hands and feet lose with my Swiss Army Knife, grabbing your free wrist for a pulse. I'm so nervous – my fingers fluttering with electrical energy – that I can't tell if you're alive or not. I peel open your eyes, say your name, feel for a pulse in your neck. This can't be how it ends – in some dusty attic, lying side by side with a paedophile.

Dr Swann comes round.

Before Neil can stop me I punch Swann hard in the solar plexus, pushing him down through the hole.

'Leave it!' Neil shouts. Swann is left half clinging, half hanging against the ladders. He's not going anywhere of his own accord. Neil goes down after him and I hear PC Felton cuff him and read him his rights. He moans, but it doesn't sound like he is putting up any resistance.

I roll you onto your back and position my hands on your chest ready to perform CPR. As I straighten my arms and take a breath, there's a tiny sound from your throat. Did I imagine it? Your eyelids flutter and your head rolls to one side.

'Dee – it's me – Harper. I'm right here, darling. You're going to be fine. You're safe. He's gone.'

You open your eyes and try to sit up, disoriented, squinting with the light. I hold out a fresh water bottle and you snatch it greedily, but start coughing and spluttering almost immediately. Then you see me and everything stops and simultaneously everything in my life starts again – after three weeks of pure torture and misery. You let me fold your limp body into mine and I hear you gently moan in my ear. It's the sweetest sound in the world.

'Have you got any broken bones?' I ask.

'Ribs maybe, I don't know...' Your voice is dry and papery. 'Oh, Dibs, it's so good to see you. I thought...'

'I know. It's over. You're safe.' I stroke your face, your hair. I want to wrap all of you against me and never let you go.

Neil has been watching silently from the hole in the

hatch. 'Let's get her down,' he says.

You wince as I put my arm under your shoulder. I know this is going to hurt. I can see from the look of you that you're injured; not just your bloody nose, there are fiery red bruises on your bare arms.

'We'll be as careful as we can.'

We get you down the ladders and I carry you in my arms to the front door. Swann has already been taken away in a police car. Tara is waiting outside beside the ambulance; she rushes forward with more water.

In daylight I barely recognise you. Emaciated, unwashed, your lips crusty and brown, your skin grey with dust. Yet, you are the most beautiful creature in the world.

You jerk suddenly as if you've been kicked. 'The little girl, Clara,' you cry out, 'we must hurry...'

'We've got her – just found her. She's safe.'

'Thank God.' Your relief turns into distress instantly as you press your palm into your hairline. 'There's something you should know...'

I nod. 'They'll check Clara over...at the hospital.' I can't bring myself to think about what depraved games Swann made her play. I slide you onto the stretcher and the paramedics cover you with a blanket.

'How did you know where to come?' Tara asks me.

'Once Clara mentioned a place that sounded like an attic, I knew Swann's own home had to be worth a try. I managed to persuade Clive to get me the addresses of hospital staff that day he let us see the CCTV footage. In fact, in my mind Clive was a suspect himself at the time, but I moved him down the list, because he was so helpful.'

As the paramedics wheel you inside the ambulance, you call out, tossing your head from side to side. 'I saw him with her in the woods near the cottage...' Your voice is trembling with fever.

I climb in after you and grab your hand. 'It's okay. You can tell us everything later when you're feeling stronger.'

Chapter 45

Two weeks later

Tara arrives exactly on time, as usual. She swings past me into the kitchen with two carrier bags and drops them in front of the fridge. Leeks, parsley leaves and two bottles of wine are poking out of the top. She's going to a lot of trouble again and I tell her I think she's amazing.

'You've done so much,' I say, squeezing her shoulder.

Tara has been vacuuming, doing the laundry, ironing, bringing books for you to read and shopping for us, while you have been recuperating.

'I didn't want you to have to leave Dee's side,' Tara told me, as she appeared with another boot-load of provisions, the day before yesterday.

'You don't have to come and cook for us, as well,' I protested.

'I insist. Anyway, I don't know what you're like in the kitchen, Harper, but Dee is terrible and you both need a decent meal inside you.'

'Amen to that,' you called from the sofa.

'Actually, I'm very good,' I retorted. 'I'll have to show you one day.'

The phone hasn't stopped ringing with friends, neighbours, colleagues, delighted to know you're safe and Alexa has been over several times, of course. She's made a point of saying as little to me as possible. I realise now that it was jealousy that made her say the things she said after you disappeared. She made me believe she knew more than she actually did, though, and I'll never forgive her for that.

You spent two days in hospital, before I had the joy of bringing you home. The fireplace is still spewing bricks, the builders can't come now until October, and there's further subsidence in the kitchen, but I don't care, because my life is whole again.

We made love for the first time the night you were discharged. Swann was only interested in children – the nasty sod – he hadn't touched you, but still, after your ordeal, I was gentle and tender and waited for you to initiate. I washed you as you lay on the bed and carefully dried every inch of your body. Then I laid naked next to you and gently stroked your skin with perfumed moisturiser. You were still recovering, so I was slow and measured. The doctors said you'd suffered internal bleeding, but, with your athletic constitution, you surprised them all with the way your body was healing itself. Despite falling around forty feet onto a rocky crag, you hadn't broken any bones, not even a rib.

You reached out to me on the bed and I curled myself around you. Making love was sublime and beautiful – I felt like it was our very first time and I was falling in love with you all over again. Afterwards, you wanted more and wouldn't let go of me. While we stayed entwined, I told you something important. I told you about the flash of new insight I'd had about my father.

'I've been targeting *myself* with the shame and

humiliation I felt towards him, Dee.' I stared into the distance. 'I didn't even realise that's what I was doing.' A beat passed. I wanted to tell you the whole thing. 'I never told you, but when my father tried to teach me football when I was little, he made me wear this heavy welder's mask. It was supposed to make me get a feel for the ball just using my feet, but I always ended up toppling over and it turned into a kind of humiliating punishment.'

You blew out your cheeks, sharing my mortification.

'That's where my anger came from; that's how it started. Sometimes, I felt rage so overwhelming I didn't know what to do with it. Hiding in the chicken coop seemed to be the only way I could calm down. I don't know why, but it became a ritual.'

'It's okay,' you whispered.

I pressed your fingers to my lips. 'I couldn't talk about it. I was so ashamed and confused – I didn't know where to start. I'm so sorry.'

'I can see how it's all bound up with your dad. Your unresolved grief and anger got mixed up together. You found an outlet for it…which was a bit…unusual, that's all. You understand it more now. We can work through it together.'

'That spell at the police station made me feel differently about Dad, somehow. I told Tara about it. I don't feel like it was my fault he left any more. It was his choice and I was only a kid. I didn't let him down.'

You curled your fingers around mine and sank your head on my shoulder. 'I'm so pleased, Dibs.'

I laughed. 'The penny dropped, at last.' I stroked your

shoulder, still marked with bruising. 'I had so much time when I was detained with nothing to distract me, so I ended up chewing things over. I thought about Clara, too. About how she seems so balanced about her father's death. Marion must have handled it so well, because Clara always speaks of him with warmth and acceptance, even though in the eyes of a child, he "left her". It made me think.' I kissed a small scratch near your nose. 'Everything feels different. When I think of getting angry now, the idea of stomping off to stew in an empty hut seems ridiculous. I don't think I need to do that anymore.'

'We'll see how it goes,' you said softly.

'Yes – I'll need to put it to the test, of course, but it feels like a thing of the past. And smashing vases and plant pots seems so…extreme now, too…so *juvenile*.'

'I think that could be the point – anger always seemed to take you back to your childhood.'

I sighed and thought of the glass I flung at the wall after Alexa accused me of killing you. It was only a few days ago, yet it seemed a lifetime. 'I don't want to get too ahead of myself, but I think I can find better ways of handling my anger.'

'And we can talk about it now. That's the big difference.'

'Yes. We can.' I cradled your face. 'I'll see someone,' I said, 'I'll make sure I sort this out, once and for all.'

Tara's meal – Mexican this time – is superb, as I knew it would be. You even have an extra helping.

'Got to build up my strength,' you say, patting your

stomach. I can't believe how well you're looking, after what happened. There is colour in your cheeks again and your hair has regained that raven gloss. You've arranged to have counselling too, which sounds like a sensible idea. Get everything out in the open.

Everyone in the village has been incredibly kind. We've had flowers and baskets left at the front door and Clara has been in and out to tell us what she's been doing. She's incredibly sparky after her ordeal; I'm in awe of her resilience. She hasn't mentioned Swann. Her sessions with Dr Pike are continuing and Marion says she's making progress, although Marion herself is spending more of her life either in a wheelchair or in bed. An incident like this must take its toll on those who have so few resources to draw on. You and I know we've been lucky.

Tara has a quick chat with me in the kitchen when you go to the bathroom. 'Has she mentioned Morrell? Does she know what happened after the party?'

'No,' I tell her in a hushed voice. 'One thing at a time. I'll tell her about the paternity test when I think she can cope with it. I'll let her know the rest after that.' I feel nausea rising at the back of my throat. 'What on earth makes a bloke want to rape a woman when she's unconscious is beyond me.'

Tara wraps the end of the tea towel around her middle finger. 'When I used to work in the clubs, we used to come across all kinds of pervy types. Ted Bundy apparently slept with women who were *dead* – I mean, can you imagine?' She shakes her head.

'It's probably all about power, isn't it?'

365

'And there's little threat of it being reported, because the victim isn't going to put up a fight.' She stops to think. 'And Gillian – does she watch or join in?'

'I don't want to think about it.'

You've told me in little bits and pieces what happened to you the night you disappeared, but I haven't pushed you. All in your own time. You're back – that's the main thing. I know that the day we found you, you'd kicked Swann in the face with your bound legs when he'd appeared with a tray of food. He was furious and climbed up into the attic to retaliate, but you kicked him again. Once he was down you somehow managed to squeeze his head between your knees until he passed out. I can't believe your courage! He fought back, of course, he'd punched you in the face before he went down.

You confirmed to the police that Swann was the man you saw with Clara at the Anderson shelter in the woods. He must have come back to the cottage when I was out looking for you. I was sure someone had been in, at the time. Neil confirmed that Swann used your phone, found your passport – they weren't hard to find in the filing cabinet – and used online passwords scrawled in your appointment diary to fake your movements. He even took a pair of my shoes and swiped a slick of your blood on them – to implicate me – before hiding the car on a busy local campsite, near Chichester. Then he caught the train to Heathrow to use your cashpoint card at an ATM.

'Sounds like he's a man who loves playing sick

games,' Neil had concluded, 'laying a trail of false clues to make us all think Diane had left the country was just one of his little tricks. I wouldn't be surprised if he was well practised at this and has always got away with it until now.'

We were taking a stroll along the stretch of river at the end of the garden one afternoon, when you suddenly felt able to talk more. It was the figure you mentioned first, the one that dashed in front of the car that night, as you drove to the village shop.

'I couldn't even be sure what it was,' you said. 'It was a fast blur and I wasn't expecting it. I thought it could have been a deer, a dog – then I realised it was a child. I stopped and got out, then climbed down the bank, pressing through the foliage and I saw her – and he was standing right behind her. The scene looked all wrong. When I realised who she was, I remembered her father had died. I didn't know the man with her was your specialist at the hospital, but it was pretty clear the creep was up to no good.'

You were collecting wild flowers and seemed robust enough for me to give you more details. I filled you in with what Neil had told me following Swann's arrest. 'He'd threatened Clara – told her he'd make sure her mother didn't recover from the cancer if she didn't go along with it.'

You dropped the sprigs of cow parsley you were gathering. 'Utterly diabolical,' you hissed.

'He knew she'd retreated into fairy tales; that it was a traumatic response, and he was banking on that continuing.' I glanced at you just to make sure this wasn't all too much for you. 'The police discovered that alongside his work with fertility treatments, he was carrying out a privately funded project into child sexuality. That's why he had free time during the day to meet her. Obviously his professional interest had turned into something else altogether.'

'Did he…?'

I took hold of your hand. 'No. Clara hadn't been…violated…'

'He didn't hurt her?'

'No – but, he played "touching" games with her. It started with the visit to the hospital after she was trapped in the castle. He was on the lookout for little girls who were independent and were used to wandering off on their own. He 'made friends' with her that day, when he heard what she'd been up to. She was exactly the kind of target he was looking for – she'd spent a whole night outdoors and relished it – so she played right into Swann's hands. He gave her an apple on that first visit, and after that, every time she went to the hospital he found a way to take her into a secluded consulting room or arrange to meet her at the Anderson shelter in the woods, luring her with books and toys. That's why her condition was getting worse, not better.'

You snatched a trembling breath. 'And *Little Red Riding Hood* was her escape mechanism?'

'The story is essentially about telling young girls to stay away from strange men. I should have seen it sooner.'

'You found her though, that was incredible.' You

leant your head on my shoulder. 'How did you track her down?'

'Clara was trying to tell us all along what was happening to her. I tried to remember every encounter I'd had with her, especially what she'd said. I was looking for anything that linked to individuals at the hospital. I considered Clive, the security guy; Dr Pike; Dr Norman; even Dr Guha, Marion's specialist. There were others who could have made visits too, a guy at the allotment; the boyfriend of a babysitter; police officers.' I didn't mention Morrell – he would get his comeuppance, but it seemed he was entirely unconnected to the abductions. 'Then I started to see a few links with what I'd witnessed in Swann's office during my consultations. I realised he'd been right behind her in the foyer in the CCTV footage, the morning she disappeared. He had a snow globe in his pocket that I'd seen in his office. I'd spotted a kid's DVD in his briefcase, too.'

'Had he targeted other children?'

'Neil is in the process of getting records from two hospitals where Swann used to work; one in Scotland, the other in London. Sadly, I don't think it will be an isolated case. Neil thinks he had developed a honed routine over time.' Your hand claps tightly around mine. 'Apparently, Swann spent most of his life in South Africa, although I didn't notice an accent. He'd always planned to go back there eventually, then a promotion opportunity came his way. He knew he only had to keep Clara quiet for a short time, then he'd disappear overseas. When he heard I was poking about, he started to panic.' I kick at the long grass. 'He left Clara for dead; tried to make it look like she'd got into the windmill by herself and couldn't get out again. He was gradually clearing the place of toys and once she'd died of dehydration, his plan was to leave the door unlocked, but blocked on the outside with rubble. Like the oubliette scenario, only far worse.'

We sat down on the bank and watched for fish. Your eyes darted back and forth and took you to another thought. 'Why did he keep me locked up for so long?' you asked.

'I think he...was working out what to do with you. Neil told me that, according to his confession, Swann was hoping you'd die from your injuries so it would look like an accident, like Clara, so you'd never get the chance to report him. He took you to an old stable near his property first, then he moved you soon after you starting smashing down the door. He found the sedatives you had with you following the miscarriage – so it was easy for him to knock you out whenever he needed to.' I threw a stick, idly, into the bustling current. 'In fact, Neil told me this morning what he intended to do.'

Your face shot round. '*Tell* me – what?'

I swallowed. I'd said too much now to go back. I took your hands between mine, squeezing them tight. 'Swann admitted he was planning to take you to the coast to force you over a steep rocky cliff – to make it look like suicide – before leaving the country. If you'd died in his own attic – it would have only implicated him.'

You snatched a breath in disbelief. 'Oh my God! He

was going to kill me. Come to think of it, I think he tried to do it earlier at the bell tower when I was drugged up to the eyeballs, but Clara came along…'

'It really was only a matter of time. He was keeping you in the attic until he was all set to leave.'

'He'd packed his bags, hadn't he? I remember seeing them when you carried me down the stairs. That would have been my last day…'

I nodded, with a grimace.

Once Tara has left, you draw the downstairs curtains and I lock the back door. It sets Clara's butterfly spinning and I smile. I've lit candles and we're ending the evening with a small glass of port and Dido on the music system.

I pull you close on the sofa and think of the facts you don't yet know. I haven't yet told you about the Morrells and their despicable date-rape set up. You're still not ready for the truth at this stage, and I'm going to have to be patient. As soon as you feel stronger I'm hoping to help you fill out the sketchy parts of that party, with the evidence from Elaine's photos, so we can press charges. I've already spoken to Neil about it. We'll get the bastards – it's only a matter of time.

You're stroking the hairs on my arm. I know there's something you want to say, but can't. I've felt it ever since I brought you home from the hospital. Is it about the baby? About me resuming infertility treatment? About us trying again for a child? We sit together, holding hands silently, enveloped in a stalemate, even though there is so much love flooding between us. Perhaps, because of it. Neither of us wants to push or hurt the other after what we've been through.

Finally, you turn to me.

'Ever since you rescued me, I've been wanting to ask you something...' Your fingers go straight to your lips. This is hard for you.

'I know.'

'You do?'

'I know you too well, Dee. I can see you've been carrying something around with you since the day I found you.'

You take a breath. 'I miss Frank. I wondered if—?'

'You'd like a dog? Our own Frank?'

You shift forward. 'We both work full-time, so it wouldn't be fair, as things stand...but maybe in the future?'

'Right...' I'd been bracing myself for something more momentous.

'That's not all, though,' you say. Another silence, while you find the right words. 'Okay. I'm just going to say it. Then you can either say something straight away or think about it. It's a big request, so I'm not expecting an immediate response.'

You have me worried now. I hitch forward to the edge of the sofa, my shoulders riddled with tension. I don't tell you that I, too, have a suggestion to make that I've been hanging on to for days. You press my hands together, your eyes wide with anticipation. Whatever you have to say, I can tell it's going to be life changing.

'When the time comes, if Marion agrees, I'd like us to...take Clara in...and be her legal guardians.' You get up, stand back, your eyes glued to my face, not knowing what to expect. 'There, I've said it.'

I'm speechless.

Because you've read my mind exactly.

I nod, tears making their way down my face. I nod again, vigorously, unable to say a word. I hold my arms open for you and you rush into them like a wave crashing to the shore.

Acknowledgements

I'm deeply grateful to my early readers: Mike Holmes, Helen Townsend and June for their invaluable insights. Thanks also to Helen Greathead, my super editor, for her excellent advice and attention to detail.

Gratitude in bucket-loads goes to Jo Dorrell, and my sister, Ruth Holmes, for constant encouragement and practical guidance in so many areas. Thanks also to other wonderful supporters: Anna Kiff and Kerry Jarrett for creative insights, constant interest and morale-boosting along the way. A special mention also to author, Daniel Clay, for always giving his time to listen and understand so well.

A big thank you to my Agent, Madeleine Milburn, and her team - I do appreciate all your hard work!

And my biggest thanks of all go to Matthew, my amazing husband, who is my first reader and always does such a terrific job of spotting all my blunders - and who supports me wholeheartedly, especially when the going gets tough.

~

Coming soon from AJ Waines:

No Longer Safe

A chilling Psychological Thriller that
will pull the rug from under you

Alice Flemming is deeply flattered to be invited to a
remote cottage in Scotland by her old University friend,
Karen Morley. Eager to please, she's happy to be on
hand to help Karen re-bond with her nine-month-old
daughter, Melanie, who has just come out of hospital.
But the idyllic scene is shattered when Alice wakes to
find a stranger dead at the end of her bed.

Karen isn't the warm-hearted friend she remembers and
appears to have a hidden agenda. Trouble is – once Alice
realises she's in grave danger - it's one woman's word
against another...

59811593R00230

Made in the USA
Lexington, KY
16 January 2017